Swimming with Dolphins

ERIN PIZZEY

Swimming with Dolphins

HarperCollins*Publishers*

HarperCollins*Publishers*
77–85 Fulham Palace Road,
Hammersmith, London W6 8JB

Published by HarperCollins*Publishers* 1993

1 3 5 7 9 8 6 4 2

A catalogue record for this book is
available from the British Library

ISBN 0 00 223945 0

Set in Linotron Aldus by
Rowland Phototypesetting Ltd
Bury St Edmunds, Suffolk

Printed in Great Britain by
HarperCollinsManufacturing Glasgow

DEDICATION

Swimming with Dolphins is dedicated to David Morris, Alan Cohen, and John Elford, my intrepid white knights. To Mr Hubbard, my lovely bank manager at Lloyds and Juliet Clark whose friendly voice comforts me in dark moments. To Signor Faenzi at the Cassa di Risparmio di Firenze. To Sam Bhadha at the St James Court Hotel and to Mr Striessnig, manager of the Savoy. All my books are always dedicated to Rino. Without him, the Savoy's River Restaurant will never be the same. To Mr Kelly and Sonia Potter at Fortnum and Mason, and Stella Burrowes at Harrods. They make my very busy life run smoothly. To Graham Harper at Ashgreen Travel who efficiently transports me. To Patricia Parkin my new editor – I hope for always – and to all at HarperCollins. To my village of San Giovanni D'Asso. To Roberto Cappelli, the mayor. To Luanna and Nicoletta, my friends. To my English class and to Manuela Meocci, Maura, Lia, and Rocco Machetti. To Antonella Guidotti whose unfailing good nature keeps me sane. To Arleen Pacht in America for her good work to better the lives of women and men. To John Lampl, Director of Public Affairs, and Louise Smith, Special Services Executive, at British Airways, my favourite flight. To Ruth Alboretti who is my friend. To Christopher Little, my handsome agent, for all his hard work. To Keita and Amber Craig and Dmitri Scott, and Che Lewis, and Kadir Shillingford, my beautiful grandchildren. Truly my cup runneth over.

'Then the time of exile began, the endless search for justification, the aimless nostalgia, the most painful, the most heart-breaking questions, those of the heart which asks itself "Where can I feel at home?"'

ALBERT CAMUS,
from *The Rebel*

'You begin by sinking into his arms and end up with your arms in his sink.'

Said by that well-
known feminist, ANON

'Puer Eternus – an arrested adolescent living in a permanent state of Peter Panic.'

MARIE-LOUISE VON FRANZ

Chapter One

Pandora lay in the hot sand, cursing herself. Shit, she thought. Why is it, every time I swear I'll never have a one-night stand, I go and do it again? She felt the hot sun throbbing on her inert body. She detached her mind from her body and gazed down at herself. She could hear the sea sucking the sand. Gingerly she opened one bloodshot eye. She saw a sleeping form beside her. 'Oh no,' she moaned.

Her mind snapped back into her body and she felt herself blushing. She raised her head and looked down the beach over her brightly painted toenails. All ten nails winked brightly back. Maybe if I didn't paint my toenails, I'd quit one-night stands.

There, on the edge of the seashore, she could see in humiliating detail the swirls and whirls of the sand where she had thrashed into a frenzied climax with an unknown man after a night of delirious dancing under the stars. Was it the man beside her? Pandora gazed at the still sleeping face. How awful, she thought. I really don't remember. In the heat of the night, with the rum-punch loosening her limbs and her hips, everything had become kaleidoscopic. The moon, the stars glittering so coldly over her head, the palm trees heaving massive sighs as the soft Caribbean breeze rippled through the spines, the sudden curl of a wave as it came restfully to the shore . . . And then the moment when the dancing had stopped and, Pandora now remembered quite clearly, all around her had fallen silent. Hummocks of bodies had lain in the sand, an empty bottle of rum on the beach; and the man had fallen to his knees and kissed her breasts. Reverend Mother would have a nervous breakdown, she had reminded herself in an attempt to stop her throbbing nipples from puckering tight as cherry tomatoes. But there was no Reverend Mother on this island and no Catholic priest either. What the hell? she had thought as she slid between his knees. And then the roaring had started and Pandora had let the waves of the warm sea wash away the rum, the night; and then there had been silence.

Pandora stirred now and sat up. Her backless cotton dress was crisp with salt. She looked at the shape next to her and saw a pair of big

9

brown eyes smiling in a friendly fashion. Was he the one? she wondered nervously.

The man rolled over affably on to his stomach. 'My name is Ben.' He put out a generous hand.

Pandora put her hand in his. 'Have we met before?' she asked. Shit! What if it was him? I can't really say *Hello. I'm Pandora. Did we fuck last night?* There had been no lessons on sexual etiquette in the convent she had attended as a girl.

Ben smiled at her. He has lovely teeth, she thought. 'Met? I guess you could say that.' He stretched hugely and shook the sand out of his tightly curled black hair. He leaned over and pulled her close to his chest. 'That was fun last night. What's your name?' He hugged her.

Pandora had to laugh. 'I'm not Whatsyourname. My name is Pandora.' She lay with her head buried in his chest. She smelled him. He was fragrant, like a cross between a lime tree and the white-starred frangipani trees that grew along the side of the ribbon road that ran around the little island.

'Welcome,' Ben said, 'to Little Egg. My island.'

Pandora heard the pride in his voice. 'You were born here?'

'Yes.' Ben sat up, cradling her head in his lap. 'I was raised by my grandmother, and I'll always live on this island.'

Pandora gazed at him. There was a shine to his face and an air about his slim, lithe body that made her wish to cling unto him. For so long she had been travelling through the other islands. Big Egg, the main island forty miles away, seemed to be peopled by drink-sodden expatriates. She had left there in a hurry. But even after only two days in the small ramshackle hotel on the beach of Little Egg, she felt she was home. Now, with her head in the lap of the man called Ben, she felt a moment of security that she had lost when she realized that her marriage to Richard, her third husband, was no longer a marriage but a graveyard of broken promises.

Ben looked down at her face. His practised eye checked her wedding finger. He saw the white give-away mark of the wedding ring now no longer there. Pandora watched him. 'I threw it away in the sea,' she said. 'When I first arrived.'

'Are you divorced?'

'From Richard? No, not really.' Pandora was aware that she sounded trite, like an airport novelette. There was so much pain bound tight in her voice, but this was a man she did not know, a man she did not trust any more than she trusted any man. 'My husband and I decided we would separate for a while. Give each other a lot of space. We sold the house and split the money. He spent some of his on a red Ferrari. I bought myself a ticket to the Caribbean. It was always a dream of mine to live on an island. Listen, I'm sorry about last night. I hope I didn't shock you.'

Ben put his mouth on hers. 'Hush,' he said. 'It was all right.' He gave her a hard, clean kiss. 'You get changed and have a shower, and then we'll go and eat with my grandmother.'

Pandora smiled. 'I'd love that,' she said, getting to her feet.

'I'll walk you back to your hotel.'

Pandora picked up her sandals and walked beside Ben.

'Johnson is my family name,' he said, holding her hand. 'My people came to this island several hundred years ago. Johnson is our slave name. When my great-grandfather was freed, he kept the only name he knew, that of his white master.' He laughed. 'Now everybody marries everybody, so we are all colours.'

Pandora felt the sand crunch between her toes. The sun was warm on her bare head. Inside her heart she could feel a small song of joy beginning to make itself heard. Perhaps, she thought, this is what I've been looking for all my life: a beach, a blue-green sea, and a man who is simple and kind. The beach she could trust. The sea could hold her in a warm embrace. But another man? Yet another risk of betrayal? Where was Richard in his red car? The song ended in a sob and she hung her head so that Ben should not know she was crying.

By now Pandora considered herself an expert on marriage. After three failures, she should know. The first two marriages were abusive and violent; the last one just came unstuck, like two bookends no longer belonging to each other. One day she was happily married to Richard, and the next the clove-hitch of their life together was missing.

As she walked in silence beside Ben, Pandora asked God to forgive her. I took vows and I broke them, she reprimanded herself. I have become one of the monstrous regiment of lonely women, trying desperately to convince myself that I am happy in my freedom . . . That was too heavy a thought for such a beautiful day. I'll put it away for later, she promised herself.

They were walking up to the cabana-style cottage in the hotel grounds. Ben squatted in the shade of a palm tree outside the door of her cottage. 'Don't you want to come in?' she said.

Ben shook his head. 'No, thanks. You get changed, and I'll wait for you here.'

11

Pandora looked at him squatting on his heels in the shade. What on earth am I doing with him? she wondered as she watched him balance effortlessly on his heels, hands elegantly curved over his knees. She wandered into the shower. There's a man who has learned a lot of patience, she thought. Maybe the peace of this island would teach her patience; help her rediscover the peace that she had lost a long time ago: Richard had an irritable temper that had kept Pandora constantly on edge.

It hadn't always been that way. Once she and Richard had loved each other, doing all the things that lovers did. Time plays tricks, though, Pandora reminded herself, soaping between her legs. She felt the scratch of the fresh sand from the night before. In any case, I have to think forwards, not backwards, now. Richard has gone to pursue his platinum-haired Gretchen, his Lorelei. Once, *she* had been his Lorelei, his waif and stray in need of love and protection. Subsequently she learned that Richard needed his woman to be his project in life, a cause, someone to whom he could offer not only succour and sanctuary but also reformation. Gretchen, with her white eyelashes demurely disguising adrenalin-high eyes, was another such candidate, and Richard, besotted, had begged Pandora for his release. There had been no arguments, only the sad thought that men, since time immemorial, have always searched for *la belle dame sans merci*. After two disastrous relationships, Pandora would not hug a third to her damaged breasts. If Richard must venture forth to slay Gretchen's dragon of a husband and ride back with her triumphantly across the pommel of his saddle, then she, Pandora, would be elsewhere.

Elsewhere was hard to be, though, when two people have architected a decade of a life together.

She smiled, more of a cringe than a smile. One day at a time, she thought.

Chapter Two

Ben's grandmother lived way up a steep hill in the mountainous region of the island.

Pandora sat behind Ben on his motorbike, her arms around his waist, her head resting on his broad back. Despite only having known him for one night, she felt amazingly comfortable with Ben.

Flying in to the island, her heart sick with ill-ease and the sense of another failure, Pandora had pressed her head against the window and looked wistfully down at the now familiar but still wondrous colours of the Caribbean reefs and lagoons. Small boats went about their business oblivious to the fact that yet another exhausted, bereft woman was flying into their island. A woman almost at the end of her tether after two divorces and a fractured marriage. Where had she gone wrong? After landing at the tiny shack of an airport, she remembered very little of the next two days. Most of it she had spent sleeping in her cabana. Shy, she was unable to communicate with the other visitors, most of whom seemed to be English and spoke in incomprehensible accents.

Now, with the sun on her back, she felt as if she had awoken from a very bad dream. No one knew her on this island. No one, of course, until her mother arrived, as arrive she must. Pandora sighed. Still, she thought, gazing up at the tall palm trees that lined the floury white dusty road, I'll have some time to myself before she rides in on her broomstick.

Ben stopped his moped. 'Wait,' he said, running back down the road. Pandora felt the sweat dripping down her legs and she grinned. Better get used to sweating, I guess. It's a very un-American activity. Huge industries made millions out of making sure American women didn't, couldn't, or wouldn't sweat. She inhaled a mixture of sweat, semen, and the scent of wildflowers that grew along the ground near her feet. Maybe I should bottle that, she thought. Women would go mad for it.

She sniffed again, watching as Ben ran swiftly back towards her. How naturally he moves! How unlike Richard, who lumbered whenever he moved. A very English, bear-like motion, knees and joints – injured by rugger – popping and cracking. Ben ran lightly on bare feet. In his hands he carried small round objects. 'Smell,' he said, thrusting them under her nose. 'Those are mangoes.'

Pandora took one. 'These are very small compared to the ones I saw in Jamaica.' Don't be so negative, she scolded herself. But enjoyment and anticipation of happiness were dangerous things: Pandora knew that to her loss. She was sure Ben wasn't dangerous, though. He didn't deserve her disapproval.

Ben bit into a mango. 'But see?' he said. 'Very sweet. Now it's mango season.' He grinned. 'The old women have to guard their patches. The small boys come up and teef from the mango trees.'

'Did you *teef* these mangoes, Ben? You speak such clear English.'

'I was not taught by missionaries. I was taught by a Mr Sullivan. He was a good teacher and would never have let me get away with saying *teef*.' He laughed. 'But *teefing* still has a special sound to it; when I was a small boy, I was a champion teef. Now I plant on my grand-mother's land up here. One day it will be my land and I'll build my house and have my family.'

Oh dear, Pandora thought as she sat astride the moped. It's all so simple for Ben. She wondered how old he was. Maybe twenty-seven. She was in her thirties. She did not like to use numbers, and always stayed in bed for her birthdays. She felt that if she completely ignored the day she was born by staying in bed and refusing to answer the telephone or the front door, those years chronicling her age would creep by unnoticed. It was hard in her first marriage to Norman who drank and to whom any event was a party. Pandora spent both her birthdays with him enmeshed in a drunken brawl resulting in black eyes and broken bones. Marcus, her second husband, was the psychiatrist she attended after the break-up of her first marriage. He was a Harvard graduate, articulate, handsome, and wealthy. Pandora's mother had been pleased with her only child for the first time in her life. Marcus turned out to be bisexual and verbally terribly cruel. In many ways life with Norman was at least real. He really drank and really beat her: she could count the bruises. In his own way, Norman really loved her, as any dependent, desperate, unloved child might love his mother. And it was this part that Marcus assured her would never change. The only problem was that after she had divorced the sobbing Norman and moved up in the world where the life of a Harvard-educated psychiatrist's wife made her rich and exclusive, there were no bruises to show the other wives. Poor women comforted each other, went shopping, supporting

14

a black eye. They gave each other sympathy like war-wounded soldiers, a cup of tea and a biscuit, and a tsk-tsk and *that bastard!* erupted out of outraged mouths. Not so among the dinner parties of the wealthy. Not a mark or a scar on her body – usually – because Marcus tied her ankles and wrists with silk scarves and her mouth with a black silk handkerchief. The words *you whore, you cunt* were incised on her breaking heart. The slam of the door of the mansion. Pandora knew she was not the only lonely, abused wife in her circle. She knew that there was a secret sorority of women who carried in the lines on their faces and the limp movements of their hands and arms the secrets kept so closely guarded behind their imposing front doors.

Richard had been a relief from all that. Big, solid, and totally English, he worked in Boston as a features reporter for the *Boston Telegraph*. Sometimes she felt that she was like a baseball glove passed from one man to another. Did they all belong to the same team? Now Richard was offering to fit his five fingers into the glove. Would he, too, prove in time that he needed the glove just in order to play a game? But from the nightmare that was Marcus, Pandora had woken up in the apparent safety of Richard's arms. Maybe that was her problem . . .

Pandora saw the top of a long tin roof and then the moped turned around a corner. Pandora felt immediate delight at the myriad colours: butterflies lifting and settling on the bushes of bougainvillaea; hibiscus bushes, far less showy, standing sculptured and gleaming, their leaves deep green and their faces permanently perfectly formed. Pandora smiled. 'Ben,' she said, 'the hibiscus remind me of the nuns at our convent, very stern and very proper, whilst the bougainvillaea look like chorus girls lifting up their skirts.' The house was enclosed by a long veranda. Over the railings bedding hung listless in the hot sunshine. Overhead, family washing flapped in the wind. Seeing the fresh cleanliness of the clothing, Pandora was aware of her own pile of dirty washing in the corner of her hotel room. She scrunched her way behind Ben, wishing she had worn shoes. It was all very well to go native, but the sand burned the balls of her feet. She was grateful for the cool of the veranda and the snap of the screen door as it swung back into place.

Ben's grandmother was old and bent, but she had bright brown eyes and she held out a surprisingly strong hand. 'Ben.' Miss Rosie's eyes were wary. 'Miss Maisy make obeah. Starting now.'

'What is obeah?' Pandora asked nervously.

'Obeah is black magic. Sshh!' Miss Rosie put her hand to her head. There was silence for a moment. What had happened to the cacophony

15

of crickets and the screaming of the parrots in the trees? The island seemed to be holding its breath. Only the sound of Miss Rosie's heavy breath in and out. 'I can hear now. She is getting ready for the killing. Night goes down and full moon come up. She cut the neck of the white cockerel.'

'Who for?' Ben asked.

'For Massah Jason. He bad-mouthed a Jamaican woman. He popped her one and she went to see Maisy in the mountain.'

Pandora was finding it difficult to follow the conversation. Both Miss Rosie and Ben were chirping to each other in a patois she could not understand. The final words of the sentences lilted upwards. It reminded her of poetry read by Dylan Thomas.

Ben grinned. 'I'll translate,' he said. 'Miss Maisy is an old Jamaican woman who lives in this mountain. She is so old, nobody knows much about her except that she is a witch. She brought her spells and her knowledge with her from Jamaica. They think she was washed up on this island after a shipwreck. Anyway, she lives up there and we were all afraid of her when we were kids. I guess we gave her a hard time. I remember her chasing me away when I went up there with Demian and Clem to pick her pomegranates. I swear that woman can fly.'

'Sure she can!' Miss Rosie snorted. 'I've seen her on many a moonlit night. Maisy thinks she's powerful, but she not as powerful as I. Anyway, I get food now. You come.'

Miss Rosie's back took on a supine shape and she launched herself at what Pandora assumed was the kitchen. She seemed to Pandora like a small but very effective battering ram. She watched Ben's quiet smile of affection as he walked into the kitchen behind his grandmother.

There was no one else in the house and the pine-scrubbed kitchen table had only two chairs pulled to it. Ben saw the question in Pandora's eyes. 'My grandfather was drowned,' he said. 'Like so many of his generation. They all went to sea, and for my grandmother life was very hard. She had twelve children and at times they had to live on coconuts and almonds. But there was always fish.' He sighed. 'My mother died when I was nine A terrible flu came to the island and lots of Little Eggs died.'

'Death came by the English doctor. He brought his foreign ways and his drunkenness with him,' Miss Rosie interrupted Ben. 'He give all these pills to the children instead of island medicine.' She shook her head. Pandora could still see the agony in the woman's eyes. 'Many died, so many. And my Ann Marie, Ben's mother. She was so beautiful. My best child. But then God takes the good first.'

'That means I'll live a long time, Grandma.'

'Sit, Ben.'

'I'll get another chair for Pandora.'

Ben sat, shifting slightly uncomfortably. Miss Rosie flurried and fluttered around his plate. 'Here, boy. Fish-head soup! I also made fried chicken for you. And your favourite dumplings.'

Pandora watched, amused. The old lady so obviously loved Ben.

Ben glanced across the table. 'I'll pass the fish soup to Pandora, Grandma. Where she comes from, ladies get served first.'

'That's right, Ben. That right. Right there. You are American?'

Pandora nodded and hoped desperately she would not be classed as a tourist woman. 'Yes, I am,' she said. 'From Boston.'

'You American women don't know how to take care of your men.' Miss Rosie took a tray of buns out of the oven. 'I worked for an American woman maybe two, three, no, maybe five years ago. No food in the larder. No washing or ironing. No changing the sheet. No wonder he leave her for an Egg woman. Egg women know how to look after a man.' She vigorously shook a shower of salt over Ben's soup bowl.

Yeah, and give them hypertension, Pandora thought rebelliously.

'Things are changing, Grandma.' Ben tried to wheedle. 'I can shake my own salt, you know.'

'Pitter patter, fish to butter! Nothing changes in my kitchen. Sit you down, girl, and I'll pass you Egg food. Best food in the world.'

Pandora sat down and slowly took a mouthful of fish-head soup. Bloated dead eyes gazed at her. Definitely heads in there, but the soup was delicious. Her stomach, made in the USA, said *I don't believe you're doing this to me*, but the tastebuds of her tongue joined forces with her rebellious sandy feet. *We're on Little Egg now and we are going to enjoy ourselves, every moment of it.*

Chapter Three

Ben dropped Pandora off at her cottage in the hotel. He shook his head when she asked him to come in. 'No,' he said gently. 'I'll go to the bar with my friends.'

Pandora frowned. Ben gave her a quick hug and left.

Pandora sat on the bed with tears filling her eyes. They had both shared such a beautiful day and now he was gone. She obviously had been quite wrong in her assumption that they would continue to share the night and hopefully many more nights together. She felt restless and the familiar ache of loneliness tugged at her heart. She knew where the loneliness came from. Marcus, damn him, had told her often enough. 'Men walk out on women like you, bitch,' he'd spit in her face while working himself up into an orgasmic rage. 'Even your father couldn't stand you. He walked out when you were twelve. What a bitch you must have been!'

'I wasn't a bitch,' Pandora whispered the words to herself. I wasn't a bitch at all. I was a scrawny, mousy, ugly little stick of a thing. My mother said I was a joke. All the other mothers on the street had pretty little girls with soft curly hair, and I had this awful red hair, huge freckles, and wild green eyes.

She wandered over to the mirror in the bathroom and bared her teeth. For years she had been made to wear braces. Her first memories of spittle-toothed kissing were embarrassing, the times when she had found herself locked into an unwilling embrace. She sighed. Mother will turn up if I stay any length of time, she thought. Like a big bird of paradise, she will flap her way to wherever I am, her nails manicured into deadly talons. She will sit and disapprove of everything I am doing, and I will crumble away into dust. Only my shell will remain. I am a failure. I failed my father. Norman failed to beat any feeling into me. Marcus failed to make me agree that what he wanted was normal. She smiled for a moment. Well, at least I stood my ground there.

Then she made a face. Dear, sweet, irresponsible Richard. He finally got so tired of me that he asked for a divorce. Richard, of all people. She felt a dreadful need to pick up the telephone and just talk to Richard. She shrugged. Anyway, she couldn't, because Richard was somewhere else looking for excitement. After ten years together, Richard had asked politely if she would mind if he changed his life. She remembered the tears pouring down both their faces, Richard gasping with pain but determined, she feeling as if her boat was slipping its mooring again. Then, in their flat in Boston, came the anger while she waited for Richard to come back from the *Boston Telegraph*. What did he know of the world outside? Pandora was now an expert on pain and suffering, and the thing you learned about both those subjects was to stay away from them. Richard, protected by a loving family and money, was a novice. But he had remained determined, so they had reached an agreement. Sell what they had, and he would go off to write his novel. He would chase his dream of a life in Europe and no doubt keep chasing a woman like Gretchen who could fascinate him in a way Pandora had obviously failed to do.

Pandora took off her clothes and had a shower. She stretched out on the bed and fell asleep, tears still bitter in her mouth. She dreamed of a fish swimming between her legs, of Miss Rosie, and of a big black witch. Just as the black witch came diving down to get her, she heard a knock at the door. Startled, she awoke and sat up, her heart pounding. 'Who is it?' she asked, frightening herself with the shrillness in her voice.

'It's Ben, Pandora.'

She got to her feet and wrapped the sheet around her. She pushed open the door. The night was black outside. She could see the light around the pool. 'Why are you here?' she said defensively. 'I thought you'd gone off with your friends.' She could smell rum on his breath.

'I've come to make love to you,' he said, looking surprised.

Pandora found herself smiling. He stood there in the moonlight looking so hopeful, she felt she was taking in a puppy. 'All right,' she said, motioning for Ben to come in. *At least I'm not alone any more.*

Ben sat on the chair by the bed. 'Will you live here for ever?' he said.

Pandora, sitting on the bed, looked back at him. 'I don't know, Ben. I really don't know.'

'Many people come to this island, sad women like you. They talk to me all the time.' He shook his head. 'They stay for a while and then they move on, always looking.'

'Men do that, too.' Pandora had visions of unshaven men on boats at anchor all across the Caribbean.

'Yes, but it's different for men,' Ben said, all the wisdom of youth on his face. 'Men have always had adventures. Not women.'

'That's a very old-fashioned idea.' Pandora was wondering if she had missed dinner. Her stomach was rumbling. 'Both men and women can have adventures. I've wanted to do this all my life. From when I had a book about a boy who used to swim with a dolphin.' She felt a surge of excitement. 'That's why I'm here, Ben. I want to swim with a dolphin just once in my life.'

Ben grinned. 'I'll show you how to swim with dolphins,' he said. 'They come here. You'll see.'

Pandora laughed. 'Ben, I'm really hungry.' She looked at her watch. 'I've missed dinner.'

'Never mind.' Ben stretched. 'We can go to my cousin's house. She will feed us.'

'How many people are you related to on this island?'

Ben shrugged. 'Almost everybody.'

Pandora picked up her dress and put it on a pile of clothes waiting to be washed in the corner of the room. She felt guilty. His grandmother was so together, she made Pandora feel like a slut. But Ben's eyes were closed. He was asleep in the chair. She smiled as she drew on a pair of shorts and a black silk T-shirt. I'm not a skinny little stick any longer, Mother. She put her lipstick on in the bathroom. Wait till you see Ben, you old bitch. Her mother's nimbus of grey hair stared back. *A black guy, eh? That's the best you can do? At least they've got big cocks, or so I'm told.* Her mother's red varnished slit of a mouth leered into Pandora's face.

Shit, thought Pandora, washing off her lipstick and walking back into the bedroom.

Chapter Four

Ben left early. He was going fishing. 'I'd love to go with you, darling,' Pandora said dreamily. Her vagina still felt the width of him deep within her. He was such a good lover. She loved his long brown back and the feel of his shoulders under her hands as they rode together into their explosive climax.

Ben stood by the bed, gazing down at her. 'I'll catch a Little Egg lobster and we will cook it on the beach.'

'You mean you'll cook it. Poor thing! How could you?'

Ben smiled down at her. 'I'll cook. No problem. Island men are good cooks. We learn at sea. No women, you see.'

Pandora made a face. 'I'll learn,' she said. 'Now I have time, I have a lot to learn.'

Time, she thought, sitting outside her cottage, holding a cup of hot coffee. The sun was rising. The air was still cool, but filled with promise. It was going to be a hot day. She lay back in the deck-chair and looked at the glittering blue pool. Behind it the sea turned somersaults in green and blue. Occasionally something big jumped to the surface and little waves scurried in the wake of escaping fish. Even in all this loveliness lies danger. Pandora's eyes darkened. All her life she had gradually built a wall around herself, like the one beside the cottage made of local stones stacked by a human hand. Brick by brick, she too had chosen the shape and the size of the stones. Now she could feel a crack beginning to open in her wall. If only, she thought, I could climb through that gap.

She got up and walked to the cottage wall. Curly tailed lizards ran in and out of the holes. She turned over a stone and let out a shriek. 'Holy shit!' she exclaimed. A translucent scorpion stood defiantly, its tail upraised, curled high over its back. Pandora backed off. Precisely, she muttered. I squeeze through the crack and I'll find a nightmare. Maybe I can't deal with that nightmare. Maybe I'll flip and never come back, like the time Marcus whipped me and I had to go to the hospital and get stitched up. A wave of humiliation wafted over her. She well remembered the young doctor's comment. 'At it too hard, honey?' Only stupid loyalty stopped her from saying *I hated every minute of it, but I'm married to a man who can't come if he isn't inflicting pain.* She remembered the looks on the nurses' faces and the dreadful pain of the stitches, but worse, far worse, was the fact that she would have to go back and before long Marcus would do it again . . .

I need another cup of coffee, she told herself. And anyway, Marcus is a million miles away in Mexico, no doubt driving small ladies with madhouse-haircuts crazy and into other mental asylums. I'm here. The weather is wonderful and Ben is the best lover I've ever had. She even allowed herself a moment of hope. Maybe this time she had found a happiness that would endure. Then she reminded herself she didn't deserve happiness. Her mother's prophecy was always that she would end up alone. Pandora heard her mother's voice. *Two old tramps on our own.*

'I'll go down to the beach,' she said very firmly to the wall. The scorpion, alias my mother, can go fuck herself.

Pandora sat on the beach and watched the fire. Ben had a very flat pan over the fire. Pandora looked away when he dropped the huge clawing monster of a lobster into the boiling water. Then she looked back. Ben's face was intently bent over the fire. Of course men had cooked for her before. Not Richard, who couldn't or wouldn't boil water. Marcus cooked exotic dinner party dishes for his exotic dinner party friends. But there was always something hysterical and disgusting about his forays into the kitchen. His food looked wonderful but tasted indifferent. He had no feel for the sensual experience of cooking, the smells and the erotic feel of the purple swell of a perfect aubergine, the virgin tightness of a small artichoke at the beginning of the season, or the deep contentment of a pile of green asparagus, an oral and sexual romp both before and hopefully after dinner.

Pandora sighed. Few people, she knew, even began to understand what she was about, so intensely and internally did she live her private life. She learned to live this way, forced into unwelcome closeness with her terrorist of a mother, a mother who stalked her daughter's maturing mind and body, thinking, as she watched her daughter grow into a presentable young woman, that she could cannibalize all parts of Pandora. Pandora always felt she was a Spartan road-runner tearing backwards and forwards between her mother's mean, ratty little house and the other world, the real world, of her school, her friends, and eventually her boyfriends. It was the teenage world that particularly transfixed her mother. All of a sudden, her middle-aged mother took on a different persona. The hard, brittle, nagging, shrieking mother was still there, but there was an unmistakable shift. All of a sudden another Monica emerged. Pandora was used to the myriad people who seemed to inhabit her mother's body. She learned to negotiate with each one from a very early age, but this Monica, the arch-eyed, simpering whore, threw Pandora. Soon she kept her boyfriends away from the house. 'Wazzamatter, honey?' WhoreMonica would say, smoothing down her cream satin blouse tight across her sagging breasts. 'Ain't you got no boyfriends? Or are we turned on by girls?'

Why am I sitting on a beautiful beach with a wonderful lover thinking about my mother? Pandora asked herself. She smiled at Ben. He was totally concentrated on his cooking. She loved him for that. She, too, knew the absolute silence that occurred when she was cooking, or drawing, or painting. In those moments no stone dropped into the empty pond of silence. Infinity and the universe stood still. God, both benevolent and benign, inclined his ear to her efforts and she loved him in those moments. Ben slowly cut a green pepper into the water. His knife was thin in the middle from much cutting, its thick wooden handle wrapped tightly with string. Pandora thought of her own shiny, red, ostentatious Swiss Army knife, the first thing she bought herself when she decided to go on her adventure. She showed Ben the hoof-pick. There were no horses on this island, Ben told her. They were all drowned in the hurricane of 1932. She remembered Ernest Hemingway's description of that hurricane hitting the Florida Keys and the death of a very fat woman thrown high into the trees by a tidal wave. Anyway, she comforted herself, it'll be a while before I have to worry about the hurricane season here.

Ben grunted. She watched him cut an onion into the stew. Without a chopping board, he sliced the peeled onion downwards. The gleaming blade created perfect crescents of white onion slices shot through with red. As she imagined the sweetness of the onion she thought of the sweet moments of making love to Ben. He had a beautiful, onion-like bulb shape to the end of his penis. It was made to be kissed. Shyly she watched him. He looked up, finally finished with the stew. 'Here,' he said. 'You put the chilli in.' He put his hand in his pocket and pulled out two round, squashed-looking vegetables. 'These are island chillies.

23

Very good for you. See? We call them bonnet chillies because they look like the hats my grandmother wears, especially to church.'

'Do you go to church, Ben?'

Ben shook his head. 'No, I don't,' he said. 'I find Jesus in my boat on the water. Jesus didn't go to church. He sat on the water and he taught his children. But my grandmother goes, and if the preacher doesn't roar and yell, she comes home disappointed. She likes a good roar on a Sunday. And boy can he roar, that old bastard! He thinks he's Jesus Christ anyway. I hate him,' Ben said amiably. 'He's a thief and a crook. He steals land from poor people.' He handed Pandora the chillies. 'Put them in now.'

The lobster, by now blood-red, stared at her reproachfully. He swam in a green gravy.

They sat beside each other on the sand. The fire cast a flickering shadow between the two of them and the sea. The ubiquitous palm trees swayed backwards and forwards, bending in the light wind. Bats swooped in arching circles. Birds called out their evening prayers. 'It's so easy to believe in God, Ben, when everything is so beautiful.'

Ben took her hand. 'Everything is beautiful, Pandora. So are you.' He said the words so simply that tears came to her love-starved eyes.

'Do you really think so?' She looked directly at him. 'I have spent so much of my life having to service men that I feel as if I'm working in a bus station. I fuel, clean, and wash one bus, then that one pulls out and I begin again on the next one. Each bus has years of personal garbage that needs attention. I straighten it all out and then off it goes to find its destination in the great big world out there.'

Ben smiled. 'I'm not a bus,' he said. 'And Little Egg is a very small world.'

'The problem is . . .' Pandora withdrew her hand from Ben's. 'The problem is . . .' And she heard a sigh reach her lips. 'Part of me is left on Richard's bus, so I don't feel free. I promised myself third time lucky. And Richard was the third time. So you see, I feel a terrible failure. You know, I was warned about him. I was told I was marrying a perpetual child. I thought Richard might grow up if he had me to love and take care of him.' She felt her face contort. Her mouth drooped and her eyes wrinkled with anguish. 'I was wrong,' she said bleakly. 'He had no intention of growing up. He will always be a selfish, ruthless child.' She sighed. 'The only part of the marriage that worked was when I was indulging him. I gave and he took. That's really the story of our marriage.'

24

Ben nodded. 'It hurts,' he said. 'I do know how it can hurt. I was hurt once. A very long time ago by a girl from Florida. We were going to get married, but the island was too small for her. In the end she went her own way. She missed the malls and the discos, all the things we don't have here and I hope we never will have.' He ended fiercely.

Pandora's nose wrinkled. The smell of the chilli peppers perfumed the air. 'What a glorious smell,' she said. 'I've never smelled anything like that before.'

'I know.' Ben grinned. 'Wait until I cook you curried chicken with island peppers.' He kissed the tips of his fingers, laughing at her.

Pandora heard the young girl in her own body return the laughter. What a universal gesture, she thought, the kissing of fingertips. She bent forward and kissed Ben's soft lips. 'How lovely to be sitting here with you on a night like this,' she said.

Ben pulled her to her feet. 'I must crack the lobster now,' he said, and he pulled her close. Pandora rested in the moment. If this is happiness, real happiness, she thought, I'll buy this for now.

Chapter Five

Days lazed by. 'Never have I had so much time on my hands,' Pandora explained to Ben. 'It's odd. With all this time, I am remembering things about the early parts of my life I've forgotten. Maybe not forgotten, but pushed away.' She was lying on her back on the beach. The blue of the water reminded her of a lapis lazuli necklace her father had bought her as a present. The green of the water reminded her of a plastic bracelet he had also brought her back from a trip he had taken into town. It had been unusual for him to leave their little town of Boise, Idaho. He had returned that time with the little crinkly white bag that contained the bracelet. Both his return and the present remained for ever in her mind. Lying now on the hot sand feeling the beat of her heart and the low rumbling of Ben's stomach, she also had another memory.

It was of herself sitting across her father's right leg. He was singing 'Ride a Ship Across the Sea', a song he had made up for her. It was a magical, intimate moment. Only the two of them there in the room. The leg, with its floppy brown sock wrinkled on his shin, went slowly, smoothly up and down. She realized now, all these years later, that she had been sexually aroused by her father's behaviour and even now the memory of it aroused her. 'Hold me, Ben,' she said, rolling over.

As they snuggled in the sand, she finished the memory. Her mother's face in the doorway and the ringing slap that threw her to the ground. 'Get upstairs, you little whore!' her mother had shrieked. 'You dirty old son of a bitch,' were the words her mother had spat at her father. 'You keep your filthy fingers to yourself.' From then on, father and daughter had moved around each other like strangers: if her father came into a room while she was there, she would leave. A deep sense of mutual embarrassment had hung between them. He had no longer hugged her or kissed her goodnight. The vindictive pleasure in her mother's eyes had remained full-time: Monica would sit at the dining table, night after conversation-frozen night, delighted with the damage she had caused. 'Your father is not a sexual man,' she would say over the washing up. 'Can't git it up, you know.' This was always followed by a sigh of self-pity.

The heat of the memory caused Pandora to shudder. 'What's the matter, Pandora?' Ben said as he lay comfortably beside her.

'An old memory,' she said. 'A very old memory. I'm sorry, Ben.'

'Don't be.' Ben smiled and snuggled up to her side. 'We have all the time in the world. Tell me how you got here.'

Ben was fascinated by Pandora's stories of her childhood, fascinated as only a man born and reared on a small island would be. His life, bounded by the sea and the beauty of the wild landscape, was still narrow in the sense of knowledge of the lives in other countries that Pandora had experienced. So for hours they would talk as lovers always talk everywhere. In no one before had Pandora found this quality of listening, the gentle silence that let her words and ideas fall from her mouth. In the silence was a total understanding. No ego, no other voice seeking to compete, struggling for domination. Ben was like the sea on a clear, calm day. The water pellucid, awaiting a never-arriving breath of air. Ben listened and in the listening she learned to love him.

For Pandora to try to explain to Ben just what it was like to live with her mother was difficult at first. Ben never really had a mother, just a wise, loving grandmother. Family relations in his life were happy and settled. He lived within walking distance of aunts, great-aunts, and uncles. He knew the sorrow of death since his father died and he suffered the loss of a man who had truly loved him. 'I miss him very much,' he said, 'but he is now with God. That is what he wanted his whole life. So when death came to him, he was ready with a smile on his face. It was his father who came to get him. His father, who died when he was twelve. Daddy could see him and talk to him. Just before he died, it was like a miracle. The room lit up with a soft, shining, yellow light. I looked across the room at Grandma who was holding his hand and we heard a voice say quite loudly in the room, *I have come for my beloved son.* Then Daddy gave a little moan and stopped breathing. I asked Grandma if she had heard the voice or was it my imagination. She said she had heard it. Grandma kissed his forehead and I did too. Then I left as the other women came in to dress him. You know, that's the only time two women will make a bed together.' He smiled. 'They say it's bad luck for two to make a bed because it means they have a body to lift.'

27

Pandora hugged him. 'You are so lucky, Ben,' she said. 'Very few people have a happy childhood.'

He shrugged. 'People want too much these days.'

'Yeah, I suppose so. My age group was taught by their moms that they all have to be rich and famous.' They were sitting outside the cottage. It was an overcast day and a cooling breeze blew across the sand. 'You'll meet Mom, Ben.' Pandora realized that she hated the idea of Ben meeting her mother. 'Mom will track me down anyway, but I'm using the excuse that I don't have a house for the moment. As soon as I do, the guilt trip she laid on me all those years ago will kick into action, and she will arrive. The thing is, she can't let any part of my life alone. She needs to tell me that everything I do is wrong. If all my thoughts don't mirror hers, then I'm also wrong. She can't live and let live. She can't accept that she has her life and I have mine. So I'm OK for a week or two, and then I get exhausted.'

Ben shrugged. 'I'll be there. I'll deal with her. I'm good with American women. Remember, I teach them to dive. They're not all bad, but many of them don't know how to be happy. Pandora, if you want a house, I have a little house out on the shore. My grandfather left it for me. You can live there. It needs a woman's touch.' He grinned.

Pandora sat on her deck-chair. 'That's really great, Ben. I've been a gypsy for far too long. I've lived out of my suitcase for over a year now. To tell you the truth, I miss running a house and cooking my own food. I'd like your grandmother to teach me how to cook island food. I really would.

'After Dad left, almost the first thing I remember about Mom is that she quit cooking or cleaning. She also quit shrieking at me. It was as if she had won a major battle. She had got rid of the competition and now the rules of the game were going to change. Apart from being allowed to go to school, I was her captive. Now, instead of grilling Dad, she grilled me. She kept going up to the school and bothering my teachers until they all looked at me funnily. I felt like saying, didn't it ever occur to you nuns that she is violent? No, she no longer hit me. She just used her mouth, until she left nothing of me. I couldn't even buy my own clothes without comment. *Shouldn't you get a larger size? Eat! You're too thin! Exercise! You slouch!* I sometimes wonder how I survived her at all. Maybe it wasn't my husbands I was running away from but her all along. Anyway, I saw Norman as an escape hatch. That's why I married him. I saw sex with boys . . . I'm not proud of this,' she said. 'I started at thirteen. But it was power. I felt powerful.

28

I didn't enjoy sex with boys or even with Norman. But I suppose I was so used to my mother's brutal way of life, I just didn't see the signs. I was only with Norman for two years. He kicked the shit out of me. That's when I met Marcus, who helped me to divorce him. I was so grateful I married him, idiot that I was. You can't marry for gratitude. Anyway, it really all began when Norman and I ran away to get married.

'Norman was six foot two, not particularly bright, but all the other girls wanted him. He had dark hair and dark eyes, and I often thought he was surrounded by a sad black shadow. My mother didn't embarrass him. No way. He ignored her mostly before we were married. He was quite nice to her, but once we were married, he ignored her or just punched her if she screamed at him. The difference was that when Norman punched my mother, her neck would flush with excitement and her eyes would widen. Shit, I used to think. She's enjoying this.

'I knew Norman enjoyed hitting me because he'd get the same wide-eyed look of excitement, the same intense tone in his voice as when he sexually excited himself with the verbal bullying. I saw it all later on as disgusting. I hated every moment of it, but when he hit my mother or screamed at her, his face was cold. I felt he knew that the faster he punched her out, the quicker she'd shut up.

'Anyway, we got the tests done and drove down to the town hall and stood in a line. Norman was as frightened as I was. We both had on our best clothes. Norman's only suit hung on his huge shoulders like a coat on a Salvation Army coat-hanger. Actually, we did get his suit from St Vincent de Paul's store. I got it dry-cleaned . . .' Pandora paused. 'To get rid of the smell of poverty,' she explained.

'The suit was perfectly clean, of course, but when you are as poor as I was, you are always aware of the smell of poverty. Of course you don't really know what poverty is, do you, Ben?'

Ben shook his head. 'My end of the island is considered the poor end of the island. We are poorer in terms of money. We're not like the governor and his wife. No one sends us invitations to the governor's cocktail parties. But we all know each other and we all care about each other. Nobody goes to bed hungry at night. It's not money that makes us happy or unhappy, Pandora. It's what's in here. I'm used to very bored tourists coming here to this island. They have money, all the money in the world. They stand here in my paradise and they say, "What is there to do?" I look at them and I think they are like empty beer bottles. Nothing inside. So I don't answer them. I take them under the water and then at night in the bar I listen to them telling each other what they saw. At least underwater they have to be quiet. Anyway, go on telling me about Norman.'

'There's not much to tell. We got married and we stayed at a little motel for a few days. Norman went out to get some beer on the second day. He came back in a bad mood and carrying a bottle of Scotch and proceeded to get really drunk. I tried to stop him. So he hit me. He hit me so hard he broke my nose. I waited until he fell asleep, and then I got my things together, jumped into the car, and went home to Mom. I never thought I would ever have to ask that woman for anything again, but I did.

'This conversation is getting miserable, Ben, and you must be getting bored. Can we go and look at your house? It sounds wonderful. I feel I need to put down some roots. All that talk about Norman gives me the creeps. Funny, you know. I thought I'd locked all those years away, but I haven't. Maybe it's having all this time to think.'

Ben put his arm around her. 'No, it's Little Egg. This island is like that. It's very small, but everything out there in the rest of the world you can find here right in front of your eyes.'

'I suppose so.' Pandora rose from her chair and felt the ever-present moisture run down her chest. 'I guess I'm going to have to get used to sweating.' She looked at Ben and laughed. 'You sweat, too.'

'Sure, I sweat.' He took her hand. 'Sweating is good for you. Let's go to the bar and get a cold beer with a slice of lemon. Then we can really sweat. Then we'll go over to the house.'

Sitting in the shade of the little hut on the beach, Pandora watched Janine clean the tables, her long arms moving lithely among the clutter of tourists. How beautiful were the people of Little Egg! Unconcerned in this forgotten haven, the so-called real world passed them by. Janine, who had been friendly from the first, smiled at Pandora. 'You're going to stay with us for long?' she asked, coming over to Pandora's table.

Pandora felt a surge of panic. Why was she frightened of this kind, helpful woman? Was it because she had been betrayed so many times before by Norman, by Marcus and his bisexual lovers, and finally by Richard? She had promised herself in her sojourn that this time when she reached Little Egg she would forgo relationships. So far her batting average sucked. She knew that with Ben she had struck it lucky. Ben so far was pure gold, but the rest of the world would have to take its time. Wearily, like a porcupine without its protective spines, she would take her own time, too. 'I hope so,' she said faintly. 'Do you think I'd like it here?'

Janine smiled, a wide, warm burst of sunshine. 'Yeah. You'll like it here all right. Except there are no men here.' She glanced at Ben. 'At least not what I'd call a man.'

Ben lifted his beer. 'That's Janine for you, Pandora. She likes her men hard. The harder they are, the better she likes them.'

Janine saw the shiver of fear in Pandora's eyes. 'Hey, honey,' she said gently. 'Some man hurt you bad.'

Pandora found her eyes full of tears. 'You're right. Some man or men did.'

'All men are bastards at heart.' Janine leaned her elbows on the bar, her gleaming black hair swung forward. 'Listen to me.' She extended a long, middle finger in Pandora's direction. Around them tourists sat chattering, above them parrots screeched in the trees. The bushes rustled in a slight wind and curly-tailed miniature dinosaurs scuttled about. 'You listen to me, Pandora. If men give you any trouble, you take off your high-heeled shoes and you womp them right on the head. If that don't do it, take a baseball bat and swing it hard.'

'You don't really mean that, do you, Janine?'

'She sure does,' Ben said ruefully. 'When she works over at Bar 666, she takes her baseball bat and if anybody gets out of hand she swings it.'

'You know your problem?' Janine stood up, flaunting her magnificent breasts. 'You Americans think too much. How about coming up tonight and giving me a hand? I got a Lion's night tonight, and boy, can those fellows drink!'

Pandora looked uncertainly at Ben. For a moment she felt confused. She did not want to lose her exclusive relationship with Ben, but she knew, like two little children in the moon, they could not live away from the rest of the world.

Ben nodded. 'OK,' he said. 'I'll bring her around about nine.' He finished his beer. 'Come on, Pandora. Let's get going.'

Pandora waved goodbye.

Janine grinned. She stood with her hands on her hips, well aware that most of the men and a few women were entranced by her breasts. She gave them a final shake and watched Pandora leave. Damn fool woman, she thought. She made a face. I'm a damn fool woman myself, with Octo somewhere off Cuba, drug-running. Why am I feeling sorry for her? She's safe enough with Ben. Janine poured herself a rum. Safe, she thought. But Octo is something else. A pirate descended from pirates. A glitter of gold in his mouth, an earring to match a heavy gold chain around his neck, and all the police in the Caribbean trying to catch him. Naw, they can't catch Octo, she reminded herself. He knows every reef and sandbar between here and Jamaica.

On his boat the shabby little cabin hid an immensely powerful engine. The hull had the most ingeniously hidden spaces for drugs. Towering over the steering wheel, usually drunk, Octo carried anything legal or illegal. Janine loved him with all her heart. For Janine, born and raised in a hut in Honduras, Octo had come early into her life and saved her.

Her big eyes fringed with long black lashes, she watched the American tourist leave on the back of Ben's moped. At least Ben won't harm her, she thought. Her womanly soul, much scarred by her years as a survivor of life's struggles, could hold out a palm branch of peace to another woman. But she was anxious for Octo to come home. Far too many nights had gone by without his warm, earthy lovemaking. Somehow, lying with his head on her breast, aware that she had the power in her back and her legs to suck him dry, she took comfort.

She wiped her hand across her brow and leaned low to take an order for rum from a pink and white tourist.

'From New York?' she said, allowing him a tantalizing glimpse of nipple.

'How d'ya know?' he said, keeping a pale blue eye on her cleavage.

'I'd know that whine anywhere,' she muttered crossly. 'All you boys sound the same from New York.' She left a question at the end of the sentence.

'Ah,' the man said, lifting first one end of his leg and then the other, as he felt an erection about to announce its presence. 'D'you know . . .'

'Know what?' Janine's eyebrows lifted themselves.

'Well, um. Are there girls on this island?'

'Lots of girls.' Janine turned her back to fill the glass. 'What sort of girls?'

'Well, you know, *fun* girls.'

Janine turned back to the counter. The tall glass brimmed with a white foam. She lowered her face into the drink, then, lifting her head, she very lightly licked the foam gently from around her full red lips. 'Sure, honey. We have fun girls. What about me?' And then she laughed.

The man stood there, his narrow pigeon chest heaving with lust, and with the driving midday heat. Now his erection was clearly visible in his skimpy black lycra shorts. His moustache under his sunburnt nose reminded her of the bristleworms that crawled in the dead reefs looking for debris.

'You can find me tonight at the Triple Six Bar on the other end of the island.'

'666? Wow. That's the mark of the great beast. Satan.'

Janine leaned forward again. 'Here's your drink,' she said. Well, at least he looks clean. You could never tell with Americans, she mused. Of all the tourists that came to the islands, they were the most confused. Italians might scream *Mamma mia* when they came; the English said nothing; but the Americans were more likely to make a great noise and then cry. What a race Americans are, she thought. What a strange people.

Maybe if she worked hard tonight and got good tips she could add to the £1,000 she had under her mattress. One thing for sure, Octo would be pleased with her. It had been a good month, this month. She gazed up at the sky. High above her the frigate birds rode the thermals. She often thought of herself and Octo as frigate birds, a species living on the edge of extinction. These birds lived by robbing others of their efforts. They swooped on the slow-footed boobies as they laboriously lifted their fishes from the waters. They stormed and mobbed the fishing craft until the fishermen, in an attempt to beat them off, dropped their catch.

'Two beers, baby, and make it fast. We're hot.'

Janine looked at the two men in front of her. She lifted up her arm to reach for two glasses from the top of the bar. Both men could see her breasts through the gap in her T-shirt. 'There's a party tonight at the Triple Six Bar,' she said, sliding the first beer down the side of the glass. She looked at them both. They were gazing at each other. Damn, she thought. There's no business there for me tonight. Maybe they'll find Mark. She handed over the two drinks.

'A party?' the older one said, rather peevishly. 'There's nothing to do on this Godforsaken rock. We should have stayed on Big Egg. At least it had discos.'

'We don't need discos here on Little Egg,' she smiled sweetly. 'You just be at the 666 and ask for Mark.'

'Mark who?' The little one had small boy shorts and pristine, white, carefully turned-over knee-length socks, both feet shod in equally pristine beach shoes.

'Just Mark. And say Janine sent you.'

33

Chapter Six

Ben stood behind Pandora at Bar 666. She felt the heat from his clean body pass through her back, and she folded herself gratefully against his chest.

Bar 666, she realized, contained all the same seeds for both love and destruction as did the bars that Norman used to haunt. What she did notice almost at once was that, unlike Norman's favourite bars, the drinking here was cheerful and the voices animated. Norman's bars had been sulky places where men hung out with their trailing partners and competed for the loudest events in the laborious days that had passed. Here, as far as she could follow the conversation, most of the men seemed to be discussing fishing and boats. What she did see, and it made her smile, was several determined ladies sitting in between their men and joining in the general revelry loudly and without fear.

Bars with Norman had meant constant aggression. There had been no such thing as a night out with Norman. All nights out with his wife in tow meant that Norman must fight for the honour of his little lady, and if a man so much as lifted his eyes from the froth on his beer to gaze at Pandora, that, by the end of the evening, was a cause for a fight. Pandora learned very early on to allow her head to drop until the tops of shoes became her only assurance. She became an expert at other people's shoes, the cracks on pavements, the size and shape of dog turds, and the floors of various bars. Even then, she was not always safe. If deprived of a legitimate arousal of rage, Norman, by the time they walked home, took her long red hair in his left hand and frog-marched her down the road to their apartment.

On their humiliating Calvary there were several stations of the Cross, the worst being the Isaac family. Mrs Isaac, with a true history of persecution to back her, always leaned out of the window. 'Let go of the girl, you putz!' she screamed.

'See?' Norman hissed loudly. 'You're making a show of yourself in front of the neighbours.'

Pandora said nothing at all, but she knew, once the front door clicked shut, his big meaty right hand would swing fast, Mrs Isaac's misguided intervention having unwittingly served Norman's purpose.

Why did she go back after fleeing her honeymoon? How to survive? A mother, who didn't want her, or Norman, who said he loved her but continued to beat her . . .

Janine was busy down at the long arm of the bar that curved under the thatched roof, open to the smooth, sidling sea. To live without any fear – what a ridiculous way to have to think! Pandora was aware it was, maybe to most people, a neurotic thought, but she knew only because of the times she was in hospital, thanks to Norman, that there were hundreds and probably millions of women who felt as she did and would understand. Norman had created physical fear in her, but later Marcus had taught her a far greater fear, the fear that her mind could disintegrate and leave her with a head full of ash and a body limp and lifeless, obedient only to the faint burning smell of the suction of an electrode to the head, the zap of obedience, and then the shuffled, slippered walk of Largactil.

Pandora bent her head and looked around her furtively. Who was that woman over there, sitting in a corner listening to a man whose knees were pressed close to hers? The woman was wearing a black print button-through dress. Her hair was matted across the top of her head. Both eyes seemed milky with cataracts. She sat with deep lines etched around her mouth. She had big ears, pointed at the top, and then fleshy earlobes and big sea-shell hollow holes that led to her brain. Pandora imagined the tides in her mind forever swishing backwards and forwards. Bells tied to rocks, ringing over the riptides. 'Who is that woman over there, Ben?' Pandora nudged him gently.

'That's Miss Maisy, Pandora. Don't you look. She has the Evil Eye.'

Just then Janine saw both of them. She left her customers mid-order and sailed down to the end of the bar. 'Pandora and Ben! You said you'd come.'

'Any news on Octo, Janine?'

Janine reached for a glass. 'No,' she said. 'But the tide's good and I'm not worried. They say there's a shipment out of JA on its way here, but Octo won't be so silly. Not after last time. Maybe I fool myself, Ben, but I live like a fool.'

'Don't we all?'

Pandora found herself laughing. 'Yes, we do. And worst of all, most of us take ourselves far too seriously. What can I do to help, Janine?'

'Can you run a bar?'

'No, but I've been in enough bars to learn fast enough.'

Janine lifted up the flap. 'Come on in. And what you don't know, ask.'

Ben sat and watched Pandora. Her face was pink from the sun and from concentration. How could anyone want to hurt her? he wondered. The thought puzzled him. Was she like a conch deprived of its hard, protective shell? When he was young, he and his friends had taken a conch from the sea and pegged the protruding foot to his grandmother's clothes line. As the sun raised the temperature of the suspended mollusc, the white gleaming body had been forced to let go of its refuge and slowly allow itself a tortured hanging on the clothes line. A conch possesses two large stalks upon which sit two brown, reproachful, gentle eyes. From that day on, Ben had been unable to eat conch without feeling guilty. The conch on the line had been so helpless; he felt that helplessness in Pandora. In truth that was the helplessness in all things that made him tender, but he knew, even as he watched, it was not so in all people. Maybe Pandora attracted evil attentions. Maybe she walked like the small soldier crabs without a shell. The others walking with her knew they must arm themselves, but she for some reason had no idea that a shell was a requisite for life.

Still he watched her bend in the flicker of the light of the bar. He saw her great green eyes flash in her thin face and his heart lurched. For how long, he wondered, would these days last with a woman who became increasingly familiar to him? So many times in his life he felt the sexual pull of a long pair of tourist legs. 'Tourists are for practice,' he heard the old men say, 'but the island girls are to marry. They keep island ways.' Ben listened well and in spite of sweet pleadings in the grapebushes from a series of pretty island girls, the furthest he ever got was a two-finger lover's dip into a heavenly, warm, wet promise.

For ten years after that, apart from the heartbreak in Florida, he had got used to cheque-book sex from the tourist women. Ben never graduated to Ziggy's class. Ziggy was the island stud. Six foot four, thighs like ironwood stumps, Ziggy roared and raved and beat his chest after a sufficiency of rum.

Tonight in the bar he was in full voice. Several women hung off his huge biceps. Pandora, filling a glass of rum and Coke, grinned at Ben. There was no fear in her smile, no wincing at the noise. Maybe, Ben hoped, he could teach Pandora to grow a protective covering. And until it was there, he would be her shell and protect her from all harm.

36

Pandora watched the two tourist men from the hotel arrive at the bar. One leaned forward and hissed at Janine, 'Is Mark here?'

Janine's eyes flashed. She lifted her chin. 'By the fishing boat on the beach,' she said. 'Over there.'

'Do they have "stuff"? You know what I mean?' The man was shaking and sniffing, his eyes pink and glittering.

'Mark has everything you want,' Janine said imperturbably. She grinned as the two men walked off. 'The customer is always right,' she said in a mock American corporation accent. 'Have a nice night!' she called after them.

Pandora shivered. Even in paradise, she thought. Even in paradise.

Slowly, from the centre point of Pandora's life – which was her hammock on the porch – her days on the island began to take shape. Ben's little clapboard cottage, built by his grandfather, sat on the south side of the island. The veranda faced the sea and a small arm of the reef made it shallow and calm. For Pandora the cottage became a sanctuary. Unlike Richard, who was untidy, Ben's cottage always shone with pride in itself. He kept the place scrubbed clean and had a collection of seashells and purple-pink fans which he picked from the bottom of the sea. The place smelled of fresh jasmine and the flowers his grandmother brought for him.

Lying in a hammock slung between two struts that held up the front porch, Pandora pushed a lazy foot backwards and forwards in the still heat. One o'clock on a cloudless, windless day. The birds were silent, sheltering under the cool green palm leaves or sitting in the holes in the volcanic face of the mountain. Ben was working all week for the Ministry of Works. Pandora daily packed his lunch. Sweet sugar bananas, homemade rolls, and salt-beef.

As Pandora lay in the hammock, her hair a wet tangle of curls, she enjoyed the thought of Ben squatting with the rest of the crew in the shade of one of those magnificent Pride of Jamaica trees, the blue-green leaves supporting the heavy burden of flashy red flowers tumbling over the tree. Often the branches of the Jamaica Pride trees lining the road leaned far forward and blessed the hot tarmac with their shade.

Lying on the porch after a quiet weekend with Ben, Pandora felt her kaleidoscopic life begin to settle. No more did the refracted rays of light split and splinter her mind. No more did the slightest sound cause her to cringe or to draw breath sharply. Even Ben noticed the difference. 'You smile with your full face now,' he said, smoothing her forehead and tracing his finger around her jaw and her nose. His gentle fingers could feel the scars left by Norman's fists and his body warily touched hers, careful never to make her feel constricted.

Where, she wondered, did a man like Ben learn so much?

He followed Pandora's lead and watched her carefully.

Pandora, lying in the hammock, remembered her first night at Bar 666. She most of all remembered the moment she heard herself laugh. It was a moment that stopped her polishing the glass in her hand. To her surprise, the glass did not shatter. It lay in the palm of her hand, its rounded belly winking at her. The laugh, still loose in the bar, carried the bells of genuine amusement, a hint of a conspiratorial giggle. A little girl laughed that laugh, and the little girl lived in the body of a grown woman called Pandora.

That night, after Janine had closed the bar, they walked her back to her house on the beach. All three held hands and the soft sand slurried at the kick of their heels as they left six tracks, soon to be covered by the rising tide. Little crabs, their arms akimbo, rushed sideways into their holes. Soft chirps of nesting birds disturbed by the heavy footfalls. So many days away from another night on the beach when, mad with rum and lust born of desperation, Pandora had been looking for a body – any body – to hold her. To hold her physically down to the earth and to staple her into the sand so that in her loss and desperation she would not go flying off into the night, to be flung into atoms among the cold, unblinking stars.

But that night, after they left Janine with sleepy goodbye kisses, they fell into bed in Ben's house, and before sex was even aroused to rock them to sleep they slept, warm arms around bent head and sleeping rosy breasts.

Pandora swung again and realized it was time to repaint her toenails. The sand had scratched away the tips of the pink. The only decision she had to make for the rest of the afternoon was whether she wished to continue the thought of her escape from Norman or not. Why, in all this happiness, must these huge, flapping memories come to haunt her? Precisely because she had what so few other people had. She had time and she was safe. And whatever welled up, she now felt she could cope with the memories. First she must paint her toenails.

Chapter Seven

At daylight, when the sun tipped the tops of the palms around Ben's house, she lay, her eyes closed, listening to the joyous morning chorus of the parrots. They could be heard screaming their appreciation of the dawn, quite drowning the gentler anthems of the survivors of the night. Whey-faced owls grumbled, clicked their beaks, expectorated little furry capsules on to the ground and settled down with a flurry of feathers deep into the trees up on the mountain.

This was Pandora's treasured moment. Lying quietly behind Ben's sleeping back, she could trace the straight line of his curled hair and then an expanse of sugar-brown neck, his smooth skin running down over his shoulders and then down again to his indented waist where his two symmetrical buttocks turned gently up to his drawn knees. Just between the sweet crack of his buttocks she could see the fur and the shape of his balls. His innocence in sleep made her smile.

Norman slept with clenched fists and an angry frown. Marcus, his hands crossed and protective of his sleeping person, was like a fortress. And then Richard. Richard slept like a small child, one thumb all but in his mouth and a hand protectively holding what he referred to as his 'plonka'.

Pandora could take her time now and catalogue what had really been a mad dash through insanity. Those memories belonged to the Richard story and today, with her escape from Norman still sitting like an unpacked suitcase in the attic of her mind, she was going to wait and tackle this attic at her leisure. There was only so much time before her mother traced her through her American Express card; she knew that once her mother's letter arrived with its aggrieved writing, she would inevitably reply.

She nuzzled the back of Ben's neck. 'Time to get up,' she said and then she laughed, running her finger along his erect penis.

Lifting a lazy leg, moist from the heat, she adjusted her left buttock, until they made their usual morning connection. A surge of excitement brought fresh sweat to her brow, and then the gentle sounds of two bodies well-satisfied. A thick grunt and then a few sounds of deep growling and Ben was content. A higher sigh, and then several, and a silence.

The parrots reasserted themselves loudly and disapprovingly. Pandora laughed as she imagined their beady yellow-rimmed eyes watching the human endeavour to find a simple satisfaction. Ben hung over her and kissed her sweaty neck. 'Coffee,' he said. 'Lots and lots of thick black coffee with sugar.'

'Oh, Ben. Do you think this will last for ever?'

Ben sat up. The sheet sat around his shoulders. He looked down at Pandora sprawled at his knees. She had gained a little weight, so her face did not look quite so gaunt or anxious. The corners of her mouth were not so tight. Her eyes that tended to loom from her skeletal face now looked less protuberant. He hated to hurt her ever, but he also was unable to lie to her. 'Nothing lasts for ever, Pandora,' he said. 'Nothing.' He spoke from the loss of his mother and then his father, and finally, not quite so grievous, but at one time in his life the possibility of the girl he loved. 'I'm afraid I don't believe anything lasts for always.' He saw her body tense and her face change. 'Pandora, think about it. I don't mean us. Just think. You are born alone and you die alone. You can love people along the way, or people can harm you, but in the end you leave this world by yourself. Doesn't matter if you're the Queen of England and people are all around your bed praying for you. Or if you're my grandfather, drowned at sea all by himself. The journey is your own.' He smiled and leaned forward to pick her up and hug her close. 'Mr Sullivan, who taught us English, also taught me about many, many religions. Sometime when I don't have to heave rocks out of holes in the road, I'll tell you more about it all.'

Pandora lay back on her pillow. Somehow Ben made everything seem so reasonable. Of course you are born alone. In some cases, like herself, not only are you conceived by accident and born alone, but you are also not wanted, even when you do arrive. Except . . . Except . . . And a stab of pure sorrow caused her to grimace.

I hurt her. Ben looked at the now familiar expression of pain that pinched her nostrils and twisted her lips in its wicked fingers. 'I shouldn't philosophize, darling, so early in the morning, and then leave you for the day. I'm sorry.' Ben felt contrite, but also puzzled. So much had happened to this woman. All his twenty-seven years were as nothing compared to her thirty-seven years of pain and rejection. He felt she had been born in a light fishing craft and had spent most of her life rudderless, scudding across waves and shorelines through dangerous reefs and atolls. Sometimes the jagged coral had pulled her down and she had struggled to right her craft. But when he had found her on the beach, drunk and desperate, his taking of her was no usual end-of-beach-party sexual conquest, but a promise to himself that for as long as he could he would take care of her and try to restore some balance in her life.

She, too, felt that they had time to share together, but of that, so far, she said very little.

'Coffee,' Ben said. 'Otherwise we'll lie here all morning and my foreman will get cross.'

For a moment's silence they lay splayed and innocent on the bed. Big bluebottle flies beat their intransigent heads against the windows. Mosquitoes squealed in for a landing. Crickets chirped. Outside the door a sugar-banana tree proudly displayed its ripening crop of fruit. Paradise is not peaceful, Pandora thought, but maybe I'll learn to be happy for today.

In many ways Pandora felt like the red bud of the hibiscus tree. There was one in the garden by the gate before she left to turn right from Ben's property to visit Miss Rosie. She picked the four-inch, tightly furled bud from its stem and examined it closely. So far she had wrapped herself in a cocoon of isolation. The only person who could pull away the gauze and come near was Ben. Behind him, at a greater distance, his grandmother. She was still very wrapped in this red, womb-like cocoon. Or maybe it was a well-chosen womb of her own. Not her mother's unwilling uterus, filled with often described fibroids. Pandora always thought of her mother's fibroids as road blocks to halt conception. It amused her to know that she attained her right to life only because she was diagnosed as a fibroid until she was four months old and too late to be aborted.

Looking at the rolled flower in her hand, Pandora was thrilled at the long yellow stamen that thrust through the flower. Yellow, dripping with pollen, it threw a three-pronged challenge to the rest of the world. *I am going to be the biggest, the best, and the most beautiful hibiscus*, the flower challenged its holder. Pandora looked down at the stem on the flower. I'll take it back, she thought, and put it in water and wait to see it open. Miss Rosie would understand.

As she climbed the stairs of the cottage, she heard the telephone ring. How odd. Ben's at work. Maybe it's Janine.

She wandered towards the telephone, a little put out by the intrusive noise. There were long-distance crackles and a few clicks. 'Is that you, Pandora?'

Pandora froze. 'Richard? How did you find me?'

'Easy,' he said, his voice sounding only a few feet away. 'Your mother tracked down your American Express address and I asked the lady at the telephone exchange. After all, there can't be all that many Pandora Townsends on such a small island. How on earth did you get there?'

I'm not going to justify myself to Richard. Pandora struggled to take hold of herself. After all, he left me. 'How's Gretchen?' she counter-attacked.

'She's well. Very well. Germany is rather different from Boston, but we're enjoying ourselves.'

'And the book?' Pandora waited in silence.

'Well, the book is taking a little longer than I thought. But I'm getting there. Look, I know this is silly, and you're a big girl now and can look after yourself, but I have been worried about you.'

Pandora found herself grinning, not an apologetic grin nor even a friendly grin. An imp of pure mischief surfaced and she heard herself saying in an even, calm tone, 'Don't worry about a thing, darling.' Towards the end, she very rarely called him darling. She heard him draw in his breath. 'Everything is marvellous.' She liked the slur on the word *marvellous*. It sounded so like Gretchen, the German bitch. 'Actually, I'm living in a little gingerbread cottage right on a beach, surrounded by coconut trees.' She rambled on, waiting for the question he most wanted to ask. 'I have lots of friends. I help Janine out in the bar. It's all very idyllic, darling.'

'Are you . . . ?' Richard's voice flattened. 'I mean, do you see any-body in particular?'

'Not in particular, Richard. I am living with Ben. He and I are gloriously happy. I do hope you feel the same way about Gretchen.' She even managed to say the words without spitting them through her teeth.

'Oh, yes, of course. Then you think we did the right thing, Pandora? I mean, taking a break?'

'Oh, I do, Richard. I really do. It's all so beautiful here. All so laid back. I feel years younger.'

'Good.'

Pandora rejoiced in the hollow tone of Richard's voice. 'I must go, Richard. I've got to go out to lunch.'

'I must hurry. I've got to meet Gretchen for dinner. She has been promoted to a senior position in her bank.'

'Wow. Great news. I bet you have a cellular telephone in your car, don't you, Richard?'

'How do you know that, Pandora?'

'We were married, sweetie. Remember?'

'Yes. I do remember. I remember lots of it very well.'

'Say hi to Gretchen for me, Richard. I must run.'

'Pandora . . .' Richard's voice came painfully down the line.

No, I mustn't, Pandora thought. I really mustn't. This time Richard is going to sort out his Lorelei for himself. She knew Gretchen well enough, after all. And if Richard wanted women's wiles, headaches, followed by raging rows and then the comfort of Gretchen's forgiving body in bed, let him have it. So far she, Pandora, had little to complain about. 'Goodbye, Richard,' she said firmly. 'And good luck.' She was glad she could not see Richard's slumped, round-shouldered discontentment.

All his life Richard and his public school friends had decreed that their lives must and should contain a large amount of irresponsibility. Richard followed his pack of merry friends between publishing parties in London and festivals in Rome and parties in Boston. Richard's role was that of court jester – instant hard copy on the delights and differences between the inhabitants of Europe and the completely other world of New York, Washington, and Boston. The rest of the continent didn't exist for them.

Now in his Ferrari with its new telephone he could telephone Gretchen the Grouch and tell her he had been held up at a meeting. No doubt Gretchen would kick her high-heeled shoe in the thick carpet and apply yet another smear of her bright red lipstick . . . Late for dinner again.

Pandora laughed at the memory that had once been painful. Now she had heard his voice, the memories did flood back. She had arrived at the house she shared with Richard at the bottom of Boston's Beacon Hill. Gretchen had been scurrying around in Pandora's kitchen and for a moment she hadn't seen Richard. 'He's in the bathroom. He will be with us in a minute.'

Something about the *us* comment had disturbed Pandora. Had she invited Gretchen to join herself and Richard for a drink? That was certainly how it sounded, but she had ignored the question mark and the three of them had drunk the excellent pitcher of martinis fixed by

Gretchen. Pandora had relaxed. Of course. How could she be such a silly, suspicious bitch? All three of them had been friends for years and if Gretchen and her husband Friedrich needed to play death games with each other, it was none of Pandora's business. Gretchen was fun, especially after three martinis, and she was showing Richard how she had escaped down the side of the house, an infuriated Friedrich after her.

After the laughter had subsided, Pandora had decided that Gretchen should be packed off home. She forbade Richard to drive Gretchen. He had had far too much to drink. 'Miss Bossy Boots,' Richard had muttered as he telephoned for a cab. 'All you American women are bossy. No fun. No fun at all.'

Pandora had ignored him, bundling a now lacrimose Gretchen into the taxi. 'Do you have money?' she whispered.

'There are other ways to pay for a ride,' Gretchen had whispered back, loudly enough for the cab-driver to hear.

'Well, just in case it doesn't work, honey, here's the fare.' She had returned to the house with Gretchen's jammy lipstick all over her face.

Later that night, leaning forward naked to remove Gretchen's lipstick from her unwilling cheek, she had seen Richard swaying behind her shoulder. 'Finished the jug of martinis,' he had said helpfully. 'Poor, poor woman, married to a brute like that.'

Pandora had turned in irritation. 'Listen, St George,' she had said . . . And then she had lowered her gaze. Around Richard's penis was the bright red imprint of Gretchen's violent red lipstick. 'Oh, look, Richard.' Pandora had held out her red smear of cotton wool. 'Our lipsticks match, don't they?'

Richard had looked down at himself and clasped his genitals in his hands. At the same time he had crossed his legs.

'So that's what you two were doing when I came in. You bastard, Richard! I'm tired of you and your string of unsalvaged women.'

She had walked out of the bedroom and spent the night sitting upright in a chair in the spare bedroom. Things between them had reached an impasse.

Richard's voice on the telephone today had brought that night momentarily into the forefront of her brain. But even now, as the betrayal caused her wound to leak, she knew that the evidence she had seen that night had done nothing to alter the fact that they no longer enjoyed each other's company. The lipstick had merely been the event that allowed the following events to flow, however hurtfully, to the inevitable implosion of their relationship.

And now Pandora was late for lunch with Miss Rosie. Damn, she thought, checking the sun in the sky. It must be after one. Her watch lay beside her bed, another unused memento of her past life.

The walk to Miss Rosie's house took her past a primary school. There, in blue and white dresses for the girls and blue checked shirts for the boys, the children sat at their desks in the cool of the shaded veranda. As she walked by, she was aware of young fresh faces smiling and hands waving at her. She found herself grinning back and then laughing as the class clown did a handstand on his desk for her. His teacher shooed him down, but she, too, joined in the general laughter.

Over Pandora's head the almond trees loomed, ready to drop their now brown fruit into the dust. Papaya trees, spindly under the weight of their heavy fruit, leaned forward as if to offer their bounty to Pandora as she passed by. Her toes, free of shoes, curled in the dust and she saw her arms now less pure in the sunlight slowly turning an acceptable colour of brown. Dogs barked and cats threaded their way between thickly huddled hedges. Fat chickens waggled their egg-laden behinds out of her way. Pandora sighed. She should really try to feel sad for herself and for Richard, but so far today it was impossible. Today, she decided, would go down in her diary as a good day, not one to be outlined in black felt pen and forgotten as soon as possible.

Ahead of her she saw Miss Rosie sitting under her grape tree with a white enamel basin in her lap. 'I'm sorry I'm late, Miss Rosie.' Pandora ran up the immaculately raked drive.

'No hurry, child.' Miss Rosie put up a staying hand. 'I sit here in the cool. Let others run and fuss. I sit quiet.' Miss Rosie sat in an old armchair. Next to her sat its long acquaintance, the sofa. Both leaked slightly but by now comfortable cliffs and valleys had been hollowed out in the aged upholstery. A murky pail of liquid sat beside Miss Rosie's feet. She had a sharp island knife and was cutting a white muscled object into slices. 'That's whelks,' she said, forestalling Pandora's question. 'I picks them every morning at daybreak. I walks along the shore there.' She pointed with her knife. 'I go with my friend, Miss Annie. We be doing that since we were girls together.'

Pandora sat, silenced for a moment. She could not remember any event from her childhood that cobbled together all her thirty-seven years. Miss Rosie could count sixty years hand in hand with Miss

Annie. Pandora remembered Mable Yerwood who had smelled. They had played skipping rope for several summers. And then she had moved. Billy Slipkins, who had taken her to Saturday matinées before she had moved again. How would she settle here on an island where nothing moved and everything was timeless? She didn't know, but she was willing to find out.

Chapter Eight

The morning chores in the little cottage were a time of celebration for Pandora. After those long, lean years of childhood in her mother's sour kitchen in the various frame houses they inhabited in Idaho, this little cottage, equally ill-equipped, still caused Pandora to smile. The fridge was old and she struggled with a thick rim of dark green mould that battled for its life around the lining of the front door. The ice-compartment was broken and triumphantly made quantities of useless hillocks of slushy ice, ignoring the pristine ice-trays Pandora bought from Mr Forgan's shop. Mr Forgan visited the little cottage occasion-ally; and he and Pandora had long meetings over cups of coffee on the subject of the recalcitrant fridge. Nothing seemed to work, except when occasionally Ben lost his temper and gave the fridge a flying kick on the side, when it retaliated and hummed and clicked back at Ben in distress. Even the fridge could not depress her. Unlike her mother's house, the air was clean. Outside the waves beckoned and the sun shone brightly.

True, her least favourite invaders were the cockroaches. Nightly they clicked their way across the floor. Armies of them took up positions behind the cupboard door, in the drawers in the kitchen, and she could hear them scratching under the house.

Going to the newly built bathroom at the back of the house was a nightmare. The first time Pandora had walked confidently into the room, she had reached for the light, only to become curlingly aware that there were many-legged creatures crawling not only around the room but over her feet. She had switched on the light and then she had screamed. Ben had come running to her rescue. 'They're only cockroaches,' he had said, laughing, as she clung to him. 'Haven't you seen them before?'

'Sure,' Pandora had said. 'We used to have them back home, but never this many. Never this size.'

Ben had picked her up and carried her back to bed. 'You'll get used to it all,' he had assured her, stroking the side of her neck. 'I promise.

Hmm. You smell sweet,' he had said, nibbling the lobe of her ear.

Pandora had reached out for him. Almost too tired to come, she had lain in the valleys and troughs of his pleasure. As she had faded into sleep, she had been aware that she enjoyed making love with Ben.

Norman's need for sex had been a mixture of animal lust and revenge for all the women he had imagined had betrayed him in his young life, beginning with his mother. Sex with Marcus had had very little to do with sensual pleasure either. For Marcus, sex was pure power, and she a praying mantis, rubbing together her mandibles in earnest prayer that he might remember that this praying mantis had no evil intentions. Ah, but then she had been too young and far too stupid to realize that it was precisely her innocence that had fired Marcus to even greater acts of cruelty.

Richard liked sex as much as he liked a good scrum down on the rugger field. At the end of some fairly joyless bouncing and the noise of a whale coming up for air, Pandora might be rewarded with a sharp slap on the bottom. Not always, though. There were times when she and Richard, away from his tedious friends, had made love. It was joyful and it was tender, rather as it was now, with Ben. Maybe that was why Pandora so happily made love to him.

She had pushed him gently off. He had lain, a smile on his sleeping face. She had wondered about Richard. How was he doing with Gretchen? Marcus, come to that; they had been together for eight years, a long time in those days of instantaneous relationships. As for Norman, Pandora always imagined him in a railway shack, rather like the one she had lived in with her dad. She had such a clear vision of her dad's thin face as he held his lantern up by his whiskery mouth and chin. 'Good night, little lady,' he'd say, giving her a quick kiss. She knew the kiss was furtive. That was even before her mother's jealous screams blew apart their relationship. Marcus had always insisted that Pandora's father had seduced her, but Pandora knew better . . .

She rolled over. I'll go to sleep now. No need to think about all that now.

Two weeks after that Pandora returned to say hello to Maxine the cook at the hotel. She was famous for her cooking. Maxine was big of brow and huge of forearm. Pandora watched her in awe as she laid into the mounds of pastry for dumplings. Her thick, gold-adorned fingers picked apart seashells for the fish soups and, under a stream of clear running water, forced the inky squid to surrender his sack to lie limp and ivory white. Maxine had a bright smile and a fine curl to her flat nostrils. She was reputed to be, along with Janine, one of the few women who could bring all male aberrant behaviour to a halt.

'So what's up?' Pandora demanded, feeling foolishly at home in this steaming kitchen on an atoll somewhere in the Caribbean.

'Not much, honeybunch.' Maxine engulfed Pandora in a vast, fishy hug. 'That bastard Len done gone to Big Egg after pussy.'

Pandora raised her eyebrows. 'Len the cook?'

Maxine nodded her head. 'How she take him, smelling of grease and onion, I don't know, but she here from Florida. Give him fare money and he gone.' Several dark heads nodded. Pandora knew how they felt. Len's temper made scorpions back off. 'He come back quiet for a time.' Maxine poured Pandora a cup of coffee. 'English teachers outside,' she said. 'Arrived this morning. Already complaining.'

'I'll go out and see if I can cheer them up.' Not everybody was as lucky as she had been when they began life on the island. In a way she felt favoured for the moment by a beneficent blessing. And, walking through the empanelled tropical dining-room, she felt like Pollyanna, setting forth to cheer the world. 'Hi,' she said, sliding into a seat next to a white, larded woman who sat with a child clamped to each thick thigh. 'I'm Pandora.'

'Do you live 'ere?'

The woman sharply lifted her left hand and slapped the girl child on the knee. 'I said shut it, din'I?' The child's wild howl floated across the pool.

Pandora tried again. 'You must be tired,' she said, gazing at the little wisp of a man she supposed must be the husband.

He nodded. 'We didn't know this place would be like this. We spent a day on Big Egg. It was all discos and Hardy's 'amburgers and the hotel 'ad two pools. And then . . .' his voice dropped, 'we came here. We're 'ere for the next two years, you know.'

'What's your name?' Pandora addressed the man, feeling on the whole he was less belligerent.

'My name is Neville, and this is my wife Doreen.'

'You can let the children go, Doreen. They won't do any harm. The pool is quite safe and the sea is not deep. It's great for kids here. Lionel is the manager here and he is really good about letting the locals use the place.'

'You mean the black people.' Doreen pointed to several young boys sitting on the side of the pool.

Pandora tried to keep an edge out of her voice. 'They are local people. This is their island. We are visitors here.' Pandora felt less like Polly-anna and more like Mary Poppins. She also wished she owned Mary Poppins's very sharp umbrella. A quick poke in the butt might get the leviathan moving.

During the discussion, the little boy had managed to wriggle free of his mother's fingers and now stood on an adjacent table, peeing happily on to the ground. A swarm of interested ants scurried to the still foaming pools. Neville got to his feet to attack the child, only to find these microscopic insects were capable of a fearsome bite. He hopped. Doreen yelled, and yet again a child was heard to howl across the quiet of the hotel patio.

Around Pandora, pastel pink and white sun-shades warded off the burning rays of the sun. She saw the handsome face of the manager, Lionel Marshal, protrude from his air-conditioned office. He fluttered two fingers at her, both of which said in Lionel's well-known code, 'Not my scene, honey. You take care of it.'

Pandora sighed. And then, hearing the clatter of heels down through the atrium leading to the hotel patio, she saw the motley crowd of English ex-pats arriving to claim their compatriots. Pandora had met them early in her stay, and had been politely but firmly evading their insistent attentions ever since. She recognized Esmerelda who was married to the weak, drunken science-teacher, Henry. They too had a string of unhealthy children whining behind them. Esmerelda, her wide cheekbones flitting with newfound power, led the advancing forces. 'Come on, you two,' she said, scooping up the pissing child and clapping Doreen on the back. 'We've got the chip-pan on at our place and the beers are all cold. Let's go.'

Pandora watched as they swept out of the hotel, amused to see Doreen point at her and ask loudly, ''Oo's that, then?'

Esmerelda tossed her cabbage-patch head. 'Oh, that's Pandora. American. She's gone native, you know.'

Pandora was shaken for a minute and then she had to laugh. It looked as if they'd given up on her at last, she thought with relief. Compared to the English crowd in their shorts and T-shirts, she did indeed look incongruous. Long ago Ben had given her a local basket with a long handle to carry fruit and food along the road. Around her she wore a cool wrap, supplied by Miss Bundy's boutique, one of the few shops on the island, and under that her swimsuit. And of course her feet were bare.

She walked past Lionel's office and smiled at him through the glass.

He opened the door and beckoned her in. She sank gratefully into the comfortable leather seat. The air-conditioning put a cool mantle over her shoulders. 'Whew,' she said. 'I never thought I'd miss air-conditioning so much.'

'You don't have to, Pandora. You know that?'

Pandora looked at him. His eyes were bright. 'Thanks, Lionel,' she said. 'I'll pass.' Pandora had heard all about the house on the hill shared by Lionel and Linus Marshal. That was the world she left behind her. That was a world that must never touch her again.

As she walked the dusty roads towards her cottage, she reflected sadly that Ben was right. Little Egg was a microcosm of all that could be found in the macrocosm of the world out there. She turned into the liquor shop for a cold beer. There, she knew, she would find Maureen.

Nothing much daunted Maureen, unless any woman unwisely laid a lascivious finger on her Edgar. She had been divorced from Edgar for the last ten years, but single men on Little Egg were hard to find. Most men took off after graduation and returned with wives from Honduras or Florida or anywhere other than Little Egg where the women ruled their men with their blood-thirsty carving knives.

'Can I have a Coors please, Maureen?' There was no one else in the shop. The sea sparkled through the back door. A line of T-shirts extolling the virtue of Little Egg hung limply on the rack, and rows and rows of shining bottles to oblivion awaited purchase. Pretty soon other women would descend after a day's work in the heat. Marie was due by, full of woe with her two tearaway kids, Shirley and Doyle. But for now Pandora sucked at her cold bottle of beer in silence. Belonging is too fragile, she thought. Even happiness is less fragile. You can be happy but not belong. At the turn of a road on a journey to somewhere, the view can make you happy, but you know you are going to move on. Like a childhood scrapbook you can paste the memory and carry it with you under your arm, but to belong, to really, really feel that the earth under your feet will remain for always, not at some point become dangerous or try to flex you off into some other place . . . She envied Maureen. This was her place. She had always been here.

Today Maureen was not in a good mood. Her bushy hair stood sentinel over her lowering brows. 'That bitch!' she said, opening her own bottle of beer with her strong teeth. 'Lizzie made it with my Edgar.'

'Oh no!' Pandora leaned forward with an appropriate look of horror. 'Where?'

51

Edgar, it appeared, yet again staggered from the bar at the hotel, and the hussy lay await in the grapevines. Incapable of defending his virtue, he succumbed to the hussy's embraces. Word reached Maureen through the coconut express. And tonight Maureen would be also crouched in the same grapevines awaiting her arch-enemy.

Pandora tried not to laugh. 'Why don't you belt Edgar, Maureen? After all, he can always say no.'

Maureen shook her head. 'Men never say no,' she said, drawing herself up on her elbows. 'No Egg man, Big or Little, ever says no. Why say no? They have no babies. Not much to do on an island. Just drink and have sex.'

Pandora took a luxurious sip of her beer. She licked the froth from her mouth. 'Not everybody on this island's like that, Maureen. What about the churches? You have lots of churches.'

'Sure we do. Old Brother Silver, he's a good man, and does a good funeral. But that black bastard Sonny?' She spat on the ground. 'One day he'll call the devil to this island and then we shall see.'

Pandora felt a little uneasy. 'What do you mean call the devil?'

'Him, that jack-ass, and Miss Maisy are like that.' Maureen made the sign of the downward cross. 'When obeah and the left-hand path join forces, very dangerous.' In the background there was a thick rumble of thunder.

'I must get back, Maureen. Thanks for the drink.'

Maureen smiled. She flapped her big, loose-knuckled hand. 'For nothing,' she said. 'I'll see you soon.'

Pandora walked along the road. Big bullets of raindrops exploded on her shoulders and between her toes. The water was warm and she lifted her face to the sky. Obeah and left-hand paths had not been part of her catechism in the convent. A flash of lightning danced before her feet. The smell of ions in the air reminded her that this was not Kansas, Toto.

Chapter Nine

Ben belonged to a local diving boat called *Kingfisher*. They were a happy bunch of men who had all been born on the island and grew up together, so for them the sea was an extended playground. The little airplane from Big Egg landed every morning at eight o'clock and disgorged an exhausted pile of would-be divers, pale and blinking in the sunlight. The newcomers usually arrived festooned with useless equipment. The experienced divers carried with them neat blue dive-bags. Around Little Egg other small islands lay, awaiting the impatient arrival of these strangers to the sea. For some, diving is a possession, an addiction.

Pandora took a while to realize just how powerful a mistress the sea was. On his days off, instead of spending the afternoon with Pandora, Ben often left her on a beach while he took off in his diving gear to explore his beloved sea by himself. 'You're supposed to go with some-one else, Ben. It says in the rules of the dive-book.'

'I'll go with someone else when you go with me,' Ben grinned. 'All week I either work on the roads or get hauled in to help at the dive operation. This is my time alone. Why don't you let me teach you to dive, Pandora?'

Pandora didn't know why. She knew she was deeply afraid of the turtle grass that grew everywhere in the reef. She carried with her two shiny, laminated pages, one entitled *Beachcombers' Field Guide: Shells*. These were shells from the tropical Atlantic, Caribbean, and the Gulf of Mexico. The shells delighted her. As she waited for Ben, she walked close to the edge of the outgoing tide and searched with fingers tingling in anticipation. So far she had carried several beautiful pink-edged conchs to the cottage. Brown-spotted measled cowrie shells. They fitted snugly into the palms of her hands and they contained the swell of the sea to her ears. The movement of her body as she swung up and down the beach soothed her. The beaches, unlike so many she had explored, were clean and without the usual rubbish or oil cast off from passing boats.

By now Pandora's island life was establishing a pattern. She rose early, as soon as the sunlight streaked the sky with its dawn fingers. The island cockerels did great battle with the green parrots, but the parrots won out. Great flocks of them screeched off the mountains to settle in the gardens of Pandora's neighbours' house. There they took mischievous bites out of the breakfast papayas, or sat in rows high up on the mango trees laughing raucously at the neighbours' vain attempt to rescue their crops. Old Captain Hardy lived next door with his wife, Mona. He had been away at sea most of their married life. Captain, as he was called, loved to sit on Pandora's stoop and tell her stories of his days in China, of the monsoons off the Singapore coast. 'Hurricanes here?' he said dismissively. 'They don't know hurricanes, not like the South China Sea where the winds go screaming behind the sails of the junks and they fly like clouds, all beating their sails.' Pandora learned to listen and not to fidget.

She was amazed to find that slowly she could walk along the road and not turn and twist apprehensively. She could enter a small shop and ask for a pair of nail scissors and find the exact change without fumbling or blushing. If she forgot to buy dish detergent, the beneficent god that inhabited this particular island forgave her with a bright smile. The first time she had run out of detergent she had stood by the sink in frozen misery, looking at her shaking hands, her neck stiffening. 'You stupid little bitch,' she had heard her mother yell. 'Can't you organize nothing?' Her ear had ached for the expected stinging slap, her eyes tightly closed.

Her mother's shrieking voice, her mother's need for constant dramas, had so polluted Pandora's life that the peace of this little island was almost a curse. When so much of her life had been fraught with the need of other people to inject their lives with tension and drama, the peace and the quiet now brought a feeling of dread. Pandora found herself waiting for the peace to go, for the calm to erupt back into the noise and the violence that were always created by her mother.

Ben had stood beside her, watching her. 'Pandora,' he said. 'What's the matter? Have you been stung by a scorpion?'

'Sort of,' Pandora had managed. Her small frame had rattled and shook. 'It's just a bad memory. It will go away again. Just give me a minute and I'll be fine.'

Ben had put a hand on her shoulder. 'Wait a minute. Nothing's worth getting that upset about. Come on. Let's go outside and I'll get you a cool beer.' Leading Pandora out of the front door, Ben had sat her on the double swing on the porch. The sun had been behind the little house and a breeze blew the strands of her sweat-stained hair away from her face. Slowly she had felt the rictus that distorted her face release its grip and the shaking slowly turning from a helpless shudder to a gentle shiver. The pain in her back had eased and she was able to take a deep breath. The garden – her garden and Ben's garden – had swum into view. While in the grip of these 'hallucinations', as Marcus had called them, she only saw a blank wall with no light, cut off in what felt like a cupboard. Thinking about it today, it was probably just that. She did have a vague memory of her mother advising the nuns to put her in the coal-hole, or some secluded place, until she finished having one of her 'fits', as they were called. These fits had only manifested themselves after her father had left. Pandora knew that, but Monica, Pandora's mother, swore blind that Pandora had always had fits.

Ben had returned to the porch carrying two beer bottles encased in beer-coasters. 'What was the problem, Pandora?'

'Nothing.' Pandora had been embarrassed. She was much too old to behave like that. 'These are nice coasters. Are they from the shop?'

'No, Pandora. You tell me. You looked so afraid. What did you think was going to happen to you?'

Pandora had felt tears stinging her eyes. 'I thought you'd be angry with me,' she had said, hating her little girl's voice.

'What about, Pandora? Why should I be angry with you?'

'Because I forgot . . .' And to her chagrin, the little twelve-year-old girl had taken over and begun to cry in earnest. Huge snotty bubbles had streamed down her face. 'Don't be angry,' she had heard herself saying. The beer had fallen to the floor. 'Please, don't be angry. I'll go and get some more detergent now. I have my allowance saved up.' She fumbled in the pleats of her skirt.

Ben had sat, amazed. This was not the Pandora he knew. This was a poor waif of a thing, a spectre blown in by a black wind, a thing whipped out of sand and dust with thatch palm for hair and sea-grass for arms and legs. 'Take my hand, Pandora, and we will walk to the sea. Come. Just at the end of the garden. If you say you have forgotten to buy dish detergent, then I'll show you something so much better.'

Pandora had looked intently at Ben. 'You're not angry?' she had said.

'Of course not. Nobody in their right mind gets cross if you forget something shopping. It happens to everybody.'

Pandora had followed Ben down the path, wiping away her tears with the edge of her skirt. Who on earth was I afraid of then? she had wondered. Such a litany of tyrants in my life.

The sea sparkled this morning. The sky was cloudless. No wind so much as whispered across the reef. Far out the jagged teeth of the sea coral sat silently. The foam ceased to cleanse the coral, but lay blue and deep. 'Here.' Ben had put his bottle of beer into the sand. 'Wash your face in the sea-water.'

Standing ankle-deep in the water, Pandora had smiled. A tiny fish was furiously attacking her left foot. 'What's he doing?' Pandora had asked as she received quite a sizeable nip from the fish.

'That's a yellow-headed wrasse and you're standing in his territory.' Ben had pointed to a stone. 'He's always there. If you bring him bits of chicken, or scraps, he will befriend you. Anyway, come on. I have something to show you.'

They had walked hand in hand along the beach. 'I wish I'd been born in a reef, Ben, and lived there safely until I was old enough to go out into the open sea. Maybe if you're given time to grow up safely, you don't live in dreadful fear of everything.'

'Maybe you don't, Pandora, but then there are people who live on this island who have never left the safety of the reef. They have never known hunger or how to be poor. When I was little, Mr Sullivan gave me *Huckleberry Finn* to read. I was horrified. I knew we had slaves in these islands. My people were slaves. But I never knew America had slaves. Our preachers always made America sound as if it was God's place on earth. Look down now.' Ben had nudged a brown pod with his foot. 'Pick it up, Pandora, and you can have all the detergent, shampoo, soap, or whatever you want.'

Pandora had picked up the heart-shaped bean pod and looked at it. 'This? Really?'

Ben had taken his diving knife out of his belt and slit open the bean. 'Now, when we go back, we "pounds it and boils it", as Grandma says, and then you will find it will lather up, just like soap. This is what all the old folk used on this island before boats from Miami came in.'

'Was life better then, Ben?'

'Some things were, I suppose. Families were tighter then. Life was hard, though. The men away all the time on ships, making a living. Then they'd come home to the wife and leave another baby to rear. Clothes came from the missionary barrels, so we wore what we could find. But there was plenty of singing and dancing on this island. Christmas night we folk from here took to the roads, all dressed in our best clothes. The men played their violins, and some had guitars, and Grandma and Miss Annie sang with such church voices with all the children about them. And we walked from one end of the island to another. People coming out of their houses to join us and to wave. Some had Johnnie cakes to give us and at the end we all had a big boil-up.'

'Boil-up?'

'Yes, that's what we called it. Captain Hardy made big tin drums full of water and he put in a big piece of the Christmas cow he killed, fish, pig, a chicken or two, a handful of red and green chilli peppers, and then dumplings all floating on top. My, Pandora! The smell of those dumplings!'

Pandora had felt the tendons along the back of her neck relax. Her shoulders had migrated from above her ears back to their normal position. 'Will that happen this Christmas?' she had asked hopefully.

'Some of it will.' Ben had rolled the pod between his fingers. 'Not all of it, because we have Miami for Christmas, but you and I can have all of it. I have my fiddle and Grandma has a boat-load of relatives all back for Christmas. She and Miss Annie cook for three days before Christmas until New Year's Day.'

'It certainly sounds wonderful. Thanks, Ben. I feel a lot better now. I'm sorry about the freak out.'

Ben put his head on one side. 'This afternoon I have to take a crew diving, but tomorrow morning I'll take you snorkelling.' He had seen the apprehension in Pandora's face. 'Don't worry,' he had said. 'We will take as long as you like to get used to the mask and then slowly, one by one, the bogey men will go away.'

Chapter Ten

The idea of looking at fish underwater entranced Pandora. When she was little, she had once won two goldfish in a round goldfish bowl at a fair. It had been evening time, the lights just beginning to prickle the dark backdrop of the lowering sky. That night all those years ago was one of her special shiny memories. Her mother, after an inordinate amount of persuasion from her father, had agreed that the three of them should walk up the long road between the neighbourly twitching curtains to pay a visit to a little local fair that took place every year in a small field in front of the train station. Frank, her father, was able to argue that, as it was his train station that held the fair in order to collect money for medically stricken members of the station crew, they were duty-bound to turn up, at least to listen to the oration given annually by the station master.

Pandora was six. She remembered the date because she was without her front two teeth. For months she had inspected the gaping holes before going to bed, but she could see no budding pearly white teeth in the bland pink gaps. Though the week was peppered with threats from her mother Monica that they would not go, fortunately for Pandora Miss Sylecia, Monica's neighbour and long-time confidante, was carted off to hospital. Pandora was elated: now she couldn't be left in Miss Sylecia's cat-pissed front room. She also felt guilty, as if she had some-how summoned a black curse on the poor woman, who left her house in an ambulance groaning and moaning loudly with 'the gas', as she was ceremoniously carried down her overgrown garden path, thereby promising an afternoon's event for her neighbours to chew over with their meat-loaf and yellow meringue pie. 'Look after my cats, won't you, Monica?'

Monica, loving all hospital events, held the exploding woman's hand all the way down the path to the ambulance door. She gave a little red peck of a kiss to Miss Sylecia's cheek. 'Don't you worry about a thing,' she said. 'I'll see to it all.' As Monica trotted back on her high sling-back heels, she commanded the admiration of the small crowd that had gathered together, summoned by the whine of the ambulance. She knew what went through the heads of those people who lived around her. After all, it was her hands that washed and brushed and combed those heads. It was her motherly advice that told women how to keep their husbands, or at times how to get rid of them. She knew who could afford to pay for a perm, a manicure, and a pedicure, and leave a nice tip at the end of it. Most of all Monica knew she had a reputation in her road that she treasured above all else. She was known as that woman who kept herself to herself. She kept a lovely home, married to a man who came home on time every night and turned over all his money to his wife – not like some – and had a little girl. Pity about the little girl, though. Rather plain and quiet. But then maybe she will blossom. They do.

Pandora, looking in her water-stained mirror in her suffocating bedroom, thought that she wasn't about to blossom now, nor would she ever do so, probably.

Perhaps her two front teeth would grow in; then of course Monica had decreed that she must wear braces. 'I can't think why,' Frank grumbled, but he held his peace. A world war over, braces were unthinkable. Still, today was the day all three of them were going up the road to the fair, and Pandora was brushing her red fly-away hair until she heard the electricity sing and the long strands stick to the brush.

Five of Frank's friends played in a small brass ensemble. Much out of time, but filled with beer, they played their pieces with gusto. Monica, wearing her most severe pleated dress, walked carefully along the grass in her high-heeled shoes. She pigeon-toed her way across the field to the refreshment tent, obediently followed by Frank and Pandora. Frank was hot and sweaty in an aged suit, but Monica had insisted on a shirt and a tie. 'After all, the station master will be in full uniform.' The refreshment tent was cast beside the splendid big black engine that pulled passengers and rolling stock for miles through the flat fields and prairies of Idaho. No one knew or cared very much where it went after that. All the population of Pandora's town just knew that the long, slow hoot of the engine told of the arrivals of the hours of the day, of strangers from beyond, and of goods and textiles to make another day's shopping in town worth while.

The station master cast a quick look at the assembled crowd and then began his speech. It was as long as it was heartfelt. He posed the question to his audience of the value of the great railways that crisscrossed the lands of our country. He spoke of the lives lost keeping those trains and their tracks safe for the wives and children of the settlers. He pointed a white-gloved hand at the rows and rows of little houses with their white picket fences and he finally wound down on a truly melodious hymn of praise to his beloved engine. Declaring the event open, he climbed up the steps of the engine into the cabin and pulled the whistle three times. Each time Pandora's heart quaked, partly with fear, for the noise frightened her, but also with a sensual need to abandon all that was going on in the little field and to push away the station master and to take off, her hand on the whistle. The train pulling faster and faster through the thick, high, golden wheat. *Goodbye, Mother. Goodbye, Miss Sylecia and the stinky cats. Goodbye, school* . . . Never for a moment did she think of a goodbye for her father. After all, it was his railway. Even if the station master wore the uniform, it was her father who washed the steaming sides of the great black iron monster and then weaved his way back to their house with his lantern in one hand and his lunch box in the other.

'I've volunteered to serve lemonade,' Monica announced. 'So you two take yourselves off and don't get into no trouble, you mind. Here, Frank. Here's a dollar for beer and fifty cents for you, Pandora. Get a ribbon or something sensible, though Lord knows I know you won't.'

Pandora smiled at her father. He took her hand in his and they walked together down the dusty, chewing-gum-strewn path towards the shooting gallery. Pandora saw, among the coconuts on the shooting stand and several cuddly toys, two fish in a bowl. She gazed at the fish, round-eyed. Lately she had been reading all there was to read about fish in her school library. At the back of the fiction section she found a story about a boy not much older than herself who lived in Italy and had made friends with a friendly sea-dolphin. Gradually the dolphin had allowed the boy to climb on its back and together they had great adventures diving deep into the warm Mediterranean ocean. For weeks Pandora had been enchanted by the story, by the wildness of the boy untrammelled by adults: just the boy, the dolphin, and the sea. Now, here, before her, were two golden fish, both looking closely at her, their eyes, she was sure, following every move. 'Do you think you could get that? I mean those fish, Dad? For me? I'd sure love to own two fish. I could take care of them myself. Feed 'em ants' eggs and things and clean them out. What do you think, Dad?' Pandora could feel her feet tapping with impatience.

Frank looked down at his daughter. The long sorrow lines deepened around his mouth. 'Your ma ain't going to like them much. She don't much like anything alive. She prefers her fish dead in the refrigerator.'

'I know, Dad, but this time I'll talk her into it. I'll promise to clean out all Miss Sylecia's stinky cats until she comes home from the hospital. I'll promise to do extra shopping. I know I can talk her into it. Please, Dad.'

Frank shrugged. 'OK,' he said. 'But don't say I didn't warn you, honey.' He beckoned to the stall-owner. 'Six rings,' he said.

'Six rings, Frank says! You'll do it. You got long arms.'

Frank smiled. 'If I get it, you got to buy me a beer, Tony.'

Tony laughed. 'If you get those damned fish, I'll buy you two beers. No one wants them suckers.'

'I do.' Pandora drew a deep breath.

The first ring went over but slipped off and fell to the ground.

'I know we are not supposed to pray for silly things,' Pandora addressed her God, locked away in the sacristy of her Catholic convent in Idaho, 'but these ain't silly things, Lord. These are your animals. I mean fish. And I'll be kind to them and look after them all their lives.'

The second ring sailed over. 'You need that beer now, Frank,' Tony said.

'Hell no! I'm just getting my eye in. You watch for the next one.'

The next one hung over the lip and then teetered for a second and fell to the ground. The fish were racing about the bowl. Pandora felt her bladder fill. 'Try, Dad. Really try.'

'Don't you worry. I'll get it for you.' The fourth throw, the ring settled securely around the neck of the fishbowl.

'There you are, little girl!' Tony tied a piece of twine around the lip of the bowl. 'They're all yours.'

Pandora held the fishbowl in both her hands. She raised the level of the bowl to her eyes and gazed at both the fish who gazed back. The larger one of the two blew a friendly bubble. 'Thank you, Dad,' she said, lifting her face for a kiss.

'Think nothing 'bout it. I always went fishing when I was about your age.'

Tony yelled for his son to watch the stand. 'Come on, Frank. I'll buy you that beer.'

Pandora followed both men, walking tenderly on her tiptoes so as not to disturb the water. When they reached the green-flapped tent filled with men, Frank stopped. 'You sit outside, honey,' he said. 'I won't be a moment.'

Tony patted her head. 'Here,' he said. 'Complimentary. On the house.' He put a round container of fish-food in her hand.

Pandora lay on a dusty piece of grass. She was aware of people, mostly feet passing backwards and forwards. As the evening got later, little fairy lights studded the tents and the stalls. Voices, emboldened by drink, grew hoarser. Young girls and boys stood in flirtatious pairs, giggling in gangs or just holding each other, wordlessly and passionately. Pandora watched the teenagers and wondered if her turn would ever come. She could never see herself throwing a punch at a boy or curling up her nose at a knowing remark. Maybe she would be one of those girls who fell in love with just one boy and then it would be for ever. But for now all that was very much in the future, and she had her two goldfish who gazed so soulfully at her, and she knew that from now on their lives depended on her.

She dropped in what she supposed must be several ants' eggs. A careful study of the list of ingredients on the side of the box recommended a pinch of assorted eggs. She puzzled over exactly how much a pinch was, but the fish seemed wildly enthusiastic at the amount proffered by her and swam happily up and down their round bowl in pursuit of the food.

Feet passed swiftly now. Men's flat shoes were outflanked by women's staccato heels as they came in search of their errant husbands. What had once been a comfortable male roar gave way to a peevish bellowing and an occasional stumbling back down the road with a whippet of a wife behind the miscreant. Pandora decided she was in danger of getting stepped on, so she stood up to see her mother's determined figure battling its way down the path. 'Where's your father?' she said, brushing back Pandora's hair with the hard flat of her hand. 'For heaven's sake, child! Pull up your socks. And whatever have you got there?'

'Dad got me two goldfish, Mum. They'll be no trouble. I'll keep them in my room.'

'We'll see about that.' These were always the dreadful words. *We'll see about that.* That could mean anything from instant annihilation to long, drawn-out terrorist tactics. It was a war of attrition for Monica. She could lead her attacks and her ambushes over a long period of time. Sometimes Pandora felt, when these attacks were launched at her father, that he only stayed in their house out of his love and his loyalty to her.

For now, though, Pandora was safe. Monica was going to pull Frank away from his friends, publicly humiliate him, and then march him home to a silent supper, interrupted only by the litany of her efforts to keep a home together for her ungrateful husband and disappointing child. With any luck, the goldfish could be sneaked into Pandora's bedroom and the whole matter could be diverted into a lively discussion as to the state of Miss Sylecia's bowels. Monica could not resist the day-to-day drama of hospital life. And then the evening could be spent with Pandora cleaning up after the cats, and Monica having a good snoop around the woman's now empty house.

Pandora ate a goodbye helping of lemon pie.

All that late summer, the fish sat on the desk in her bedroom where she did her school work. She remembered that bedroom very well indeed. It was by far the most attractive of the bedrooms she had ever had. Frank's never-ending transfers took the family down all sorts of train-lines and into all sorts of accommodation, but this summer still stood out, lit up in the neon fairy lights of that summer evening when her prayers were answered and she got her two fish.

Frank thought the fatter fish was the female, but he admitted he knew nothing about sexing fish. Pandora decided to believe him anyway and she called the putative female fish Dinah after Dinah Shore, who had such a huge, big, earthy voice. The male she called Bing after Bing Crosby because she loved his sticking-out ears and his way of looking like a lost little boy. She watched her Bing mouth his ants' eggs and then remembered Bing on the screen on a Saturday afternoon mumble his first notes into his mouth, rolling them around his tongue to feel if they were in the right shape to escape from his lips.

Pandora talked to her fish all the time. That autumn the woods at the back of the railroad tracks turned a deep golden brown. The leaves came tumbling out of the wind and the branches, amputated of their hands, stretched towards the sky. Something had happened that autumn to the fishes, Pandora could not now remember exactly what. It was so long ago. The turtle grass in the water around Little Egg had awakened some distant fear, linked, she was sure, to that episode. But more than that she couldn't, for the moment, recall. More baggage in the attic. She knew it was there and one day it would reappear.

A perfect day for snorkelling. Ben sat up in bed, clasped his hands around his bare knees and gazed out of the front door. Pandora snuggled down beside him. 'Let's make love,' she said. 'I've had dreams about fish.'

'We can make love and then go snorkelling,' Ben suggested. 'We have all morning ahead of us.' Ben looked down at Pandora. 'Before or after your cup of coffee?'

'Right now,' she said. *What a terribly late age to discover that fucking can be fun.* The thought slid through her head as they moved slowly and teasingly together.

'You wait for me,' Ben said. 'Sexy American woman.'

'No, I won't.' Pandora felt herself rising rapidly to the pulsating one-pointedness that would finally let her plunge down a throbbing slope, each throb more heartfelt than the last.

Once down and back, firmly on their well-remembered bed, she waited for Ben. Finally, after a last gasp and a moan, he took a deep, shaky breath. 'You'll have to get coffee for me this time,' he said. 'And how about sausages and bacon?'

'OK.' Pandora was up. All her muscles hung loose. Her joints felt stretched, and even her usually tense facial muscles felt loose. I can't live on a beach for ever and make love to Ben, she thought. Somewhere outside in the real world Richard exists. Do I really want to divorce him? Is there anything to hang on to there? Somewhere, probably closer than I'd care to think, my mother is raging.

The local bacon, seasoned in thyme, splattered. Red tomatoes oozed succulent seeds into the penumbrae of white surrounding the brilliant yellow of Miss Rosie's eggs. The aroma of fresh coffee and sharp, slightly singed toast raised Ben from his post-coital slumber.

'If only life could always be like this, Ben.' Pandora put the tray down on her side of the bed. She sat, watching him seriously. 'Maybe if I go snorkelling, I'll find out why I'm so afraid of water. I do splash in it, but I don't trust it.'

Ben wiped his mouth with the back of his hand. 'Islands give you time to find out lots of things,' he said. 'That's why I hate Miami. No time. No time to listen.' He climbed out of bed, carrying both plates, and Pandora looked across at his back as he walked towards the little caboose at the back of the house. Two steps down and then two up led to the little kitchen where food was prepared. Pandora felt like pinching herself, it was all so pretty. So clean.

Don't dwell on bad things. Don't worry about time or for how long. Just accept that for now this is your happiness and somewhere in my not so very nice life I earned this time.

She got up and located a bathing suit. Lime green. It suited her.

Chapter Eleven

'This is the bay for snorkelling.' Ben smiled at Pandora. She was standing rather awkwardly in her blue fins. 'Do they fit?' Pandora wiggled her feet.

'Yes, they do,' she said. 'But I feel like a walrus.'

'Just walk backwards and fall into the water. It's very shallow here.'

Pandora, holding her matching blue mask and snorkel, took two lurching steps back and fell rather noisily into the quiet cove. She came up grinning. 'Well, that's chased away anything worth looking at.'

'They'll come back.' Ben was busy spitting into his face-mask. Pandora watched him carefully. 'This spit will stop the mask steaming up. Give it a try.' Ben slipped his mask over his head and then moved across to Pandora. 'Here. Let me help you. Don't panic. Just breathe through your mouth. In and out. In and out. See?' Pandora nodded. 'Now I'll put the mouthpiece between your lips. Hold it there and continue to breathe. In and out.' He took her hand and they backed gradually into deeper water. 'Now you can see the water is waist-deep. Just put your face gently on the top of the water and breathe in and out of the snorkel.'

Fascinated, Pandora saw a flotilla of purple striped fish dashing about between her legs. 'Wonderful!' she exclaimed and received a mouthful of salt water. Choking, she pushed off the mask.

'Next time, don't talk. Just stick your thumb in the air.'

'I'll certainly remember.' So far Pandora was pleased. She was not as frightened as she had imagined she might be, but then the still nearby ocean floor was clean with pure white sand.

Ben held her waist and then stretched out her legs behind her. 'Now float. Stay flat on top of the water and just look around you.'

At first Pandora could only see stones and rocks. The little flotilla of fish had gone. But then she saw something flat and crumpled lying right underneath her. One large round eye looked back at her. She jolted upright, spluttering. 'It was the eye,' she said shivering. 'It was like the eye of one of my fish.'

Ben held her arm and bent down. 'Look. It's only a baby flounder. It can't hurt you. There's nothing to be alarmed about.'

Pandora took a shaky breath. 'I know,' she said, 'but it just reminded me of the fish I had. There's some memory – something horrible about what happened to them – that keeps nudging at my consciousness, scaring me.'

'Let's try again, Pandora. We have all the time in the world.'

She obediently flattened out and began to kick her fins. Slowly, with Ben by her side, she followed the underwater sea wall formed by ancient formations of coral. For a moment she hesitated at the mouth of the shallow lagoon, but Ben took her firmly by the hand and pulled her through. Now the water lay deeper and she saw a brilliant shoal of bright blue fish gazing up at her. To begin with they were quite far down, feeding off the bottom of the sandy stretch between great coral antlers. Pandora was breathless with excitement. She pointed furiously at the fish. 'Spotted parrot fish,' Ben said, speaking to her for a moment above the water's surface. 'Watch me.' He took a huge gulp of air and then he dived down between the fish. Amused, Ben lay on the bottom of the sand, the fish gliding over and around him. How at home he is in the sea, Pandora thought. How very at home. It's me that's so clumsy and alien. I'm always an alien, I suppose, wherever I go.

She adjusted her mask and then took several strokes by herself. Far down below her, Pandora saw a flat triangle lying close to the sea floor. There was a long whip-like tail. For a moment Pandora thought she might panic. She felt the air in her chest get faster. She steadied herself and looked behind. She could see Ben. He was moving up beside her. Then she looked down again. The ray – she recognized it as a spotted eagle ray from one of Ben's charts – had not moved. She moved her legs until she was right over the fish. They stared at each other. To her surprise, the ray's eyes were blue. Most of all she was surprised to find that the ray seemed to look at her with total comprehension. The eyes were filled and luminous with intelligence. She lay over the great ray and then he cast a last look at her and began to flap away into the darkness and the shadows.

Pandora lifted her face. She was beaming with pleasure. 'Did you see that?' she said.

Ben nodded. He tipped his mask up to the top of his head. 'He's an old friend of mine. I call him Man Ray: he seems almost human.'

'He's wonderful, Ben.'

Pandora lay in the warm blue water, her body relaxed and her mind afloat. How could I have wasted all those years so miserably? Not any more.

They both rolled over together and started slowly for the entrance of the cove. Ben was leading Pandora through the entrance. The tide was tugging behind her shoulders. And suddenly she was aware of a long line of turtle grass blowing around her face-mask and slowly touching her fingers and her legs. She felt the distant memory hurtling into focus: she did remember what happened to the fish. She began to lash out, as frantic as she had been all those years ago. She felt water fill her lungs and then she lost all control.

She felt Ben pulling her through the water, his elbow tight about her neck. She knew it was not Ben she was fighting; it was the river, the river that ran behind the railway station and fed the thirsty trains through a system of pipes and pulleys and filters. The stream was white in late autumn, full of old tin cans and used condoms. Rats lived in the banks. Pandora avoided the river as much as possible.

It was a cold November day and Monica was grumbling about the state of her bedroom. 'I'll do it when I get back from school, Mom. I'm late and I have a maths test. I'll have to study on the bus.'

'You spend too long staring at those fish of yours,' her mother shouted at her retreating back.

Pandora fled for the bus. Once safe inside she sat down and pulled out her maths book. Maths was hard for Pandora. English came so much more easily.

The day was long and the ride back equally exhausting. She could hear her mother moving about in the kitchen. She ran through to her room to put down her school books and then she noticed the fishbowl was no longer there. Just a small round polished place stood empty of the bowl and of the two fish who gazed at her so lovingly every afternoon. 'Mom!' she shrieked. 'Where are my fish?' She barged into the kitchen.

Her mother was bending over the stove, her hair still latticed and stiff with hairspray. Her nails clawed open an empty cake tin. For once the pale blue iris eyes looked shifty. 'I threw them things out, Pandora. Winter's coming and it ain't healthy to have all those dirty little eggs floating around.'

'You threw them out? Where did you throw them out?'

Monica pointed out to the backyard. 'Down there where the sewer-pipe reaches the river.' Pandora grabbed her mother by the shoulder and pulled her out of the back kitchen along the ground. Monica gritted her teeth. 'You always were a wild child. And one day you'll get your just deserts.'

Pandora was past listening or caring. She paused by the water-pipe. It leaked sour grey water from age-old underwear and snot-encrusted handkerchiefs.

'There's the bowl.' Monica pointed down among the filth and the weeds.

Pandora peered down beside her and saw the fishbowl sitting upright on the bottom of the river. She jumped into the river and, immersing her face in the grease and the stench, she struggled to get a grip on the bowl. Finally tearing away at the rotting weeds and swallowing mouthfuls of the slimy water, she pulled the bowl to the surface. She tried to stay afloat with one hand flailing frantically. The other held the fishbowl which proved to be empty. Her mother ran up and down in a straight line, screaming and panting. 'Mother of God! It's my daughter! She's drowning! It's a sinful thing she's done, but Lord forgive her!'

Pandora felt herself lose her grip on the bowl. She fell back into the water and the weeds and the fronds of the slippery grass washed across her face. She opened her eyes and felt perfectly calm. If I could die now, she thought, I'd be happy. No more of this life, dear God. I want no more of it.

What seemed like hours later, Pandora felt rough hands on her face, pushing her head to one side. She was on the bank, throwing up, and she felt as if she might never stop. An old can of Campbell's Tomato Soup gaped beside her in sympathy. And then the tall figure of her father bent over her. 'Ah, darlin',' he said. 'Whydja do that?'

He picked her up in her sodden school uniform and carried her home. 'I'll get you two more fish,' he said as he tucked her into bed after a warm bath.

'I never want to own anything again. Never again.' That night there were no grateful prayers to God from the little bedside in the shack by the train station. Only a bald spot where the fishbowl used to sit.

'Pandora, stop kicking.'

Slowly she could hear Ben's voice intruding on her terror.

'Pandora?' She felt him hold her upright in the water and remove her mask. He held his cheek tightly against hers. He waited while the tears coursed down her face and then the sobs slowly subsided.

'You did all that to save two goldfish?'

Pandora nodded. 'I know it sounds mad,' she said after she explained the story, 'but apart from my father, they were the only things that I loved. And they loved me back. It was as if . . . Well, I can't explain this. All the love I needed to give to my mother I gave to them. Does that make any sort of sense? You see, my mother very rarely smiled. Every day when I came home, the fish were pleased to see me. They waggled their tails and they raced around the bowl. I talked to them a lot because Mom was either over at the hairdresser's or she was at the neighbours'. There was really no one to talk to at home. She didn't allow animals. She said they gave her an allergic reaction.'

'Well, you're OK now.' Ben hugged her close. 'But don't throw any more of those panics on me again, Pandora. Tell me what's bothering you before you get in that state.'

They climbed out of the rock pool and lay in the sun. Somehow the recaptured memory seemed to have exorcized some of the fear: her panic had not been illogical hysteria – what her mother called one of her 'fits' – but had been the natural response to a scary incident, made worse by years of repression. I'll practise swimming among the turtle grass every day, Pandora promised herself. After all, I came here to swim with the dolphins.

Chapter Twelve

The moped turned the corner into the drive of the cottage and Pandora kept her drowned head close to Ben's back. She was ashamed of her behaviour, but also shaken. Now she just felt tired. The juxtaposition of a beautiful sunny day, the clean sea, and the wondrous fish . . . and all she had managed to do was to turn it into a nightmare for herself. 'Don't worry,' Ben reassured her. 'I have people panicking all the time. It's quite normal. And you were in no danger. I'm just sorry it spoiled your first snorkel. We'll try again soon. Here. You lie on the hammock and I'll bring you some of Grandma's sweet lime tea.'

Pandora lay gratefully in the hammock. She pulled her wrap around her and felt that familiar moment when the heat of a drying body draws into itself the still-wet bathing suit. 'You'll ruin your kidneys that way,' her mother scolded . . . She was asleep before Ben was back with the lime tea. He watched as she lay on her side, her knees drawn up and her hands and arms wrapped about her sad face, and he did not have the heart to awaken her.

Monica did not have much to say when Pandora turned up on her doorstep two nights after her run-away wedding with Norman. Pandora held her suitcase in one hand and tried very hard to shield a battered nose and black and bulbous eye from the all-seeing neighbourhood. Though God knows, she comforted herself, a black eye is no strange occasion in a town like this. The door opened by itself. The town was still safe enough to leave the key in the latch, and for that Pandora was grateful. She dreaded for some reason having to knock on her mother's door. Somehow the act of knocking was an acknowledged submission and an act of contrition. *Forgive me, God, for I have sinned.* Yes, indeed. Father O'Hanlon would agree most heartily. She had sinned. The vows were for better or for worse, and already she had torn apart her vows and left the marriage.

She stood, her face numb, her injured eye bulging and blue. Small drops of blood fell from her nose and she tried to sniff to keep the stains from her white jacket and blouse. That much-loved jacket she had chosen weeks ago to go away as Norman's bride. She pushed the door a little further open and there in the yellow light of the hall stood her mother.

For once her mother's hair was dishevelled, her glittering eyes pink, and her mouth trembling. 'So, you thought you'd run out on me like your father did, did you? You little tramp. Don't think I didn't know you'd gone. Miss Jones was there registering her dog and she saw you both giggling and whispering. Well? What have you got to say for yourself now, you stupid little whore? Look at your face.' She walked up to Pandora and tipped her face to the fly-blown light. Pandora had always hated that light. It hung on a long piece of aged flex from the high ceiling in the well of the stairs. From time to time Monica had made it her business to wage war on the daddy-long-legs and the flies. Pieces of sticking paper hung in long rolls from the flex, and various bodies in differing stages of decay swung to and fro, casting shadows.

The shade used once to be white Bakelite but was now deeply yellowed, like an old man's toenails. But for now, while Monica was examining Pandora's face, there were at least two new dead daddy-long-legs to study. Pandora had always thought of her own father as Daddy-Long-Legs, and before they had both been thrown out of their paradise together, it was on those long legs she would sit and pretend they were riding across the fields and the woods. She could feel tears well in her eyes. If Dad had been there now, Norman would be hauled out of bed and made to behave.

Anyway, she had had enough of Norman and tomorrow she would go down to the Honeydew Grocery Store and ask for her old job back. She had been the store supervisor; before long she could save up her pay cheques and get a place of her own. All that she decided as she stood waiting for a breath of kindness from her mother.

'You won't get rid of him that quick,' Monica said, anticipating in that uncanny way she always had Pandora's private thoughts. 'He'll be back and he'll be begging. Well, I got to go to work in an hour or so. You can get back the use of your old room. I planned a cold plate of eggs and ham and cottage cheese for myself and Miss Sylecia. Her gas is much better. No salad or onions. You can get it ready for me. Remember to boil the eggs for exactly four and a half minutes. Leave the fat on the ham. It's good for you. Don't you do anything stupid like throwing it away.'

'I won't, Mom. Can I just get upstairs and change?'

Monica went off into the kitchen and Pandora hauled herself hand by hand up each familiar step. Three steps on the side, the tear in the green and maroon patterned stair carpet. She used to sit for hours during the evenings at the very top of the stairs while the black and white television fluttered its pictures through the ajar door, and her parents' voices rumbled backwards and forwards like distant storms in the prairies. Mostly they sounded like dust storms, dry and high-flying, a promise of rain to calm the dust. But often Monica's voice would crack through like a slice of lightning. 'You just listen to me, Frank!' The roll of thunder she could put on the F of Frank was ominous, presaging the crack of the sound on the k which made the cups in the corner cupboard rattle.

Now, years later, Pandora, an embittered bride, entered her own childhood room, the one with the writing table still polished, the chair pushed neatly into the knee-hole, and the same round bald space that used to contain her fish. She put her suitcase on the floor and she began to cry. Not just for herself or for Norman, or even for the marriage. It was a marriage she had orchestrated. She had no one to blame but herself. It was more a lament for a life ill-spent. How often had she left this and other rooms as a child to go out to bars and coffee places with her teenage friends, and ended up in the back of a car, handing out her wares as easily as if she were offering strips of chewing gum? Not all the girls were as bold. Indeed, she knew with a crippling sense of shame that she was by far the easiest 'lay'.

Want a girl for a date? Take Pandora. She'll open her box for anyone. That, she knew, was the joke around the block.

At the convent she ran, huddled and unseen, up and down the corridors, always a little late, always crumpled and always out of breath. The nuns sighed over children like her. 'What do you expect?' her class teacher asked the head mother. 'The poor child has moved schools almost every two years. The girl is illiterate.' Little did Mother Eliza know that once let out of school Pandora made up for all her educational dysfunction by being very busy with the boys. To her, sex offered no pleasure; it was just a moment of power among many. Learning to second-guess her mother taught Pandora more about psychology than any class offered at her high school. Norman just wanted to get into her pants the moment he met her, because he had his own reputation to uphold. Pandora had kept him waiting for a good long week.

Several chocolate milkshakes had slipped down her throat as she watched his big Adam's apple bob up and down his neck. He had huge mechanic's hands and the thick fingers wrapped and unwrapped themselves round her ankles under the table. Pandora sucked the milk-shakes slowly and suggestively through the straws, making pretty little pink forays with her tongue. She stretched her foot under the table and dared him to pin her shoe between his thighs. 'Saturday, Norman,' she whispered as they pushed away the table. 'Let's do it Saturday.'

At least Norman had a mattress at the back of his mechanic's shop. The place was none too tidy, but he had the foresight to put a clean pillow at the head of the mattress and a blue and white striped blanket spread over the grey ticking. 'My, what a pretty little blanket, Norman,' Pandora said, swinging her white square handbag.

Norman smiled. Pandora really liked the way Norman smiled. He had deep-set sad eyes, but occasionally they could catch fire, and then his long, sad face looked quite appealing. Pandora hoped she could make Norman smile rather often.

'Want a drink?' Norman opened a fridge behind his pick-up truck and took out a beer.

'You don't have any root beer, do you, Norman? My mother says it's uncouth for a girl to drink real beer.'

Norman paused for a while. 'I don't have any root beer, but I do have a Coke. Will that be OK?' Norman's voice was shaking.

Pandora always enjoyed this moment just before events began to unfold. This was like the movies. Here she was, perched on the side of a chair by the mattress. The prop, of course. Lit by hundreds of lights. Men crouched behind the movie cameras whispering instructions. Sound booms hovered over the mattress to catch every groan, every moan that might occur. This was no ordinary, everyday movie; this was Pandora Productions' *Pandora – Queen of Porn*. Open the box and out came all the equipment ever needed to turn a man witless with lust. So far all there was in Pandora's box of porn were three pornographic magazines (payment from a willing client) and a black suspender-belt with red garters.

Today she was wearing the suspender-belt. She had purchased two 15-denier silk stockings and was swinging a very white pointed shoe held on by the very tip of her big toe. Now the director was calling for silence. Pandora sipped her Coca-Cola, alas! not through a straw. A wasted moment of tension, she felt, but still it was Act One, Scene One.

Norman, clutching his bottle of beer, approached her chair. He bent his head and put his thick lips over her mouth. He stood for a moment savouring the minute. 'No, not like that, Norman,' Pandora said. She made an invisible signal to the lighting men. 'Just look what you're doing. You're messing up my hair and my lipstick is all over your face.'

Norman stood sullen. 'Ain't we goin' to get on with it?'

'*Aren't we*, Norman. *Aren't we*. Didn't you learn anything at all at your school? Now, let me just clean off this lipstick with my nice clean handkerchief, and then you can hold me and kiss me properly, like James Dean kisses his girls. As a matter of fact, you look a little like James Dean. He's so cute.'

'Shut up and let me kiss you,' was all Norman could manage.

Pandora slipped her eyes upwards. Cue camera, lights. Act One, Scene One, Take Two.

Norman had a slightly different version of the forthcoming event, and threw Pandora down on the mattress with such force that she was winded. He tore off his belt with one hand while he pulled up her skirt with the other. 'Don't be in such a hurry,' Pandora chided. 'You'll tear my stockings.'

'I'll get you a new pair,' Norman grunted.

Finally, with Norman's jeans on the floor and his underpants flopped beside them, he struggled impatiently with Pandora's suspender-belt. After grappling a hold on the elastic waistline, he pulled with all his might and was rewarded with a shot like a pellet from a gun. The stocking holder hit him in the eye, but at least all the studs were pulled asunder and he could get down to the business of getting laid.

Pandora lay passively under his big heaving body. This was going to take time, she thought. He was no express train, like some of those boys who entered the tunnel, who let out a few loud whistles and then were finished. Neither, thank God, was he a nervous type who dripped the contents before entry and then effected a dry and embarrassing run. No, Norman had screwed a few women in his time and had obviously enjoyed it. She looked at the large, clean garage. She knew he'd left school and owned his own house. His father was dead and his mother was in south Florida. That was really when Pandora first thought Norman might be a possible way out of a life of sorrow and boredom with her own mother.

Obviously not. Here she was again, back in her mother's house in her own room, without the goldfish.

Cold ham. Miss Sylecia's several applications of powder covered Pandora's eye. Miss Sylecia was thrilled to be the first to get the scoop

74

for the street: *Monica's girl came back two days after her honeymoon with a busted nose and a black eye.* 'We weren't expecting you home so quick, Pandora. What happened? Lover's tiff?' Miss Sylecia laughed in breathy gasps. She showed rotten stumps of her yellow teeth.

'Something like that, Miss Sylecia.' Pandora passed the cold ham. She hated the pink perspiring pieces of pork with their white shining skirts of fat. Monica always insisted on globs of white cottage cheese, boiled eggs sliced to show their lemony yellow sulphur-centred cupolas. Pandora put down the plate and waited for her mother to bring the iced tea. She waited for either the sound of a car or the tinkle of the telephone. Where was Norman?

Monica brought in the iced tea and sat heavily down in her own personal chair. Monica's chair had a high back and she could lean against it without disturbing her hair. 'Iced tea for everyone?' Monica enquired brightly. Her eyes were alight. At last, here was some excitement. Excitement was what she most missed in her life with Frank, her terminally boring husband.

Pandora noticed that her mother had painted her nails her usual scarlet, but she also knew that to achieve such a high gloss required endless patience. One layer of nail polish, much shaken, the little ball-bearing banging and bouncing up and down in the bottle, and then the moment of the quick turn of the wrist and the frown as the threads, caked with last week's polish, relinquished their grip. Then an overcoat of see-through polish to hold and immobilize the arterial blood sprouting from each digit. A maximum time of puff-cheek blowing, and then the red again. Finally, hands held high in the air, delicately waved to and fro, and the fingers were ready, full of promise.

What did Monica's fingers promise? Pandora wondered. Certainly they would never be found curled around a hot and hairy pair of balls. Monica probably wouldn't even know where to find such things. Her proud claim to Pandora was that only she and the Virgin Mary had achieved virgin birth. She had thought of going up to the convent and seeing Father Dodd about her miracle, but Frank talked her out of it. Anyway, she always said afterwards, one look at peeky Pandora with her slightly buck-teeth and eyes like green tea, everyone would know it was an accident of the devil.

Pandora looked at her own hands. So far she had chewed two nails fully down to the quick and scraped off most of the pink polish. She wore a pleated grey skirt and white blouse with a Peter Pan collar. She so much wanted to pretend that those awful days had not happened, that her eye was not swollen and hurt, and above all that her wedding ring, which sat on her left finger and did mean so much to her, was always going to stay there. Maybe once she and Norman could talk again, she could find out what had upset him so.

She had known that he could be moody and bad-tempered before she married him, but he could also be kind and sweet. He loved small cuddly things like kittens and puppy dogs. He was proud of her and she knew that. Any boy who stared at her when she was on his arm had best beware. The only other man who had that kind of authority was her father . . .

She glanced down at her plate and at her pale frosty glass of iced tea. There was a difference. People feared Norman. They had respected Frank.

After finishing the iced tea, she telephoned the garage. She waited. There was no reply. Just before she got ready for bed she telephoned the apartment above the garage, their apartment with the new double bed. There was still no reply. She lay in her own small bed feeling very young and very sorry for herself. It was then that she had known with a dreadful certainty that this marriage was going to be a disaster.

Chapter Thirteen

Monica had gone off to work the next day. 'Seeing as you're here, slumping about in your nightdress, you might as well give the house a good clean,' she had said to Pandora. 'Fix a sweet smile on that sullen face of yours. And then, when I come back, I'll go by Norman's and see if he's home.'

'No thanks, Mom.' Pandora's hands were in the sink. 'I'd rather go round myself.'

'Don't be so silly, girl. I can handle Norman. He just needs telling where to get off. Besides, you can't stay here for longer than a few days. One thing to have a newly-wed quarrel. But that isn't the end of the marriage. You clean up and I'll go round after work and put the fear of God into that no-good layabout.'

'He isn't a layabout, Mom. He works very hard on those trucks and he fixes them well. He's just got a bad temper. That's all.'

'Your daddy never hit anybody.'

'I know, Mom. I know. He just went out that door one day and he never came back.' Pandora felt the Palmolive soap in the kitchen sink slip through her grasp. It slid with such force that it flopped out of the sink on to the floor. 'No husband of mine is ever going to walk away from me like that, Mom. Not if I treat him right. And I intend to treat Norman the best way I can.'

'Are you saying I didn't treat Frank right, young lady?'

Pandora sighed. She didn't need this endless, tortuous discussion yet again.

'Let me tell you, your daddy adored me until you came along and spoiled my waist and gave me those veins on my legs, so I could no longer wear short skirts. You ruined my marriage to your father, you flirtatious little minx. I had to haul you off him.'

'He wasn't doing anything, Mom. We were just playing together.' Pandora stood very still. This was the first time the subject had come up since the incident. They were both in the kitchen, and behind them stood the open door where her father traditionally sat with his belt unbuckled and his legs outstretched. Pandora could feel the smell of him, the sooty smell of cold air around his iron-grey hair.

Monica looked at her daughter's face. Monica's peculiar eyes groped to see how much damage she could inflict on this evil child of hers who had so captivated her quiet, kindly husband that he was prepared to walk out on his shrew of a wife. Monica knew that she was a shrew. She revelled in her history at the hairdresser's. *Don't mess with Monica* was the word down there. In the store, managed by Monica, life ran like the trains. Tick-tock went the clock. Shunt-shunt went the bodies of the ladies under their hairnets. Oh yes, Miss Monica was a holy terror, a holy terror who always carried a crucifix in her pocket which she shook when irritated. The Virgin Mary was her special friend, and a Hail Mary was like a royal command from Monica to get things temporal seen to rather fast.

This time, Monica thought, she'd save her spleen for a visit to Norman's house. So she smiled. 'I must be going,' she said, ignoring Pandora's statement. 'Make us a nice plate of cold Spam and radish. I like a cold salad after a hot day at the store.'

The door slammed and Pandora stood in the quiet of the house. Should she try the telephone again? Maybe not, not if Mom was going over there anyway.

She began to clean the kitchen. It was not so much that it was dirty, because Monica was not the sort of woman who kept a dirty house. The house was far more flaking with age, so that surfaces had been repainted. Not meticulously, like Dad used to paint, but paint splashed on paint, so that the grooves attracted and held dirt. Monica did everything very quickly. All surfaces were wiped down, so that corners eventually accumulated small balls of dried food. Pandora decided to change into her jeans, get out the Clorox, and really give the whole room a scrub. Maybe if she could tackle the kitchen and then the living-room, the day would pass by quickly and Monica would come back with an answer.

She must give her marriage another try. Pandora was not a quitter. Her dad taught her that, even though in the end he had quitted. Well, she wouldn't. She didn't want to live somewhere in the universe not knowing the whereabouts of the man she had vowed to love until death us do part.

Miss Rosie's lime tea was refreshing. Ben woke Pandora by pushing the hammock lightly and then bending down and kissing her on the forehead. 'You look as if you've been chasing little lizards in your sleep,' he said.

'No.' Pandora sat up. 'I dreamed I was cleaning up my mom's kitchen. The time I ran away from Norman after we were married.' She sipped the tea.

'Do you want to tell me about it?' Ben sat cross-legged on the floor.

'Don't you ever get bored hearing about my unsuccessful life and relationships with men?'

'Not really. Not at all. All over this island people are all telling the same stories.'

'Do you think any marriages are happy, Ben? Ever?'

'Sure I do. Look at my grandma and grandpa. They were happy. Not all of the time. Sometimes things were hard. But they had love and patience. Yeah, it can be good.'

'Well, not for me it isn't. Mom did go and see Norman, and he said I could go back if I wanted to. No sorry, no explanations. Just that I could go back. So I did, Ben. I packed my suitcase, said goodbye to the kitchen floor which had never been so clean and shiny in all its life, and I went home to my husband. Tell you what, though, Ben. The rest doesn't get any better. Let's do something fun together and I'll tell you the rest later on.'

Ben stood up and shaded his face with his hand. 'Wind is swinging south,' he said. 'Looks like a good day for fishing. I could call Octo and see if he's around; we and some of the boys could go for a picnic on Fire Island. Would you like that?'

Pandora finished her cup of tea and threw her arms around Ben's neck. 'I'd love it,' she said.

'I'll get the boat ready, Pandora. You get a cooler with beer and a sharp knife. With luck, we'll catch yellowtail or dolphin.' He saw her face pale. 'Not that kind of dolphin, silly. It's a fish. No one here would hurt a dolphin.'

Pandora smiled. 'Maybe we might see one, hunh?'

'Not so much this time of year. They tend to come down in March to get away from the cold weather. But you never know.'

Pandora hurried into the house. For a moment she felt transfixed between these several worlds. The bleak, dark, dangerous world of Norman, which intruded into this paradise. Then the even more secretive, horror-stricken years with Marcus painted an evil-shaded purple. And finally Richard. There was a passage in Pandora's Bible that always reduced her to tears when she thought of Richard. She did not know

79

the passage by heart because she had left her Bible long ago in the convent, but she did remember King David's grief when he told God of his friend's desertion: 'Yea, mine own familiar friend, in whom I trusted, which did eat of my bread, hath lifted up his heel against me.' All those wasted years: she had now time to take off some of the Band-Aids and let the sea air and the sun heal the wounds. One day she might be whole again. The gloom lifted at this thought and she rummaged about in the ancient fridge looking for ice for the cooler.

Ben's boat was fourteen feet from stem to stern. She was painted white with a light blue flash. She had two seats in the tiny cockpit and two box-seats further back. She was made of fibreglass and Ben assured Pandora she was almost impossible to sink. Pandora reminded Ben that she had almost no knowledge of little boats. The years she was Marcus's wife the boats tended to be motorized gin-palaces. And Richard's attempts at rowing only seemed to result in catching crabs. Still, as she sat in her seat with Ben by her side, she appreciated the little boat. First it chirped like a cricket and then thrumped when the powerful 75 HP engine at the back picked up speed. Ben lifted the anchor, laid it wet and dripping on the front of the boat, and then turned the boat away from the shallow water and zoomed it into a curve up the reef.

The boat responded like a ballet dancer. It lifted its nose and tucked in its tail. Behind, a huge foam, like the tutu of a dancing swan, creamed across the water. Ben, half-standing, watched the sharp coral beneath the waves. 'You really have to know these reefs,' he said. 'See that old can there? That's really sharp. It can take the bottom off the boat.'

As they passed other houses, Pandora could see boats being winched and hauled in and out of the water. Those being winched on to their trailers belonged to the early fishermen with their big catches of wahoo and yellow-fin tuna. 'See the frigate birds?' Ben pointed and laughed. 'They're bastards, those birds. Too lazy to catch anything for themselves, they wait.' Two men sitting on the rocks were flailing and flapping at the birds as they streaked in, their enormous wings stretched out and their greedy claws waiting.

Octo's boat now fell in behind Ben's boat. 'What's your boat called?' Pandora asked.

'*Shalom*,' Ben answered. 'It means *peace* in Hebrew. I like the name, and it certainly brings me peace. A day out on her, and I'm happy and calm and nobody can rattle me, not even old Janine. See that big sucker over there with the two engines and the big cabin? That belongs to

Octo, Janine's man. He's big-time trouble, but if you don't trouble him, he'll leave you alone.'

Pandora gazed across at the giant of a man on the large boat. He was naked except for a pair of swimming briefs. His arms were massive. He looked as if he pulled mango trees out of the ground in his spare time. His face was carved in an interesting fashion. Half a nostril was missing, Pandora realized with a slight shudder. She could see Janine's magnificent torso stretched out on the roof of the cabin. 'She looks as if she's wearing a pink shoelace,' Pandora remarked.

'She is. And not around her ankles either. Anyway, she's Octo's woman, so no one will bother her.'

By now, many of the boats were heading for the break in the reef. These were the famous reefs where Captain Kidd and Blackbeard used to hide their treasure, especially this one on Little Egg. Ben was squaring up the *Shalom* between a series of poles. 'There is a huge tide here, Pandora, so I'll race across it and then keep going. I can't turn for a good while because there is a very famous rock called Bluer's Rock, which we have to avoid. Hold tight and I'll try and read the waves, but occasionally we're going to slap down.' He looked down at Pandora's face. 'OK?' he said.

She nodded enthusiastically. 'Sure thing,' she said. 'Let's go, partner.'

Ben smiled as he pushed the throttle forward. Pandora was not the usual spoiled American girl. She was good fun. He felt a little part of his heart melt, and then he reminded himself what his grandmother always said: 'Old song, child. My mommy sang it to us girls all those years ago when our brothers went to other countries to get girls.

> *'Island girls, you get a wife.*
> *Foreign girls, they give you strife.'*

As he shot through the reef, Ben immersed himself in the tumble and the roar of the waves that came at him. He heard the wild shuddering of the straining engine bite and buck across the waves. He was reminded of his grandmother's words and he acknowledged a truth in them. Though in Pandora's case she seemed to have made such a mess of her life, she really was a small castaway. She looked much better now since they had been living and loving together. He was surprised at the animal straightforwardness of her need for sex, how much she enjoyed his body, and her own climax. The tumbling water reminded him of their moments in bed together, the sheets damp with semen and the dripping honey between her thighs. Ben had been wary of the new breed of American women who descended on Little Egg with their money and their rapacious eyes. Sex for them might easily be available with green dollar bills on the tables at Bar 666. But the few times he took these women home he found the sex thin and disagreeable. No joining of two pliant bodies with an urge to explode into each other, rather a cerebral approach and a back-achingly long performance to get the woman to come. For a long time Ben remained celibate rather than find himself with one of these creatures in tow. Pandora, though, from the moment they joyously connected, contented him.

Now she sat, her knuckles white on the side of the boat. Ben eased back the throttle and the boat planed out. 'See?' he pointed. 'Look over there. Watch carefully. Flying fish.' A few feet away from the boat Pandora could see silver flecks of fish lift themselves out of the water, small wings outstretched, and then, in a flying glide, slip back down again.

By now all the faster boats were well ahead. Pandora could see Fire Island. It lacked the mountains that protected Little Egg. It was low and flat. Ben pottered slowly. 'Don't let's hurry. They can do all the catching, and we'll get there just in time for eating. After lunch, we'll snorkel again. There is no turtle grass on Fire Beach Bay for you to worry about. It's all soft white sand. I'll show you how to catch the lobsters and we'll take one home for supper.'

Ben put his arm around Pandora's shoulder. The boat comfortably took her time approaching their eventual destination. Why can't life always be like this? Pandora wondered. She knew Norman would have liked the fishing, but too many people made him angry and uncomfortable. Marcus would frankly have been very, very bored. There was nothing perverse to pursue. Richard, without his built-in gang of playmates and volleyball or tennis after tea would have been striding up and down the island after ten minutes trying to find something to do. Hopefully Gretchen is keeping him busy, she thought.

As they approached the murky shadows on the sea floor, Pandora gasped. 'Look, Ben! That must be a man swimming.' She could see a vast back and two strong arms. And then she saw the big jaws and the long nose with two straining nostrils.

'That's a really big old sea turtle. Oh boy!' Ben's face lit up with pleasure. 'Look at him go!'

The turtle let out a huge belch, its mighty guts rumbling. The stale smell of old squid and dead sea creatures enveloped the boat and then the old leviathan looked into Pandora's eyes – his, so old and yellowed with wisdom, and hers so green and lost. He dived and she leaned over the boat and watched him go. You've lived for so long a time and kept yourself safe, old turtle, I think I'll try doing the same.

As they came closer to the reef on Fire Island, the waters changed colours. Where there were clean sandy bottoms, the water was a limpid green. Dark, menacing colours closed over jagged coral rocks. At times the sea was blue and untroubled. Slowly, slowly, Ben picked his way between coral heads and around smooth boulders. The shadow of the boat was sometimes before and sometimes behind them, but he was sure of foot and his hands and feet spoke the language of the sea and of the sand.

Finally they rounded the corner. Seven or eight boats lay beached while clumps of Little Eggers sat in the water gossiping. Some were up under big banana trees that gave shade. Already the small boys were gutting the fish they had caught on the way over. Pandora waited until Ben had anchored the boat and then jumped into the water. She looked about her and smiled. Hopefully, she thought, we'll find time to walk somewhere together. Just by ourselves.

Chapter Fourteen

Pandora recognized many of the faces that sat under the trees on Fire Island. In the sand someone had built a big square brick barbecue. On the spit already, a big grey fish was turning slowly, its pink flesh cracking through the crisp skin. The woman turning the spit smiled at Pandora. She had a lap full of fresh limes which she cut expertly and squeezed over the fish.

'What kind of fish is that?' Pandora asked, feeling a little shy among this crowd of people who all knew each other so well.

'That fish is grouper. He is fat fish. You the American girl with Ben?'

Pandora blushed. 'Yes,' she said. 'I stay at his house.' She looked anxiously at the woman. She so much wanted her approval.

'Ben is a good boy. He is my cousin through the Fletcher side of the family.'

Pandora laughed. 'You're all related, you know.'

'Everybody is related to everybody. My name is Lucy Fletcher and yours is Pandora Townsend.'

'It *was* Pandora Townsend, Miss Lucy, but I really don't have a name. I'm sort of divorced, or at least I'm on the way to my third divorce. My last husband's name is Richard Townsend. I'm really sort of just Pandora.'

'Really.' Miss Lucy squatted herself comfortably on her haunches. 'It seems to me that women in America change their husbands often. So many women come here like you, alone.'

Pandora sat on the sand. It was warm and she felt comfortable talking to Miss Lucy. Miss Rosie and Miss Annie she now considered her friends. Although they put their hair up in bright red rollers for special occasions and painted their nails and wore their best frocks (as Miss Annie called her dresses) they were serious women, unlike so many of the women Pandora had surrounded herself with for years. With Norman she had had no friends at all.

In Marcus's crowd the idea of friendship never occurred to any of them. The trick was to damage and to destroy. The latest piece of gossip from the night before was a necessary acquisition. During those years Pandora largely remained silent.

Richard's friends did have friendships going far back into nannyhood: Richard's best friend was his nanny. The men all had affairs as fast and as furiously as their Peugeots or Aston Martins could take them across town.

Pandora sat with the familiar dull ache in her heart. Why Gretchen? What did he see in her? She gazed down at her slim brown thighs and her brown feet partly buried in the sand. Gretchen had thighs like marble rolling-pins and buttocks that would win her trophies at the Idaho State Fair. Still Pandora smiled at Miss Lucy. 'Women don't leave their men, Miss Lucy. The men just get bored and leave them.'

'Not on this island, they don't.'

Pandora could see Ben talking with his friends. He was happy and relaxed. 'How do the women stop their men leaving?' she asked, intrigued.

Miss Lucy picked up a lethal knife. It was sickle-shaped and it looked as if it were intended to cut grass. 'We find our man with another woman, we cuts the woman like this.'

Pandora jumped as the blade flashed past her face.

'Men go drinking at the bar and get kind of big talk. Come home and hit the wife. But then we gets them the next day. All over the island. Listen.' Miss Lucy was in a good mood to tell a story. 'One white woman come here. She married to Public Works' officer. She think she better than all us dark women on the island. Hunh! One day she run off with Bridie's husband. Now he is a good-looking man. Lots of women look at his pants. But Bridie has his pants well tied down.' Miss Lucy squeezed another lime over the fish and gave it a fast twirl. 'Now one day, after the dance, and the sun not yet up, Bridie can't find her man. So she go hunting. She find him and that white woman in the bushes.' She spat on the sand. 'That harlot of a woman, naked! So Miss Bridie beat her with a stick all the way back into town. You should have seen her dance and howl! All lights went on in the village! All women lean out, give her a lick for Miss Bridie! I tell you, no man drop his trousers for months on this island. We women take care of our own.'

'Didn't anything happen to Miss Bridie's husband?'

Miss Lucy shook her head. 'Shame enough for him. Miss Bridie go see the white woman husband. Said the island was too small for her and the white woman. So last thing the white woman saw was Miss Bridie waving her off at the airport.'

'Wow! I wish I'd known you a long time ago, Miss Lucy.'

'Little Egg women had to be tough. We all grow our own vegetables and fruits. We dig on the mountain.' She paused for a moment and ran the knife down the back of the fish. Then she nodded. 'All done,' she said. She covered the coals with sand. 'Let the fish sit for a while. It come better off the bones. No, when all the men were away at sea most of the years, we women made money with our eggs or our chickens or whatever. Or if we didn't have money, we barter. Miss Annie's cakes are the best on the island. When she and I were little girls and hungry, we used to go to the cousins down east and clean their yard. She could give us a covered pan of coco plums. So we would take that to school for lunch. On the way home we could pick almonds and coconuts. Nobody ever went hungry. But work was hard. Miss Annie was planting yams when her baby boy was born. Almost didn't get into the bed at all!' She giggled. 'Now you go and tell the others fish is cooked.'

'I will, Miss Lucy, and thank you for talking to me.'

Miss Lucy watched the girl go. Somebody done took her backbone out, she thought.

After an excellent lunch of freshly caught fish, fried Johnny cakes, which looked like dumplings, and yam, Pandora lay stretched out in the sun, half-asleep. Ben was asleep, his arm protectively across his eyes. Behind her Pandora could hear a furious argument developing, and then a large lumbering shadow walk away. A flurry of sand spread over her prostrate body and she sat up. She saw Janine's hurt face. She was leaning on a palm tree. It was Octo walking like a vexed grizzly bear, making for his boat anchored a little way off the shore. 'Can you carry me home, Pandora? Octo's in a bad mood, so he's leaving now without me!'

'Is he angry with you, Janine?'

'He's always angry with everybody all the time, that Octo.'

'Then why do you stay with him?'

'Why do any of us stay with any of them?'

Pandora hunched her shoulders. 'You're right, I suppose. I did, three times. At least I had the sense to get out of the first, but the second, I only got out because I thought he'd kill me if I didn't. And the third . . . Well, he asked to go away with another woman. So I haven't much to boast about.'

Janine slid gracefully to the ground. She had covered her tiny bikini with a white T-shirt. Her shining black hair hung loose and her large eyes, with their double fringes, looked seriously at Pandora. 'I've been with many men. Oh, poy! I expect you've heard the island gossip.'

Pandora nodded. 'I listen, but I don't believe most of it.'

'Well, in my case it's true. Octo came and got me out of a slum when I was just a child. He taught me how not to get pregnant and he sold me to men or women or whoever would pay. He never beat me like the other men who beat their girls and boys. He always fed me well and took care of me. I love Octo.'

Pandora's mouth fell open. 'How can you love a man like that? A man who made you a . . . Well, a prostitute, I suppose?'

Janine looked at Pandora. 'Honey, where I come from in the slums of Honduras, that's what all children learn to do early. Have sex. Sex means money. Money means food. Food means life. Haven't you ever made a fool of yourself over a man?'

'Yeah. I have. His name was Marcus. The funny thing was that he was supposed to be rescuing me from my first husband who beat me. He was a psychiatrist at my local hospital. He looked at my face. I looked as if I'd run into a train. I told him the old "door" story, but he wouldn't buy it, of course. I remember he said very matter-of-factly, "If you'd run into a door, you'd have a big bruise across your nose as well as two black eyes. Nope. That's one sock in the eye and then another." That's how I met Marcus. What an evil bastard he turned out to be!'

'In my life,' said Janine, 'I have noticed a type of man who likes to rescue women. They pick them up and dust them off and take great care of them. Then, when they feel they have sufficiently reformed them, made them completely dependent on them and so forth, they get bored and then they become cruel. Like small boys tearing the legs off soldier crabs.

'Octo is not like that,' she continued. 'He is not cruel at all. He has a great sadness to bear. Here on this island, you will hear about the island sickness. That's all it's called. You also hear about the depressions and the sugar sickness. They are all related, you see, because so many of the families had to marry each other. Strange children were born. Many died at birth, they were so deformed. Many were hidden away by the families and you never see them. Octo's mother was one. No one has seen her for years. They say she has the face and the shoulders of a cow. A huge, great forehead, and a thick pelt of hair. They say all sorts of things about her, but when she got pregnant with Octo, she was afraid they might take him away from her. So she went into the mountains and stayed there for years. Nobody saw Octo, and eventually everybody just believed that they both died. One day, Octo thinks he must have been about eight years old, he came down the mountain wearing clothes made with thatch palm. And he walked into the school house and said he wanted to go to school. Various missionaries and the school teachers tried to get him to tell them where his mother was, but he never would. They even tried to follow him, but those mountains are a warren of chalk caves, and only Octo knows how to get through them. She must be quite old now, but he loves her with his life.'

'Have you seen her?'

Janine shook her head. 'Nobody's seen her. She doesn't want to be seen either. He takes care of her. If he gets caught or goes to jail, she knows where to find me, and I've promised Octo I'll take care of her. He has his moods, Octo does, but I really love him.'

'I can see that.'

Janine smiled. 'Come on. Let's go for a swim and you can tell me all about your psychiatrist. Here on this island, we don't believe in such things. Miss Annie always says a good purge will cure anything.'

Ben was still sleeping, so both women walked down to the powdery dry sand and then fell gracefully into the bath-like sea. Pandora surveyed her toes sticking out of the water. 'I feel unsinkable in this sea.' She looked across at Janine.

'It's the salt. There is so much salt in the ocean, you feel as if you could float for ever.'

Pandora envied Janine. Janine really loved Octo, and listening to Janine Pandora realized that she had never really loved anybody. Certainly not Norman. He was a way of escaping her mother. She had certainly thought she loved Marcus, but now she realized that much of Janine's description of reforming a woman then torturing her applied to her relationship with Marcus. But then, how could she have known? There were no government health warnings stamped on his forehead. She remembered her first appointment, made by the hospital social worker just before she left the little local hospital. Even after all those years, Pandora remembered the social worker's kindly face. 'Don't be afraid to tell him everything, honey,' the woman said. 'Remember, half the hospital beds are filled up with women whose husbands beat them regular-like. I don't understand it myself. It must be the drink.'

'I think Norman hits me when he's sober, too,' Pandora had replied.

After the disastrous honeymoon episode, Norman did let Pandora back into the house. He never had much to say before they were married, but now he said even less. Pandora cleaned, washed, and cooked, and then waited for Norman to come back from his favourite bar. The night might end up with him lashing out at her or it might not. When she told Norman she had been given an appointment to see a psychiatrist, all he said was, 'Good. At least a nut-doctor might find some loose screw in that silly head of yours. Is my shirt ready for tomorrow?' Pandora was relieved. Norman could be very touchy about whom he allowed her to talk to.

Lying on her back on Fire Island, floating over the pure white sand where no turtle grass grew, Pandora felt safe enough to examine the second part of her nightmare.

She walked down a long white corridor in the psychiatric wing of the general hospital. Fortunately she didn't know anybody in the General Hospital at Boise, Idaho, and her mother knew nothing of this appointment. The nurse who accompanied her was a small, compact woman. She had a thick gold wedding band on her finger. She looked very happily married, Pandora decided. Happily married women had a clean white light about them. They had a bounce in their step. They laughed a lot. Pandora couldn't remember the last time she had really laughed with Norman. It must have been months. They moved around each other like submerged icebergs, she full of fear and he full of rage, except when he crudely coupled with her and then fell asleep, leaving her crying.

Pandora knew she looked awful. She had on a black suit that was shiny with too much wear. She hid her stringy neck with a pink scarf in an attempt to brighten up her outfit. But she knew the pink clashed with her red hair. Her left hand gripped her handbag. She packed three handkerchiefs, hoping she would not cry, and her shoes, though dusted and cleaned, turned dismally up at the toes. She just did not have the money to have them resoled. The nurse knocked on the door.

'Come in.'

At least the voice sounded nice.

The nurse gave Pandora an encouraging push and then closed the door behind her. The psychiatrist was standing by the window, looking out over a fresh meadow. She could see the soft green light of the trees reflected in the mirror behind the great desk. On the desk a brass sign read, 'Marcus Sutherland, MD.' Pandora looked at this long, slender man. In fact she found herself staring at him. He was tall, very tall indeed. Taller than her father. His skin was milk-white, as if he'd never been in the sun. As he continued to gaze out of the window, she realized the man had a completely round face. A golf-ball of a face. No chin at all. Very shiny, flat ears to the head.

There was still a great silence in the room. Dr Sutherland turned and faced Pandora. 'Why have you come?' he said. Weariness and disapproval mapped his face.

'What a fool I was.' Pandora rolled over on to her stomach. 'You know, Janine, I reckon he saw me coming. Looking back, I must have been the perfect little idiot, just waiting to be taken for a ride by a man like that.'

Janine snorted sea-water and stood up. 'In my life, I have had many men. But most men have macho. American women laugh at macho. They think it means men drinking and swearing and showing off. It doesn't. To me, macho means that a man, if he is a man, lives by rules, and one of the main rules is that he is good to his woman. I don't mean he doesn't hit her. Men do hit women everywhere. But a macho man is not cruel. If he hits a woman, it is because he is angry. But your man sounds bad. You say nothing about him, but I see his face, like a vision. ¡Madona mía! Such an awful face.'

'Can you see visions, Janine?'

Janine laughed. 'Yes, and I can tell fortunes. Here, give me your hand, my friend.' Pandora held out her right hand. 'No. Give me your left hand first. That is the hand God made you with. Look! You have a broken heart, early on, as a little girl.'

'My dad left one day. He waved and he was gone.' They were both standing now on the edge of the sea together, Janine, so much taller, the water dripping off her shoulders, and Pandora small, her face lifted, listening intently.

Ben lay propped on one elbow, watching them both. He was glad Janine had taken Pandora under her motherly – well, perhaps not motherly – bosom. Pandora needed to open her eyes and to look around her. Ben worried about her as if she were a small child. In a way she was just that. When her father walked out on her, a part of Pandora closed down. She could run a house, she was a good cook, she could race around on his moped. But for so much of her life she had been this unhappy little child, chained, as far as he could see, to this scorpion-

90

fish of a mother. This morning a fax had come through to the Telephone and Wireless office. Fortunately Ben took the call before Pandora awoke. *Arriving next Friday. Be there to pick me up, Monica.* Ben thanked Mrs Scott and tucked the fax away. Today was not a day to be spoiled by Pandora's mother.

'You see, Pandora, if you now look at your right hand at the top line, your line of the heart, what a mess! How many boys when you were young?'

'Lots,' Pandora said and made a face.

'No money for all that sex?'

Pandora shook her head. 'Guys don't have to pay for sex any more in America. It's all free.'

'The babies that come after are not free.'

'I know.' Pandora looked at her hand. 'I was lucky, I suppose. Norman kicked me so hard when I was pregnant they had to do a hysterectomy, so I can't have kids. Anyway, I don't want kids. What if I turned out to be just like my mom?'

'Aye. You have a terrible opinion of yourself. Look at you. You're small and pretty. You have hair like a sunset. Why don't you sign on with Octo and we'll both go to Rio and make a fortune?'

'Hey, wait a minute! Who's going where?'

'I'm telling Pandora that she and I will go with Octo for the Rio Carnival. We'll both make a fortune. Rio men like women with red hair and green eyes and skin like the inside of a banana.' Janine ran a finger up the inside of Pandora's arm. 'You must drink all that creamy milk in America.'

'Can you tell me more about my future, Janine? I know Marcus has gone for good, but what about Richard? He's my third husband and he has gone off with my friend. At least I thought she was my friend.'

Janine took Pandora's hand again. She saw Ben's face watching carefully. Oh damn, she thought. Whatever I say will hurt Ben. He is falling in love with Pandora. She lightly traced a diverging line that ran alongside the heart line. 'Your Richard has a lot to learn,' she said. 'He is young for his age, and greedy to play too much. His time will run out, but you must wait.'

'Do you think we'll be back together again?'

Janine winced at the pain in Pandora's voice. 'Who can tell?' she said. 'For now I have Octo. For now you have Ben. Why more questions, Pandora? Why must Americans be certain? Two certainties: you struggle through your mother's womb alone and finally you die alone.

The first you cannot dictate, but the last you must do your best. You owe it to your ancestors that you die a good death.'

Ben put his arm around Pandora. 'Don't let Janine chill you with her moods.'

'My mother was a great voodoo priestess from Haiti. When they were driven from there, they went to Honduras. That's where Octo finally found me. By the way, Ben, I'm coming back with you and I'll show Pandora how to sing for the dolphins.'

'Can you really do that?'

'Of course you can, Pandora. You can talk to all things. God made them with his wind. Even rocks are made with intelligence.'

'You talk to rocks?'

'Yes. I talk to everything. Beetles, lizards, scorpions. Always I talk. Come back now to the trees and we will get ready to go.'

Standing under the banana tree Pandora felt she had taken a far journey. The wind had moved across the island and the sea was flat, almost too lazy even to suck at the sand. The blues and greens were like giant rolls of Italian silk. The other boats were already on their way, most of them out of the channel and out to sea. So only the three of them stood in the falling four o'clock shadow. Ben put on his sea-cap and Pandora pulled on a T-shirt. She could feel the tingle of too much sun. Janine ambled to the boat and hoisted herself on to the beam end. 'I'll watch you out,' she said to Ben. 'I been taking boats out of this reef when you were on your mummy's titty.'

Pandora laughed. How much she had missed in those years as a friendless little girl in her mother's grey, arid yard.

The little boat pointed its nose out to sea. Pandora stood beside Janine, who pointed at fish as they passed through the coral heads. 'Here,' she said, indicating two big barracuda. 'They live there always. Here only eat barra after the ants have tasted it. If the ants die, the barra is poison. Fish-poisoning is bad out here. I had an uncle. He ate a wall-eyed jack. Poisoned him. He was like a dead man. Twenty-five years ago, he ate that jack. Still comes back the poison. Now, see those two triangles on the shore behind us? Watch. Ben will line them up, and then we will go through safely.'

Pandora watched Ben carefully as he swung the boat and then straightened her out. He gunned the engine full throttle and then the boat picked up speed. For Pandora, it was thrilling. Beside them the flying fish escorted them out of the reef. Janine had a small shell in her hand. She stood at the back of the boat, blowing through the shell, the sound hardly audible over the threshing of the engine. But Pandora could just hear it. A high, clear, joyous sound. A sound that would make all living things want to unite and to sing. Janine stopped blowing and turned to Pandora. 'Not today,' she said. 'It's too early yet. But they will come.'

Pandora sat in silence in the boat. Ben dropped Janine off at the hotel. 'Do you think Richard is all right, Janine?'

Janine shook her head. 'That bastard dumps you for your best friend and you worry about him? OK. Octo is in a bad mood tonight. I'll come to your house for supper, and I'll bring my looking bowl. OK? Maybe you can see him.'

'Just by looking in a bowl?'

'Not just water. A few other things as well.'

'You mean magic.' Ben pushed Janine off the boat. 'Don't forget, she's the voodoo daughter.'

As they took the boat up the shoreline, Pandora gazed at Ben. 'Aren't you nervous, Ben?'

Ben shook his head. 'Janine is a good witch, not like Miss Maisy. Anyway, these islands are full of magic, demons, and ghosts. Why not?' He shrugged. 'Mr Sullivan used to teach me about your Shakespeare and his ghosts. How about the ghost of Banquo, hunh?'

'I didn't do any Shakespeare at school, Ben. I was an awful dummy, I think.'

They tied up and climbed out of the boat. Hand in hand they walked towards the cottage. It was as if they had both been away for a very long time together. The yard looked fresh and the little cottage lay anew in their eyesight. Pandora sighed. 'I'd like life always to be like this, Ben.'

Ben kissed her. 'So would I,' he said. 'But it can't be, Pandora. It just can't be.' He said it with such desolation in his voice.

Chapter Fifteen

Talking about Marcus had upset Pandora. Usually she left that part of her life well hidden away. Although Norman upset her, she at least understood her motive in choosing him. Partly it had certainly been to get away from her mother, but partly it had been pity. She had felt sorry for the big, lonely man. Somehow she was certain that if she were a good enough wife, she could make him happy. But Marcus had been like a black box for her. Now, while she waited for Ben to come back with some fish, she tried to recapture the memories of that first morning in his office.

She remembered the words 'Why have you come?' and she also remembered Dr Sutherland's long white fingers pointing to the chair by the massive table, empty except for the sign that gave his name.

'The hospital social worker sent me here.' Pandora opened her handbag and tried to flush out a little piece of rolled up paper with her appointment written on it. But somehow the handbag had decided to have a party all of its own, and it had disgorged its distended contents on to the floor. Pandora's lipstick rolled loudly across the tiled floor. A spare pair of black tights lay sprawled beside the lipstick. Pandora blushed. She felt her pale skin take on a bright red shine. Between the black tights and the lipstick the doctor must think she was a hooker of some sort.

'Pick it up like a good girl, and I'll have a read of your notes.' Dr Sutherland's voice wasn't from Boise, Idaho. It sounded New York, Pandora thought as she scrabbled on the floor. She watched him surreptitiously as he bent his sleek head over a folder that seemed to have appeared from nowhere. His hands were long and slender. His nails, she noticed, had no half-moons. They were very carefully manicured and buffed until they shone. She was not sure, but she thought they were painted.

Now she was on the floor picking up her lipstick, she noticed that he wore black lace-up shoes. Most of the doctors around the hospital wore loafers; the younger ones even wore sneakers. But these shoes looked terribly, terribly expensive. So did the suit. Finally Pandora restored order to her handbag and sat straight up in the chair. Her hands clutched the handbag and her feet did not quite touch the ground, which made her feel very childish.

'I see, Mrs Banks, you have been referred to this hospital on several occasions, and you have been admitted as an in-patient three times. The last time, your face was fractured. Hm.' He leaned back in his chair and then suddenly lunged forward. 'There, you see? Right there.' He pushed his fingers into Pandora's left cheekbone. 'Hardest bone in the body to break. He must have taken a real crack at it. What did he do it with? His fist?'

'No.' Pandora was still wincing from the memory. 'He had an iron bar.'

Dr Sutherland leaned back. 'Yes, that would do it, I suppose. Let me see. Broken fingers. Six cracked ribs. Did he ever use knives or threaten you with guns?'

'No.' Pandora shook her head. She felt so naked in front of this man. She had never discussed her life with Norman with anybody. Of course her mother knew Norman hit her. They both ignored the subject. 'You always were a clumsy one,' was her mother's way of getting around an embarrassing black eye.

'Was your husband in trouble with the police?'

'Oh no. Never. Norman's not like that.'

Dr Sutherland smiled. 'Most of them are never in trouble with the police, dear,' he said. 'Wife-beating is a secret crime. It takes place behind closed doors and nobody interferes. Do they?'

'No. They don't.' Pandora looked down at her hands. They were shaking. She remembered the times she had stuffed handkerchiefs into her mouth to muffle the screams. How Norman held his big hand over her mouth and her nose, almost choking her.

'You lost a child,' he said with something like sympathy in his voice.

'Yes. He kicked me down the stairs when I was four months pregnant.'

'I'm sorry if all this is very painful for you, Mrs Banks, but if you will trust me, I will try and help you with this perilous situation you are in.'

'Perilous?' Pandora was quite shocked by the word. 'I don't think it's that bad.'

'Maybe not, Mrs Banks. But my last client died.' Dr Sutherland wrote out a prescription. 'These will keep you calm, dear, and I'll see you again next Monday. Try to stay calm, and make a list for me of the things that make him angry.'

Dr Sutherland stood up. He towered over Pandora, but his handshake was firm and he took her proprietorially to the door of the consulting room. Pandora found herself quite comforted. Here was a man who knew how to make things better. Dr Sutherland had the same certainty that her father had. Her father's trains always ran on time; she was equally sure that Dr Marcus Sutherland would regulate things for her.

'I nearly forgot to tell you,' Ben said when he arrived back carrying a thatched palm basket. 'I have a fax from your mother. She will be here next Friday.'

'Oh shit.' Pandora stood in the kitchen.

'Is she that awful?' Ben put the basket down and put his arms around Pandora.

'She's not so awful now, Ben; she's too old to hurt me, except for some of the things she says. It's more that there were bits in my life when she was very cruel to me. Not just when I was a child, or even when I was with Norman. Mostly she tried to make me stay with Marcus because she liked to be the mother-in-law of a psychiatrist and visit us in our big house. I can't forgive her for that. I try, but I still feel very bitter.'

'You know that whatever you do, good or bad, it follows you, Pandora.'

'Well, I didn't do much that was very good so far, did I?'

Ben smiled. 'I must have done something very good,' he said. 'I caught a yellow-tail tuna fish. Come on. I'll show you how we spice fish on this island.'

Slowly, as Pandora chopped the onions into tiny shreds and added the hot little chillies that made her fingers sting, she forgot the nightmare that was Marcus. Ben cut the fish into thick cutlets and then, with a major sharp knife, he slit the side of each cutlet like an envelope. Now, with the mixture of green peppers, chilli and onions, this fish was ready to be cooked. He took a pile of grated coconut from the fridge and then pressed the liquid out through a sieve. 'That,' he said, throwing away the remaining solids, 'is what we call trash. And then this is the pure milk. In the old days my grandmother collected the oil on top of the milk and we used it for lamps.' He poured the coconut milk over the fish and then cut a tomato and laid the bright red pieces across each piece of fish. 'Now we can put it in a slow oven and wait for Janine.'

They sat watching the sun set over their little boat. Pandora very much wanted to ask Ben why he was so adamant that they could not stay together, but she still felt uneasy with such a question. For once she was at peace with the world and with herself. She loved Ben. He was simple and uncomplicated. She loved to make love with him. The sad thought crossed her mind that she could never ever give him a child. As she sat beside him on the old rusty swing, she felt a mixture of lust and sadness well up inside her.

She gently took his fingers in hers and moved them down to the space between her swimsuit and her skin. Ben's face and eyes lit up. She always loved the joy in his face when they were about to make love. He moved his fingers gently, exploring her slightly parted lips. 'You still smell of the sea and the heat of the sun,' she said, pulling herself on to his lap. As she moved her thighs across him, she dropped her swimsuit and sat naked, straddled across his thighs. In a moment he had removed his shorts and was kissing her nipples.

As he positioned himself inside her, he swung the old swing with his heels. At first slowly and lazily, as Pandora lay in his arms, her head on his chest; then she raised her hips and moved down on him harder. She took his mouth in hers. 'Faster,' she said. 'Faster.' Ahead of her she could see the bright red ball of the sun about to drop into the sea. She wanted to climax like the sun, to plunge deep into the sea and then stretch out in space for ever. With a gasp she felt herself move on a rising tide. Deep down inside and below any point of her body that she knew she owned she felt as if the whole island was moving with them both. The bottom lip of the sun kissed the sea and then slid faster and faster to its rest.

Ben erupted and Pandora lay back laughing. 'Paradise,' she said. 'That was great. We must try this swing more often.'

Ben held her in his arms. 'Many babies are born on these swings,' he said. 'Hey. We'd better get cleaned up, or Janine will be here and we'll be running around naked.'

Janine was late, very late, but that was predictable. 'She has to look for plants on certain parts of the mountain.'

The fish was cooked. The embers of the fire were burning low and Pandora had her head on Ben's shoulders, almost asleep, when she heard the sounds of feet crunching on the sand towards them.

'Sorry.' Janine was standing in front of the fire. 'I'm late, but I had to look for a root that grows in the swamp.'

Pandora knew the swamps. They were dark brown mud and smelled of long-dead things. Mangrove struggled to survive in the sludge. The swamps were inhabited by fierce crabs. Some were blue, but the most ferocious of all was the white crab. Its flesh was delicious, but it had a huge fighting claw and if not held properly the claw could pierce a man's leg. Ben often picked up a white crab and chased Pandora.

'It's OK, Janine.' Ben stood up.

'I'll just go in and shower the swamp mud from my feet. Ugh! I hate the place.' Janine's eyes were very bright, even in the dying fire.

'You look as if you have fireflies in your eyes, Janine.'

Janine laughed as she went into the cottage. 'And you two look as if you've just made love.'

Pandora blushed. 'How do you know?' she said.

'When two people make love, there is a golden thread between them that lasts for days. I can see the cord between you. Take this bowl and sit by the fire and just look into the water. The secret is not to think of anything at all. You need to empty your mind. You practise, and I'll get washed and changed. After we have finished, we can eat. You must be famished.'

Pandora sat cross-legged on the sand with a small blue bowl of liquid in front of her. 'I'm not hungry. I'm too excited.'

Chapter Sixteen

When Janine had finished her shower, she returned to the porch and walked around the yard talking to herself. 'From this plant . . .' She pulled a strip of leaf from the banana tree. 'The banana is not a tree. It is a member of the vegetable family . . .'

Ben busied himself with the fish. 'Do hurry, Janine. I'm starving.'

Janine looked up at the sky. 'See?' she said. 'See that bright star over by the moon?'

Pandora stared. 'I think so,' she said, a little nervously. 'I was never very good at that sort of thing.'

'Well, from now on you are going to practise looking at that star every night. Tonight I'm going to catch it for you in that bowl of liquid that I have given you to hold. Watch carefully.' Janine, wearing a long, flowing kaftan, raised her slim arms up high. In her fingers the small round bowl seemed to capture the cold light of the moon.

Pandora stood up beside Janine and gazed at both the woman and the bowl. Now Janine's face had lost its sexual promiscuity. Her mouth was a straight hard line. Her nose no longer flared with laughter and her eyes were still full of dancing fireflies. Around her Pandora felt as if she were being pulled into a blue haze.

'Let go, Pandora,' Janine said. 'Let the aura take you over. We will both be wrapped as one. Now look into the bowl.'

Janine put the bowl in Pandora's hands. Pandora looked down into the black water. 'I can see a star. I really can.' She threw her head back and gazed at the bright star above her head, which was now twinkling in her hands. 'What a miracle! What do I do now?'

'Ask your star a question.'

'Where is Richard?' She felt the question burst out of her. Until then, she had been unaware that she cared so much.

The star bobbed and swayed and then the water cleared. Very clearly Pandora could see Richard sitting by himself in what looked like an empty nightclub, his head in his hands. He seemed either asleep or very drunk. Then the water went dark. 'That is the man you love?' Janine asked gently.

'I don't know if I love him or not, but he's my third husband and he was very kind to me. I feel responsible for him.'

Janine made a face. 'That man has a lot to learn about life.' She looked at Pandora. 'But then, so do you.'

'Let's eat!' Ben bellowed. 'Once you women get into all this island magic, a man's food gets cold. And I get scared crossing the swamps at night.'

'Why the swamps?' Pandora asked.

'That's where the ghosts of those that were pirates were buried. Often they hung them off the yardarm and then chained them by the twenties and thirties and tied them down in the swamps so the crabs would eat them. Make them fatter and sweeter.'

'Ugh, Ben. That's a very disgusting subject for dinner. But the fish is fantastic. I reckon I could do this dish for my mother.'

'Your mother's coming for a visit?' asked Janine.

'Yeah. I wish she weren't, but she follows me like one of those frigate birds. Do I get to keep the bowl, Janine? And can I see things in it if I practise?'

'Sure.' Janine picked her teeth. 'Anyone can do it. People all over the world have looked into bowls of water to read either the past or the future. But you must be responsible. Remember that. There is both good and evil at the same time. They co-exist. Satan has free will and he has his followers. So if you find yourself being drawn away into something that seems evil and against your will, you chant your word of power and keep the sound moving until you are safe again.'

'My second husband was evil, the psychiatrist. He preyed on defence-less women and then tried to . . . I can't explain it really . . . It was as if he wanted to own you, both body and soul. When I first realized he was interested in me, not only as a patient, it sounded all so exciting. He said he would be my Svengali and change me from the ratty little piece of shit I was into the sort of woman that all men would die for. All I had to do was to follow his instructions. What an idiot I was! Unbeknown to me, he had a whole string of ladies he was playing Svengali to. All on pills, coke, and heroin . . . And pain. Plenty of pain. He took his sadistic pleasures very seriously.'

Janine put her hand on Pandora's head. 'Let go of that painful thought for tonight. You must train your mind not to jump from one place to another like a frog. Now you will sleep and see your Richard. He does not look happy.' She put her finger up in the wind. 'The wind is moving, and Octo will be coming in on his boat. I must go to him.' She smiled. 'Tomorrow we discover your word of power. It will be a special day. No food until late.'

'Again?' Ben was sitting on the porch, wishing they were making love, not talking magic.

'You can eat as much as you like, Ben. No men are allowed anyway. Only women.' Janine threw back her head and laughed at Ben's face. 'Women have always had their magic. That's why we will always be the stronger sex. Men can make as many rules as they like, and we women will always break them. All men fear women.'

'Even Octo?'

Janine gazed at Ben. 'What do you think?'

'OK, OK. Even Octo. And now you're going to teach Pandora all sorts of secrets so she can poison my food and make me droop near other women.'

As Janine walked away, Pandora took Ben's hand. 'Don't be silly. I'm very tired. Let's go to bed. Look, Janine's gone. And I'll clear up the dishes tomorrow.'

'You go to bed, and I'll wash up the things. Anyway, you'll be dreaming of Richard.' Ben had seen the sorrow in Pandora's eyes when she gazed into the bowl. He felt an awful ache in his own heart as he picked up the plates and took them to the sink. As much as he loved her, he knew she could not stay. Not on an island this small. He knew also that he could never leave. When she finally left, she would remain in the sky above him, his star.

Chapter Seventeen

After seeing Richard's lonely face in Janine's bowl of water, Pandora did dream about Richard all night long. The sight of him sitting seemingly asleep and alone at a table upset her dreadfully. The dream began with their first meeting at the theatre in Boston. Marcus loved to be seen at the theatre. By now Pandora had been married to Marcus for three years and had very few illusions left about who Marcus was and how he behaved. That night she was wearing a high-necked black silk robe lined with silver fox fur. The night before Marcus had pulled a silken cord tightly around her neck and the red marks were livid against her pale skin. She tried not to touch her neck because she knew Marcus was watching her and it would give him retroactive pleasure to know she was still in pain. Her voice was hoarse, but fortunately she didn't have to say much. Reginald was with them.

Reggie was a transvestite prostitute and a special friend for Marcus. Occasionally, if she had taken a sufficient amount of pills, Pandora made up a threesome in bed with both men. This night she knew she was doped, but she had taken some belladonna which made her wide green eyes luminous.

She saw Richard sitting several boxes over. He was with a much older woman who was wearing a very expensive black mink coat. Pandora smiled at her own quick appraisal of the coat's value. If you come from the wrong side of the tracks, you notice things like that for the rest of your life. You save aluminium foil, string, and you water down your hair shampoo. Richard was wearing a dinner jacket. He must be English, she thought. Only Englishmen can wear dinner jackets and not look like ducks.

She gazed at him and he gazed back. For a moment they were so lost in each other's eyes that she became afraid Marcus would notice. She looked sideways. Marcus was caressing Reggie's knee. He was repeating the latest scatological joke chasing around the streets of Boston.

Somehow Pandora knew she would see Richard again. She took one last look at him and smiled. He smiled back and lifted a hand as if he were carrying a glass. Ah yes! In the bar. Marcus seldom left his seat for a drink. For a man who was obsessed by sex, he was quite uninterested in food or drink. Pandora loved both good food and wine. The prospect of a glass of champagne pleased her.

The play was *A Streetcar Named Desire*. Fragile as she felt watching the play, she realized how well Tennessee Williams understood human life with all its miseries. So well, in fact, that she wondered if that was the cause of his own undoing. Sometimes knowing too much was to allow for too much pain. Far better to live at an even level than to suffer the internal dramas that were inflicted on the women she knew who attended Marcus's weekly group sessions. She, too, of course, was expected to attend. Still, as the lights went up, she looked over at Marcus and, touching her neck gently, which she knew would please him, she whispered hoarsely, 'I'm just going to the bar to get a cold drink, darling. Is that all right?'

By now she had learned that Marcus expected a slave mentality. He glanced at her and nodded. He was busy talking to a mutual friend, another deviant. His head was thrown back, his eyes arched coquettishly, and she could hear the high trill in his voice. He waved her off with two little fingers.

She got to her feet, slightly unsteady because of the pills, and walked from the back of the box to the bar that served the surrounding boxes. 'I had to see you.' Richard was direct. 'I've had dreams of a girl like you all my life. Red hair and almonds for eyes. By the way,' he was very red and sweating, 'I don't normally pick up,' he looked at her finger, 'married ladies.'

Pandora blushed. 'I don't normally go for a drink with a married man.'

'I'm not married, actually.' His voice made Pandora want to laugh. She had never heard a more British *actually*. 'Shall I get you a drink?'

'Please. I'd love an ice-cold glass of champagne. A light champagne, if you will.'

'Fine then. Hang on a minute.' He turned to the barman, who seemed to know him quite well. 'A bottle of my usual,' he said.

Pandora found herself smiling again. How nice to be with a man who had such personal authority. Marcus had none, except when he screamed and bullied women.

Richard handed Pandora a tall, fluted glass of champagne. The glass was well-chilled and the champagne soothed her throat. 'That's my Aunt Norma I have in the box tonight. She, bless her cotton socks, used to sneak me care-packages of cakes and sweets when I was away at school as a boy.'

'I never could understand how the English could send away their children so young.'

'Oh, I don't know. In England, you're off to prep school at seven and then public school, so we're all parentless most of the time. You get used to it. And sometimes I used to go to Aunt Norma's place for the hols. I don't really see much of the old dear, but she's over here on a holiday. How do you like the play?'

Pandora sipped her drink thoughtfully. 'When they come to take Blanche away and they ask her how she will live, she says, "I have always relied on the kindness of strangers." It cracks me up every time.' Pandora laughed, then felt tears well up in her eyes.

Richard gazed at his feet.

I've embarrassed him, she thought.

'Well, if you ever feel the need for a stranger to rely on, here's my card.' He handed her a white card. *Richard Townsend* it said, and it gave his address in Boston.

'I'll be going back to Idaho tomorrow, but thank you all the same. I will keep this card.' She put the card in her handbag, never dreaming that one day it would be her ticket out of Marcus's life for ever.

After the show was over, Marcus wanted to go to a gay bar to do some serious flirting, but Pandora refused. 'I'm too tired,' she said. 'Besides, I have all the packing to do tonight. We're on an early flight tomorrow morning.'

For once Marcus didn't make a fuss. He hated packing and she, like a good slave, did it for him. Anyway, they'd have a better chance of a pick-up without Pandora . . .

Pandora awoke in Ben's arms with tears in her eyes. 'I did dream about Richard, just like Janine said I would.'

Ben snorted. 'Janine and her silly sisters, with all their sorcery, will get us all into trouble on this island. Albert the Police Chief hates all three girls.'

'I didn't know Janine had sisters.'

'She has, and they're all as mad as each other. They make magic pills and potions for the girls on the island. Voodoo is much different to obeah, you know. Albert was having an affair with Mr Lauren's wife. He didn't go into the grapebushes. He thought he was far too clever,

104

so he met her in the graveyard. One night Janine and her sisters put Baron Samedi's black frock-coat on one of the graves and put his black stove-pipe hat on the corner of the gravestone and waited behind a frangipani tree. My goodness, Albert got spooked! The whole island laughed and pointed at him all week long! He is a very bad man. He doesn't think he's God; he *knows* he's God. He takes away people's lands and their money.'

'Why do they let him do that? In America he'd be jailed for stealing.'

'There are no laws on this island.' Ben handed Pandora a cup of tea. 'Here there is a weak governor and corrupt people who want to sell off as much land as they can. There are good people like my grandmother. She does what she can, but she is old now.'

Pandora felt quite disoriented, half-awake from her dream with Richard, and half-sitting in the peace and quiet of Ben's cottage. 'Sometimes I think there are no rules anywhere, Ben. Particularly when you think that Marcus was supposed to be a psychiatrist who was there to help women like me who got married to violent men and then were too ashamed to get out. My mother wouldn't help me. I told you. Her attitude was that I had made my bed and I certainly wasn't going to lie on hers. At first Marcus seemed very kind and understanding. I looked forward to those Mondays when I would walk along the cold corridors and just be able to talk about me. He often let me talk for a few extra minutes. And then one day he suggested I join these group therapy sessions that he held in his house for women with the same problems. He said it might help me to understand myself if I listened to what other women went through. At first I said I didn't think Norman would allow me out at night, but Marcus said he'd talk him into it. After all, our marriage was improving and Norman hadn't hit me in the face for quite a while. I didn't tell Marcus about the kicking in the stomach.

'But I did go. Norman didn't make a fuss at all. I put on a new dress I made from an old tablecloth and I bought some new shoes and set off. My, it felt unusual to go out at night! As a family we never went out at night. Night was dangerous. Night was when my father would listen to the television or watch football. My mother locked all the doors and windows. It was a dark and dangerous world out there, especially for girls. My mother was convinced, and she convinced me, that there were white-slave traders lurking out there. So even when I was a teenager I had to be in as soon as it got dark or my mother'd give me a good belting.

'Anyway, I drove Norman's truck up this lovely driveway. All around me there must have been at least twenty cars. Some really expensive Caddies, but a couple of trucks like mine. So I didn't feel too bad. I walked up these three marble stairs and the door opened and a man with white gloves showed me in. The clinic was at the far end of the corridor. He didn't say a word. He just walked beside me. He had silver eyes, like dollars, and they were round and staring. He took me as far as the door of this clinic and Marcus was there.

'All around him were women who seemed to be drinking glasses of wine. He offered me a glass of wine, but I asked if he had a beer. "Norman doesn't like wine. He says it's cissy stuff," I explained. "Well, you're not in Norman's house now. You're in mine. Would you like a glass of wine?" "I'd love to try some," I said.

'"Ladies," Marcus said, and they all stopped talking. "Let us meet our new friend. May I present to you Mrs Pandora Banks. When we've settled down, we can all have a little session at explaining what we are all doing in this room."

'I tried the wine, Ben, and it was lovely. Then we all sat in this circle and to my amazement each woman talked about everything that had happened to them. Right in front of each other. I found it very hard when it was my turn. Very hard indeed. In fact I started crying. I felt so disloyal talking about Norman like that, but Marcus said that's why the subject never gets discussed. Women keep it secret. That's true enough. I kept it secret at work. Only my mother knew. Some women had much worse done to them than what Norman had done to me. At least Norman just punched me and kicked me. He was violent in bed, but not kinky. Lots of the women seemed to be married to men who did weird things to them, like tied them up and whipped them, or stuck things up inside them. Awful! It made me really sick to hear it. Little did I know then that one day that woman would be me.'

'It's over, Pandora. It's all over now. You can put it behind you.'

Pandora shook her head. 'It is never over. Never. Not when your mother did not want you to be born. You feel as if you don't exist. If this makes sense, there is a person I know called Pandora Banks, and then Pandora Sutherland, and now Pandora Townsend. I know those three people because they have their names on suitcases and passports. They have faces I cannot see in the mirror, though, and they have bodies I cannot see either. I can, of course, put clothes on them, but I couldn't tell you what they look like. In between the three Pandoras is a grey cloud. She's a she. A woman, I think. I'm not sure. But she is like ectoplasm and she drifts about. Some days I can't see her at all.

Sometimes she's quite there, really . . . My God, Ben! You're looking at me as if I'm mad! Maybe I am. But I always believed, even when I was that unwanted, abandoned little girl, that if I could swim with the dolphins, then that is what I should do. Maybe the dolphins will show me who I am in this universe and if I have a place at all.'

'You're in luck there.' Ben went over to a drawer in the kitchen. 'I have my *PADI Open Water Diver's Manual*, and we can begin lessons today. Or at least until those giggling girls arrive to take you away to the women's cave. Silly bitches.'

Chapter Eighteen

For her first diving lesson with Ben, Pandora joined a session of beginners in the pool at the hotel. She was grateful that she was now evenly tanned; she did not much like looking at the crowd around her who reminded her of uncooked shrimps. Except for a large woman called Eve. 'Why are you here?' she asked Pandora.

Pandora was busy raising her hands above her head with her mask on her face and then slowly submerging herself in the swimming pool. She gazed at Eve's eloquent brown eyes, forgot she was underwater and choked.

'Sorry.' Eve hauled her up by the elbow.

Pandora leaned against the side of the pool and gasped for breath.

'Not much to lay in this crowd,' Eve grumbled. ''cept for that guy. Who's the divemaster? He's got all the right things in all the right places.'

Ben moved over to Pandora and took her arm. 'OK, honey?'

Pandora smiled back. 'Sure, I'm OK. I just forgot to keep my mouth shut.'

Ben moved across the group. Eve smiled. 'He's yours, I guess.'

Pandora watched Ben's back retreat. 'Sort of. I'm still married.'

'So'm I! The schmuck won't come diving. Says all it is is lonely people looking for nooky. But it ain't, you know. I'm doing this course again as a refresher because I ain't dove in years. But it's like an obsession. Once you're down there, you're free, like nothing else I can describe. Not even a bird is free like that. Do you want to be my dive-buddy? You can't buddy up with your friend, because he's the divemaster. But I'm a pretty good diver, you know.'

Pandora smiled. Her heart was racing. Just the thought of being down way under the waves was exciting, but also frightening. One of the things Marcus had taken away from her was all her confidence. Or what was left of it after her mother and Norman had made their best efforts. Now Richard's defection with Gretchen left her slowly realizing that there was only one way out of this bottomless, bitter, black hole that she too had dug for herself, and that was to take risks and decisions for herself. So far Ben and his grandmother had been gentle first steps. Janine had given her an inkling of just how strong a woman could be. Now Eve standing in front of her was making her an offer of real friendship. Before, her friendships with other women were based on traditional women's power-play. Gretchen, she realized, had always intended to have Richard, not so much for love of the man but more because she was bored and Richard was amusing company. Besides, English country gentlemen were chic in Boston. The women around Marcus were either part of his heavily manipulated group of women who partly funded his very expensive lifestyle by the amount of drugs he pushed at them, or even more personal groups of friends who lived closely and excessively on that tightrope between sex, drugs, and danger, the only place where the very bored can feel alive.

Here and now though, standing waist-deep in the little, rather shabby hotel pool, Pandora began to feel a real sense of a shadow of what could be herself. She lifted her hand out of the water and looked at it very carefully. This was no white, limp hand waiting for the manacle to take her away for a ritual torture. This was a warm brown hand that made cups of tea and coffee for her love in bed.

'How old are you?' Eve's voice broke her concentration.

'I'm thirty-seven this year.'

'Well, I tell you what, honey. This is a good island. A real good island.' Eve had a deep furry voice. She sounded as if she had been sipping sea sand through her gills all her life. 'I came here when I was just twenty-four. I was running for my life from Tampa, Florida. In them days, there was no such things as battered wives. You put up and you hushed up. Anyway, one night he was out to blow my brains out, so I hopped the plane in Miami. In those days, you had to take one of those little clipper planes, and I got here and I stayed washing up at the bar and doing this and that. The bastard never found me. He died, God rest his soul, ten years ago, and I met Pat in Florida at the race track. I can't get that man into the water if I tried, but he's just so good to me. So it can all go right, you know. Just give it time.'

'That's what I'm doing.' Pandora adjusted her mask. 'I'm just going to give it time.'

They both slid under the surface.

*

Pandora and Eve parted on the agreement that they would indeed be dive-buddies. 'Tomorrow we get to try the diving equipment. You'll like that. We'll go real slow.'

Pandora chattered into Ben's ear all the way back on the moped. She knew she was talking far too fast and into the wind, but she could feel the sense of excitement buzzing through her body. When they got to the cottage, Ben parked the moped.

'I'll make an omelette for you, Ben, and then I need a sleep.'

Before she slept, Pandora licked the salt off Ben's nipples and he pulled her to him. By now the fit and the comfort of their two bodies reminded her of two perfect conch shells lying under the water with the milky foam moving one to another. No effort of will. The quietness and the perfection of the hot shaded sun sent them, still united sexually with each other's bodies, to sleep.

Chapter Nineteen

Janine produced Julia and her youngest sister Jane. Ben was not in a good mood, but agreed that he would go out with Octo and his friend Ziggy. 'Don't you put any curses on us,' Ben warned Janine.

All three women shrieked with laughter.

Pandora sat on the step of the cottage feeling a little confused. This morning had been such a warm enchanting moment, meeting Eve who seemed so solid and real. And now she was about to go off with Janine and her sisters to play with magic potions. Actually, she really felt like staying at home with Ben and just spending a quiet evening together. 'We are not really going to do witchcraft, are we?'

Julia, who looked as if she could have been Janine's twin, giggled. 'I intend to put a curse on a woman who has her eye on my husband.'

'Seriously? This sounds rather more promising.'

'Anyway,' said Julia, 'apart from Ben having a night out shark-fishing, we'll have a woman's night out. I've brought a bowl of chicken, rice, and peas. Jane made the dumplings, and Janine cheated and got ice-cream from the ice-cream shop. I worked all day, not like you housewives. Gossip, gossip, gossip. To go to work is child's play, Janine, and you know it,' Julia continued. 'When my husband comes home from lunch, it's where's his yam?'

'And what about his salt on the breadfruit?'

'Hunh. You are a lucky woman with Octo.' Jane's face was hard. 'And someday we'll all get tied down with children.' She looked at Pandora. 'And you?'

Pandora shook her head. 'Three husbands, but no children. Anyway, I'm not sure I'd be much of a mother.'

'Come on. We'd better go. The light is failing and it's a long climb.' Janine led the way.

Pandora very quickly realized that all three women were very used to climbing the mountain. Soon she was puffing along behind them. Jane carried the food in a thatched palm basket. The handle around her head held the basket at her back. Pandora wore sneakers. She felt silly, but she knew her feet would be cut to ribbons by the sharp stones. All three women seemed impervious to any pain at all. They made their way up the trails, pushing away overhanging purple hibiscus. 'Look up, Pandora.' She did as she was told and could see nothing at all except bare, dead tree trunks and some organ cactus.

'Look at what?' Sweat was stinging Pandora's eyes.

'Look hard at the corner, like a woman's elbow, of the tree ahead of you.' Julia stepped across a lump of white volcanic stone and pulled out a long green creeper. 'See? Here are our wild orchids. These with the purple throats and yellow tongues are called banana orchids.'

Pandora's eyes widened. She had only ever seen one orchid in her whole life, and that had been the orchid Marcus pinned to her wedding dress the day he married her. In her hand she held a delicate little flower with an innocent face. How, she wondered, could such innocence be transmuted into the monstrous inky black orchid with its evil purple tongue that she had worn? The orchid had seemed so inappropriate on her wedding dress, even before she married him. Did God in his great innocence design all the beauty of this island, or did Lucifer, his fallen angel, have the power and the free will to twist the architecture of the flower and the minds of men?

'Pandora's daydreaming. Come on. We must be at the cave before the light goes to begin this spell.'

Far away, as they walked in amicable silence, they saw a falcon wheel and tumble in the sky. In his talons he was carrying a big fish. Big enough for Pandora to see the last pink rays of the sunlight flash on its wildly flapping tail. 'Oh, poor thing!' she muttered.

'That's no poor thing,' Jane retorted. 'That's Octo sending his falcon with fish for his mother.' They stood for a while and saw the bird fall. 'No one has ever seen her, you know,' Jane said, 'except Octo who loves her. The old people say she was put away by her family and fed, but when she was pregnant, she ran away.'

'I know,' Pandora said. 'Janine told me the other day. I can't imagine living all by myself up here in the mountain. I think I'd go mad.'

Julia laughed. 'All you Westerners with your busy minds go mad in half an hour left alone. You all think too much. Here there's not much to think about. We're nearly there.'

In ten minutes they stood in front of a big hole. Inside the floor was clean with sand. 'This is our family cave. Now, even at the back, we have chests stored with linen. When the hurricane season comes, we will get out the bedding and clean it and also keep fresh water and tins of food ready.'

Pandora stood at the door of the cave and looked out over the trees that tumbled over the mountain. The light had originally been a sun-flower yellow slowly changing to a pink, a very delicate pink, and was now slowly climbing down a paint-box of colours, now from the pinks to a gentle violet, and then, as the sun hovered over the water, the sea went red. The four women stood with their arms around their waists, just watching. Pandora had seen the sun go down many times on the beach, but they were so high in the mountain they seemed to be looking down as if they were no longer humans, just disembodied spirits. Pandora imagined floating above the sun as it immersed itself into the sea. She could put out her arm and she would stretch all the way across the mountain and push the sun down herself.

'You lack power yet,' Janine said quietly.

Pandora jumped. 'You can read my mind.'

'Most people can read each other's minds. A thought travels on an electrical impulse. Once you design and understand your own electrical field, you can plug into other people's fields.'

Pandora's eyes widened. Julia and Jane had gone into the cave. The night was getting very dark. Bushes stirred as hefty parrots made ready for sleep.

'Then there are no secrets from those people who know their own powers. The truth is,' Janine said slowly, 'there are no secrets any-where. The only thing that limits you, Pandora, is you. Come on in and we'll have supper before Jane begins her smelly concoctions.'

'So, you've been married three times, Pandora.' Julia's voice was neither nagging nor inquisitive, just generally friendly and interested.

'I'm not very proud of it, but there you are. My first husband beat me physically. I was so grateful to my second husband who rescued me from my first, I didn't realize he was an emotional sadist.'

'What's an emotional sadist?' Jane asked, licking her fingers after a plateful of curried chicken.

'He liked to hurt people and humiliate them sexually.'

Janine shoved Jane in the ribs. 'You know. Like those videos Virgil tapes off the satellite TV station. The dirty movies he stashes under the counter of his electrical shop.'

'Those?' Jane's eyes widened. 'Were you in one of those?'

'Yeah. I suppose so. You see, when I was with him, he gave me so many pills. Much of the time I had no idea of what was happening. He had quite a lot of us as his patients. He said he was doing research into the problems of why women get beaten. And after a while we all got hooked on the drugs and then he asked me to leave Norman and marry him. By this time Norman didn't care much. He had fallen in love with a cute little barmaid.'

'I'll bet he didn't beat her,' Julia said.

'No, I don't suppose he would. He was probably far happier with her than he was with my miserable face.'

'Well, your face isn't miserable now.'

Pandora laughed. 'But my mouth is hot. Those peppers burn! Anyway, finally Marcus got caught videoing one of the other patients in an orgy with three other women. Thank God I wasn't in that one. Poor things, they were all out of their minds on his pills and booze. He had this frightening voice. He could either sound like a snake about to strike, which scared the hell out of me, or he could talk you into a hypnotic trance. The awful thing is that we all trusted him. We all believed him, that he gave us those pills and therapy sessions for our own good. And then of course, after the sessions, the pills, and the booze wore off, and you forgot whatever went on, you certainly had no idea that there were a crew of people filming a few feet away. Once we were married, he took me away from the clinic. I never saw those women again.'

'Did he go on tormenting you?' Janine pushed a piece of fruit into Pandora's hands.

'Yes, he did. Long weekends when I'd be unconscious from Friday night until Sunday evening. I remember waking up a little, just to drink more and take more pills. I remember the pain, though. The terrible pain. But rarely any marks except inside me. And if he used something like a club. Sometimes he whipped me.

'Anyway, he got caught. Some bright cop had been watching the clinic and began nosing about. Finally Marcus and his friends got careless and a batch of videos were found in one of the houses belonging to one of the so-called nursing staff. Because of Marcus's connections with the judge's family – two of the judiciary beat the shit out of their wives – there was not much of a splash in the newspapers, but they were all warned and left town for a good long time, too.' There was venom in Pandora's voice.

'It's OK to learn to be angry, Pandora.' Janine's face was a long silhouette in the light from the small fire at the centre of the cave. 'Anger can be very healing. Don't be afraid of it.'

'I've been angry for so long, Janine, I don't know how to let it go.'

Janine put her hand up. 'Pandora, it will go in time, and I will teach you. Anger can be attachment. Then it is no good. It fuels the evil. It makes a bright fire brighter. Clean anger kills the attachment, like a rosemary bush cleans the fire out of the sand. One sweep and all the black embers are gone. Poof! Just like that. You look at the floor of our cave. What do you see? White clean sand. Enough of my talking now. Julia, who are you hexing?'

'Leona. She's been after my William for months now. Every dance she tries for him. He's a big weak fellow without a brain to his head, but he's a good husband.'

Janine and Jane both nodded in sympathy. 'Well, what should we do? I think we'll put three white cockerel feathers as a warning for the first time.'

'I'll tell you about Richard another time,' said Pandora. 'I want to see Julia's spell.'

'Leona is no fool,' said Jane. 'She sees cockerel feathers, she knows it's us or Miss Maisy. She has no fight with Miss Maisy because she is cousin. Maybe two days' bat's blindness to begin?'

'I have an amulet here for William.' Julia took out a highly polished square of thinly cut black coral. 'That piece belonged to my mummy. She gave it me many years ago. I'll put that round William's neck with a thick rope of gold, and he'll wear it proudly.' Julia grinned. 'If Leona so much as touches it, that black coral will tell me. So tonight I get the cockerel from our land ten minutes away. Come, Jane. You walk with me. Too many duppies up here.'

'What are duppies?'

'Oh, that's the island name for ghosts. They are the people who die and can't let go of material things. Sometimes it's the house; or they were very rich and they can't take their belongings with them, so they haunt the night. You can smell a duppy. It's a sour smell, and there is always coldness around them. Next time you open the door of a house, wait and see if you feel cold. Then there is a duppy living there. Shut the door and go away. There is no happiness when a duppy lives in a house.'

'Well, Ben's cottage feels happy. Really happy. I wish my mother wasn't coming to visit. She'll just go on and on about Richard and what a fool I was to let him go.'

'Why did you let him go, Pandora?'

It was a very unexpected question for Pandora. She always said *because he ran off with my friend,* but now she realized that was not the answer at all. 'I think I grew up, Janine, and Richard didn't. I think that's the real reason. It wasn't Gretchen. It wasn't any of that. It was being married to a surly, sulky little boy, and I got bored. So really, when he offered to leave, after the initial shock of it all, I realized I'd be much better on my own. I still love him and at times I miss him, but you can't stay in the sand-pit for ever. I'm thirty-seven now and I want to do something with my life. Not just become another attachment to a man looking for an unpaid housekeeper. I want to do something for me.' Pandora's voice stopped. She heard the squawking of a chicken. 'Oh no, Janine. What are they going to do?'

'They are going to cut his head off and then sprinkle the blood in a circle while Julia . . . Anyway, you can watch.'

'I'm not watching them cut off the poor thing's head. I'll stand outside the cave and you call me in when it is all over. I'll come in and watch the rest.'

Pandora stood outside the cave. She put her hands firmly over her ears and gazed up at her special star. Somewhere Richard was under that star with his usual crowd of friends, and somewhere else Ben was hunting shark with Octo. And tomorrow she would have another diving lesson.

'You can come in now.' Janine took Pandora's hand. She pulled her into the cave. The body of the decapitated white cockerel lay like a feather duster in the centre of the circle. Julia, with the dismembered head, was just finishing drawing the circle with the beak; the bird's tongue lay hanging out. In her hands, Julia held two small velvety skins.

'I call to you, Great Mother of Darkness. I, Julia, of the Horus tribe in Haiti, call to you for an answer to our prayer.' Outside the circle Jane was holding a pair of white goat-skin drums. As Julia's voice rose, the skins of the drums began to vibrate.

'Look,' Janine said. 'The Great Mother is listening.'

'Great Mother, we greet you, we three sisters, and ask for your help.' The skins began to hum with the vibrations. Pandora felt hot and then cold and the hair on the back of her neck was standing on end.

Julia lifted the two little skins and put one and then the other on the dead chicken's eyes. 'May these skins of bats blind Leona for two days as a warning that sisters do not destroy sisters.'

116

The drum was throbbing all by itself. 'Put your hand on the drum, Pandora,' Janine said quietly.

Pandora reluctantly walked over to Jane who held up the left drum, and she put her hand out gingerly to touch she knew not what. Under her fingers she felt a warm, sweet, steady beating, and over her whole pain-racked body she felt a part of her empty soul fill with the loving throb of that universal beat.

Pandora slipped on to the sand, clutching the drum to her heart and she sobbed. The three other women sat with her until daybreak.

Ben was waiting on the stoop of the cottage. The walk down the mountain had been long, but as all four women walked calmly side by side, Pandora felt peace inside herself as never before. Janine passed her small berries and fruits. 'What's this?'

'This is from the naseberry tree.'

For a moment they broke ranks as Julia lifted a long stick up to the top of the tree where the biggest berries clung. There was a spattering of naseberries and then a scamper between the women and the ants to get to the berries. So this is what inner peace feels like, Pandora mused, munching on the sweet flesh of the brown fruit.

Jane carried both drums with her in her basket. 'Those are our mother's drums, and they are sacred to us from our days in childhood. My mother said that before all the world began there was first the Great Mother and she gave birth to all living beings. And then one of her sons tried to usurp her position and put a spell on her so that she was no longer immortal. Before she left her physical body, she asked her eldest daughter to cut out her heart and to cut it into several pieces, one for each daughter to carry in a drum. Our family have had these two drums for generations. We play them for guidance and we hear the love of the Mother of the Earth in them. You felt it, didn't you, Pandora?'

Pandora nodded. 'I felt such a strange feeling of peace. It was like I had been all jumbled up inside myself. There were holes made by my father. Deep scratches made by Norman. Disgusting swamps by Marcus, and then all this venomous ink by my mother. And then of course the grey, messy, undecided, paralysed person called Pandora. Last night and even now all these things are so much clearer. Just the four of us walking down the mountainside, everything feels clean and decent.'

'Except for Leona's eyes,' Jane said. They all laughed.

117

Finally at the bottom of the mountain they kissed each other goodbye and Pandora wandered along the side of the road, dreaming. The walk back to the cottage took her past beautiful pools of trapped sea. The ironshore was sharp, but within the pools tiny multi-coloured fish swam in and out of baby coral fans. I'm a bit like that baby fish, I suppose. And soon I will be confident enough to go out into the sea and swim with the big fish, and hopefully, eventually, with the dolphins.

Early morning drivers offered her a lift, but she preferred to walk, listening to the flap of washing on a line as the sun kissed the sheets clean. The scuttle of little sideways crabs pre-guessing her footfalls. The hens calling the children before school to collect their new-laid eggs. The poisonous ackee trees. 'Ah yes. The tree that is festooned with bright red, pear-shaped fruit.' It was one of Ben's first stories: 'If you cut the ackee and eat it before it is ready to be eaten, you will die. It carries a dreadful poison. But the way to deal with the ackee tree is to let her think she fools you. You stand under the ackee tree one night when the fruit is sweet and plump and you laugh at the tree. "You silly old ackee tree! Ha ha!" You button up tight like a woman in a graveyard dress. Then you go away. Next day the tree is laughing at you, its fruit all open and ripe to pick.'

'Is that a real story, Ben?' she asked as she walked up the steps of the cottage. 'I mean the one you told me about the ackee tree?'

'It's a story my grandmother always tells. But she is better at patois than I am.' He held Pandora gently. 'Was it all right up there in the mountain? I was worried about you.'

Pandora hugged him. 'I was worried about you, Ben. We saw the falcon take the fish to Octo's mother, and I knew you were out after shark.'

Ben nodded. 'We caught four. Big ones. All black-tip shark. They'll go to market in Tampa, Florida. What happened up in the mountains with those silly women?'

'Nothing much, at least I don't think anything much happened. We might check and see if Leona's car is at the hospital. She might wake up with a bit of a fright. Other than that, I felt this drum beat . . . It was like a huge, loving, human heart, if you can imagine what I mean. I suppose it is the sort of heartbeat a baby must feel in its ear when it nurses from its mother's nipple. A sound that wills life and happiness into that little body. Does that make sense to you, Ben?'

'Yes,' he said. 'It does. It feels like that twice for a man. Once in his mother's arms and then again when he finds the woman he loves and he lies on her breast and both sounds are one born of the other to sustain him to the end of his life.'

They stood blinking in the sunlight at each other, holding hands, and smiling. Pandora knew that it was not to be her breast for Ben, even though the thought hurt her, and Ben in his turn knew also that their time together had a limit. But for now they were content. 'I'll get you some breakfast, Ben. Then we must go and do the second part of the diving course.'

Chapter Twenty

Eve was waiting by the pool. The group of divers had by now begun to learn each other's names. Today Pandora and Eve were learning the basic information about the buddy system. ' "*You should always dive with a buddy who stays nearby at all times*," ' Pandora read aloud from the *PADI Open Water Diver's Manual*. 'So,' she said to Eve. 'You're my official buddy.' In spite of the intensity of the night in the cave, Pandora felt elated. Today they were to do their first shore dive and the excitement sent electric tingles up Pandora's spine.

As she pulled on her diving suit and carefully checked her equipment, Pandora realized she had never really belonged to a group before. Stuck with her mother, isolated by Norman, and mesmerized by Marcus, she had always been alone. Here in the hot sunshine she could hear Eve talking to another tall man with predatory blue eyes. They had obviously been dive-buddies in other parts of the world. Pandora watched the man and then shook her head. No, she smiled.

'What are you smiling at?' Eve whispered, turning away from the man.

'I was telling myself, no more adventures with six-foot psychopaths. And that friend of yours looks like he's trouble.'

Eve sighed. 'Yeah, he's trouble with women, but he's an excellent buddy. Nothing scares him. Absolutely nothing. Diving can be quite a dangerous business. Your life is really in your buddy's hands.'

'Do you trust me that much, Eve?'

Eve inspected her torch. 'Yes, I do. I watched you and you always seem so vulnerable and out of it all, but inside you I can see a core of steel.'

'But I do get panic attacks. I'd better tell you that now.'

'Don't worry. Most new divers get panic attacks. And then Ben will teach you a way to breathe, and that's also where your buddy comes in.'

By now almost everyone was kitted up and ready to walk down to the shoreline. Pandora felt the water rising to her waist. She was quite used to the feeling of the water rising, but she was not used to the clothing. Her diving suit felt heavy.

Eve squeezed her hand and then stuck her thumb up. OK, Pandora nodded, and then remembered she couldn't be heard. She could see Ben leading the fifteen or so divers into the deeper part of the reef. There a sunken treasure ship had lain for over two hundred years. Slowly pushing herself along with her fins, Pandora followed Eve down under the water. Before, when snorkelling, she had swum above the fish, an interloper in their world, and the fish had always looked upwards at her shadow and then hurried about their business. Now she was among the fish. Two blue, spotted parrot fish came to stare straight into her mask. One stood on his head for her appreciation. The other swam beside her until it was chased away by a very large red snapper. Dinner, thought Pandora, but then, captivated by the silver glitter of the fish's scales and the red bands running down its sides, she realized that she would be unable to take this beautiful creature's life. Eve pulled her around and pointed down at the sandy floor. Pandora watched but could see nothing. Then she noticed a flicker of a tail: a big eagle ray rose a few feet and lightly flapped away from the approaching divers. Pandora felt little bubbles of elation.

She followed Eve as they dropped even further down. She saw the outline of the old sea-wreck. Ben swam up to her and knocked on her tank to gain attention. She followed him. At first she found herself aghast. A huge slimy head was sticking out of a hole in the side of the sunken boat. She knew it was a moray eel. Ben had explained that, though moray eels can bite viciously, he had known and befriended this eel for many years. The eel looked too much like Marcus. Even as she happily played underwater, Pandora also knew in the back of her mind that her mother was getting ready to visit her island paradise and she resented it bitterly. If only she could hold back the days and put her shoulder to the door that separated her mother's life from hers, maybe she could hold this contented bubble of peace. The water around her was full of purple and orange coral heads. Fish joined her. A posse of small barracuda patrolled around her and then did a right turn and peeped off, leaving her face to face with a shark.

Panic. She felt her chest tighten. Her hands began to wave and her feet splash without co-ordination. She couldn't open her eyes . . . Then she felt a hand firmly take her shoulder. She knew it was Eve. By now her air regulator had fallen out of her mouth. The other reassuring hand took her own mouthpiece out and Pandora was able to take a few deep breaths of air. She opened her eyes and felt the panic subside. Eve gave her back the dropped mouthpiece and returned her own. Both of them gazed at each other, Eve with worried concern, Pandora with a sort of delight. She had panicked, but she had managed to survive. Maybe in this awful, tangled life of hers she was beginning to get a hold of herself.

Yes, her mother was coming. Even now, the nylon peekaboo blouses would be sitting in neat piles on the drab ironing board in the brown varnished house. The ladies at the hairdresser's would all have been informed of Monica's momentous trip to the Caribbean to see her erring daughter. 'First she marries a no-good man. Then a psychiatrist from Harvard. And now she's running away from a reporter from the *Boston Telegraph*.' Pandora could hear her mother's smoke-cracked voice, the slight whistle of emphysema in the air . . .

Eve tapped her tank. The shark had circled around again. Pandora felt her body tighten, but Eve held her hand. She made an *It's OK, buddy* sign and then Pandora watched this six feet of muscle glide in and out of the wreck. The wreck, she realized, was like her life. The wreck had holes full of beautiful, gentle, kindly fish. But then there were also the scorpion fish which could poison you, or the stingrays which were capable of passing volts of electricity through your unsuspecting feet. Marcus the moray eel, Norman the shark, and Richard . . . Well, Richard was a clown fish. But Mother would have all the news. She made it her business to keep a tight rein on all three of Pandora's ex-relationships. Particularly on Marcus.

Ben made the return signal. Slowly buddies got together and paddled back to the shore. It was evening light when they surfaced. Pandora was always amazed at how early the evening light descended upon the island. She checked her diving watch, her present to herself before leaving Boston. Four thirty-six. The light was still yellow ochre, but just a tinge of pink was blushing through. She stood up in the water and was shocked at the feeling of gravity all around her.

Eve slipped off her tanks and then helped Pandora with hers. 'That was a great dive, you know? You handled yourself well.'

Pandora blushed. 'Well, at least I managed to control the worst of it.'

'Sure. And once you've seen your first shark, you won't panic again.'

'I was an idiot really. I was thinking about other things, Eve.'

'Never mind. You'll find the more you go down and the deeper you go, you'll leave this so-called real world behind you. I promise, diving gets to you. It brings peace down there. Let's go and grab a beer. I want to tell Chuck, your psycho-connection, about the shark. I reckon it's a black-tip. He's probably got a photo.'

'Do you think he'd give me a copy?'

'Sure he will.'

Both women struggled up the beach carrying their equipment. Pandora felt the slight soreness of her muscles as she carried the tanks, now empty of air. After she stashed and washed her equipment she walked to the bar with a new self-confidence.

Janine was at the bar with Octo. 'I saw a shark.' Pandora's eyes were shining, and she knew she had a silly grin on her face. Normally she would try and contain any excitement until she was alone where there would be no disapproving look or cross word to make her feel foolish. 'I'll take two beers, Janine.' And she waited, happily jostled by the crowd around the bar. Another difference, she noticed. Normally other people touching her or pushing up against her made her nervous and hostile. But here in this little round thatched hut packed with people, she felt no threats; just other people who, like herself, had spent the afternoon sharing a thrilling experience. 'Did you see that big grouper chase away the barracuda?'

Pandora watched for Eve who was threading her way through the fairy lights that lit the way towards the bar. Islands of tables and chairs surrounded the bar and Janine moved quickly around the tables. Grunting, Octo told stories from his place on a high stool, his huge thigh quivering with the memories of the last blue marlin competition. Most of the talk that evening was about next week's fishing and marlin-hunting. Janine had promised to take Eve and Pandora in their boat. Pandora was determined to go, even if she left her sulking mother behind.

The sun splashed early into the sea that night. Chuck of the bullet-blue eyes and 'Danger to women' written all over his forehead arrived with his roll of film. There indeed was a colour slide of the shark. 'Yeah,' Eve said, 'that's at least six feet.'

Chuck nodded. 'You wait till next week and they get the blue marlins in here. Then you'll see sharks.'

'Could I have a copy of the shark picture, please?' Pandora cursed herself for feeling so shy, but she very much wanted to send Richard a copy. She wanted to convey to him that she was not just a mousy little housewife waiting for her genial journalist husband to come home, but a woman who was sitting among many others on a hot Caribbean night, drinking beer and enjoying herself. She gazed around the beach. On some hammocks slung under the coconut trees couples snuggled and giggled. At most of the tables, colour slides were being examined and plans taking shape for the next day's diving. Only one more day before her mother arrived.

Then Eve said, 'Let's get in a night dive. We could do a dive in the morning and then have the afternoon off, and then dive in the evening.'

Ben was moving across the bar. 'Grandma invites us to eat tonight,' he said. 'Do you want to go?'

Pandora smiled. 'I'll go anywhere for your grandma's food, Ben.' She kissed Eve good night.

Chuck watched her walk into the night. 'Pretty woman. Why's she so afraid of men?'

Eve shrugged. 'She thinks of herself as a piece of shit, so she attracts shit. She's getting better though.'

'Maybe I can help.' Chuck sprawled in his chair and put the bottle of beer to his mouth, straining the froth through his teeth.

'No, not you, Chuck. You're a good buddy, but you're lousy to women.'

'I know,' Chuck said. 'I just can't help it. I love women so much. All that pussy waving at you. I guess I was born in a lucky age. There's my old man pushing a lawn-mower for the last thirty years of his life, married to my apple-pie mom, went to college, wore button-down shirts, and what does he have to show for all his efforts?'

'What?' Eve was interested. Chuck did a lot more humping than he ever did talking.

'A triple by-pass surgery and prostate trouble. That's what he's got. Here I am about to hit the big four-O and I can have anything I want. I tell you, diving is the sexiest racket I know. All these poor, lonely, horny divorced women come down here and all you need is to buddy up with them, a bottle of Jamaica rum, and POW! You have yourselves a party.'

'That's one way of looking at it, Chuck, but I'm glad I'm happily married to a guy I love. There's lots of couples here who care about each other. Anyway, I think you've got a touch of the big four-O worries and won't admit it. What happens at forty-five, hunh? or fifty? Are you still a walking gonad chasing younger and younger girls?'

124

'Ah, let me buy you another beer, Mother Eve, and quit philoso-phizing.'

'OK, if you quit the bullshitting.'

Later Eve watched Chuck walk from the table. His method was impeccable. He had big, broad hands which lightly stroked a cheek here, a thigh there. A pat on the head or a kiss on the forehead. A special squeeze on the flabby forearm of the woman who last paid his bills in Antigua. Ah, the Chucks of this world, thought Eve, glad that Pandora was safely away with Ben.

Chapter Twenty-one

Pandora spent an anxious night in Ben's arms. He had soothed her the best he could, but he could feel that beyond all the words and the kisses of comfort, there lay such an awful ravine of pain in Pandora that the most he could do was to act as a strong oar in the leaky little boat that was Pandora's only safety in this life she had chosen for herself. 'I'm just a piece of shit. That's what my mother's going to say, Ben, you wait. Give her twenty-four hours and she'll start.'

'You're not a piece of shit, Pandora. You're lovely. You just let people treat you badly.' Ben was holding her close, her head buried in his chest. Finally, an exhausted Pandora fell asleep in his arms.

Monica stepped off the eight-seater aeroplane loaded with exploding suitcases and string bags. She was hot, sweating, and predictably cross. 'You didn't tell me the damn thing stopped in Tampa, Pandora.' Monica extended a grey face for a kiss.

'It usually doesn't have to stop, Mom. Maybe they had to check something. Anyway, I've hired a car and I'll take you straight to the hotel where your room is air-conditioned.'

Monica grunted. 'Whose money are we spending?'

'Mine, Mother. Mine. Richard and I split what we had, after all the spending he did. He will, no doubt, make a fortune writing his novel, and I'll be a happy beach-bum living here on this island.'

Pandora drove along the ribbon road past the few shops that served the island's needs. As she passed each doorway, hands reached out and waved. At a large bulky building, Pandora stopped the car and said, 'I've just got to run in and buy you some Coke, Mom, for your fridge. Do you want to come in with me?'

As they walked around the shelves stacked with food, Pandora could feel the rising disapproval in her mother's face. The wattles of her neck were going red. Always a bad sign. 'So, you're not staying in my room with me?' Monica demanded as they walked past the shelves of cereals.

'No. I'm living with Ben.'

126

Monica snorted. 'Another no-good man who'll treat you like a piece of shit, I suppose?'

Inside herself, Pandora was amazed to feel Ben's presence. He was waving an oar at her, mouthing *She didn't even last twenty-four hours.* 'No, Mom. Ben's not a shit. He's great to be with, and we make each other very happy.'

'Here, Pandora. Grab that box of Metamusil. The food here is bound to make me constipated. I hope they have Preparation H over here. I've brought some with me, but my haemorrhoids are acting up something terrible.'

Pandora obediently took down a box of Metamusil. She looked at it and for a moment felt her usual tinge of sorrow and pity for her mother. The box assured its owner of the joys of big, bland movements of excretory happiness regularly every morning, to be followed by the less pleasant moments of the return of the delinquent haemorrhoids to their rightful place in the scheme of Monica's body with the daily application of Preparation H. The sounds of Monica's excretory life had been part of the orchestra of Pandora's life. The cigarette permanently dangling either from her mother's flaked lips or her fingers was an adjunct to that memory.

Now, with the basket full, they both stood sweating at the checkout. While they waited, Pandora picked up the local paper. 'It's the Governor's cocktail party next week,' she said. 'All week long they'll be fishing for blue marlin, and on the last day the Governor gives a party and everyone goes. Would you like to go?' She knew her mother would love every moment of such an event and that she could trade off her day in the boat with Octo and Janine if she planted her mother firmly in the one and only beauty parlour on the island for most of the day.

'That sounds nice, dear.'

Pandora knew her mother was pleased.

'And is this pretty lady your mother?' A big, booming voice broke the silence between Pandora and her mother. 'I can see the resemblance in the eyes.'

Monica's mouth pinched itself into a disapproving little drop of vinegar. Captain Billy laughed. He'd seen these relentless pursuing mothers over the years, chasing their daughters from one island to another, and he liked Pandora. She was no fuss.

'What's happening on Big Egg these days, Captain Billy?'

Captain Billy shrugged. 'Not much, just bigger cars, bigger expense accounts and corruption. Nothing new.'

Pandora packed the items into the shopping bag. 'Come on, Mom. I just want to say hello to Miss Christine.'

Miss Christine in the next-door shop was bent over her sewing machine. She looked up as she saw Pandora's shadow fall on the floor of the shop. 'This is my mother, Miss Christine. I just called in to say hello and see how you are.'

'Ah well, we're doing fine. Nolan is on Big Egg trying to get some justice done. Sometimes I think he's right, you know. We should be independent of that awful place.'

Pandora could see that Monica was bored. 'I'll be back to see you in a few days, Miss Christine. I must get Mom settled in the hotel.'

She got into the car and turned on the air-conditioning.

'Whew! How can you stand everybody knowing your business like that?' Monica frowned. 'Everyone is so forward here. Where I come from, you keep your business to yourself.'

'I know, Mom. I know only too well.' Pandora remembered the days of sitting in bed waiting for Marcus to return with some of his drunken, sexually delinquent friends. Nobody in the city to talk to. Here on this island, the arrival of a car at any door was immediately wired on the coconut telegraph. For Pandora, after the lonely years of her life, this lively intervention in everyone's lives was like an elixir. Mornings could be spent with Miss Rosie describing the history of the day before. Next week, with the millionaires' fishing boats in, the island would sound like a wasps' nest of speculation. For now, though, Pandora knew she must settle her mother as comfortably as possible and endure an evening of her mother's favourite form of conversation: the long saga of her husband who left her, and the brave, heroic attempts to bring up her daughter who then let three men slip through her fingers.

'I have a letter from Richard. Remind me to give it to you,' Monica said as she squeezed her broad beam out of the little hire car.

Pandora felt a tug. Maybe Richard had finished playing. Maybe the letter was to say his Peter Pan days were over.

Later Pandora took Monica down to the bar at the hotel. Janine, she knew, would cope well with her mother, but she was prickly with embarrassment at the idea of her mother meeting Ben.

As it happened, she needn't have worried. Ben came by for a beer at eight o'clock, and by then Monica was mellow with rum. 'I checked your room,' Ben said, smiling at Monica. 'You weren't there, so I thought I'd catch up with you both down here.' He took a swig from his bottle of beer.

Monica looked up at him. Her eyes were wary, but all she could see was a wide smile and big brown eyes under a thatch of sunburnt hair. 'You be good to my girl,' she growled. Her bright red fingernails on the right hand clenched around her cigarette.

'Of course,' Ben said, laughing. 'I'll take good care of Pandora for you. See she stays out of trouble. OK?'

Monica visibly relaxed, and Pandora gazed at Ben thoughtfully. Really, at times Ben could be so sickeningly sycophantic. But it worked on women. It certainly worked on Monica. From now on she would dote on Ben.

Ben returned her look, and the lid of his left eye dropped drastically. Pandora giggled. Ben made her feel like a child again. He gave her time to recapture all those lost years, those years that she needed to have back to find out who she was.

Chapter Twenty-two

Pandora was glad that she had joined Chuck and Eve on the two dives the day before. The night dive, while at first fiercely frightening, soon welled into a sense of adventure and wonder. At night, with her torch picking out browsing fish, she no longer felt herself an intruder. Here, under the water, swimming in deep shadow, breathing evenly, she was beginning to find a real power in herself. She swam with Eve but without requiring Eve's bulk for protection. She swam with Chuck and realized again that she was not asking for his masculine approval nor his presence to free herself from fear, but that she too was eager to explore this huge unknown world that had lived for so many years in her imagination.

Now, with Monica complaining about her high-heeled shoes and the heat, Pandora was able to smile. 'Come on, Mom. You'll be OK once we get to your hotel room. And I'll order you a rum punch.'

'And a good-looking guy to go with it,' her mother retorted.

'I'll do my best.' Pandora walked up the sandy path to the room she had first shared with Ben. She had hired the room reluctantly because she treasured those hours of lovemaking with Ben and also the beginning of her fragile feelings of her past that had surfaced so surprisingly. Before the island, life seemed to be a series of sequential events, most of them awful, but at times some of the occasions brought some moments of unprepared happiness. Busy in her daily life, she had never had time to take her life and look at it like a child through a kaleidoscope. Life before Little Egg was like a long, straight, mariner's ruler. You walked inch by inch from the beginning when you were born until the farthest inch which was when you died. Here she discovered not only time – ages and volumes of hot, water-filled hours in which to do nothing but float in a sea of memories – but also people like Miss Rosie, Janine and her sisters, all spending time talking *woman's talk*. 'Go away,' Janine would say to Octo. 'We want woman's talk.' And Octo took Ben by the elbow. 'Woman's talk no good for a man's head. They different people.' And they would shamble off to the bar to play pool or dominoes.

Monica sat down in a rattan chair in the air-conditioned hotel room and sniffed. Her cigarette was out and her mascara leaked down her face. 'Hang on, Mom. I'll call for a couple of drinks, and then I'll get you a wash-cloth to wipe off your face.'

'Wash-cloth hell. I'll take a shower.' Monica stood up and began to pull up her tight, polyester, polka-dotted dress.

It was then Pandora remembered her mother's flaunted nakedness. Her mother's smell had always repelled her as a child. Other mothers, whose little girls sat beside them while they had their hair enmeshed in great punitive rollers and hissed and steamed away the long Saturday mornings, always seemed to smell of sweet, light, edible nibbles. Pandora imagined a tooth full of chocolate mint with a hint of vanilla ice was the right smell for a mother. Not ever for Monica. Monica smelled of tobacco, pink floury face powder, and a musky smell that overpowered any bottle of perfume she might shake over her person. Now, as the dress came off, the smell of stale airport sweat also hit Pandora's guarded nose.

'The bathroom's over there, Mom. I'll turn on the shower.' Pandora hurriedly moved over to the bathroom. She heard her mother's shuffling walk coming towards the open bathroom door. Pandora held a white bath towel in front of herself as if to stave off an attack from a bull. Again, to her surprise, as her mother's pendulous belly partly obscured her greying pubic hair, Pandora felt a pang of pity for what had once been a fine, firm body. Now the belly was as wrinkled and soured as the discoloured limes that lay under the lime trees. Her thighs bulged with blue veins that reminded Pandora of the clinging mangrove swamps, all held together by gnarled, bunched knots. Her mother's pale blue eyes, with their startling black irises, gazed at Pandora. 'I've put on a little weight since the last time I saw you, honey. But I can still attract the men.'

'You get in the shower, Mom. You'll feel a lot cooler.'

Pandora watched her mother turn her body and lift her head to let the water run down her face. The flaccid back was streaked with rills of water which then spread over the towering buttocks. As Pandora patiently held the towel in her hands, she realized she had lost an enemy. She may not have gained a mother, but she had indeed lost an enemy all the same. At least there was the possibility of peace between the two of them.

131

The towel was warm and white in her hands. She felt a familiar throbbing and then the faint, slow vibration of that loving heartbeat. Ah, the drum! Of course. The drum. Universal love, always the gift of women to each other, and from us to men. She saw Janine's face.

'The water's gone cold.' Monica's peevish voice split the moment.

'Don't worry. I've got a towel. Here.' Pandora wrapped the bath towel around her mother. 'You look much cooler. How do you feel?'

'I'll tell you after I've had a rum-punch. My goodness, Pandora! The girls back home were so excited when I told them I was going out to see my daughter on a Caribbean island.'

Tears were in Pandora's eyes. Many, many years had passed since Monica had referred to Pandora either with pride or by the word *daughter*. 'I'll call the bar,' she said.

Chapter Twenty-three

Janine brought over the rum-punches. The glasses were running with beads of water. Titanic ice cubes floated on top. 'This is my friend Janine,' Pandora said.

Monica, lighting up a cigarette, looked quizzically at the woman. 'Has my Pandora been keeping good company while she's been on this island?'

Oh shit. Pandora knew the next line by heart.

Monica took a large slug of the rum-punch and then another. 'All we two women got in the world,' she continued, 'is our good family name.' Monica's eyes filled with practised tears.

Pandora looked at Janine.

'Your Pandora's a great girl, Mrs Mason. We all love her here.'

Pandora relaxed. She felt Janine fall into her usual patter of tourist chatter.

But Monica was not going to be deprived of her moment. 'It's all very well running away to an island in the Caribbean, but she's got a perfectly good husband at home waiting for her to come back.'

'That's not true, Mom.' Pandora felt the old familiar flame of anger begin to burn brightly. 'That's not true at all. Richard left me for Gretchen, and he doesn't want me back.'

Janine shot Pandora a sympathetic look before sliding out of the door. 'I'll see you tonight at work, Pandora.'

Monica looked up sharply. 'So, I'll be all alone on my first night?'

'No, Mom. I'll have dinner with you and then I'll go and get changed for work. My shift isn't until ten o'clock, and you'll be fast asleep by then.'

Monica sucked moodily on the straws buried in the few remaining ice cubes. It was a sound that had infuriated Pandora in the past, but her peace held.

She could manage now to deal with all of her mother's emotional manipulating, but not the clash of their two memories. Her mother's version of how her daughter's life took place, and her own. This was why she had so dreaded her mother's visit. The only agreement was that her father had abandoned both of them. Even then there lay the question of why. On her mother's side was an unexpressed allegation of sexual malpractice stopped only by her maternal care for her daughter. Over Pandora's head hung a puzzled question mark. Really Marcus was the main source of contention. As far as Monica was concerned, Marcus had been framed by a few malcontent women who had tried to seduce him. Pandora as his wife was not allowed to testify in court. Monica even insisted that the videotapes of the sexual orgies were fabrications, and the fact that Marcus was found guilty was just further proof of corruption in high places. The subject of Marcus was like poison ivy between them, with no antidote.

Monica by now used Marcus as an excuse to lash her daughter, but it was Richard she really wanted to see her return to. His large and influential family. To her yearly visits to the Townsend estate where she stood among the family gatherings which smelled of money, gazing in awe at the silver and the chandeliers. How could this very plain, unenterprising daughter of hers end up with three husbands, when Monica had only had one and lost him?

Monica rummaged in her bag. 'Here,' she said, pulling out a fat letter. 'It's from Richard. I talked to him on the telephone before I left. He says he misses you very much.'

'Oh, Mom! Must you telephone them all? I bet you even telephoned Norman.'

'Sure I did. He's my first son-in-law. He's doing real fine. He has two children and the cutest little wife. I see her all over town. "You know, Mrs Mason," she said to me when she first came to the beauty parlour, "I can't think why these awful stories got out about my Norman beating your girl Pandora. He's a real quiet man. Wouldn't hurt a mouse." That's what she said, Pandora.' Monica tipped the glass and loudly sucked the last of the watery rum. 'I don't know, girl. Marcus is about to marry again. I saw his picture in the society paper. And his new little bride looks so young! She looks just like you, mousy little thing.'

Pandora shivered. She'll be more than just mousy soon enough, she thought, looking at her mother. Soon she'll be anorexic and drugged to the eyeballs. Those were the murderous memories that haunted Pandora the most. Those awful days and nights when her body lost control of itself and her mind bent like corrugated iron in the wind as voices and fingers and tongues giggled and licked and probed. Then the shuffling sounds as people made their way off to their bedrooms. And then the silence. Sometimes Marcus asleep, satiated, or more hopefully the bed empty, but the sheets slimy . . .

'Do you want to go for a swim, Mom? The sea's perfect right now.' She desperately wanted to get out of the room and away from the memories. To be washed by the sea and shriven by the clean white sand.

But Monica had not travelled all this way with her carpet-bag full of grievances to let Pandora go quite so lightly. 'You get me another of those rum things first. Then we'll see. No, I'll go get the damn thing, and you read that letter. I want to hear what Richard has to say.'

'That's my private letter.' Pandora was amazed at the authority in her voice. 'I'll read it when I feel like it.'

Monica grinned a wolfish grin.

Pandora sighed. Of course, Monica knew what was in the letter. She had steamed it open, just as she had felt it her right to violate Pandora ever since she was born. *I carried you inside me for all those long months, and you owe me now*, was one of her mother's favourite sayings. *Yes, indeed. You owe me.*

'I'll put on my new sundress and head for the bar. According to my hotel meal-and-bar plan, I can drink until I drop. You want a drink, too?'

'No, thanks.' Pandora held the letter in her hand. Her feelings towards Richard were ambivalent. Away from him on the island she felt unconcerned. Moments of regret for the good times they had together, but slowly, as she lived so simply within the kind confines of her relationship with Ben and her new friends, all that past life slipped away and the daily delights of the sun and the sea took over. Had Mrs Johnson had the operation? Did Miss Laverne go to Miami to attend her sister's wedding? Was the boat coming in, bringing with it fresh tomatoes and crisp cool lettuce? *I never thought I'd lust for a fresh tomato* . . . Pandora willed herself to hold on to the happy present, to leave the less happy past.

Two photographs fell out on to her brown knees. One was of Gretchen standing by Richard's red Ferrari. Gretchen's blonde hair was tied back in a bandana. Her very blonde skin was never touched by the sun. She was wearing dark glasses so her albino pink-rimmed eyes were shaded from the light. Ever since her treacherous behaviour, Pandora felt Gretchen reminded her of one of those white stringy caterpillars found under cabbage plants.

135

Gretchen had warned Pandora enough times that if she did not look after Richard in the 'European way', she would lose him. Pandora always laughed. The European way of taking care of men seemed to Pandora archaic, or even Dickensian, in the fawning and the fluttering and flattering that occurred when *daddy* came home. It was always Gretchen who leapt to her feet to give Richard a drink when he came home from the office. Pandora was usually wrist-deep in the basin in the kitchen. Friedrich, Gretchen's husband, was always being patted and poodled while Gretchen served both men their food at the table. Friedrich played golf all weekend, with Gretchen sitting demurely on her plump German bottom on a shooting stick. Richard played rugby football on Saturday afternoons while Pandora curled up on the sofa in the drawing-room of their home and watched television. And on Sundays Richard took off with his friends and a cooler of beer to go fishing. Pandora quite happily spent Sundays wandering in the Boston Museum of Fine Arts or rambling along the Charles River. Often she would meet Gretchen at Pier Four for lunch. Gretchen usually arrived loaded with shopping bags; most of the table-talk would be about the cost of the clothes. After half a bottle of wine, it inevitably turned to Friedrich's insatiable need for sex, which made Pandora wince with embarrassment and mutter that she and Richard were just fine. Which indeed they were.

After Marcus, Richard's healthy, uncomplicated, robust lovemaking was healing. It lacked all the delicacy and the time that she had to spend with Ben, but then Richard, as she well knew by now, was English. His attitude to women, as far as she had been aware, was that they were there to be mounted upon pedestals. Pandora had always felt herself reverently treated as if, like his mother's prized tea-set, she might break in tiny pieces. And all that was really expected of her was to listen to all his school stories, share all the jokes with his chums round the dinner table, and be a 'jolly good sport'. *Jolly good* was Richard's highest accolade. He said it when she managed not to fall off his horse and he also occasionally said it after sex.

'To tell you the truth, Pandora,' said his letter now, 'Gretchen and I have been going through a bit of a bad patch.'

Pandora snorted. Gretchen was probably cleaning out Richard's bank account. Friedrich was a wealthy industrialist and he let Gretchen do whatever she liked, as long as she played the perfect hostess and had an obligatory orgasm once a night. Gretchen thought this piece of male philosophy was cast in stone and brought down the mountain by Moses.

136

'You give him his pleasure and you make him feel like a man.'

'You mean you come every night, Gretchen?'

Gretchen's rounded cheeks flushed. 'Well, not every night, silly. All women know that you just fake it and give him a little kiss on his *strudel* and he feels satisfied.'

Pandora giggled. She couldn't see Richard getting round to sex every night, especially when the night before a rugger match was sacred to the team. And as for kisses on his *strudel*, it was hard enough to get Richard's *strudel* out of his old blue school pyjama bottoms.

'I'm sitting outside on the veranda with my typewriter,' the letter continued, 'and I am gazing at the heat haze on the hills. There are four sheep and two goats up there, and the shepherd, lazy swine, is fast asleep.'

Richard, the intrepid reporter, reduced to novelizing about sheep rather than spending his Hemingway quest years fighting among the villages in Tuscany against the Germans. Well, I do hope he does write the definitive novel, Pandora thought.

The rest of the letter gave a list of old friends who had visited them, mostly old school friends. Nights singing old school songs by the fire. Days devoted to walking up and down mountains. Pandora remembered all that walking. She supposed the English walked up and down mountains because they only had a few in England.

'Anyway, must finish now. Gretchen is arriving with enormous cakes and she counts the pages I've written. The awful thing about writing a novel is that it takes so much writing. Hope you are well and happy. Please write to me and send a photograph. Heard from your mother. She sounds in fine form.

'Lots of love.' And there again was Richard's childish, sprawling signature.

Pandora heard Monica walking up the path. She saw her push the swing door open with her left shoulder. 'I've brought two back. One for me and one bought for me by a guy called Chuck. Boy, they build them big in Florida!'

'Mom, don't you think you're a little too old for all that?'

'Never too old. Never too old to fall in love.' Monica, her cigarette clenched between her teeth, began to shamble in a circle around the room.

137

Chapter Twenty-four

Because Monica was now on the island, Pandora realized that her perspective changed. To please her mother, she put on a dress and attended the little white church at Peas Pot Bay. There a more gentle pastor talked of the things that mattered to the parishioners. A fire had wiped out a family home, and money needed to be collected immediately for the forlorn family who stood in the centre aisle of the church, their hair singed and still smelling of last night's smoke. Pandora was amazed and touched to see her mother put a twenty-dollar bill into the collection plate.

The congregation prayed for rain. Mrs Julie Jones sang 'Rock of Ages' and then everyone sang to a small upright piano a hymn composed by Arthur Bliss over the spot where his wife had drowned with his three daughters, 'It Is Well with My Soul'. Pandora daydreamed about the little piano that must have been hauled through these treacherous reefs on a boat filled with pilgrims fleeing persecution in their past lives.

The whole community shook Monica's hand and she received invitations to various church events. She walked back to the hotel beside Pandora. 'Why, these are real nice people, Pandora. I'm not one for church,' she said, loudly sucking on a cigarette, 'but that Mrs Jones! What a voice she has! She should go on Christian TV, you know.'

'I think she's happy here, Mom.'

The first week went by, Pandora followed Monica around the few shops, poking and picking for trinkets to take home for the ladies at the hairdresser's. 'I promised Marcus and the little lady I'd buy her a piece of black coral.'

'You'd better get hers made in the shape of a cross.'

'No, now, honey. Don't you be so jealous. Marcus was a good husband and he was always very nice to me.' Monica sighed in the heat and the sweat. 'Such fine manners.' Monica looked at Pandora's face and decided to back off. This last week she began to realize that Pandora was starting to have a very firm grasp of her own reality. Must be those awful girls, Monica decided. 'That Janine friend of yours,' she said. 'She's a no-good little whore.'

This only made Pandora laugh. 'She's a very good whore, Mom, and an excellent friend. On Saturday I'm going out fishing with Octo, her lover, for marlin. I've made an appointment for you to get your hair done while we're out, and then in the evening it's the Governor's cocktail party, and then a dance on the beach.' The same beach, she remembered with affection, where she'd first met Ben.

Monica's face lightened up. 'That'll be lovely, dear.'

A day off, Pandora rejoiced. So far, after tucking her mother up in bed every night, she had little effort left for Ben. He was always waiting for her, sitting on the veranda with the mosquito coil blowing a grey mist around the swinging chair, a six-pack of beer in a cooler beside him. She marvelled as she walked up the drive that evening at how he could sit, sometimes for hours, just gazing up into the heavens.

'What are you thinking about tonight?' she asked as she slipped into his arms.

'I was thinking of the grouper. They're running at the moment. Look. See the ring of water round the moon? That'll be rain, but it should be good weather for the big fish on Saturday. Octo's boat is old, but it has the power to pull hard. She's used to these seas and these reefs. Octo and I will fish. If you just do what Janine says, you see, we stand a good chance of bringing in a big one.'

Pandora lay still, curled in Ben's arms. Up in the mountain she could hear the drums pounding. Janine must be up there with Octo, praying for the blue marlin, she thought. 'What do you honestly think of my mother?' she asked. 'I know you haven't seen much of her, but what do you think?'

Ben shook his head. 'It's difficult to say, Pandora. I see those women when they're young and they're pretty, and they come down here for sex and diving. But then, after saying how much they want to live here, how beautiful the island is, how wonderful the way of life, they get bored and go back to their towns and their cities, and this is just a dream they bring out now and again to look at, to wonder if they should have stayed. Your mom has sadness written all over her face. She is like a boat that has lost a race. I don't know what she wanted for herself, but she didn't get it.'

'She didn't get it from me, either. I guess I was her only chance, and her last chance, and I blew it all along the line. Oddly enough, though, down here where everybody is related, everything is family: some family is good family, some is bad family, but I realize that, either way, everybody accepts each other. Now I don't get angry with Mom any more. I just think of her as being old and rather frightened. She's really trying to behave, and so far she hasn't even chased Chuck, other than to have a drink or two with him, and he really gets a kick out of her. I haven't seen that side of her at all, you know. I think all the laughing and joking sides were kept for the shop. Then she had this series of miserable houses to go back to, and Dad usually laid off from some railroad job or another. Life can't have been much fun for her.'

Ben opened another beer. 'No, it can't.'

There was a scented silence between them. The smell of fresh sea salt on Ben's smooth skin and the tang of Ambre Solaire on Pandora's shoulders. The only sound heard was the squeak of the swing as it moved lazily in time to Ben's bare feet. Soon the rocking rocked them both, locked together, mouth to mouth. Ben could feel deep, gentle crevices inside her warm vagina, and Pandora could feel the ebb and flow of his probe until he caught her urgent need, like a great fish, to leap out of herself up into the bright, moon-streaked light of the sea all around them. She led and he followed and they lay warm and panting in each other's arms.

'Couldn't it always be like this, Ben?'

Ben stood up and pulled her to his side. They walked down across the beach into the sea. The ripples rose and covered their knees. 'In films, Pandora, in books, yes, it could always be like this.'

'But in truth?'

'What do you think?'

Pandora dived into the water and let the waves break over her head. She found herself sobbing and then she turned her face to the night sky. The tears still coursed down her cheeks. 'But I'm so happy, Ben. I've never been so happy.'

'Listen.' Ben lay beside her in the water. 'Listen to the drumming.'

The drums had stopped pleading and now they were singing. Straining her ears, Pandora could hear a song.

'That's the mothers' song. It's played on a conch shell by Octo's mother. It is rare to hear this song.'

'What is she saying?'

'Oh, it's an old song about this island. It captures many people and shows them how to be heart-happy.' He put his hand on Pandora's chest. 'Life means moving on. Always parting. But with gladness.'

Pandora lay in the sweep of the sea. The drum had given her this soul-peace before, and she knew she must stay until that peace was welded like fire coral into her heart and could not be touched or disturbed by hurt or cruel human hands. Hands that wished to dig out parts of herself to shore up a lonely, miserable existence. There were to be no more mistakes.

She wound her legs around Ben and they made love gently in the sea, like two watery jellyfish washed with the blues and the purples of the rising sun.

Chapter Twenty-five

Saturday was a fine, hot day. Ben hugged his head tightly. 'Get me coffee please, Pandora. I have such a headache!'

Pandora put on the coffee-pot and waited for the familiar smell of roasted Blue Mountain Jamaican coffee, mixed with the smell of the brine from the beach. The smell was not just of coffee and sea; it also contained the putrid, dying smells of seaweed picked over by small crabs and flies. The smell stung in her nostrils and reminded her of the big boats gliding into the island's main reef the night before. The dock had little mooring; it was just a large chunk of concrete strutting out to sea. Ben explained that in the old days they threw all the old heavy American cars into the dock and then poured concrete over the lot. 'Plus a man or two we didn't like.'

The coffee boiled.

'Some of those boats from Florida look pretty awesome, Ben,' she had said.

He grinned. 'Yeah, but they don't know the waters like we know them. That's what we've got going for us. Pack something to eat.'

Pandora shuffled together a pile of curried Jamaica meat patties. Ben could eat these by the dozen. Two chests of beer, and they were ready to go.

Monica had been organized by Trish at the beauty parlour, so Pandora now felt free to enjoy her day. Close to the dock, cars were parked and families descended. Women with their hair in fierce red rollers hollered advice to their husbands. Small boys begged to go, but Octo explained to his little friends that the action would be too fast. The whip of the fishing lines could be lethal and the spearing and the killing of the fish allowed for no distraction. Janine wore jeans and a red T-shirt. For once she looked seriously dedicated to today's activity. 'I hope we get a big one,' she said, hugging Pandora.

Octo stood, surveying the competition. The three motor-boats moored out on the reef looked like serious contenders. A catamaran was already out of the running, having torn her hull coming into the reef. The dock stank of buckets of bait. Every fisherman had his own concoction. Octo's mother, Blossom, had promised a special brew which included various barks and flower essences from the mountain. Rumour had it that Miss Maisy had been bribed by Conrad to give him several pints of fish-heads heavily laced with Haitian voodoo promises. Miss Rosie just laughed when Ben told her, and hugged him and said, 'The best man catch the biggest fish, boy.' She was down on the dock in the chilly blue dawn of the new day.

The three big boats from Florida took off first. Conrad and his crew pulled ahead of Octo who seemed to want to wait until most of the boats were out of sight. Pandora was so used to Octo that she was quite taken by surprise at the curious stares he received from the tourists who stood in deep rows, watching the boats leave. It was not so much that Octo was huge, but more that the disfigurement to the shape of his head and his long trailing arms made him look so much like a gorilla. Today he wore no shirt and his fur pelt gleamed in the sun. 'I have a red shirt ready for him when he sits for the big one,' Janine confided in Pandora. 'Till then he sweats too much.'

Ben, Pandora knew, was nervous. She could feel him standing beside her, flexing his arms. 'By the end of the day,' he said, 'God willing, they will ache with the pulling.'

The frigate birds were duelling in the sky, crashing down with four-foot flapping wings at the buckets of bait left on the dock, awaiting the arrival of some of the smaller boats. Pandora could see them coming down the reef. Only Conrad's boat had gone ahead, but by now she had been on the island sufficiently long to recognize the boats and friends. Octo had been sitting on a barstool, positioned by the huge fish weights. He stood up and the crowd moved back instinctively. He gazed around at the crowd and then yelled, 'Come on, Janine! Let's go and get him! Ben, take the buckets. Pandora, don't forget the beer.'

The old boat sat low in the water. She was named *Blossom* after Octo's mother. Pandora felt a slight sense of guilt that she was not as sure as Octo was that they would win the trophy. The other three boats from Florida looked so purposeful, so jam-packed with the very latest equipment. In fact, the night before, there had been ferries out to the three boats so that the islanders could admire the equipment. But out of loyalty Pandora refused to go. Monica, escorted by Chuck, came back most enthusiastic. 'They have everything you need,' she said, settling herself at a table at the bar. 'An inside toilet with a bath, and colour television in the living-room. Think of it!'

143

'They're hoping to catch fish, Monica, not watch TV,' Chuck teased her.

Monica smiled and Pandora thought how much younger her mother looked after a few days away from her old life in Idaho.

Now, as she clambered aboard, she applauded herself on her ability to find her way about the boat without falling down or slipping. No longer did Ben have to keep a worried eye on her. She took herself off to the galley and set the bottles of beer in their cooler under the sink. There was a swinging stove for boiling or cooking, and two big, long bunks for sitting or sleeping. The chart stand was a step above and protected from the elements by a piece of makeshift roofing. Two old chairs with thick buckles and leaking horse-hair sat at the back of the boat. High up, so high up that Pandora often feared they'd capsize, was a steering wheel and the power controls. While searching for fish the boat could be controlled from that great height, but when the fight began in earnest, the main control cabin was behind the two seats.

For now, as Octo ran around the boat casting off from the dock, Janine quietly coiled ropes. Ben checked the long rods in their holders, hundreds of feet of thick line on their spools. The boat rocked under Pandora's feet and slowly pulled away. She could hear the local island crowd and the children cheering for Octo. 'There'll be other boats from Big Egg coming over,' Octo remarked, 'but we just feel about a bit and see what's moving.'

They motored slowly and lazily for the first hour. Octo sat in a chair with Ben in another, drinking beer. 'Would you like a beef patty, either of you?' Pandora heard her rather middle-class voice cut the silence. She was worried that without food in their stomachs, the two men might get drunk. The empty beer bottles were piling up and she could see two bottles of tequila under the sink. She saw Janine smile at her and nod. She went off to get the patties. Maybe she was not just an outsider with pretentious worries. Maybe all women worried about their menfolk. Nothing wrong with that.

Octo sank his teeth into the hot spicy pastry. 'You make this?' he said incredulously.

Pandora nodded. 'Miss Rosie taught me.'

'Pandora's a good island cook now,' Ben said.

They idled along, waiting, Pandora felt. Waiting for what? But it felt unlucky to talk about why the waiting. Rather like stepping on the crack of the pavement.

Octo grunted. 'Let everybody else throw their bait and then we watch to see where the marlin come in. They know more than a man knows. This is a fish that likes to fight. He knows man, many men, are out there looking for him, and he'll come in and decide to fight. Or maybe he won't.' Octo climbed up the tower. He pointed across to the west. 'Marlin jumping over there!' he said.

Pandora ran up the tower behind him.

'See?' Octo held her head in his big hands. 'Watch. Don't breathe or you'll miss the jump.'

And then she saw the fish. He had the hook from one of the Florida boats in his mouth. For a moment he stood on his tail in the water, being pulled by the engines which she could hear gunning the boat furiously forward. The great fish arched his body and dived. As he went, the sun caught a flash of blue mixed with silver. 'That's the big one, I think,' Octo said slowly to himself. 'He's diving now. Let's just see if he gets off their line.'

Octo watched the competition through his binoculars. Every so often he'd call Ben. Ben would take a look. 'Tourist fisherman,' Octo said. 'Moving him too fast. They'll tire before he will.'

Conrad went cheerfully past. 'Maisy's spell sure helped me out! I got a twenty-five-pound tuna already. You caught much yet?'

Octo leaned over. 'No. We're waiting for the marlin.'

Pandora watched both Ben and Octo. She sensed yet again a great patience in both the men. Even Janine, who was usually always in motion, squatted quietly on her heels, a bottle of beer in one hand and a patty in the other. Little boats fussed and pulled in fish. Gulls quarrelled with boobies. The frigate birds attacked the smaller boats and were beaten off by small boys with broomsticks. 'No-good robber birds,' Ben remarked.

'But they're so beautiful,' Pandora said as one huge male in full mating cry soared over them, his underpouch bright red with passion and his mind on things other than fish.

Octo roared with laughter. 'Ben, you getting too straight. We're all robbers and thieves. My grandfather was a pirate. He made a living from here to Jamaica. Today the police leave us alone. Today we're clean. Good feeling. God knows and not before long, I'm going to give up this way of life, marry my Janine, and settle down.'

Janine, leaning over Octo's chair, her eyes alight, kissed him on his big, misshapen mouth. 'You really mean that, Octo?'

'Here,' he said and he took her slim, long-fingered hand and put it on his heart. 'Feel my heart beat?'

Janine nodded.

'That's for you,' he said. 'All for you.'

Pandora felt her eyes fill with tears. Would there ever be a day when a man would say that to her? She thought she had it once with Richard, but really it was a trick, an illusion. Richard's life was not an illusion, but it produced the illusion which was Richard and that was what so confused Pandora in the beginning.

Ben, sensing her fragility, hugged her. 'One day, Pandora, you will come back to the island with the man you love.'

'And you,' Pandora laughed, 'will be married to a pretty little island girl with six babies, a girl who doesn't go "Oh gross!" when you boil the whelks.'

Not much was happening, but the boat to the west had obviously lost the marlin. A shark was pulled in by a boat behind them along with several large grouper.

'OK,' Octo commanded. 'Let's get out the salt and the tequila and get fishing. I feel fish moving in my veins.'

'It's true, you know,' Janine commented as she filled the cooler with yet more ice. 'The more tequila that man drinks, the closer he gets to the fish. You know, sometimes I wonder if Blossom didn't mate with one of those fish-men they say live out there.'

'I know what you mean,' Pandora said. 'He has the most amazing eyes. They can swing all round his head.'

'My Octo,' Janine blushed. 'I know that sounds silly, but if he really means it, I would be so happy.' Both women carried the new ice box filled with beer and tequila to the aft of the boat.

The sun was low in the sky and they had caught three barracuda, four tuna of not much size, and some grouper. Pandora caught several parrot fish and then bitterly regretted it. They were so beautiful. She lost all sense of pity when one bit her fiercely on the leg. Ben laughed. 'We call them Old Wives. Mean as hell when you catch them, but good to eat.'

Pandora was feeling hot and sweaty. Boats were turning and the sun was going down. So far Pandora had enjoyed the day, but it had been long, hot, and arduous. Octo and Ben seemed to have consumed an enormous amount of tequila with beer-chasers. Octo was roaring stories and occasionally making dives at Janine who kissed him back with unrestrained passion. Pandora was sitting on Ben's lap. He drank more slowly, but she just sipped at the beer. 'I've got to go to the Governor's cocktail party with Mom, Ben. I can't drink tequila.'

Ben giggled. 'At least I don't have to go. Us niggers, as they call us on Big Egg, don't get asked. Anyway, why should some Englishman tell us what to do?' This was Ben's favourite subject. But he was interrupted by a roar from Octo.

Pandora had always in her dreams from childhood thought of fish as gentle victims of man's aggression. Not for a moment did she expect to feel an awful, primeval fear of this giant that rose out of the water. The fish was bigger than the boat, she was sure of that. It was not just the size of the fish that made her afraid, but also the fact that she saw in its cold round eyes a hatred, a wish to take on a fight with this object that stood in the way to the food that it had unwittingly snatched from its own territorial water and was now being denied. The fish wanted the succulent bait and the fish was quite willing to fight to the death for that morsel. After all, the blue marlin was king of the Caribbean, and no puny boat with a drunken, tequila-swigging, strange-looking creature was going to get in his way.

Ben left his chair and headed for the controls. The fish jumped to dive, but Octo pulled the line so hard it broke the back of the dive, so the fish sounded and sat for a moment brooding under the boat. Octo took another swig. 'Hold on, girls!' he rumbled. 'He's going to make a run for it. And that's better than if he comes up under the boat. I'll give him line to go.'

The fish read Octo's mind and came straight up beside the boat, lashing the water with his tail. Pandora was panic-stricken. The fish was going to pull them down with him, she was sure of it.

Octo screamed obscenities at the fish, and for a moment they both stared, man and fish. Then, with an audible groan of wind through its gills, the fish sank again. 'We got him, Ben! The hook's well in. He can't get off. Now it's just how long it takes to tire him.'

As far as Pandora was concerned, it took a very long time. The fish lunged, and Octo pulled back. At times he passed the rod over to Ben and peed off the side of the boat. Octo was in a world of his own. The girls, Ben, the boat, the island, none of it mattered. It was Octo and his fish. Pandora realized he didn't even care if it was the fish that would win the trophy or not. It was a pact between a blue marlin and a man who loved to fish. Both man and fish claimed not only ancestry but also ascendancy and what was going on now was an ancient battle, far older than the islands themselves.

The sun was well down when the great fish finally gave up. There were no histrionics, just Octo finishing his last bottle of tequila and saying, 'Now I pull you in, my friend.' His huge arms strained to their limit. His shoulders creaked with the effort. At last Pandora could see the fin cut through the water. Octo tied the fish to the side of the boat, and they limped into the harbour.

Octo and Ben were too tired to unhitch the fish, so they let other willing hands lift the marlin with the winch. 'Four hundred and twenty-five pounds,' sang out Conrad. 'Biggest yet.'

Pandora knew she must leave to collect her mother. 'I'll be back,' she said to Ben who seemed to be laid out on the anchored boat in a stupor.

'I'll take care of them till you get back,' said Janine. 'They need to sleep. They don't have waitresses like me for the Governor's cocktail party anyway. They bring the white girls from Big Egg.'

Pandora used her mother's shower to get rid of the smell of the fish and the gasoline. She pulled on a black cocktail dress and did her hair.

Monica was garrulous, but pleased with herself. Her helmet of hair had been softened by Trish who also cut out all the perm, so Monica's face had a younger, gentler look. They walked up to the hotel and down the receiving line. The Governor blinked his weak eyes at Pandora and shook hands very politely with Monica. Monica was ecstatic. 'I've never shaken hands with an important person before,' she said.

All evening Pandora seethed. She hated the way the confident British ex-pats strode into the hotel, shaking the Governor's wilting hand. His mousy wife stood beside him. She reminded Pandora of a wind-up doll. 'How marvellous!' 'Really!' 'So wonderful to see you, darling!'

What a farce, Pandora thought. A little pimple of colonialism prac-tised on a faraway island. She could hear the loud voices of the teaching profession chattering up to the main lobby, then quickly dispersing and spreading like poison ivy. The food was handed out by blonde-haired, blue-eyed girls especially brought over from Big Egg for the occasion. How remote the two segments of this small island really are, she thought. Today she saw clearly the Little Eggers with their best suits and their well-dressed wives, trying to take the chance to talk to their Governor about the very real and worrying issues of the island. The many ex-pats were involved in education in theory, but in practice they were doing as little as possible until their two-year contracts were up and they were gone, blaming their failure to educate the children on everything except the teachers' lack of interest. Pandora knew all about

148

the situation from two teachers who really did care. She could see them both standing by themselves, ostracized by the others.

There were several exceedingly wealthy couples who had big houses on the island. Million-Dollar Fishing was a time to open the houses and throw parties. Their interest and contribution to the island was nil. However, the Governor shook them all by the hand, turning away from the small deputation who so earnestly begged support for an improvement in the airways service to Little Egg.

'Come on, Monica.' Pandora felt an arm about her shoulder. It was Chuck. 'Let's go and have a free dinner on the immoral bureaucrats from Big Egg, shall we?' Pandora knew she owed it to her mother to at least sit through dinner, but she blessed Chuck for his inclusion.

As they ate their way through plates of chicken curry and fried yam, Pandora did notice that Chuck, for all his bragging and boasting, really did seem to get on with her mother. Monica, in Chuck's presence, seemed oddly at ease. The need to bully and to rear into arguments seemed to leave her. Chuck made her laugh with his rude, crude attitude to life. She made him gentle with her startling little pretensions. Chuck, Pandora noticed, no longer drank beer from a bottle.

After coffee was served and before the speeches were made, Pandora slid away. She was sure that Ben would be gone, but she did so want to find him and Octo and Janine. She took off her high-heeled shoes, cursing the blisters they had given her, and she ran down the path and along the road to the harbour.

As she turned the corner, she could see that all the watchers were gone. The moon was alight, casting cold shadows on the great fish as it hung on the weighing hook. It took her a moment to see Octo sitting on a stool beside the fish. He had his huge arms around the fish's head. 'It was a damned good fight, fellow,' he said. 'It was a damned good fight.'

And she realized that Octo was crying.

She tiptoed back to the boat and found both Janine and Ben sitting quietly in the moonlight. 'What's the matter with Octo?' Pandora asked, mystified.

'He won,' Ben said slowly. 'Octo won. He has to go on living. That's what hurts.'

Janine pulled Pandora down beside her. 'You take Ben home and I'll wait for Octo. After a while, he'll be ready to eat.'

Pandora helped Ben up and they both walked quietly by the fish as it hung silver in the moonlight. Both eyes still glared at Pandora. This one would not live to fight again, but then the world was full of eyes that looked like that. Norman's, Marcus's, but no, curiously enough, not Richard's.

Chapter Twenty-six

All night long, Pandora dreamed of the big fish. Entwined in her dreams were memories of Marcus. Those memories made her turn and groan in her sleep. Then there were memories of fishes with Richard in the river in Devon where they took their holidays away from the strain of Boston and his work as a newspaper man. These memories were happier. The night seemed long, but Ben did not wake up. He was so exhausted, he lay flat on his back. Pandora got up several times between dreams, partly because the dreams were so real that she felt if she did not get on her feet and walk around, the dream might swallow her and hold her for ever in its horror. After such a wonderful day, the sight of the magnificent fish hanging on the dock unleashed so many subconscious thoughts in her head. Why did she have such a difficult head? She knew it had troubled her all her life. Other children had difficult mothers, but they shrugged their shoulders and got on with life. Other women got beaten. They, too, often stayed with a fatalistic acceptance of their fate. The women Pandora met in Marcus's therapy group accepted much of what he was doing to them. Some even connived, but no one married him. Only Pandora. Why on earth did she marry Marcus? She sat out on the floor of the veranda, holding a cup of fragrant coffee in her hand.

It was two hours before dawn and the night was crisp and brilliant. The stars pinholed the black sky; her star in particular shone brightly. Marcus, then, from the moment she first saw him, seemed to have the deepest understanding of her as a person of anybody she had ever met. He saw her raw and mutilated places, but also he could see her strengths. Those strengths were the defences she had built against her mother's attacks. The raw pain was the pain of the abandonment of her father and now a further failure of her marriage. Marcus saw in Pandora a very malleable female creature.

Within Marcus lived a twisted soul. As a small boy he tortured animals. That information only came out in the trial, but during his courting of Pandora, he could see so gleefully that she was an exquisite creature to torment. Sufficiently fierce to hobble, should he break one of her legs, she was insufficiently capable of communicating pain, so he had her caught like the flies whose legs he pinched off one after the other. Pandora bore his rough sexual attacks without sound. But where he mostly scored were the moments when her face would turn away and her eyes filled with tears. Then, rearing up from some volcanic cave of rage, he would begin to attack her verbally. Of course he must be right. After all, he was a psychiatrist.

He reserved these amusements for their private dinner engagements in their own home. Pandora dreaded their dinners together. The staff would serve the courses and then leave for the evening. Slowly, as the corrosive words slipped through his thin mouth, she learned about herself from Marcus. In defence she reached for wine and then for more wine. Finally the litany exhausted itself and Marcus was bored. At the beginning of the meal a pretty, though anorexic, woman sat in front of him, her hair a halo round her face, and her green eyes wary. Now, hours later, he ordered this dishevelled thing, evicted from its carapace, too drunk to do much, to crawl to her bed. 'I'm going out,' he'd say. 'I've had enough of you.' And with great relief she would hear the door of the car slam and the wheels grind on the stones. Slowly, holding the walls, she would make her way to the bedroom. Often she would retch up the wine and then shake, her whole nervous system suffering a St Vitus's dance. Thankfully Marcus was not there to see it. This then was the woman that first met Richard.

Not a woman, not a person, not even a thing. Just a hollow box with a painfully scratched surface . . .

Pandora sighed and finished the coffee. Richard was now very much on her mind. So much of the island had healed her. Even her relationship with her mother was now tenable. Why could she not resolve how she felt about Richard? She would ask Janine's advice. With that comforting thought she quietly placed her coffee cup in the sink and climbed back into bed beside Ben.

Pandora was really surprised to see Chuck and her mother breakfasting by the pool. They were in such earnest conversation that Pandora felt loath to interrupt. Finally the smell of bacon and eggs overcame her embarrassment and she pulled out a chair and sat down. Monica gazed innocently at her daughter. 'Oh, no. It isn't what you think at all,' she said. 'Chuck and I have an idea to go into partnership here on this island. Don't we, dear?' Monica put a possessive hand on Chuck's arm.

'Sure. Your mom and I reckon we could open a beauty parlour with your mom's business experience from her store in Idaho. And I could sell my diving photographs and equipment. What do you think?'

Pandora looked at them both and then laughed. Her mother had her usual cigarette dripping ash on to the tablecloth, and Chuck was wearing his see-through gold lamé bikini bottoms. His gold chains gleamed in the sunlight and his tow-coloured hair stood up on end. 'So, you two have spent all night talking business?'

'Not all night,' Monica admitted. 'We have changed clothes since dinner, if you've noticed.'

'I have. Sure. I think this island could do with another beauty parlour.' Pandora wolfed down her breakfast, kissed her mother goodbye, and ran off to find Eve.

She arrived on the dock puffing and panting. 'Gee, Eve. I had such a good day yesterday, and just now I had breakfast with Mom and Chuck. They're getting on so well together, I can't believe it.'

'I can. Your mother is the kind of strong woman who can deal with Chuck. And in a funny way, Chuck will take care of her.'

'I even kissed my mom this morning. I know this sounds childish, but I just naturally leaned over and kissed her as though I'd been doing it all my life.'

Eve grinned. 'Anything can happen on a Caribbean island, especially on Little Egg. Let's get our gear and go. I'm desperate to get underwater.'

By now Pandora felt very much at home in the sea, but as she allowed herself to sink slowly, stage by stage, she looked around her. Would she see a phantom of the great marlin which no longer hung from the hook? She knew the fish had been sold to a restaurant in Florida, an undignified end for such a warrior. But still, deep down in the stillness, was he here watching her?

They were making for Pirate's Wall, a drop-off point that fell away for thousands of feet. Once they reached the place, Eve made a thumbs-up sign and Pandora began her flight. Weightless and free, the only sound was the air from her bottles and a few bubbles. She swooped and glided. Close to the wall she could see a suspicious moray eel, his heavy trunk half out of his hole, his teeth clicking disapprovingly. Down this far, there were not that many fish, just the silence and the freedom, the sense of other. In a way Pandora realized there was also the sense that had always been elusive to her, the sense of self she had so long mislaid. Did she ever have it? Probably yes, but that small

153

twelve-year-old sense of self had walked out, holding her departing father's hand. And so far it had shown no sign of returning. Yet here, alone but with Eve nearby, she felt a contentment, and again that pure stillness of the heart in contemplation. In contemplation of what? Only here could she sense the infinite. Maybe the only other example would be to stand on the moon. The hand that had wrought this landscape must be a mighty force. It was within that circle of force Pandora had first felt the stirring of an understanding, too small yet to comprehend. Out here again she felt it grow in her belly.

Eve was making signs to rise to another stage. They beamed at each other through their masks. They took their ascent sufficiently slowly to avoid the bends. Pandora blessed the island. To come to this place was the best thing she had ever done.

Chapter Twenty-seven

Eve had to leave. 'I've enjoyed the time with you, Pandora. We've been great buddies.'

'Thank you for all you taught me, Eve.' Pandora hugged Eve joyfully. 'I guess I'll have to find another buddy now.'

Eve grinned. 'Well, it won't be Chuck.'

Pandora's eyes widened. 'Why not?'

'Because I saw your mother sign up with him this morning.'

'Mom? Are you sure?'

'Yup. And they looked really happy.'

'You don't think they'll get together, do you, Eve?'

Eve shrugged. 'Well, I got together with my old man after a lifetime of swearing that I'd always be an old maid.'

Pandora waved to Eve as the aeroplane flapped both its little wings and flew over the hut. Eve was going back to the normal world, to shopping malls, to city noises, to people who didn't know each other. Pandora didn't envy her at all. Today, she thought, I'll go shelling. There had been a considerable wind a few nights before from the south, so Pandora headed for the south shore, towards Miss Rosie's house.

Walking barefoot along the beach, she came across old Mr Logan leaning disconsolately against his small fishing boat. His left hand was pressed tightly across his eyes and his teeth were chattering. As Pandora passed the old man, he opened two fingers, and a rum-soaked eye watched her approach. 'You Missy Pandora?'

Pandora nodded. 'Yes,' she said happily, hoping her cheerful manner would improve his hangover.

'You a good Christian woman?'

'I hope so.' Pandora felt startled. She was used to the direct island way of talking, but old Mr Logan was a legendary drinker and a wencher. She felt a little leery of the man.

'Come over here and sit, girl. I'll tell you 'bout what happen last evening. I was at the bar up the road with my friends playing dominoes, when that no good Jamaican nigger woman Sandra . . .'

Pandora flinched. She hated to hear the Jamaican community so maligned. But Mr Logan was too far gone in his story.

'. . . she come up to me and she calls me a cocksucker and a liar.'

Pandora tried not to laugh. Mr Logan must be in his eighties, she thought. His face filled with a mixture of fear and rage.

'And then she said, "Oh, Mr Logan. I very sorry, but you'se going to die." "To die?" I say. "Who say I'm going to die?" "I done visit Miss Maisy," she say, "and she done obeah on you. I very sorry, Mr Logan, but you shouldn't have two-timed me with that Dulcie woman."'

'Did you two-time her, Mr Logan?'

Mr Logan nodded his head, and a sly smile spread across his face. 'Can I help it if Dulcie hides in the grapebushes behind the bar and calls my name as I go home, full of rum and love? The woman needs loving. A man needs loving.'

'But you've already been loving Sandra, Mr Logan.'

'I know.' Mr Logan put his head in his hands. 'I axed Miss Maisy if she'd lift the curse, and she won't, so I punched her in the mouth.'

'That must have been a great help, Mr Logan.'

'Now, I am thinking if I go to Reverend Havegood and tell him all what happens, and get repentance, maybe the curse will be lifted.'

Pandora judiciously gave the matter some thought. 'I don't see why not. Reverend Havegood is a mighty loud preacher, and if you truly repent, God will forgive you.'

'You think so?'

'I know so,' Pandora said with surprising conviction. 'We all make mistakes, and we all are forgiven. I think you should go and say you're sorry to Miss Maisy for a start.'

Mr Logan grinned. 'Say sorry to that old witch?'

'Why not? Probably nobody's ever said sorry to her. They're all so frightened of her.'

'Ah well, Miss Pandora, I'll take your advice and go up to her house, sit on her legs, and kiss her up.'

'You try that, Mr Logan.'

Whew, Pandora thought as she walked along the beach. All of them eighty years old and still at it. Must be the heat.

She stooped into a small shallow pool dynamited out of the ironshore.

156

She could see a tunnel leading out into the sea. She ducked down and then saw a lace murex lying on the white sandy floor. She picked up the shell, pleased with herself, and still amused by Mr Logan.

By now she was hungry. Ben was teaching at the swimming pool, so Pandora thought she would go and inspect Miss Rosie's pots.

She could hear the sounds of Miss Rosie pounding conch when she swam up to Miss Rosie's beach. It was weekend time and family were arriving from Big Egg. All of Miss Rosie's natural remaining children were married and working. Pandora had a great admiration for Miss Rosie. She woke every morning at four, bathed in the sea, and then began her day.

Pandora called to her through the palm trees. 'It's Pandora, Miss Rosie. Can I visit?'

Miss Rosie came towards her, wiping her hands on her apron. 'Just in time,' she said. 'I cooked chicken, peas, and rice for lunch.'

Pandora sat down at the table and Miss Rosie continued to pound. 'How do you get the conch out of its shell, Miss Rosie?'

'Like this.' Miss Rosie picked up a fresh conch, lifted her fearsome machete, and hacked a three-inch hole in the neck of the shell. Then she picked up a piece of wire and slowly wound the conch through the hole. 'Young folk put the conch in the freezer until it dies, and then they pull it out. Young folk like life so easy now.'

'Isn't it better to have washing-machines, and stoves, and all those things?'

'I have a washing-machine, but I hang out all my family clothes. The sun cleans them and dries them better than round and round in hot air. I do like to go out and unpeg my clothes. Feel my arms full of sun-dried linens.'

'I know what you mean,' said Pandora. 'I do Ben's clothes and my own, and I like to hang them out to dry.'

Miss Rosie passed Pandora a steaming plate of chicken, peas, and rice. The bonnet chillies made the dish succulent.

'That's not just chilli, is it?'

'No. I get pimento seeds from my cousin in Jamaica. Those are nuts from the big peppers. Good, eh?'

Pandora nodded. 'You know, it's a funny island, Miss Rosie. We have all these different churches full of people, all praying to the same God, and then we have Mr Logan and Captain Lawrence and all their cronies drinking their lives away. All the tourists come in with their bad habits. I don't know. It must have been very peaceful when you were a little girl.'

'Yes, it was peaceful. And God-fearing. But we had no medicine, except what we got from the mountain. Rosemary tea for fever. Fever-leaf tea for the same. Tops of papaya trees for kidney troubles. But so many women died in childbirth. During the winter, when the boats couldn't anchor and it was too rough to fish, we all starved. Some shared what they had, but many didn't. Mr Jones in his shop did his best with the missionary barrels, and we all ate roots, mostly cassava. I remember walking down to the north side of the island to find coco-plums for my mother.

'It was hard, but sometimes I think we were happier.' She sighed. 'I don't know, child. But you look better.'

Pandora finished her plate of food. 'I sure look fatter.'

Miss Rosie was done pounding the conch. She began to rub the white meat away from the blue-black intestines.

Pandora watched. 'Do you think,' she said tentatively, 'women from other places can come and make their lives on a small island like this?'

Miss Rosie looked shrewdly at Pandora. 'Other islanders, maybe. But no, not people from big countries. They get island-fever after a while and have to go. Often they take their men with them. After a while the men's feet get jittery in their shoes and the salt water starts flowing in their veins. Then comes the depressions. The visions of their homeland. The turtle, the grouper a-running. Island food. Mr Logan told me he travelled on his ship all the way to China, but Chinese food was no good compared to Little Egg food.'

'I guess you're right, Miss Rosie. I'm happy here, and I want to stay, but I also know I'm still married to Richard and I really want it to work. I feel so stuck. He's out there writing me letters about being unhappy. I'm here thinking about him. It sucks. It really sucks out loud.'

'American slang!' Miss Rosie was hugely amused. 'Well, you have to plough your own canoe, as we say here.'

'Quite right, Miss Rosie,' Pandora laughed, deciding not to correct the woman's speech. 'I was thinking of asking Janine if there was an island way of going back to the beginning of the whole thing, I mean when I first met Richard, and almost working my way through it all. In America we go to psychiatrists and they are supposed to work it all out for you. I'm not likely to try that again.'

'Here we have the dreaming caves. They are right at the edge of the cliff. Janine can tell you all about it because the idea came from Haiti.

They specially prepare you to go into the cave and you stay there for however long it takes for the dream to be over. Often, they do it if a person is sick in the head, but you're not sick in the head.'

'No, I know that, Miss Rosie. I'm sick in the heart. I'm like this lace murex shell. You can look at me and there is nothing inside. I feel like that story in the Bible when Jesus chases out all those wicked demons, but then he warns if you don't fill up the places they took, more will come in. That's what happens to me. I let people into my shell who then take over, and I'm not there any longer, just this other person. I need to get Richard out and then to find myself before I can ever begin to think about him as a person separate from me. Does that make sense?'

Miss Rosie nodded. 'Yes, it does,' she said.

'But if you go to the dream caves and redream all that part of the life that bothers you, can you change anything while you are dreaming?'

Miss Rosie thought for a moment. 'Not exactly,' she said. 'You see, you say you have no self. You are like a person who casts no shadow wherever you go.'

Pandora nodded. She was beginning to understand.

'Now all shells that are empty invite guests. You left this self when you were a little girl.'

'I guess I did. I always imagined that I was somewhere in some part of the world with my father, that even if I woke every morning and did my hair and cleaned my teeth, I could look at the world around me, but the real me was walking along a train track talking to my father. He'd have his lunchpail in one hand, and I'd have my hand in his other hand. My hand in his left hand, the lunchpail in his right. We would all be sitting at school in the convent on long wooden benches, like railway lines, and he would sit beside me and we would share our lunch together. One half of my plate was his and the other half mine. Nobody noticed because the nuns read religious stories during lunch, so he and I could sit quietly together and then go out into the gardens for play-time. We would sit together and read the train tables from all over America. He said a man could take a lifetime learning all the train tables.'

'So I guess, when I ran away with Norman, I let Norman fill my shell. When my body hurt, I knew at least I was living. When I put my hand on my head and my head hurt back, I was there. I suppose with Marcus it was the same, but different. When he hurt me sexually, I knew I existed sexually. I didn't know anything else except to be

159

screwed by boys, mostly boys who didn't care for me. So sex hurts. It makes you feel bad and ashamed. The nuns certainly thought that was right. Then, of course, there were the words. Marcus was the one good with bad words. *Childish, helpless, useless, look at you . . .*'

Miss Rosie listened to the hurt litany and sighed. Maybe the dream cave will help this woman find the child forever travelling with her lost father and return her to the present.

Pandora's voice switched to audible affection. 'Really, it is Richard I need to understand. He carried my shell for so long that I think he felt he had to run away and find out who he is. What is so confusing about Richard is that we were happy together, and then we just became unstuck. Anyway, thanks for listening, Miss Rosie. I don't always talk this much.'

'You should do more, Pandora. All of us have boxes and secrets. It does no good to store them away. Don't forget your shell. And walk safely.'

Pandora strolled back along the beach and realized she had never told anybody about sharing her secret life with her father. The idea was so sacred that to mention it to anyone made her fear he might suddenly disappear. Now, as she stopped to pick up a helmet shell, she gazed at its deep brown back. The colours were orange and brown and it had symmetrical-looking teeth. Beside the shell lay an empty cigarette carton. Tonight I'll ask Mom if she knows where Dad is.

So far Monica's reply had always been vicious. 'What do you want to know about that piece of white trash for?'

Maybe the best time to ask was when Chuck was around and her mother was on her best behaviour. Pandora walked slowly down the beach. There was a shadow following her, but it did not look anything like her. The shadow was tall and thin with wide shoulders. In his right hand he swung a lunchpail.

Chapter Twenty-eight

Monica was in a good mood. 'I've extended my ticket,' she said enthusiastically.

Pandora tried to look pleased. Yes, it was a good and comfortable thought that she and her mother were able to talk to each other and even occasionally to hug and kiss each other. But Pandora had been looking forward to getting back to her quiet life with Ben. Monica's presence brought back too many memories, uneasy memories. Pandora very much wanted to live in the future now, and not in the past. And this was why she wanted to make a clear decision about Richard.

She waited until the hotel held its happy hour, when all the expatriates descended like carrion crows for a free rum-punch. Usually the doctor could be heard bragging loudly about his latest fishing prowess, or various groups of divers would be chattering volubly about what they had seen on that day's dive. The scene was so familiar and now so dear to her heart in so many ways.

Ben was walking towards her smiling, and she smiled back. If only, she thought . . . But she knew what Ben had said was right. As much as she loved the island, there was more that she wanted to do with her life, and her restlessness would soon take the smile off Ben's face and put lines of worry between his eyes.

She sat by Monica and Chuck who were still deep in their plans for their new business venture. By eight o'clock Pandora was famished and a little befuddled with rum. 'Mom,' she asked, amazing herself with her audacity, 'whatever happened to Dad? Did you ever find out?'

Monica cast a quick glance at Chuck, who leaned forward.

'You haven't told me much about your old man, Monica,' he said.

'There's not much to tell.' Monica lit her cigarette. 'We got married young, you know, and I got pregnant, and we both made each other pretty miserable. One day he picked up his lunchpail and he just left.'

Pandora felt her heart beating hard. 'But did he ever contact you? Tell you where he was or what he was doing?'

'Yeah, I got phone calls from all over the place. Sometimes postcards. Last time I heard, he was working in Arizona.'

'So he's still alive, then?'

'Oh, sure, your dad'll live till he's a hundred.'

Pandora knew to leave the subject alone for the moment. She had pushed as far as she dared. Monica, she realized, was quite happy for Chuck to know that there was a man still in the picture. It wasn't maternal affection speaking.

Pandora ordered a steak for dinner and sat quietly wondering about the dream caves. I suppose Buddhist monks stay in caves for years, she thought, so it's not such an unusual idea. The nuns often went on what they called retreats. But to relive all those years with Richard could be so painful. Not the hurtful times, the times of treachery and dissatisfaction. More the regrets for the times when they had fun together and enjoyed each other's company. Still, it was worth a try, just to come to a decision one way or another. His present disgruntlement with Gretchen was now seismic and his letters made Pandora smile. She lay back in the chair and listened to the sea.

The guests sat eating their dinner under striped umbrellas. Small curly-tailed lizards ran about the stone walls making hazardous dives at dropped bits of food. Maxine the cook stood behind the buffet-style bar, smiling hugely. The moon beamed over the island. My father is still alive, she thought, and I can at least go and find him.

She felt as if a tiny hole had been cut in a hedge and a little light shone forth.

Monica was getting quite drunk. She and Chuck were rolling in their chairs, slapping each other on the back and roaring with laughter. In an odd way, Pandora felt both Chuck and her mother were like characters. They hung on to life with both hands. They had little grasp of life or emotions other than their own immediate needs. The world swung round them while they hung grimly on. Much of the grimness was hidden by quick jokes and the sound of unhappy laughter. 'I've got to go, babe.' Chuck gave Monica's arm a final pounding.

'Aw, come on, Chuck. Let's go back to my place and have some fun.'

Chuck paused for a moment. For a woman in her early sixties, Monica was a really good lay. Though her body was thick and her breath reeked of cigarette smoke, she could give head better than most of the frigid women he tried to toss off. He didn't have to worry continually about whether she orgasmed or not. She usually came before he did. But no, tonight he had a little applebun waiting for him. She had big, straining tits and he bet her pubic hair was as blonde as the thatch of the hair on her head. 'Nah,' he said. 'I've got business to see to. I'm helping Sam set up the *Sea Vixen* for a trip tomorrow. I'll see you tomorrow for the second dive. We'll buddy up.'

Monica smiled a misty-eyed smile. 'I know where that cocksucker is going,' she said as she lurched towards her cabin with her arm around Pandora's waist. 'He's off to screw that little blonde who arrived yesterday. Men! They're all the same.'

They got to the door and Monica fumbled with her key. Pandora took it gently from her, pushed the key into the lock, and helped her mother across the floor towards the bed. 'Don't put me to bed like an old woman, Pandora. Stay with me for a while and we'll have a drink. I've got a bottle of Jamaica rum in the bedroom and it's really good stuff.'

Pandora very much wanted to leave, but she was stuck. In the old days before she came to the island, she would have made her excuses and left. But here on Little Egg people gave each other time. Also a part of Pandora was getting quite fond of her mother. Chuck brought out a gregarious sense of fun in Monica that Pandora had really never experienced. 'The old dickhead will be dipping into that young girl, and the well will be as dry as a bone. You watch him hobble tomorrow. His prick'll be sore as a Christian bone through a cannibal's nose. Serves him right.'

'Mom, not all men are bad.'

Monica slumped down in her chair. She poured two large slugs of rum into glasses and handed one across to Pandora. 'They're not bad, dear. There's nothing bad about men. They're just a different species. In my day we had to put up with it. "Ssshhh! Your father's had a bad day at the office" or "Don't upset your pa." Men were gods. Now?' She shrugged and then she grinned. Both her stocky feet were planted on the ground. 'I'll tell you a little secret.' Monica took another swallow of rum. 'This stuff'll ruin the ass of a cowboy. I've decided that I'm going to marry Chuck.'

Pandora sat silent for a moment. Then she said, 'Does Chuck know?'

'Well, he does and he doesn't. He knows I have quite a little nest-egg and he has no money. He's not getting any younger, and together we get on well enough. I'd like to get married on the beach under the palm trees at the hotel.' Monica poured another drink.

'But, Mom. He'll never be faithful.'

'Oh, neither will I. You'll see, Pandora,' Monica's words began to slur, 'you'll see. Chuck and me we can make good business together, a real good business.'

'Can I help you get into bed, Mom? You look as if you're going to fall over any minute now.'

Monica nodded.

As Pandora adjusted the pillow under her mother's head, Monica's eyes filled with tears. 'What's the matter, Mom?' Pandora was scared. Monica so rarely showed weakness.

'I've got something to tell you, honey. It's a confession, really.' She sniffed. 'Your dad,' she said, her voice sinking slowly into a drunken slumber, 'your dad never did those kind of things to you I said he did.'

Pandora stood by the bed. 'But why did you ever say those awful things then?' She was furious. 'Why did you do that to both of us?'

'Why? I guess I was jealous. I was always jealous of the way he loved you, from the moment you were born. He loved you far more than he loved me. Look in my handbag and you'll find his last address.' Monica fell asleep.

Pandora carried the postcard back to her own house. The hole in the dense dark bush had been getting bigger, and a much brighter light shone through.

Chapter Twenty-nine

She didn't wake Ben up. She just sat by herself on the porch swing holding to her ear the conch shell given to her by Miss Rosie. Far away she could hear the sound of distant colder seas. Arizona . . . What do I know about Arizona? She wished she had learned more about geography from the wizened little nun who had lived most her adult life behind the high convent walls, but whose ability to extol the great beauty of God's divine America excited all the children in the class, except Pandora. Only railway trains and railway tracks excited Pandora. All she needed now was to invoke her father's presence.

She moved up a little on the swing. Arizona. Ah, Arizona. She could hear his voice. 'It's a long, long straight track out that way. Flatter than a beaver's tail. You can see for miles in Arizona.'

Tomorrow she would talk to Janine. She really did want to clear up her feelings about Richard, to allow him back in or get him out of her system. At the moment he was a stubborn thorn in her side. He either wrote euphoric letters that hinted that all was well, or sent disconsolate letters wishing she were back.

One such letter lay beside her. Christmas coming. He was going back to Boston. The novel would never be completed. He preferred the adrenalin-high of the reporter's office. He didn't like Germans and Gretchen was going back to Friedrich.

Pandora sat quietly. Too much was happening and all at once. What she needed was a break. A few days asleep in a cave while the universe reorganized itself around her sounded like a good idea. She trusted Janine and the girls. They would take care of her.

Slowly she got to her feet, but when she lay down beside Ben, she found herself crying. She realized that her mother's confession had washed away feelings of guilt and dirt. It was as if she had been sitting behind french windows, but unable to see through to the garden because of the dark, dirty handstains across the glass. Now all of a sudden – and that was the shock of it – not only were the panes clean but also she knew where her father was. He was no longer a shadow. He had a body.

She should be furious with her mother for all those years that she had lost with her father, but now, looking at her mother's face, she felt more pity and sorrow. She did remember her ninth birthday when her father brought her back a blue lace dress with a full, dark blue underskirt that rustled like tree leaves when she walked. Along with the dress were a pair of black, shiny, patent leather shoes and white frilly ankle socks. It was 19 February, the day of her birthday. She had gone to school, as usual, knowing that her father was bringing her back a present. Her mother started that day with a sniff and a parcel which contained a compendium of card games. Pandora thanked her, oblivious then, but understanding now: she and her father played card games in the evening. 'I'll bring a cake for you after work,' Monica said.

Pandora nodded. There would be no friends to share the cake. She knew that. However, the cake and her father's presents gave her such a feeling of delight that she spent the whole day at school with a rapturous smile on her face.

Monica was late back from work, but Frank arrived with his parcel, and while Pandora ran upstairs to open her present, he set the fire in the parlour and got the glowing copper kettle boiling. Pandora pulled the dress over her head and buttoned up the little pearl buttons that ran down the front of the dress to her waist. The arms were long and each wrist was covered with a soft white mist of lace. Of all the dresses Pandora had ever dreamed of owning, this was the ultimate. She swung her hips and the taffeta underskirt billowed and rippled. She pulled on the white lace socks and then the shoes. She ran across to the bathroom and gazed into the mirror. Carefully she cleaned her teeth and then ran a comb through her hair.

'I'm ready to come down, Dad,' she said from the top of the staircase. 'Close your eyes and don't peek until I say so.' Slowly and regally, Pandora walked carefully down the stairs. She stood for a moment in the door of the front parlour. Frank had pulled the curtains against the grey February afternoon. The fire glowed cheerfully. He had put a big birthday card on the mantelpiece and the kettle sat on the hob, hissing with pleasure at the sight of the child. 'You can open your eyes now,' Pandora said. She stood in the doorway on tiptoe to seem as tall as she could.

Frank's face lost its lines. He blushed. And Pandora giggled.

'Dad, you look like a kid again.'

For a moment she could swear she saw tears glitter in his eyes. He cleared his throat and then put out his arms. Slowly Pandora put her arm around his waist and they began to waltz. *One-two-three, one-two-three*. The dress swung out in time to the movement . . .

A well-known step, a key in the lock, and a shadow stood looking at them. Monica had that look that then so frightened Pandora, but now she knew it was the face of a woman unloved who had given a man a girl child to love. An intolerable gift. Frank and Pandora stood still. Pandora felt her heart beating. 'I'll get the cake ready, Pandora. You go upstairs and take off that dress or you'll get it messy. Frank, I need more coal for the kitchen stove.'

Pandora lay there wondering about memories, such many-layered things. An action created years ago and misunderstood by time and experience. Was Richard a misunderstanding?

Janine consulted her charts and looked at the rosemary growing on the mountain. She, Julia, and Jane took Pandora to various caves. 'You have to find a cave where you feel comfortable,' they warned her. 'Somewhere here you'll find a cave that you will feel you have always known. Take your time and hunt by yourself. There are hundreds of caves up here.'

Every morning after the first dive, Pandora took herself off into the mountain to look for her cave. At first she was quite frightened of the road weaving through the thick mountain jungle. After several weeks, she found she became acclimatized to the various noises of frogs and crickets. She realized that the mountain creatures, like the fish in the sea, all had territories and habits of their own. So now, having arrived as an alien on an atoll in the Caribbean, she had a friend in the moray eel in the wreck, another in the dog who eagerly awaited her choice morsel of chicken and allowed her to pat his huge ugly neck, and yet more friends in the lizards who fought vigorously against each other as they defended their homeland on the mountain.

Ben teased her about her dream time, but said it had always happened on other islands. 'Not here so much,' he said, 'because we always had the churches and they sent away the witches and the sorcerers.'

'But I can see no harm in it. I just have to find the right place, that's all. I want to do this just after Christmas and then go and find my dad. Then I'll come back for the summer and I hope I'll know what I'm going to do next. You know what you're going to do for the rest of your life, don't you, Ben?'

Ben laughed. 'It always makes you cross, Pandora. Yeah, I know I'll stay here. Get married, have kids, visit Miami, and always be glad to be back.'

Pandora made a face. 'I hope I have answers. I sometimes feel I have too many choices.'

They were sitting on a promontory that jutted out into the sea. A frigate bird was flying overhead with an overloaded beak, and Pandora laughed as the fish wiggled free and plopped back into the water. The infuriated frigate bird dived straight after it, but it was too late.

As she stood up to watch the bird climb back into the thermals at the top of the cliff, she saw a small cave. It looked like a room built out of a turret of a castle. 'I think that's my cave, Ben,' she said excitedly. 'Look up there. Doesn't it look wonderful?'

'Wonderfully high and wonderfully difficult to get to, you mean.'

Pandora grinned. 'I'll race you up there,' she said.

They both began to move through the bush. The trail got steeper and steeper, but Pandora felt she had been given wings on her feet and a sweet wind in her chest that allowed her to fly up the mountain to the mouth of the cave.

She was standing, waiting for Ben. 'What happened to you?' he asked breathlessly. 'Did you take running medicine?'

'No, not running medicine.' She ducked her head and then stood upright in the little hollow chamber. The walls had been washed millions of years ago by the sea and then, when the mountain first left the floor of the ocean, the water ran back from the hollow it had created, leaving a room of generous proportions. The floor was clean and in the left-hand corner Pandora found a little bat clinging upside down. From where they both stood, the sea looked miles away. The path to the doorway dropped steeply so, once inside the cave, all that could be seen was a huge, bursting blue sky and the sea. The sea gazed back at Pandora, some of it jade-green, some of the stretches deep blue, and then long streaks of the reef, the tops of the cruel coral hidden by the chuckling innocence of white spume.

'I would hate for anything to go wrong for you up here,' Ben said, looking straight down at the sharp-toothed ironshore below. 'Not all of your dreams will be good dreams, you know.'

'I'll bet,' Pandora said. 'But I trust Janine. And, Ben, I've got to get my act together. I know that's an awful cliché. Everyone who comes here says at some point *I've got to get my act together* in a whining voice and then goes on doing nothing about it. But I really mean it. I want to achieve something in my life. I don't want to be rich or famous, just loved, Ben. I want to be able to find somebody to love me and for me to love back without all the hurts and the treachery. Why isn't it possible for two people just to love each other? To look out for each other?'

Ben shook his head. 'I don't know,' he said. 'But if you find out, you tell me the answer.'

Hand in hand they walked gingerly down the path.

Chapter Thirty

Janine said that the dream time would be best before Christmas. The reasons, she discussed with Miss Rosie, were mostly to do with the sea turtles. Apparently there was an old sea turtle that lived at the foot of the cliff and often, when he'd been swimming miles and miles back to his home on Little Egg, his exhausted voice could be heard on the shore as he lifted his head from the water to expel the air from his huge lungs. He was known as the singing sea turtle, and when his voice was heard, then was the time for the magic potions to be made. Then was it a good time for a dream to be dreamed.

Monica was most sceptical about Pandora's plan. 'If you don't stay married to Richard, you'll have to find another man. And with your luck you'd do better to stick to him. At least he's kind to you and he doesn't beat you.' Monica was about to leave the island with a promise that she'd see Chuck next year. 'I nearly landed him,' she confided to Pandora in her wheezy, nicotine gasp of laughter. 'Anyway, honey, I can't stop you doing what you want to do and I can't see any real harm in a few days' shut-eye off the booze and the cigarettes. You'll come out looking a million dollars.' She paused a moment and then said gently, 'Anyway, honey, I want to thank you for a swell holiday.' And tears began to roll down her face.

Pandora put her arms around her mother's shoulders and hugged her. 'It's OK, Mom. Everything's OK now. Don't you worry. I'll telephone you as soon as I leave the cave and tell you all about it.'

'You know something?' Monica's face was bloated and red and a stream of slime slid down her lip. 'You're a good kid. A really good kid.'

Pandora hopped from one foot to the other in embarrassment. This was not like her cold, tight, repressed mother. Other passengers were watching this piece of drama, probably thinking that Monica was drunk. Pandora heard the boarding call and, putting her arm around her mother's waist, she gently shepherded her into the little waiting room and wiped her mother's running nose with her handkerchief. Monica sniffed and then blinked. 'Time for another rum before we go, I hope?' she said.

Chuck was at the waiting room's bar. 'I had a rum all lined up for you, little lady.'

Pandora sighed with relief. After giving her mother another hug, she turned and walked away from the airport.

Standing at the lip of the mangrove swamp across the runway she could just make out the blurred face of her mother at the little round porthole. She waved and waved until the plane was just a dot over the sea. Somehow their reconciliation had left a freedom in Pandora not to dwell on the pain of being unloved or unwanted. Her mother was now an ally in this world, and goodness knows, Pandora pondered as she walked over to talk to Miss Rosie, allies were very necessary in this world full of walking dead, people who were born in body and not in spirit, who endlessly looked for the born in spirit in order to steal away a piece for themselves. Or so the island legend went.

Miss Rosie was pleased to see Pandora. She had been boiling her fish-heads for soup, and several cats sat around in the sun, their dusty whiskers raised in the sunlight. Every so often Miss Rosie threw a piece of fish at the ever-growing audience and an ear-splitting concerto of cats exploded into puffballs of ears and tails and high-arched backs. 'Janine tells me you will sleep soon.' Miss Rosie stopped stirring. 'You have chosen well. That cave is a good space. Clean, and nice, and close to the creator. But you listen to me, Pandora. Those who have done you harm in your life will try to make you give up your dream. You must not leave the cave for any reason.'

'What do you mean *those who have done me harm*, Miss Rosie? They can't touch me in a dream. It's only dreaming. It's not real life.'

'Everything is real life, Pandora. When you dream, you go elsewhere, but your body lies still. Your "sensa", we call it on the island, that bit of you that exists for ever, can go anywhere. This time your sensa must stay within you because you are dreaming of the past. Those who seek to hurt you will come because they know in their black hearts that they are guilty of taking your sensa away from you. In your dreaming you are demanding it back. So there will be struggle. Not so much the first man. He is too busy in his present life. But that second man of yours, he is a bad man, and he will try to torment you. Do not leave the cave, whatever you see or hear. Do not leave.'

'What sort of thing might I see?'

Miss Rosie shook her head. 'I cannot tell you because if I do I upset the dream.' She looked up from the stew. 'Sit,' she said. She handed Pandora a bowl of the stew. 'You didn't like my stew at first, did you?'

Pandora blushed. 'No,' she said, 'but then I didn't like a lot of things a few months ago. Now I hope I'm not so stupid.'

'Not stupid, child,' Miss Rosie said. 'Not stupid. Just ignorant. Life elsewhere gets so difficult and then people don't think. Even here, now, we have televisions and people don't have to think. They watch and they get told. "Ah!" they say. "So that's what I think!"'

Pandora relaxed in the sun. She was really rather nervous about this idea of going to sleep and dreaming this dream that Janine seemed so determined she should try. Miss Rosie chattered on about the events of the day and Pandora leaned up against the strong spine of a thatch palm and felt life could never get better. Tomorrow was Sunday and they were all off for a Little Egg picnic.

Sunday morning was a perfect day for an Egg picnic. Pandora and Ben slid past their local church, pulling Ben's little white boat on its rusty old trailer. Voices were raised in praise of God, but Pandora always felt closer to God on the sea than she did in church, and many of her church-friends would follow after the service. Anyway, by now Reverend Mother would consider consorting with spirits and owning a sensa such pagan idolatry that Pandora must already be due for years of purgatory, if not hell itself.

All along the road, boats and trailers were pulling out. Once round the elbow of the island, down by the bar, Ben tipped the boat into the water and Pandora checked the cooler. Four boats went ahead of them. And then Ben turned the key and the engine responded. Ben removed the anchor from under his special rock and Pandora took the boat out into a long luscious curve up the reef and then turned and cut across her own wave. The boat bumped happily across. The engine sounded pure and ready to go the five miles it would take to get to the picnic spot. Pandora nodded. 'You have a beer, and I'll take her out of the reef.'

Ben looked up at her small, determined, brown face. What a change in her! he thought. Here she is running a boat through a dangerous reef, diving without fear . . . But then Ben had always seen the possibility in Pandora. She had been like a seafan when he first met her, one of those little purple fans that waved their gentle fingers at you, but at the sound of a voice or a footfall, they were gone, way down in their holes. Now Pandora no longer flinched. Her eyes no longer sought permission from other faces to smile. He hoped the dreaming would help her make up her mind. He sincerely hoped so. He knew more than others who did not spend the nights with her how much she twisted and turned. Ever awake, he listened while she talked of a future without Richard. 'What will I do with myself? Without a man?'

'Don't think that way,' Ben would terminate the conversation. 'It isn't an either-or.'

'You're hopeless, Ben.' Pandora threw pillows at him and they made love.

The waves were high, coming out of the reef. Pandora stood up, gazing down at the slashing teeth of the rocks underneath. She was reminded of Miss Rosie's advice. Carefully she steered way out to sea until the riptide was well behind her and then she turned the boat towards a small island where they were to picnic.

After a while the sun grew too hot for her, even with the white canopy overhead, so she passed the steering wheel over to Ben. Throwing out a line, she sat with the wind in her face and the rapidly receding palm trees of her own island. 'Do you think they'll spoil Little Egg like they have the big island?'

'I suppose so,' said Ben. 'I hear several plots have been sold up on the north side to Americans, so it won't be long before we have Big Macs and Pizza Huts. The kids will be pleased, but it will change the island for ever.'

'Can't it be stopped?'

Ben shook his head. 'Not really,' he said. 'We have good church members who are our elders who do their best, but then,' he laughed bitterly, 'one of the most prominent church-goers does all the selling. I don't mind people coming here or sharing what we have, but what I do mind is when Little Egg is just an expensive playground, a place for outsiders to come and to leave their litter, fool with our women, ruin our reefs, get drunk, and then fly out again. You hear them, you know, on their last night. "Wait until I hit New York and tell them what fabulous ass you can get down here!" "Rum's dirt-cheap and the diving! Why, I saw more sharks off Little Egg than I did in the Red Sea!" After a while, it sounds like a very boring record. So I take a few days off and go up to the south shore and fish, or just live quietly and then I come back and I feel not angry any more, just sorry for so many of them.'

There was a pull on the line. 'I just caught lunch!' Pandora sang out.

She pulled the hand line in and felt the fish fight back. For a moment she felt guilty that she was going to kill such a beautiful creature. But then this was lunch, so she buried her liberal conscience in a practical flurry of hauling in the fish and running a knife neatly behind the gills so that it did not suffer, then she took the hook out of its mouth again.

'Good-size red snapper.' Ben was delighted.

They could see the water change colour as they drew near to the picnic area. Pandora was used to the usual picnic area, but this time, by general agreement, the participants had decided to choose this tiny little island just south of Little Egg. It was famous for its six-foot iguanas, and Pandora so much wanted to see such prehistoric monsters. Also, if there were dolphins, that's where they were most likely to be found. It was not yet the season, but Pandora just wanted to see the place.

Slipping her arm around Ben's waist, they lined up with the triangles on the shore and went roaring through. Pandora knew Ben could find his way with his eyes closed, but it still gave her a thrill. The motor thundering, the water parting over the bridge of the little boat, and the coral fangs only a few feet away.

As soon as they tied up, she took out her flippers and her mask. 'I just must cool off, Ben. I'll be back to help in a minute.' She slipped her mask on and pulled on her flippers. Once so alien in the water, she immediately felt at home.

First she swam out across the reef to the great coral fans that she had noticed on the way in. Lying calmly on the water, the sun hot on her back, she watched two black French angel fish playing with each other in and out of the fan. All around were shoals of red squirrel fish and blue parrot fish. She turned on her back and for a while she just paddled by herself, conscious of the beach far away and people scurrying about. Before these last few months on the island, she would have been afraid of being out here on her own, or indeed anywhere on her own. Quite why she was so afraid of aloneness she wasn't sure; she only knew that she had never never allowed it to happen. Her father had always been there: if he were away, she knew he'd be back. When he had left for good, and she had needed to leave the stranglehold of her mother, she had immediately chosen Norman, followed by Marcus, and then Richard, and then Ben as soon as she had arrived on the island. But Ben was not in any way tied to her. He was Ben. He came and went as he pleased. He had achieved an autonomy that in all her thirty-seven years she had failed to do. So, she thought as she rolled over in the water, hopefully this dream will end with me being able to achieve my own autonomy. *What I want* – she mouthed the words in the water – *is to be completely happy inside myself.*

She stretched out her arms and put her face in the water. The Dead Man's Float, they called it in her school days. She felt the soft, sweet sound of the drums played by Janine. The velvet tones of the skins. All is one; there are no fragments.

Pandora thought about that. When she had left the water, she asked Janine, who was cooking, about it.

'*All is one, there are no fragments* means that everything is interconnected, unless you wish to fragment yourself, Pandora. The universe is seamless, like a huge silken fishing net. Always being knitted to meet all the new conditions that are created by other forces. You can be one of the knitters or you can be one of the forces.'

'You can't be both, or you will fragment.'

'Good. You can think about that before you go to sleep.'

Pandora walked down to the boat to get the bucket with her fish. Most of the men, having tied up the boats and organized the wood for the fire, were exercising their male prerogative of lying in hammocks over the sand, drinking beer and telling sailing stories. Beside Janine's food a familiar lump of barracuda lay on the ground. The ants discovered their unexpected good luck. The barracuda was not poisonous.

Pandora busied herself with her fish. She gutted it and cleaned it. Janine roasted peppers and yams and then shared several plates with Octo who was roaring the biggest fish story of them all.

Later, she set off with Ben to look for the iguanas. They did not have far to look. Quite close by, two large iguanas blinked sleepily at the two human beings. Pandora stood quietly. 'Aren't they beautiful?' she said. 'I've always wanted to see an iguana.'

Ben pulled some leaves from a nearby tree. 'Offer the big one a nibble,' he said.

Pandora reached and offered the six-foot creature the leaves. Very shyly, he shuffled forwards and began to munch at the leaves. 'Dreams can come true, can't they, Ben?' Pandora said, laughing.

'Sure they can.' They crouched, watching the iguana in the sunlight.

Chapter Thirty-one

Pandora had never put her life so completely into anyone's hands before, except in her relationship with Marcus. So it was with some sense of trepidation that she finally allowed Janine to make the final arrangements.

To keep herself occupied while they hunted for plants and waited for the singing turtle to arrive, Pandora took a job as a divemaster at the hotel. Christmas arrived gathering her Christmas coat fronded by green palm leaves rather than the traditional red flannel. Father Christmas, arriving after a bibulous trip on the little aeroplane, was suitably ho-ho-hoed into the hotel and the guests and the children ate their roast turkey and chestnut stuffing with sweat pouring down their faces. Pandora was tired all Christmas Day. She had an emotional telephone call from Richard who was begging her to come back. The argument went back and forwards, but still Pandora told him she needed time. 'How much time?' he demanded.

'At least until October, Richard.' October had always seemed a lucky month for Pandora. 'Let's make it October.'

'I love you, Pandora. I really do. I was an idiot.'

She could hear Richard sobbing down the line. He was always good at crying. She put the telephone down and went to join Ben and his grandmother.

Octo and Janine were sitting on the balcony, Octo with his huge, misshapen face and body, grinning from the one side of his face. Jane and Julia and Maxine the cook were all sitting or squatting under the stars. On the tables were plates of fish and yam, fried breadfruit, pound cake, fresh beef and pig. Pandora could not bring herself to eat the poor cow. The owner had sold the poor beast off in lots, but not before chasing it through five gardens with shouts of 'Cow! Cow! Cow!' tearing the night air. At moments like that, the island was raw and primitive. Maxine had spent all year feeding the pig whose watery snout and eyes lay glaring suspiciously at Pandora as if she should have been her saviour. Pandora was warned by Ben in the early days not to go down to Maxine's pigpen and play with and feed the pig. 'One day Miss Maxine will come with the boiling water and the scrub brush and Octo with his knife. Then we'll have roast pig.'

By now Pandora accepted in an almost three-point turn that her central world, so far seen through an eyeglass with USA stamped across the lens, was forever shattered. There were other ways of living and other ways of thinking. None of them subversive or dangerous, just different. Leaving aside the pork and the beef, Pandora filled up on the fragrant chicken and fried fish dishes.

Octo produced his old fiddle and Maxine her guitar. At first they played Christmas carols and Pandora watched their faces as they sang. '"O Little Town of Bethlehem, how still we see thee lie".' Such were the stars in a different hemisphere that shone so brilliantly at night. What perplexed Pandora, sitting there in the cool, cricket-less night, was that, for all the rhetoric and all the Bible-thumping that seemed to resound across America and now the Caribbean islands, the message to the people was so simple: a baby was born two thousand years ago who would teach us to love and serve God. She tucked her hands over her stomach. She knew what it was to hold a baby in her womb.

Soon the music changed and Octo gave his rendition of 'Who Put the Pepper in the Vaseline?'

Miss Rosie laughed and stamped her feet. 'I'll sing you a song of the old days,' she said, and softly began.

> '"The singing turtle calls to all who pass by.
> 'This is the way to paradise,' he calls with his cry."'

And as she was singing she stood up and began to walk out to the shore. Behind her Octo and the others followed, singing along with her. 'We are calling the turtle in,' Janine explained. 'He is still very far away.'

Pandora stood with her arm around Ben's waist and they looked out into the blackness.

'Grandmother says you won't be here this time next year,' said Ben.

There was a tightness in Pandora's throat. 'I don't know where I'll be, Ben. Anyway, how does she know that?'

'She just knows these things in her bones.'

'If I go away, and then I do want to come back, what would you feel about that?'

Ben looked down at her with a golden smile on his face. 'I'd like that fine.'

177

'As long as I promised not to take you away from the island?'
Ben nodded.

'I wouldn't. I promise. First I must sort Richard out, and also I must go and see my dad. I never knew that a father could be so important in a woman's life. I've always felt this huge part of me missing. Here I was, made from the union of two people, a man and a woman, and somehow only the woman side of the equation mattered. There's a whole side of me left ungrown-up because he wasn't allowed to be a dad. Just the few times I can remember him without her making it bad and threatening. Like at Christmas . . .' She drew a deep breath. 'I always knew it was my dad that filled my stocking. He'd tiptoe into my room in his huge squeaking boots and then fill my stocking and go *ho ho ho* softly and I'd sit up and say, "Hello, Santa Claus," and he'd put his finger on one side of his nose and go, "Hello, sweetheart," in a Santa Claus sort of voice, and then he'd leave the room. That used to be the best sleep I'd have all year, that night.'

Drowsily, slowly, they cleared the tables, later laughingly splashing at each other in the water. Slowly the sun rose over the party and gradually, quietly they all faded away.

For Pandora it was a blissful Christmas. No one had seen the turtle, but stories abounded about the change in weather patterns. The gulfstream had moved and changed the climate in Europe. Il Nido was blowing off course. Miss Rosie warned anyone who would listen that they must prepare for hurricanes. 'It will be a bad season next year,' she said. 'My linens are ready. My tins and my warm clothes. After a hurricane, it's the cold that kills people. The sun don't shine for days and the water is dirty.'

Maxine laughed. 'Miss Rosie loves hurricanes,' she said to Pandora. 'She changes the sand in her cave every April and waits.'

Pandora was getting anxious. In her mailbox that day she had found a delighted letter from her father.

> Darling,
>   Do come and visit me. I have a nice little house right near the train track. I'm painting the back bedroom just for you. Please send me a photograph. And here is one of me.
>   Your loving, Daddy.

178

There was such a lump in Pandora's throat when she looked at this picture of her beloved father. Still the same, just grizzled around the edges. I must get on with this dreaming, she thought.

She felt so squeezed by events now. Not only did she have her future with Richard hanging over her, but she also had the long-awaited letter from her father. Most of her wanted to do what she would usually do, which was to rush off to see him. But slowly she was learning to pace herself, to set her priorities so that one event, well thought out, flowed into the next event after careful planning. Far too much of her life had been spent reacting to other people's kaleidoscopic lifestyles. Now Pandora had her hand firmly on the steering wheel of her own little boat in life.

She sat down and composed a letter back to her father.

> Dear Dad,
> I have a few things to finish up here, and then I'd be
> delighted to visit with you . . .

The rest of the letter was about the island.

Just the tension of not knowing what to do about Richard was tiring. She wanted a resolution soon.

The turtle had arrived late. Octo had heard him coming in one night in his fish boat. 'He's here, Janine. Your friend can begin her dreaming.'

Janine was pleased. She could see Pandora getting more and more unsettled as the weeks went by, the telephone calls increased, and letters flooded Pandora's box. Now Richard was threatening to arrive and Pandora pleaded with him to leave her alone. 'This is something I have to sort out on my own,' she said. 'It has really nothing to do with you. It has everything to do with *me* as a person. Who am I?'

'Island mumbo-jumbo,' Richard said peevishly down the telephone. 'Soon you'll be telling me you're weaving grass skirts with missionary bones around your ankles.'

'Don't, Richard,' she pleaded. 'Don't trash something I care about and you just don't understand.'

'Well, I'll give you till October. I'm going to spend the summer in South Africa with the Dugdales. You remember them, don't you?'

'I think so, Richard. I think so. It all seems so awfully long ago.' She was tired by now, really tired. Indecision, she decided, was the most wearing of all emotions.

'Friday, as the sun goes down, we will go to the cave.' Janine was calm. She and her sisters were sitting in a circle around Pandora's yard. All the last-minute instructions had been given. 'Remember. Whatever happens, you don't leave the cave. You may think you are awake, but you're not. You can't change anything going on in the dream. It's your dream, and you are the dreamer, but you can see parts of your life that you wish you had done differently. Do you understand that? That's the bit of the dream that will help to make you decide when you wake up. Sometimes it works and other times it doesn't. But if you are prepared to dream as honestly as you can, it will work.'

'You mean you can dream dishonestly?'

'Yes,' Janine said, 'just like in real life. You do something because you think it will impress people, but really it's dishonest because it wasn't what you wanted to do.'

'OK,' Pandora said. 'I'll do my best. But it all sounds like a bit of a magical mystery tour.'

'It is,' said Jane, and she fell over backwards laughing.

Now there was no more laughing or joking. Pandora was instructed not to eat or drink anything on the Friday, but just to lie outside on her swing and watch the sea. Beside her she had a glass of milky liquid, the sleeping potion. All she had to do when her mouth felt dry was to sip a little. Not too much, just enough to moisten the lips, she had been told.

Ben stayed quietly in the house with her. He often just sat and held her hand. 'You never did this?' she asked him.

'No. I didn't need to, except when that girl did my head in. I felt like I had a head full of chopped meat. But Grandma sent me off on the boat for three days and said my head would fall into place.'

'I don't make your head into chopped meat, do I?'

'No, you don't. But you've got lots of other mess in yours that needs to go.'

'You know, one thing I think I'm really looking for is a home. Not a house really, or even a country, but a place where I can feel at home. I have been in exile for so long in so many places. My mother always saw me as a rebel, someone who always fights back. But it's not really that. Maybe Dad will be the answer. Maybe my heart will find a home with him.'

'Maybe.' Ben went back into the house, his shadow leaving, the sun burning her face.

She wanted to say, 'Ben, come back!' but she couldn't. The liquid made her sleepy and dislocated. She was not very sure where she was.

Later, much cooler – that's how she knew it was later – she heard voices. Janine put her hand on her shoulder. 'Drink this,' she said.

Pandora nodded weakly and then felt Octo lift her on to a stretcher. She heard him grunt and she smiled. Only Octo grunted that way. Various hands lifted the stretcher and the procession wound its way from the foot of the mountain, as the sun fell with its usual sudden sharpness into the sea, splitting the water into blood and wine. As they carried Pandora up into the mountain, the tourists from the hotel could see the flaming pine branches bobbing and weaving through the jungle. 'What on earth is that?' asked a hotel guest.

'Pagan idolatry,' said the doctor, snorting into his rum.

'It's someone going to a dream cave to redream their life into some sort of order,' Chuck explained to a trim little diver. He knew it was Pandora and he wished her well. He also wished he didn't miss her mother quite so much.

In the last moment of consciousness, Pandora saw Janine's face. When Janine was concentrating, her face often reminded Pandora of an Arab scimitar. 'Nothing can hurt you or harm you, Pandora. If you awake, drink more juice. Someone will be here to watch the cave, but it will be your sensa that will be tempted to go out to change something in your past. Remember, you cannot change the past. You can only use your knowledge of the past to change the future. Can you hear me?'

Pandora nodded. She just wished to get on with her dreaming. She heard the drums slowly beating, the one sound that to her made all things flow together, the way things should be. The honeyed sweetness of the sound filled her head and then her body. Finally the music, her present, took her into the first memories of the past.

Chapter Thirty-two

The very last sound was the drums of Horus floating away on the breeze that blew through the holes in the rosemary bushes that flanked the opening to the cave. Although Pandora's eyes kept shutting, she was still occasionally able to open them to see a star shining in the night. She felt the soft sand beneath her body and a pillow under her head, filled with wild herbs. All she had to do now was to let go, and go back into the past, untie the last knot that was Richard.

The first memory arising seemed to have nothing to do with Richard or their life together. In fact, it was a shocking memory. She was a small child standing up to her knees in a greasy cold bath with a large object that looked like a piece of wood floating behind her. She was very small, her head only just reached the top of the tub, and she had to hold on to balance herself from falling over. But the menace of the thing was that it followed her from the plug-end of the bath down to the shallow end. She was screaming and then a pair of rough hands lifted her from the bath and dumped her on the floor. She felt a sharp slap across her face, and heard her mother's voice say, 'You filthy little thing. Now look what you've done!'

Pandora sat on the floor watching her mother remove this thing from the bath and flush it down the toilet. From then on Pandora realized that she was unclean.

Maybe that is where I begin with Richard. The thought of that memory so upset her, she raised her head and sipped some of the liquid beside her. She wanted to dream coherent dreams, not confused, upsetting dreams. The liquid calmed her and then she slid into a room in Idaho.

She was wearing a pencil-thin black skirt and a white blouse, and had expensive diamonds in her ears. As she sat on an old-fashioned brown swivel seat in front of a brown Victorian lawyer's desk, Pandora felt an alarming shift in her universe. No longer was she the observer observing past events. She was in the present and observing the events which were to follow. Her breathing became deeper.

Outside the cave several eyes were watching. Jane, fully awake, pleased at the transition from observer to participant in her patient; old Maisy, waiting to see if she could tempt the witch doctor to lose a client to death by falling.

'Mrs Sutherland is my client, Mr Townsend. She has no need to talk to the press. However, she decided to give just the one interview as long as the whole text can be vetted before it is used by your newspaper.'

Vincent Singer was Marcus's lawyer and one of the many participants in Marcus's pornography ring. Pandora watched Mr Singer's face. He had a long dark chin. A small moustache covered two swollen cherry lips and over those lips hung a long, predatory nose. His eyes were small and set too far apart. A cast in his left eye gazed firmly at the reporter's left ear. A cruel figure made even more unsightly by the blackened and cratered teeth he retained in his head. His teeth reminded Pandora of an old dog, one of those scabrous, lean, prowling animals that lurked in the corners of dark streets and leered as she passed by. All his life, Mr Vincent Singer looked as if he had eaten shit. Shit like me, she thought, and then she looked up at the reporter.

'I am Richard Townsend,' he said, putting out a clean, white, firm hand to take Pandora's limp, carefully polished right hand. Yes, he was the man she had met once before at the theatre when she and Marcus had been on a trip to Boston. Obviously, to keep up the appearance of respectful formality in front of Marcus's lawyer, Richard was treating her with the courtesy of a friendly stranger. 'I'm glad you've offered to talk to me about this case.' He scratched his head. 'To an ordinary fellow like me, it all seems very complicated.'

Pandora knew Mr Singer could sit behind his desk, wearing a mask of innocence. He, after all, had never been caught. I know, she thought, that all that will happen is that Marcus will get struck off for a while, and they will all begin again. 'You were part of it all, Pandora. You sought out Marcus. You agreed to the group therapy. You agreed to act out your sexual damage in order to eradicate the power of the subconscious memories. Why are you sitting there at the desk waiting to tell this man lies about your innocence? There was nothing innocent about you. You were an active participant.' She could see all these thoughts go through Mr Singer's head. So many of these notions might well be true . . .

Waves of shame and guilt half-woke her up.

She heard Marcus's mercurial voice close by. 'Why not end it all? After all, women like you from your background don't ever change.

You go from abusive man to abusive man. We men can tell your type. There's a certain smell about you, like a frightened, cornered mouse about to amuse a cat. And you are amusing, Pandora. You frighten so easily. All you have to do is to come to the door of this ridiculous little theatre you have created with your friends, and I'll take you by the hand and we will go back to that lovely big house we owned with the green sweeping lawns. Remember your horse Tommy? Well, Tommy misses you. He really does.'

Pandora's eyes filled with tears. She could feel them running down her cheeks. She half-opened her eyes and she saw Marcus as she had first seen him. His head quizzically bent, his round billiard-ball face . . . But this time he was not looking aside; he was looking straight at her, his big, hypnotic eyes drawing her towards him. 'No!' she said firmly. 'Definitely not.'

Now she was back in Mr Singer's office. 'You must forgive Mrs Sutherland. She has been under a lot of pressure lately,' he said.

Pandora blushed. 'I'm so sorry,' she said. 'I will try and concentrate.'

'Well then, perhaps, Mr Townsend, you might presume to begin with your interview.'

The reporter gazed at Mr Singer incredulously. 'You don't really expect me to interview Mrs Sutherland here, do you? In an attorney's office? Good heavens! I was hoping to take you out to a very good lunch at a superb place I have just discovered, if one could call anywhere in Idaho superb.'

Pandora felt a smile. It had been such a long time since she smiled. She was afraid the corners of her lips might crack and fall off and then her lips would fall on to the pristine cleanliness of Mr Singer's table, leaving her with only a set of teeth. It was such a silly thought, she realized. She must take another pill. She consulted her watch. Another quarter of an hour to go before more walking oblivion. At least the pills didn't humiliate her. As far as she could see, almost all American women survived on pills. Pills to get up, pills to lie down, headache pills, menstrual pills, happy happy pills. How ever did her mother's generation cope? They didn't; they smoked cigarettes and hated their children. Like Monica hated . . .

There go my thoughts, she observed. All over the place. Guinea pigs run amok. Maybe I ought to stay with old Vincent, at least he can stop me burbling. 'Come along, Mrs Sutherland. I know you're upset, but I'm very good with women, and we won't talk about the business at all. We will just have lunch and get to know each other. How about that?'

Pandora gazed at the man and found herself smiling. He had a flop of fair hair falling over a narrow forehead; a cool, gentle face with big, grey eyes. He wore an old but silky Harris Tweed coat over an immaculate suit. She looked again at Singer. Oh screw it, she thought. I don't have to stay here. 'Thank you, Mr Townsend. I'd like to have lunch with you.'

Pandora stood up rather precariously, but the reporter was by her side, one hand tucked solicitously under her elbow. 'Just relax,' he said.

He really does understand women, Pandora thought as they made their way across the thick pile carpet and through the big, Victorian door. The reporter banged the door hard behind him. 'That,' he said, 'was like something from *Alice in Wonderland*. Haven't you heard of the book?'

'Heard of it, of course. But I can't say I've read it. I'm afraid I don't read much.'

'Well, I'll get you a copy. But your story sounds curiouser and curiouser. Still, we're not going to talk about any of that today. I have a whole week in this Godforsaken place, and I expect you to entertain me. By the way, I always knew we'd meet again, after that night in the theatre. Please call me Richard.' He shook hands with Pandora informally and walked her resolutely to an open sports car. She was pleased that their first meeting was evidently an important memory for him, too. 'My Jag. What'd you think? I wanted a red one, but they only had racing green.'

Pandora didn't care. She needed a pill. 'Do you think you could find me a drink?' she said. 'I'm a little thirsty, and I feel a little dizzy.'

Richard looked alarmed. 'Sure thing,' he said. He opened the door of the car and sat her down. 'You sit tight, and I'll get you a glass of water from across the road. I'll be right back.'

Pandora took out her sunglass case and tipped out four pills, enough for the next few hours. Oblivion, absolute oblivion. Whatever anyone wanted of her, they could have. After all, she wasn't there at all. The pills blocked off all thoughts, all feelings, all remorse, and all guilt. Why not?

She swallowed the pills dry-mouthed. By now she needed no liquid. For a moment sitting in the car seat she heard the cry of a baby. How odd, she thought, looking around her, the pills still not totally effective. Then she saw in front of her a tiny child, almost a child. Its legs were crumpled up to its stomach. Its head was huge and there was still an umbilical cord wrapped round the body. But the mouth was open and

185

baby wails came through its quivering lips. Pandora knew she must leave the car and grasp the baby. She knew that baby. It was once her baby, though she lost it before it had life. She struggled to get up, but she found herself anchored to the seat. She began to cry.

Tearing sobs split her chest apart. She felt Richard's hand on her shoulder. 'Don't cry, Pandora. It's all over. It really is. Here, drink this cool water. You'll feel better.'

Pandora looked up through her tears at Richard's wide grey eyes. He, too, looked down at her pale green eyes. He had never seen such a look of torment in a woman's face.

'The nightmare's over now, Pandora. They've got all the people concerned. Your husband has left the country.'

'Yeah, he skipped his bail, but he'll be back. Those sort always will, and there'll always be idiots like me who get taken in by it all and then it's too late.'

By now the pills were beginning to take hold. Pandora took a handkerchief out of her handbag and a mirror . . . Goodness! she thought. What a mess I have made of my face!

Richard smiled at her. 'You may think it's a mess, madam, but I would like to tell you, it's the prettiest face I have seen in a very long time.'

Chapter Thirty-three

Pandora smiled at Richard, partly because the pills put a permanent smile on her face, and partly because there was something endearing about his English accent. He stood there looking down at her rather puzzled. 'You know,' he said, 'I don't quite know what I'm going to do with you. I usually expect to find tarts – oh no! I don't mean that, my dear. It must have sounded awful.'

'What is a tart, Mr Townsend?'

'Please, it's Richard.' Richard blushed. 'Well, a tart is . . . an English word for the sort of woman who usually gets involved in this type of case.'

Pandora raised her eyebrows. Nothing he could say could hurt her. 'None of us were "tarts", as you put it, Mr Townsend.'

'I have offered an apology. Please forgive me. I'm new at this sort of thing. And please do call me Richard. And I promise I won't be so crass again. I was sent here in such a hurry. I haven't even had time to read the notes. Except I know your husband skipped bail.' He saw her wince and he cursed himself. 'So, really, until the front desk told me that you were willing to do an exclusive story, I had very little information to go on. Anyway, we can't sit on the side of the road for ever. Where would you like me to take you out to lunch? And we will talk about everything except the case. How about that?'

When she smiled, Richard thought her face looked like a tea-rose about to lose all its leaves. What was left of the impression was the faint smell of summer and a whisper of pain. What on earth could have happened to the woman that she could sit there looking so elegant, so beautifully manicured and coiffed, and yet so frighteningly vulnerable? Richard knew when he was hunting that the most vulnerable doe would often stay behind, offering herself for the life of the rest of the herd. He could see Pandora was uncomfortable in her role as interviewee, but there was a resolve to her in the office that morning that made Richard realize somewhere deep down inside the woman lay a steely competence. 'Why don't you take me to the

Triple Sec? It's a good quiet restaurant where we can talk and I haven't been out for ages.'

Richard could believe that. When the story of the Monkshill Clinic orgies first made national news, most of the women concerned were either moved to other clinics, where they could not be traced, or disappeared on cruises with their husbands. Marcus had left the country, so Pandora was free, but pinned into her big white mansion by a howling and baying press. Still, that story was yet to come. For now, Richard drove her competently and gravely to the restaurant she had chosen.

In turn, Pandora looked at his classic English profile. She assumed it was a classic English profile. She had seen the odd painting of English gentlemen hunting, and she could imagine Richard in long black riding boots. The brain blocked off the riding whip. It knew too much about that subject.

Once inside the restaurant, there was a cool silence between them. Damn, Richard thought. I ought to have brought Hortense along. At least she'd chatter. Mistresses like Hortense have their uses, other than sex, sometimes. He'd left Hortense lying on the end of his bed, mending her tights with nail varnish. 'Oh, Richard,' she had said as he was just about to leave the room. 'You will come back and we'll have a go at all that orgiastic stuff.' She'd got up, too. 'She won't make me jealous, will she? I mean, I don't care to meet you with my nipples rouged with lipstick and dripping ice-cream.'

Girls from New Jersey were good in bed but terribly tiresome. Perhaps it was just as well Hortense had the week to herself. God help the apartment when he got back.

They both sat facing each other. Richard knew he wasn't up to doing this interview. He had absolutely no experience of the subject of sexual abuse, but he had been sent along because the editors felt if anyone could get a story out of this woman it would be Richard, the star stud. Looking at Pandora, Richard felt a familiar surge of lust. He could never resist a challenge. The story would take care of itself. Besides, she was rich and pretty. And although Hortense was a good lay, she had no money. Richard felt he had a future here with this very vulnerable woman. She would be easy to lull into a false sense of security, with Richard playing the serious strong man in her life. Then, once married, he could return to his Peter Panning and fly all over the place, this time not attached by stage-wire but with a golden thread, all paid for by her.

For a moment Richard tried to move himself into the next chair so at least there was not quite so much physical distance between them.

But Pandora's shoulders flew up under her ears and her hands clasped themselves prayerfully. Space was what she needed, and probably for a very long time.

The waiter bent over Pandora solicitously. She gazed at Richard anxiously. He realized that most of the polish was fabricated and that under the silk hat and the gloves was a very small-town Idaho girl. He smiled at the waiter. 'We're not ready to order just yet,' he said. 'Pandora, would you like a drink?'

Pandora nodded. Would she ever like a drink, her thirsty brain throbbed. 'Sure. I'll have a . . . a . . .' No. Not there. She could not ask for a vodka with a beer-chaser. She controlled herself and smiled. 'You suggest something, Richard. Something long and cool and refreshing.'

'What about a gin and tonic with a twist of lemon?'

'A double, please,' she found herself snapping.

Richard made a note in the back of his head. *She can drink.*

'I'm sorry I sounded so rude, but I'm just really tired and a little flustered. I've been under house arrest with the damned press, but with you having an exclusive, they've all backed off. Thank God. You order lunch for both of us, please. I just can't seem to concentrate today. Forgive me a minute, and I'll be back.'

Pandora walked to the washroom. There she locked the door, sat on the seat, and popped an upper. The way this was going, she was going to be asleep in her food. Yes, he was nice. Yes, he had excellent manners. For so long now she, like so many of the other women, had been trained to be the life and the soul of any party. And Richard for sure was no party. She had no intention of seducing him or, for that matter, having anything to do with any man ever again. Marcus and his friends had opened her eyes to a world that was unimaginable to a small-town girl from Idaho. Still, she had promised this interview for that very reason. Hopefully enough abused women going for help to clinics would have the sense to check them out thoroughly through their doctors or their women's centres, not just blindly blunder into an even more abusive situation as she had.

She waited while the pill tingled at the back of her spine. She walked to the mirror and looked at herself. Her eyes were now alight again. Her smile seemed less cracked. She must think of something they could talk about.

Richard was sipping a whisky and soda when Pandora joined him at the table. 'I looked at the menu and the steak looks wonderful. So I've ordered us a shrimp cocktail followed by the steak and then,' he said, his face shining with delight, 'my favourite.'

Pandora waited. The restaurant was famous for its pastries and cream-filled desserts. 'What did you pick?' she said.

'Apple pie with fresh cream. You know, Pandora, we had a cook in Devon who could make the lightest pastry crust you could ever imagine. It was like eating butterfly wings. And then you tasted the apple with a little cinnamon, and then the cool, heavy Devon cream . . . I don't suppose,' he said in a sudden consternation, 'we will get Devon cream here, will we?'

'No,' Pandora said, taking a deep breath and a large mouthful of gin. 'No, I don't think Devon cream is available here.'

A horrid vision of Hortense's nipples flashed across Richard's mind.

Dear God, Pandora prayed. This is going to be a long lunch.

By the time they had consumed two bottles of wine, conversation had very much loosened up. Richard explained that there was a little railway line that travelled between Axminster and Uplyme to Charmouth, where he had played tennis in the summer holidays, and that even now that the awful bureaucrats had slashed everything to bits and ruined England, he could still fondly remember the spongy seats of the train, and the white antimacassars, and the thick leather straps that held up the windows, and the sign in the corner of the carriage that a five-pound penalty would be applied to anyone improperly pulling the communication cord.

Pandora on her part relaxed and told him about the clackity clackity train tracks that ran all day and all night through her childhood. How she could put a nickel on the line and then collect it and how later in bed at night she could feel the weight of the train in how much it had squished the nickel.

'Good heavens, Pandora! It's three o'clock. I'll have to get you back to your house. I have an appointment with that awful Singer. Unctuous old bastard, isn't he?'

'He just wasn't caught. That's all. They'll lie low for a while and then start up again.'

Richard sensed she was ready to talk, but felt here was not the place. 'I'll take you home and come over in the morning, and you can give me breakfast. How's that sound?'

Pandora smiled. She was tired. The urge to throw herself into the man's arms and tell him everything was overwhelming, but she knew she must wait. At least she could go home to her own house and let the pills take their effect. There were no more strange sounds filling the air. No more people milling around, talking in shrill voices. Nobody invading her bed or her body. She belonged to herself now, and that gave her a feeling of infinite relief.

Chapter Thirty-four

Tuesday was never one of Pandora's favourite days, but since Marcus had disappeared, hopefully for ever, she had sacked all her staff, except Marian . . .

She tossed and turned in her sleep, vague feelings of the sea pulling her into its arms. Voices around her bed. 'She's all right.' Janine lifted Pandora's sleeping head in her arms and gently kissed her on the lips. 'She's far away from us now, but her dream is going well. Poor woman, though. There is so much to tell and in the telling it will make her suffer.'

Janine left the cave when she saw Pandora's chest evenly rising and falling. Outside she looked at an anxious Octo. 'We have two more days before the turtle sings his last song and dives deep for the season. She'll be finished by then, Octo. Don't worry. Julia is staying here today, and tonight I will take over. Tonight will be a difficult night. Miss Maisy has been busy all last night, and the moon is in the third quarter. If anyone jumped to their death from one of our dream caves, we would be run off the island, and the old bitch knows it.' Janine kissed Octo. 'You go to your mother, and I'll get back to the bar. Julia is on her way. She won't be long.'

Julia was on her way, but she was fuming all the way up the path because, in spite of her days of frightening blindness, Leona's sight was restored; unchastised, she still proceeded to pursue Julia's husband. On the way up, Julia took her time collecting small beetles. These were used, when dry, to make a necklace and then burnt with a special incantation. If all this doesn't work, she thought, what I will do is what all Little Egg women do. I shall take off my high heels and break them on her head. Julia stomped on in a very bad mood.

Silently, one paw raised then replaced by another, a four-toed grey and white cat crept towards the cave. Offrey had been Miss Maisy's since kittenhood. Some said Offrey was Miss Maisy. Today Offrey was just a cat with a mission. He ignored the lizards sunning themselves on the rocks. He watched the trees for edible baby birds, but above all, he must get to the cave before the girl did. She was moving slowly, bending down now and then to collect a dung beetle. Offrey grinned. Fat good that would do her. Leona was paying Miss Maisy well enough for protection.

The cool opening of the cave before him caused Offrey to pause and to raise his head and sniff. He saw the girl lying in the pillowed sand. He liked the fan of her copper-red hair and the curl of her eyelashes on her cheeks. Offrey liked beautiful things, and the girl was beautiful, he decided.

Pandora awoke with an unpleasant taste in her mouth. She reached for her glass of water by the side of the bed. All these pills, she murmured. I must give up taking quite so many of them. She lay back for a moment and listened to the quiet of the house. She knew she must get up. Usually she rolled over, took more pills, and then slept all day until the evening. The nights she spent watching television or, if she felt up to it, she climbed into her car and took herself to a supermarket where she shopped for cart-loads of produce. At Alberto's All-night Super-market she was a favourite. So much so that she knew that Angela on the check-out register was two months pregnant and suffering from nausea. 'Try taking ginger pills. Works like a charm,' Pandora advised her. Mr Koshka had awful back trouble and was going for an operation. 'Try DMSO.' She explained the whole theory of the medicine to him, and mentioned how they used it on professional athletes. Pandora knew she was lucky. Although her photograph had been in the newspapers along with many of the others in the scandal, she had not been called to witness. So the whole neighbourhood stood united in their sympathy with the poor, misunderstood wife of that dirty psychiatrist of a husband.

By giving an interview in which the neighbours would realize she was just as implicated as all the other women, she would lose the hard-earned respect she had won in her role as Mother Christmas. But even playing Mother Christmas did not fill that blank inside her soul. Even at the worst moments, when Marcus was raging at her or physi-cally abusing her, she at least felt she belonged somewhere. Where? she asked herself too often. Where the hell do I belong? Perhaps the answer was to Marcus. Maybe she had a soul of putty that got handed to her father, given back. Her mother didn't want it, so she handed it to Norman, who threw it back. And so she gave it to Marcus. Maybe that's why she stayed. At least I belong to someone. At least when I walk into a room, another human being's eyes connect with mine. Now I belong to Alberto's All-night Supermarket. When I walk in, eyes flash, faces turn and smile. There I know I'm a person.

After paying the bill Pandora moved on. She carried all the boxes into the all-night Salvation Army shelter. The officers were always pleased to see her.

Then, and always as if she must, she found a diner on a freeway and parked her car. She usually asked for a double vodka and tonic and then sat in a seat by the big picture window. Cars flashed past, illuminating her thin white face. Even as she drank glass after glass of vodka, the void was not filled . . .

The front doorbell rang. Damn! I've overslept. She pushed the button to the door intercom and said, 'Yes?'

'I'm fearfully punctual, Mrs Sutherland. If you're not ready, I could always come back.'

'No.' Pandora pulled herself up into a sitting position. 'I'll press the button and you let yourself in. The maid should be here shortly. Can you make yourself a cup of coffee? The kitchen is down the hall on the left. There's also toast and marmalade or eggs. I'll be down in a few minutes.'

'Jolly good. I'll get going. Do you want anything to eat? I'm good at breakfast-making.'

'No, thanks. Just coffee. Lots of it.'

Pandora showered and dressed. Once this interview came out, or even before, she would have to sell the house and leave. She did not want to stay on and experience the looks on her neighbours' faces. She knew that was cowardly, but then she didn't care. According to the accountant, she had a generous amount of money in her own bank account, and Dr Sutherland's instructions were that the house and its contents were to be handed over to her. So at last – and the irony of it all made Pandora smile – she was a rich woman.

She would not, of course, embarrass her mother by going home, but she would send her a sizeable cheque. Other than that, she had no idea at all of what she would do with her twenty-seven-year-old life.

After her shower, she towelled herself dry and squirted herself with Shalimar. She pulled on a black aerobics leotard, and a pair of bright pink wool knee-length socks, and then picked out a pair of soft pearl earrings. Her face still felt rigid from the pills. I'll have to wait to put on make-up later, she decided.

She hurried down the stairs to the main hall. She could hear Richard clattering in the kitchen. What a change from Marcus! He was always so quiet. Often Pandora felt he practised silence as he did Tai Chi. Endless ripples of swirling black silence.

After a pretty fearsome crash, she heard Richard shout, 'Oh, sod it!' and she turned the kitchen corner just in time to see the Italian espresso machine explode and the coffee grains fly across the room. 'The coffee grounds on the ceiling are really most artistic, don't you think?'

Richard stared at Pandora standing in the sunlight with her auburn hair tied back in a pink band. Her lean body in the leotard relaxed against the door for a moment, and her wide green, dappled brown eyes smiled.

'I'm hopeless,' he said, hoping that this piece of self-disclosure would rouse in her a sense of pity.

The eyes widened as the extent of the damage became obvious. 'Oh dear. Marian will not be pleased with you at all.' The thought of her maid's displeasure made Pandora smile broadly. 'Marian has no time for men anyway. No time at all.' Richard stood, holding his left hand gingerly with his right. 'You forgot to put the water in, right?'

'Right.'

'Now you've burnt your hand, yes?'

'Yes.'

Pandora sighed. 'I'll get you some fresh yoghurt and you can stick your hand in that for a while. The pain will go away and you won't even scar.'

'How do you know that sort of thing, Pandora?'

'Trade secrets,' Pandora said shortly. 'I've been burnt more times . . .' Richard saw her face change, and the mask come down.

Damn, he thought. That was careless, but with her it was like walking on alligator shells, only the buggers were all full-grown and likely to snap your leg off. Blowing up her kitchen didn't help. Pandora's head was throbbing. By now she would have downed at least three cups of coffee. She knew she was angry, but she couldn't control herself. Why, Richard asked himself, oh why am I not in bed with Hortense and her huge nipples instead of standing here holding my burnt hand? Maybe he would send himself a telegram. 'AUNT DIED LAST NIGHT IN LIMERICK. COME HOME SOONEST.' The thought of the rest of the week with this woman suddenly wearied him. Yes, she was beautiful. She was from a very poor background, but the psychiatrist chappie certainly taught her well. She spoke with a mid-Atlantic twang and, judging by all the cookbooks in the now ruined kitchen, she was at least interested in food. Richard judged women by their love of food. Sex could come later. He was hungry, he realized. Very hungry.

Pandora took out a pot of plain yoghurt and said, 'Stick your hand in that.'

Feeling extremely silly, Richard did as he was told. A door down the hallway opened and a loud voice said, 'Are you up, Missy?'

'Yes,' Pandora shouted. 'I'm up, Marian, and there's been a little accident in the kitchen.'

Richard faced the kitchen door, his hand encased in the yoghurt pot, feeling very defensive.

Marian took one look at Richard in his yellow waistcoat, old tweed jacket, and Loeb shoes. Her eyes narrowed. 'I did not know you were expecting a visitor, Missy. I'm sorry.'

Pandora's face was very white. 'Marian, I really do need some coffee.'

'You go next door, honey, and this gentleman can help me clean up.'

Richard looked startled.

Pandora, through her dreadful headache, had to smile. 'Marian runs this house,' she said. 'I don't.'

Privately, as Richard ineffectually swabbed at chunks of coffee grains, he thought American women were way out of line. Not Pandora. She was the quietest American woman he had ever come across, but women like Marian? A paid servant giving orders like that? Well, it could never happen in England! Except, he thought ruefully, for English nannies. But then they were a breed apart. They were not born like other little girls in cabbage patches; they were discovered in stinging nettle beds. Maybe he'd try some nanny charm on this lady, who was moving at a huge speed. 'Have you worked here long, Marian?'

'All my life.'

'How interesting.' First ball obviously bounced wide. Try a second. Richard came running up the cricket pitch and let go gently. 'Have you a family here?'

'No.'

She didn't even try and bat that ball. OK, he decided. Let's just get on with it and hit the wicket. 'Are you married?' he said.

That one worked. 'Married?' Marian by now had a fresh pot of coffee on the stove, a pile of toast sitting by the toaster, a white plate with butter on it, and a jar of Fortnum and Mason's English marmalade. 'Why would I want to tie myself to some no-good lazy man like a ball and chain on my leg for the rest of my life?' Her voice topped the sound of the orange juicer.

Pandora's face peered around the door. 'Richard, don't get Marian on the subject of men, especially when I'm desperate for coffee. Come next door with me and please try to stay out of trouble.'

'Not all men are bad,' Richard managed to say before leaving the room. 'Some are really quite nice actually.'

Marian rolled her very black eyes in her ebony face and scowled at the yoghurt pot. 'I was going to use that yoghurt for my cheesecake for Missy's supper.'

'I'll take her out to supper, Marian. I'm sorry, really I am. If I take Pandora out, then I can say I had a hand in making the cheesecake, and we can be friends.'

'Not till you get those grounds off the ceiling, we won't.'

Richard left quickly. His famous nanny charm didn't work this side of the Atlantic.

'Will I really have to climb up a ladder and clean off all those coffee grains?' he asked Pandora. They were sitting in a very elegant breakfast-room.

'No,' Pandora said. 'She'll do it herself.'

A few minutes later coffee was on the table and Richard sat eating his toast with his most favourite marmalade in the world.

After Marian cleared away the breakfast things, she also removed the yoghurt pot in a very ungentle manner from Richard's hand. 'It works,' he said. 'It really works.' Then he remembered Pandora's face. 'Anyway, I've ruined a cheesecake for your supper, so I told her I would take you out to dinner instead. How do you feel about that?'

Pandora by now had thrown back her obligatory three cups of black coffee. The brain was beginning to move. Little chinks of light, like the strobe light Marcus had in the basement, began to shoot out. 'I don't know,' she said softly. 'I haven't been out to dinner for so long. I've almost forgotten how long.' She hated going out to dinner with Marcus because he always used the event as part of an evening's titillation. If it was a night of bondage, he would tie a silk band around her right wrist and she would sit through an elaborate meal knowing that home meant hours of being spread-eagled on the bed while he fondled her with brushes that teased and tingled. And then came the pain. Always the pain. 'It makes a man omnipotent when a woman moans in such sweet agony,' he once said to her. 'Every woman has a sound like a violin, a sob between agony and ecstasy, and that is where I have the control. Your problem, dear, is that you don't enjoy it.' He then put his face very close to hers. 'That's why I find you so fascinating, and that's why one day I will find that moment.' Pandora's eyes rehearsed those memories as she looked at this big, rather jolly Englishman who was artlessly munching on toast and marmalade. She frowned. He was spreading crumbs everywhere. Then she relaxed. Marcus wasn't here any longer, so it didn't matter any more. 'I think I'd love to go out to dinner,' she said.

Richard really very much wanted a copy of the *Daily Telegraph* newspaper and a bit of peace and quiet to digest his breakfast. He'd trained Hortense to respect his morning's lifelong habits. Breakfast, a read of the *Daily Telegraph,* a quick check on who was thanking St Jude for what, and then a shuffle off to the bathroom with the sports section. He always reckoned you could tell a man's character by the way he had his breakfast and read his newspapers. More importantly, he noticed these days, the young go-getters didn't shuffle off as if they might or might not be going to the bathroom. No, they strode to the loo, making a bald statement. Richard felt old and he knew he *must* get on with this interview. No *Telegraph* today. 'Shall we start talking about your life with Dr Sutherland?'

Pandora nodded. 'I guess we must,' she said. 'Let's go into my little sitting-room upstairs. It's quiet up there. I always thought of it as my safe place. Nothing ever happened there, you see.'

For a moment Richard was stricken with pity at the look on the woman's face, that she should be so grateful for some small safe place that was hers. He followed Pandora up the stairs and was pleased to see that Marian was indeed up a long ladder cleaning the ceiling. He caught Marian's look of disparagement as he passed by.

Pandora pointed to a room across the hall from her bedroom, and then she disappeared. 'I'll be back in a second,' she said.

Richard sat down in the child-sized chairs and stared at the room. It could or must have been a child's room. An old bed with a thick prune coverlet was squashed into one corner. A school desk well-inked. He lifted the lid. There were school books in there. *Pandora Mason* was written on each fly-leaf. On the front of the lid of the desk there was a picture of a tall man whose shoulders blocked the sunlight. 'That's my father,' Pandora said.

Richard dropped the lid of the desk with a loud bang. 'I'm sorry. I didn't mean to pry.'

Pandora smiled. She had around her shoulders an old dressing-gown. It had chocolate brown and cinnamon squares. Her hands played nervously with an old silver cord belt. 'I hope you don't mind,' she said, 'but this is my old dressing-gown from when I was twelve. Marcus let me move my own bedroom stuff in here. It was so kind of him, you see. I was so naïve in those days. So very naïve.'

Richard couldn't really think of anything much to say, except, 'I think most people are naïve, Pandora. Most people don't begin to imagine what happens in the big bad world of ours. I certainly was when I first began working on the *Boston Telegraph*.' Then he thought again of the first time he had seen Pandora. At the theatre in Boston when he had taken his aunt out for the night. 'Must be Jung's Law of Synchronicity,' he said out loud. 'I saw you years ago at the opera in Boston.'

Pandora smiled. 'The pills blot out almost everything. But I do remember seeing you. Still, the pills are why it is so difficult to remember anything.' With the wistfulness of an obedient child, she said, 'But I will try. I really will.' She sat on a small chair and then moved to the ground where she sat cross-legged, playing with her toes.

Richard got out his notebook from one of his bulging pockets. 'I was going to be professional and bring a tape-recorder, but I think those things are awfully off-putting. So let's just try it this way. OK?'

Pandora wiggled about a bit and then she was still.

'Everybody who has followed this case knows that the women who were involved in most cases were respectable middle-class housewives, except for a few paid prostitutes.'

Pandora nodded. 'Yeah. Every week a group of us who were abused women met together for a consciousness-raising group. First of all we'd all say our names and then tell each other what was happening.' Pandora's voice had gone off now into a singsong pattern, as though she had been wound up like a talking doll.

'Pandora.' Richard leaned forward. 'Pandora, stop.'

Pandora shook herself. 'Sorry, Richard.'

'You're not talking to me, Pandora. You're just repeating a pattern. It sounds like you've been brainwashed.'

Pandora's eyes suddenly came alive. 'You're right! It did become a sort of brainwashing. After weeks of that, all the women knew each other very well, and then we'd have our private therapy time with Marcus. My goodness! The women used to compete for his attention.' Her voice softened. 'He was always so kind and so gentle to me, Richard.

199

It wasn't until I was married to him that I realized he was dangerous; not just mad, really dangerous. By then it was too late.' She pulled the dressing-gown around her thin shoulders. 'The trouble is that in between these fits of madness, he was kind again. He took me travelling. He bought me pearls in Hong Kong. All the clothes I could wear. I really don't know if "normal" people, that is, people who have never felt this terrible addiction, can *ever* understand what it's like.'

'If he telephoned you tomorrow and said to come and join him, would you?'

Pandora looked at Richard. 'You know, I've thought about that lots of times. I really would hope not, Richard. I honestly mean that. But there's that awful part of me that feels if I hear his voice again, I'll go. There are some men like Marcus. They are the Pied Piper of women. He knows women so well, he can get them to do anything he wants them to do. It's almost as if he is an emotional heroin-pusher, and without him, you're lost. My buzz has gone, if that makes sense. He was my high. When I was with him, when he gave me his whole, undivided attention, I glowed. My whole body felt alive.'

In front of Richard, she shook back the dressing-gown and her back straightened itself. Her hair took on an electrical field of its own and her face shone. My God, she's so beautiful, Richard thought.

'Look at me, Richard.' She stretched her arms above her head and then she jumped lightly to her feet. 'Dr Marcus Sutherland and his No-Name Wife attended yet another reception, yadi, yadi, ya.'

Richard sat stunned. How on earth was he going to make any sense of this to his normally staid readers? 'Do you think if I put those words of yours down, my readers will understand them?'

Pandora nodded vehemently. 'Sure,' she said. 'And not just women. Men can get addicted, too. Remember Antony and Cleopatra?' She got up and began to pace about the room. 'It's just that women tend to put everything they've got into their relationships, and men don't. So a disproportionate amount of women do get into these awful degrading relationships. Then they can't get out. God knows what would have happened to me if Marcus had not been trapped by the police.'

'What do you think might have happened?' Richard said quietly.

'I think I'd have finally killed myself out of self-disgust. Many did, you know. It's a you that you don't know or understand. It's part of you that you know exists, like the wild animal in you that was never properly tamed, and it just takes a ringmaster like Marcus to use his lash, and he can find it.' She paused and then looked very tired. 'I think

I'll go to bed now and just have a little sleep,' she said in a voice quite like a small child. She climbed into the bed and turned over, the rusty springs squeaking in protest.

'Can I take you out to dinner tonight, Pandora?' Richard found himself eager to get to know this woman. Not for his readers, not for his newspaper, but for himself.

'Call me at seven, Richard. That would be lovely.' Her long eyelashes curled on to her cheeks and she was asleep somewhere deep, deep in a labyrinth, Richard felt, where no one could reach her.

Richard went back to the office and looked down at a blank sheet of paper. 'The Pied Piper of Women', he began his headline. Good heavens! Here was this man who could get all these women to do anything he wanted, and all *he* could manage was Hortense. He telephoned his flat, or rather he corrected himself, his apartment. 'Yeah?' His ears were assailed by the sound of chewing gum. 'Hortense speaking. Whadya want?'

'It's Richard, Hortense. I just needed to ask if you kept that pile of newspapers recording the Marcus Sutherland trial.'

'Nope.'

'No? Hortense, what do you mean *no*?'

'Hey, Richard. Don't give me all that aggression. How about saying "Hello, Baby! I missed you!" or something nice like that? Or have you been too busy fucking Mrs Pussy-Power?'

Richard winced. 'Sorry, Hortense. I'm just tired. No, I have not been fucking Mrs Sutherland. She's rather a sad, lost woman, if you must know. I just needed those papers for research.'

'Sorry, hon. I took them home to line the guinea pig's cage. Didn't think you'd need them. They'll be pretty much pissed and peed on by now. But I can take them out, if it will help.'

'No, don't bother. Thanks a lot. There's always library copies. I'll be home Saturday night late, so don't stay up.'

He heard Hortense's throaty gurgle. After today's discussion, he never wanted to think about sex again.

Chapter Thirty-five

In Pandora's dreams – and she dreamed all afternoon – the night was wild. She was somewhere very far away, high on a clifftop. All that talking about Marcus had made her uneasy. The thoughts of his face and the remembrance of his staring eyes and his mouth . . . She felt that odd taste in her mouth again, the same taste she felt in the early hours of the morning. Her body twitched and her mouth felt dry, except for this oily, fishy, sludge taste. Through the winds and the whirling mists she heard a voice say quite clearly, 'Spit it out. Just go to the door and spit it out.'

She struggled to her feet, feeling nauseated, but somebody stood beside her and put a finger in her mouth and removed the offending object. Gently she felt her hair calmed and her forehead stroked. And then she sipped a little liquid and was asleep again in her little bed in Boise, Idaho.

Octo crept out of the cave and joined Janine. 'Look,' he said, as he showed Janine the slime on his finger. 'Maisy's got to her, you know. Pandora was trying to get up. She would have jumped.'

Way back in the bushes, the four-clawed cat's eyes blazed with anger.

Richard spent a rather frustrating afternoon telephoning psychiatrists for advice. 'Well, could be she's suffering from de Clerambault Syndrome,' Dr Springfield suggested. 'She pestered him because he was famous. You know, that sort of thing. Women often do it.'

Dr Horst suggested erotomania. 'She's infatuated with him because he had power over her. Absolute authority. Very difficult case, in my opinion. Does she want therapy?'

Richard felt as if Dr Horst had more than just a professional interest in erotomania. He sounded as if he were drooling down the telephone.

'I have one lady who wants spanking every time. I get paid.' He shrieked with laughter.

Richard put the telephone down rather sharply. Suddenly he felt an urge to jump out of a very precarious, much larger world where people did absolutely unspeakable things to each other with no remorse.

He spent a lot of the afternoon fiddling around with paperclips. After he'd made a particularly long chain, he got bored and decided to try the old trick of lighting matches and building a bridge. It was hot and he wanted a sleep. Finally he moved over to the old sofa in the reporters' room and fell heavily asleep, dreaming of fishing for trout in Devon, and, to his surprise, dreaming of Pandora sitting next to him on the bank. He woke with a start and realized he'd better get back to the hotel to change for dinner.

He realized, as he dressed for dinner rather more carefully than usual, he was not in the habit of taking his interviewees out to dinner. Nor, on this case, did he have an expense account for doing such a thing. Richard knew he was a spendthrift. He had a large salary from the *Boston Telegraph*, a very glamorous apartment in Boston. Hortense was another expense, but he felt, as he wandered around his hotel room, she was not going to remain an expense for very much longer. The trouble with Hortense, Richard pondered while he adjusted his Italian silk tie, was that while Michelangelo's *David* was a joy to look at, as was Aphrodite rising from a seashell, or even stepping modestly out of the bath, wrapping herself in a bath towel, Hortense was more likely to harangue him from her perch on the lavatory seat. Shelborne School for Boys had never led him to give any thought to women's excretory behaviour, except to congratulate themselves as boys that they had penises and girls didn't, which obviously made boys superior to girls. Living with Hortense had given Richard a severe sense of educational deprivation. 'Clutters', otherwise known as Mr Clutterbuck, was dead keen on sex education. He was the first master to throw multi-coloured condoms like confetti at the boys. But he failed to mention girls like Hortense. He did give a lecture on inexperienced girls and the need for lubrication. 'Vaseline, boys. Lots of Vaseline.'

Richard found Hortense profoundly boring the first time they made love. She gave a loud shriek of satisfaction, followed by a fart, and then fell asleep. The bottle of Vaseline lay untouched on the night-table, and Richard's prick looked at him with obvious disappointment. 'We have a lot to learn about this one, old man,' he said in mitigation.

Richard was fond of Hortense. She swept away all or nearly all of his inhibitions. The one sacrosanct moment was his shuttle from the breakfast table to the loo with his *Telegraph*. Try as she might, Hortense could not undermine him. She once tried lying on the floor and refusing to budge. 'My shrink says you are withholding intimate information from our relationship.'

Richard heaved her not inconsiderable weight from the floor. 'I just want to shit,' he said desperately. 'I just want to open my newspaper at the gardening pages, have a read, then a little think, then I can begin my day. There's nothing wrong with that, is there, for fuck's sake?'

Still, Hortense had taken Richard in hand, and from a rather shy, diffident, public school boy with a love of literature, she had produced a very confident young man-about-town.

At least, he had been a confident young man-about-town until today. Where do you take such a beautiful woman to dinner? A woman who one minute is a glamorous, eye-catching beauty, and the next a broken flower? Pandora reminded Richard of when he was small and he picked the grey-headed dandelion-clocks and blew them away in one breath. Pandora blew away to almost anywhere.

In the twenty-eight years of his life, he had always felt that most people lived their lives on fairly predictable railway lines. He was unusual in his close-knit Devon family. There were five boys, all programmed to enter the Navy, the Army, the Civil Service, or the Foreign Office. Richard, the youngest, was destined for the Church. He remembered his father's shocked face when he declined to read theology at Cambridge. 'Sins of the flesh, Father, you know how it is.'

'But, my dear boy! You can be married.'

'I know, Father,' Richard said earnestly, 'but that's only to one woman.'

His father left the drawing-room, muttering and twitching at his lapel.

Richard telephoned the desk at the hotel and asked to be advised of the best restaurant in town. '*Le Beau Rivage*, sir. Shall I make reservations?'

'Thank you,' Richard said, and he was conscious of a tightening in his scrotum. I will not, he solemnly promised himself in his hotel bedroom somewhere in the boondocks of Boise, Idaho, I will not fall in love with this woman. Boy! If I think Hortense is trouble, what would this one be like?

Pandora was sitting, shaking with nerves at her dressing-table. Marian was brushing her hair. 'You look darling tonight, Missy. You go out and have a good time. You ain't been out, except for your charity work, for months. You can handle him. He's a push-over.'

'I'm just not used to talking to anyone for any length of time, Marian.'

'I know, honey. Just get him to talk about himself. That's all men require. See?' Marian brought over a black-sequined, tightly fitted dress. 'You wear that with that pretty little matching hat with the little red poppy on it, and you'll look a million dollars.'

Pandora slipped into the dress. The tight skull-cap accentuated the mass of her red hair. Her eyes were at least alive. At times Pandora thought her eyes would never again light up with a smile, that her face would grow to resemble the faces of the tramps she so humbly served. 'How is it,' she said, 'that for all these months I've sought penance and my peace among those poor and homeless people, and tonight I've promised to go out for a meal with a man I hardly know, and no doubt to a meal that could feed a whole shelter?'

'Quit thinking so much, Missy. Just go out and have a good time. Sometimes I think you think you're going to live like Job for the rest of your life.'

'In other words,' Pandora said, smiling at Marian, 'you're saying I should lighten up, hunh?'

Marian grinned. It had been such a long time since she'd seen Pandora really smile.

Chapter Thirty-six

Richard arrived to pick up Pandora in a rented limo. This was a sudden decision of his. Somehow even the Jaguar didn't seem special enough for her, and bustling about trying to catch American taxis was certainly not his line. He tried whistling between two fingers and got his hand covered in spit. Besides, Idaho taxis ignored English gentlemen, Richard decided. His hotel provided him with a stretch limo, an immaculate chauffeur, and dark tinted windows. He would have to tell Miss Horrocks, his terrifying secretary, that he needed the car for secret getaways. Fortunately, Richard was never short of material for his sagas, which one day he hoped he could put into a novel. Then he could sell the whole caboodle to the film industry and spend the rest of his life chasing women and sipping fine wines.

All this went idly through his head as he felt the flow of the limousine and compared it with his first car, a little rounded Morris Minor. The back seat had been too small for fornication and the front only roomy enough for heavy petting. Geraldine Patch, his first sexual conquest, did nonetheless do a good job hanging over the front seat on a hot day with the roof rolled down. Enough of a good job for Richard to have sought the elixir of sex as often as possible. His last ten years, after his first encounter with Geraldine, was a fairly fly-blown memory of mounds of bodies at parties, several amatory escapades in beds piled high with thick winter coats. Other men's wives. That he only did when the wife was irresistible and the husband very far away. Richard had no intention of submitting himself to the sound of the legitimate key in the lock or the humiliation of a quick exit with his trousers around his ankles. It all ranked alongside his habit of reading the newspaper by himself in the bathroom and not whistling for taxis between his fingers.

The limousine drew up. The chauffeur opened the door and Richard, straightening his shoulders, began to climb the stairs to the house. Marian let him in. She made a face that caused Richard to wonder if he had toothpaste on his cheek or dandruff on his dinner jacket. 'She's in there waiting for you,' Marian informed him. 'Now don't you go upsetting her. You understand that?'

'I very much hope I shall give her a very good time, Miss Marian.'

'You do that.' If Marian had a spare set of teeth, they would by now be clamped very firmly round Richard's ankles.

Richard walked as manfully as he could, knowing that Marian's eyes followed his every move. How the hell can an old woman like that reduce me to feeling like a six-year-old? he asked himself. He paused at the door to the drawing-room and knocked quietly.

When he saw Pandora standing by the marble fireplace, he stopped breathing. Years ago his mother had a flapper fashion book. On the cover was a woman, also standing by a white marble fireplace, one elbow planted on the mantel, the mirror reflecting the back of her head, and the long, clinging gown of black sequins aching to be touched, to be stroked, and then to be shed, like the skin of a snake, to the floor. Richard had been in love with the woman in the picture since he was five. And here she was. 'You look marvellous, Pandora,' he said, hoping his voice wouldn't squeak.

'Do I really, Richard?' Pandora spun around. 'Look. Can you see my little cap with the red poppy? Isn't it pretty?' Tonight she had a little colour in her cheeks.

'I have a car waiting for us, and dinner is booked.' Richard looked at his watch. Actually he wanted to get away from this house, from Marian, and the whole disgusting business of Dr Marcus Sutherland. He really just wanted to take a beautiful woman out to dinner and to enjoy her company.

'I'm ready,' Pandora said simply. 'I have my coat.' She put on a large cloak made from a shimmering cloth of gold, and then put on a pair of dark glasses. 'Shall we go?' she said. She put an arm on Richard's, and then walked down the corridor, past Marian, who smiled like a corpse. Rigor mortis about to set in, I should hope, Richard remarked to himself. A few terms at St Thomas's Medical School, before he was ignominiously thrown out for leaving a dead leg in a nurse's locker, taught him the rudiments of anatomy.

'Good night, Missy,' said Marian to Pandora. 'I'll be waiting up for you.'

'Oh, you don't need to do that,' Pandora said lightly.

'I do indeed.'

Pandora shook her head. 'Marian takes such good care of me.'

They walked down the steps to the gleaming car. 'Wow!' Pandora put her gloved fingers to her mouth. 'What a car!'

Richard laughed. He was glad to see the small urchin show through the sophisticated Mrs Sutherland. The chauffeur held the door open and Pandora slipped in.

'I'm looking forward to tonight, Richard,' she said, her small face only inches from his. Her pink lips smiling, and all around her a halo of wonderful-smelling Shalimar.

She smelled, he decided, leaning back very firmly in his seat, like his idea of an evening in a Persian garden. They would lie on a bank of myrtle leaves while scarcely dressed young women tiptoed around, dropping delicate bits of food into their mouths. Then, as the sun rose, he would finish the meal by licking ambrosia from between Pandora's breasts. 'Turn right here, sir?'

'Er, yes. I think so.' Richard cursed life. It was all so literal.

Pandora sat gazing out of the window. For the moment, the colour had drained from her face again. Richard put a hand on hers. 'I'll have to leave this place, you know, Richard. I can't stay here. It's too haunted.'

'I can imagine that, but all that can wait, just for tonight. I want us to have the night of our lives together. I've booked us a table at the *Beau Rivage*, and we will wine and dine the night away. What you need, Pandora, is fun.'

For a moment, Pandora felt a frozen flash of anger against this young man. Fun? That, at this moment, was just what *he* needed, and that was just what *he* was going to have: FUN. She watched him and thought, No, I'm being unfair. He has been kind. 'All right,' she smiled. 'For tonight we will just enjoy ourselves.' She had six hours of pills inside her and a spare in her purse. Pandora knew how to have fun. After all, Marcus, when he was in an erratic mood, insisted she entertained him. This was the same demand now, but more kindly meant.

The restaurant was dark, which was just as well for Pandora. Anyway, dark glasses on, she would not be recognized. Richard loved the ice-cold gloom of the place. The settings were all still in the twenties. A long steel bar ran down the length of the room and the bottles, ranked row upon row, twinkled in the lowered lights. 'It used to be a speakeasy,' Pandora explained. 'Everybody so liked the place that when the new people took it over, they kept it looking like this, but upgraded the food.'

Away up the other end of the room a small combo was playing slow jazz. The room was quite full, and Pandora could see Deiter Rosen scribbling in his notebook. For tomorrow's newspaper, no doubt, she thought.

They sat quite near the band and Richard took the menu. 'Cocktails?' he asked.

'Thank you. A gin and tonic, please.' She was comfortable. Richard was not difficult to be with.

He looked over the menu. 'What would you like to eat? I see they do a very good swordfish steak.'

'Oh, no. I'll have a fillet of sole, please, with a little spinach.' She smiled at Richard. 'What are you going to have?'

'Everything!' Richard grasped the menu with both hands and ran his eye down all the delicacies there were to offer. 'You don't know how much I'm going to miss all this wonderful American food when I get back to England. I go on leave, when I get back to Boston, and then I'll stay in Devon with my mother and father. And then it's good old nanny food again.'

Pandora watched while Richard ate his way through plate after plate of food. He drank two bottles of wine and reminisced about his childhood. 'You're not bored, are you, Pandora? I know I'm going on a bit, but it's quite lonely in Boston. I don't know many Americans, except Hortense, of course.'

'Who's Hortense?' Pandora's female intuition smelled *girlfriend*.

'Well . . .' Here Richard wished he had kept his mouth shut. 'She's a woman who's been very good to me. And at the moment –' he paused to see if an idea might flash into his head – 'yes, at the moment, she's plant-sitting for me while I'm here with you.' He emphasized the *with you* by putting his hand on Pandora's cool hand as it lay on her knee.

Pandora smiled. What an awful liar he is, she thought. 'Are the plants very difficult to look after, Richard?'

'Oh yes! Dreadfully, I collect orchids, you know. Have to be misted and dusted, I think. Anyway, Hortense does all that for me. Very good girl.'

'Do you have a girlfriend, Richard?'

Richard fingered his collar. 'Well, no, Pandora. Not exactly. I get involved with girls now and then, but on the whole I'm a bit footloose, as we say in England. My other four brothers are all married and terribly respectable. One is married to the bank. He has a wife and three children. Gareth is married to the Navy. He has a wife and four

209

brats. Then there's Jason at the Civil Service, with a wife and one. And then old James at the FO. Only just got married and about to sprout. When we all get together, it's all fearfully maternal and babies and nappies and bottles. Michael's wife Delilah is a bit of a dipso with hippy trimming and she insists on feeding her brat in front of everybody.'

Pandora found herself getting drawn into the matrix of the Townsend family life. Soon she found herself taking a vivid interest in who Aunt Mary had left the family silver to and why Cousin Jonathan had hanged himself from the bough of an apple tree. 'Why?' Pandora asked.

'He left a note saying he could never have sex, or something of the sort, and old soddy said he'd probably had a better orgasm that day than he ever would for the rest of his life.'

Pandora decided to change the subject. 'Shall we dance, Richard? Look, they're playing that very old song from the fifties. "Love Is a Many Splendoured Thing". You know that's from a real-life story? She was a doctor in Hong Kong, and half Chinese. He was an English doctor and married.'

Richard had his arm around Pandora's waist and his face nestled in her hair. Holding her for the first time in his life, he felt he was holding a presence that had always been there waiting for him. Girl after girl, woman after woman, had all been held in those arms, but never yet had the fit been perfect. Never before had the soft crevasses of the bodily terrain mixed and melded until two flesh did become as one. They moved dreamily to the music, their heads on each other's shoulders, Pandora smiling comfortably and Richard falling further and further down that chasm called Love.

Janine, the weaver of the dream, smiled. 'Look at Pandora's face! Good things are happening.' And indeed the face on the sand looked softer and the lips were stretched in an amused smile.

Chapter Thirty-seven

By the end of the week, Richard knew he was not going to leave Pandora in that great big house alone. Not just because he pitied her or felt that she was a victim in a cruel and unusual case of abuse, but also because he had fallen in love with her flower face, her sudden smile. And when she was not locked away in some dark and dreadful memory, he loved her sense of humour.

All these thoughts threw him into a quandary. First, Hortense, far from tending his plants, of which he had none, was telephoning the hotel, demanding his return. 'My tarot card-reader says there are black clouds above us, Richard. We need to connect. You understand? The energy between us is unstable.'

Richard muttered back at her, '. . . working, furiously, darling . . .' And then he wondered how the hell he could tell Hortense it was all over and he was in love with a woman like Pandora.

He could hear Hortense's voice now. 'Wow. Heaviness.' But would Hortense go away quietly? Then, if he could oust Hortense, he could file his copy of the story and take Pandora with him back to Devon. There in the family house near Charmouth, they could spend some time together and hopefully Pandora could realize that he, Richard, was just the man to love her and take care of her for the rest of her life.

Richard felt embarrassed. His views on marital love and faithfulness were culled from books in the school library, which had put him off the whole business for life. First-hand he had witnessed what he could see as dreadful unions of unloveliness among his own family. He was unsure that Pandora would fit into any of that picture. Surprisingly, though, Pandora never seemed to stop wanting to hear about his family. 'You see,' she said earnestly, tucking her legs up under her, 'I had no family. Only my mother, who really didn't like me. So just to think that you have all those people who love you and care about you and wonder where you are, I think you're really lucky.'

*

They were at dinner the night Richard was proposing his plan to invite Pandora to visit him in England. His piece would come out in the Sunday edition of the *Boston Telegraph*, and they could meet at Logan Airport by the carry-out live lobster tank, and be gone. Nobody read the *Boston Telegraph* in Charmouth. He was leaving tomorrow so that he could spend Saturday touching up the piece and then use what was left of his energy to say goodbye to Hortense.

The little dinner was relaxed and comfortable. Richard had brought along with him some notes that he wanted to check with Pandora. They had just finished dinner and were about to drink their coffee. Pandora was more relaxed than usual. She had cut down on the pills. Richard's presence soothed her. He was always calm and good-humoured. The nightmare of Marcus's ever-changing moods didn't exist with Richard. He hung like a big bright balloon in a blue sky of his own making. 'Harum scarum,' Monica would call him. Dishevelled, untidy, late – always late – but always smiling and Pandora could do with a lot of smiling. For years there had been little to smile about.

Richard's forehead was creased. 'I've been trying to get this bit right, Pandora. Why, if you had money in your account and a car and the freedom to go anywhere you wanted to go, did you not just leave? I'm sorry to ask you that again. You've given me various answers. One of them is that he had your prescriptions for all those pills you were on, and you needed them. The other is that you had nowhere to go to, except to your mother, who said you'd made yourself a very rich bed and you were to lie on it. But surely there must be a further answer.'

Pandora sighed and then she felt that moment within when her tiny, newborn self blew helpless bubbles with its lips and said through its sobbing little mouth *Help me. I'm so helpless.* She felt the unformed fingers in her mother's womb flap at the pointed scalpel as it sought to root her out like an unwanted wart. Helplessness, eternal incapability, and then the hours lying helpless, dirty, starving and unwanted, in a cot at the back of the dining-room, far away from her mother's whining voice . . . 'Anything is better than nothing,' said Pandora, looking evenly at Richard.

'Hunh?' Richard sat, gazing at Pandora.

She sighed again. 'Just put down that for the unwanted to be wanted for any reason is better than being unwanted. To be wanted even for sexual abuse becomes a type of relationship. To be bullied and screamed at, at least you hear someone's voice. You think they care enough to bother to abuse you.' She leaned forward and Richard saw the tears in her eyes. 'And the awful thing is that you are grateful. At the end of the day, you are really grateful. If he doesn't scream too loud, you're grateful for that. It turns into a kindness. If he doesn't say anything that is so cruel it hurts for days, you are grateful for that. Always behind the unwanted is the need for love. And they will look for it anywhere they can.' Pandora sat back and wondered if she could slip a couple of pills. 'I've got a headache, Richard. I'll just take a couple of aspirin.'

'Of course.' He gestured to the waiter for another drink. Bloody hell, he thought. How do I get all this in? At times, Pandora made Richard uncomfortable, uneasy. In an odd way he felt he was spending time with someone who had been living in her own concentration camp and had survived. Or sort of survived. Pandora reminded him of a bejewelled stick-insect with one of its wings missing.

Pandora took the drink. She sat back in the chair and she breathed out. Richard had nearly caused her to touch bottom, nearly reached the side of herself that she most feared. Now she could cope far better with the fear. It was far more than fear that assailed her at times. It was a cosmic consciousness of sheer horror that she existed at all. She knew she was not alone in that fear. Other women in the group had also voiced their concerns. Also it was instructive, amidst the disgust with which she viewed herself, to see that it was not she alone who crawled through the beds of the sexually perverse, but that other women, equally needy, equally wanting, took the same course. Disgust served her master secret well. There was little discussion among the women about their evenings. Later, when Pandora was married to Marcus, there were no women to talk to at all, except Marian whose eyes stayed hooked and lips tight.

Pandora knew, as she sat with Richard at dinner, that she had found herself a white knight, a man who, she could see, had fallen in love with his idea of who she was and who would now take her under his protective wing and nurture her for the rest of her life. Another cross-roads, she thought, watching Richard pay the bill.

She got up and followed Richard out of the restaurant.

In the drawing-room, Richard made his proposal. Pandora listened with a sweet smile. 'I would love to go to Devon for a holiday with you, Richard. That sounds really fun.'

Richard pulled her close to him. He felt for the first time in his life as if he had a heart that could actually burst. He imagined great choruses of joy and exaltation opening in the skies. He saw troops of choristers followed by the entire corps de ballet leaping about the room. 'Pandora,' he said as steadily as he could. 'Someday, Pandora, I would really like to marry you.'

Pandora opened her green, mottled, drugged eyes and looked into his face and said, 'Yes, Richard.'

Janine watched Pandora, asleep in her cave, slip her thumb into her mouth.

Chapter Thirty-eight

Sunday didn't give Pandora much time to organize her arsenal of drugs. Sunday didn't give Richard much time to get rid of Hortense. 'Screw it, Richard!' she bellowed, huge tears running down her face. 'You can't kick me out after all these months. Look what I've done for you! I've cleaned out your psyche. I taught you that to fart is not a mortal sin.'

'For that I thank you,' Richard said humbly. Why do women make me feel so guilty? he wondered. 'Hortense, we said this was not a committed relationship, remember?'

'I remember, I remember. But my psychiatrist says you are afraid of commitment. You really want to commit, but you can't. You just can't. It's like emotionally you're constipated.'

'Your psychiatrist, Hortense, is only concerned with my bowels.'

'Well, it's all there, isn't it, Richard? I mean, all that bad stuff goes down there and churns around, you know. Like hate and jealousy. You don't love another woman, do you, Richard?'

By this time Richard was sitting in his library chair by his window that looked out over the beautiful brick square nearby. Hortense was tearing at her clothes.

'Look at me, Richard! Look at my body. Don't you want me any more?'

'It's not a matter of sex. It's nothing to do with it. I've just fallen in love.' He lay back in the chair. 'Quite wonderful, really. Quite like magic. One day you're an ordinary man, just living your life, which is sometimes happy but mostly sad. And then *ping* goes that little bell. You know the kind Tinkerbell always had for rescuing Peter? And there it is. It really does exist. Moon in June. I never believed this would happen. Hey, Hortense! What do you think you're doing?'

Hortense was struggling to climb on to Richard's knee. 'Make love to me, Richard. Just make love to me. Just once more.'

'I can't. I'm sorry, but I can't. I never thought I'd ever say no to an offer of sex, but my heart is elsewhere. Doesn't that sound silly?' he said. 'I sound like Dornford Yates.'

'Was he an English psychiatrist?'

'No.' Richard shook his head. 'He was a silly idiot who always got into trouble with women and cars.'

Hortense's eyes still dripped. She climbed off his knee and then she looked at Richard very seriously. 'Does this woman know what you're really like, Richard?'

Richard looked solemn. 'What do you mean *really like*? You're not about to give me one of your ghastly lectures, are you?'

'Not really. I'm just going to point out to you that you know you are totally irresponsible, incapable of holding a job for very long, and chronically unfaithful, and you're a spender. That's all.'

Richard stared at Hortense and then he sighed. 'I know all that, Hortense, but I'm a changed man. Really I am. For a priceless treasure like that, I'll be faithful for ever. It will be like holding Venus in my arms. The original, the dream of all lovers. Dante had his Beatrice, and I have my Pandora.'

'Samson had his Delilah, don't forget that. And look where it got him.' Hortense put her skirt on. 'OK, Richard. I'll go. But I hope you know what you're doing. At least I kept you straight. You couldn't lie to me. I hope this woman is one tough woman, or you'll destroy her.'

'Don't be so silly, Hortense. I'll do nothing of the sort. I'm taking her home to visit my family. She'll get a divorce, and then we will be married happily ever after. Don't cry, Hortense.' Richard felt wretched. He put his arms around her sturdy little body and kissed her. 'I'll miss you, Hortense, and I'll introduce you to Pandora when I bring her back to Boston. You'll love her. You really will.'

'Yeah, right.' Hortense wiped her nose with the back of her hand. 'I'll be the one explaining where you are and why you're late.'

'I'll be a changed man. I promise, Hortense. Really. Look. Why don't you cheer up, and I'll take you out to dinner. After you've cleaned out all your stuff. We can drop it off at your place, and then we can go to Regina's for pizza. Sound good?'

Hortense nodded. She raced around the flat, rescuing clothes and shoes; make-up, hairspray and panty-hose from the bathroom cabinet; cold cream from the fridge; and boxes of Tampax from the kitchen cupboard; and finally, breathlessly, said, 'OK. Let's go.'

Richard looked around the flat. Once the cleaner had a go through, the flat would look immaculate and he would never again throw his underwear on the floor or leave all the dishes in the sink for the one day of the week the maid came in to do the work.

216

'It's amazing,' he said as they got into his green Jaguar, 'how a man can change so suddenly.'

Hortense, hedged about with her belongings spilling out of the boot and the back seat, looked unimpressed. She was clutching a big tub of sweet-smelling geraniums. 'This is all balls, Richard, you know it.'

Richard, arms outstretched, was driving as he imagined he would were he Dornford Yates on yet another caper in the south of France. He pulled up at Hortense's loft along the wharves. The sea bellowed and the gulls tumbled. Hortense took a huge armful of her clothes up the stairs. Richard dutifully carried the rest. 'Okey-dokey,' Richard said, stemming any more tears. 'Let's get going for a pizza and a great night out.'

Once back on the pavement, he tried his Gene Kelly impersonation. '"Singing in the rain! I'm singing in the rain . . ."' he yodelled.

'It isn't raining.'

'OK then. We'll try "April in Paris".'

'It's August in Boston,' said Hortense bitterly, 'and it's fucking hot. Let's get going.'

In the roar and heat of Regina's, Richard let Hortense do the talking. He sat back and sipped the rough chianti wine. Hortense looked intensely at Richard, trying to talk sense to him. Hortense was a sculptor. Her gnarled hands gave her a much older look, but she was genuinely fond of Richard. Now she was losing him. She was trying without much success to warn him not to damage yet another woman. 'Richard, how many women have you fallen in love with in your life?'

'Hundreds, Hortense. Hundreds.'

'How many married women have you slept with?'

Richard took another mouthful of wine. He opened his eyes. 'I'd better have another slice of pizza. I'm feeling sloshed. Quite a few, in answer to your question. Lots.'

'And how about women like me?'

'Hortense,' here Richard put his hand to his heart and burped, 'I was only unfaithful to you twice.'

Hortense gave an indignant snort. The man was impossible.

'But you see,' Richard said, his eyes gleaming with truth, 'when you meet *the* woman in your life, all that goes straight out of the window. Sorry, dear,' he said to his next-seat neighbour when he had been slapped in the face by his table napkin. 'I feel so happy, Hortense. Please be happy for me. Please. Don't sit there looking miserable.'

By now Regina's was closing down, but Richard was in full swing.

He picked up two bottles of chianti and a box of their unfinished pizza. 'Let's go and finish this at your place, Hortense. I feel like a little wassailing, don't you?'

Hortense made a face. 'OK, Richard,' she said. 'You climb into the passenger seat and I'll drive.'

Richard, beaming, his arms full of wine and pizza, folded himself into the car. He lay back in the thick leather cushions and said, 'Sunday, she and I will be up there,' and he pointed to the ceiling of the car. 'Up, up, and away.'

Two hours later, Richard lay in Hortense's big, black, Victorian tub. Both bottles of wine lay on the floor plus half a bottle of whisky. Hortense's small round face was at the other end of the bath. 'Do that again,' Richard said. 'That feels nice.'

Hortense tickled Richard's testicles with her toes. Richard gazed at his enlarged prick sticking out of the bubbles.

'Up periscope!' he yelled. 'Enemy about.'

Hortense was laughing hysterically. She put her hand under his balls and rubbed them gently. Then she took him in her mouth and they moved lightly in the warm, scented water. Just before she felt he was about to come, she sat astride him. She felt the rush of the semen and she bent down and kissed him on the mouth. Richard, you louse, she thought. You've betrayed her before you've even laid her. Poor bitch.

She got out of the bath and left Richard snoring. She dried herself off and climbed into bed. She always knew it would end like this one day, and it hurt. But at least this was the last wound. He was out of her life. He would now blaze his way through another woman's life. She would miss his warmth and his humour and above all his energy and enthusiasm, but the child who never grew up in him she could do without. 'Nanny Hortense is giving up on Richard,' she said to herself as she rolled into bed. No more nannying.

Much later she heard Richard slosh his way out of the freezing bath. He tried to get into her bed. 'Fuck off, Richard. It's late and I'm tired.'

'But I'm freezing, Hortense.'

'Towel's in the kitchen. Get dry and get going. Good luck.'

'Bloody women,' Richard muttered to himself. 'Never know what they want.'

He dressed and let himself out of the loft.

'Jolly rude of her to swear at me after I took her out to dinner and then laid her.' Hortense was always unpredictable. Not like Pandora.

He shifted in his car-seat. He really shouldn't have shafted Hortense, but then it was for old times' sake. And it was positively the last time, he promised the sun as it just peered over the skyline. He wished it were the moon. Oaths taken by moonlight in literature were far more powerful. He sighed. Today he would get the story filed and tomorrow he'd be out of there with his beloved.

Chapter Thirty-nine

Marian hugged Pandora. 'I'll come to the airport to see you off,' she said. Marian had packed six Louis Vuitton suitcases, a hatbox, and a make-up bag for Pandora.

Pandora was staring at herself in the mirror. 'You know, Marian, I'm not even divorced from Marcus yet, and I've already said yes to marrying Richard.'

'That's your trouble, Missy. You always say yes to everything. Why don't you try saying no sometime?'

Pandora laughed. Then she realized that she was really laughing from deep inside her belly. She hadn't heard herself laugh like that in years. Marian smiled. It was good to see and to hear the life and the flame come back into Pandora's face. 'Richard makes me laugh, Marian. He's enormous fun. He's full of enthusiasm.'

'And he's no good.'

'Oh, you say that about all men.'

'And I'm right.' Marian's mouth was a thin black line.

'After Marcus and all I've been through, I really don't care. The lawyers are working on a divorce settlement now. It looks as if I'll have plenty of money of my own, and I'll spend some time with Richard. Hopefully, it'll be third time lucky. The first time was stupid. The second was silly. And this time it really will be for ever. It's got to be, Marian. I'm getting scared. I look in the mirror and I see those wrinkles around my eyes. I've got cellulite on my buns. Pretty soon, I'll have a face like a used brown bag. I'm getting scared of growing old.'

Marian shook her head. 'Get along with you,' she said. 'The car is waiting.'

Pandora looked through the frosted window of the familiar limo. She watched as she pulled away from the decadent life she once lived, promising herself that life with Richard would be different. Marcus, she felt, had been a black cloud in her life that had slowly slipped into her soul like a shroud. Marcus had engaged on a long, slow series of seductions and semi-seductions. Richard, on the other hand, was like a meteor, a sudden cobalt blast from the other side of the universe. With Richard she felt she was putting on those three-dimensional glasses handed out in cinemas, and she and he could now sit together in their cinema seats, holding hands, eating sweet popcorn, and watching the rest of the world struggle by on its weary way.

The car pulled up at the airport and Richard was waiting with a porter to take her bags. 'My Venus,' he said, enfolding her in his ape-like arms. He hugged her and twirled her round and round until she was quite giddy. 'I've been up all night, terrified you might change your mind. But here you are.'

Little clots of people were standing and staring at them both. Richard's loud English voice boomed across the airport. 'Come along now, darling. Tickets all arranged.'

Marian, who was watching the event, smiled. She couldn't help liking Richard. She hugged him before they left. 'You take care of her well, or you have me to deal with.'

'I will. Oh I will.' Richard hugged Marian.

''Bye, darlin'.' Marian hugged Pandora.

Pandora saw tears in Marian's eyes. 'Don't cry. I'll be back in three weeks. While I'm away, think seriously if you want to come and work for me in Boston. I really mean it.'

Marian smiled. 'Thank you,' she said. 'Have a good trip.'

'Come along, Pandora, or we'll be late. I've booked us two first-class tickets, and it's champagne all the way.' He hurried Pandora past the news-stands where he could see her face very prominently displayed. Once they were in the first-class waiting lounge, Richard relaxed. 'Champagne, darling?' he asked her.

'No, thanks. What I need is coffee. Lots and lots of coffee.' The pills were making her hands shake and the walls of the lounge bulge in and out.

'You suddenly look awfully white. Are you all right?'

'Sure, Richard. I'm just scared of flying. I'll take a couple of tablets and then I'll calm down.'

Richard went to the bar and organized a brandy Alexander for himself and coffee for Pandora. While he was waiting for the drinks, he looked back at her slender figure in a brown box suit. She wore a matching brown hat with a small veil. By her feet she had her jewel case. Richard started to hum. 'Oh how happy,' he hummed. It was his Pooh Bear happy-song. Richard usually hummed when he was this ecstatically happy after a particularly good orgasm, or if he had hit a cricket ball

221

over the boundary line. Today he was humming because he had just met his angel, the one God had tucked away in a special velvet-lined drawer marked *For Richard Townsend*. The words *Very Special* had been added by his guardian angel. Richard did have a slight nip of guilt, a little twinge on his left shoulder where his guardian angel was reminding him that he had already told a whopping lie to his best beloved. It had been the editor of the *Boston Telegraph* who had given him the first-class air tickets. 'Get the broad out on the first plane. We don't want the other papers to get to her. Keep it exclusive, Townsend.' Only a little white lie, Richard replied, and continued to hum his way back to where Pandora was sitting.

'Richard,' she said, 'you're making a frightful noise.'

'No, I'm not,' he said, genially plonking himself down. 'I'm humming because I am really happy, Pandora. Do you know how happy I am?'

Pandora swallowed the pills with the coffee.

'I could sing you the whole of a Puccini opera. Or do you like Gilbert and Sullivan instead? "A wandering minstrel I . . ."' he began. Several of the first-class passengers were looking distinctly worried.

'No, please don't sing me anything, Richard. Just sit down and drink your drink. We'll be boarding any moment now.'

Richard beamed at her.

'Once we're on the plane, you won't mind if I put on my eye-covers and go to sleep, will you, Richard?'

'Not at all, darling. I'll sit right beside you and guard you all night to see that no evil bears or wolves come near you. I'll fight off tigers. I'll sink sharks.'

'Richard,' Pandora said quietly. 'Calm down.'

'I am calm. Quite reasonable. I'm always calm.'

Pandora was asleep before the plane reached its cruising altitude and the seatbelt signs went off. Tenderly Richard put her pillow more firmly under her head.

'Haven't I seen that face somewhere?' the young cabin steward asked, his nose wrinkling at a nagging memory.

'Don't think so,' Richard said cheerfully. 'Madam has just flown in from Hong Kong.' He put out the reading lights. Soon the cabin would be in darkness.

Across from their seat he saw a man with a copy of the *Boston Telegraph*. He was talking to the woman next to him. 'I think that's all baloney,' the man said loudly. 'They do it because they like it. All this long-winded psychology is crap.'

Richard felt his fist bunch up. He heard his breath whistle through his nostrils. He was so furious, he glared at the man until the man blushed and huddled away in his seat.

'I think,' he said to his chilly little wife, 'that that man over there is quite mad.'

Richard, with infinite delight, let out a deep growl.

After eating his own dinner and Pandora's, Richard fell asleep, snoring loudly. The terrified couple took turns during the night to protect themselves and their possessions.

Chapter Forty

Waiting for Richard and Pandora at London's Heathrow Airport was the Reverend Philip Townsend. He was a gigantic sight. He wore a dog collar under an ancient V-necked cricket jersey. Over the jersey he wore a very old, battered tweed jacket. His trousers were stuffed into the ends of his socks, and he wore white English plimsolls. 'I brought my brolly in case it rained, dear boy,' he said, giving Richard a mighty thump on the back. 'And this must be Pandora. How marvellous! If we whip along right away, we should be home for a late lunch. Mummy just can't wait to see you both. She is so excited.'

'Can I drive, Daddy?'

Pandora, still startled by the eccentric vision of Richard's father, was rather amazed at a grown man referring to his father as *Daddy*, but then the English, she thought, with their mummies and their nannies . . . Who knew what it all meant?

'Oh, no, Richard. You know I don't let anybody drive Jenny. She may be old, but she's steady as a rock. Never gives me any trouble, ever. Never had a traffic accident in my life, my dear.'

Richard shook his head at Pandora behind his father's back. He wiggled his ears at her and she found herself laughing helplessly.

The men loaded the car. Pandora's eyebrows raised when she first saw the car. It was a mammoth. Behind the back seat there was a further single seat that looked as if it swivelled. 'For shooting crocodiles in Kenya,' the Rev. Townsend explained. 'Now I just use it to shoot left-footers.'

Pandora smiled uncertainly. 'Left-footers?'

'Catholics.'

'Oh.' Pandora immediately made a mental note not to mention the nuns or the fact that she was a Catholic.

'You get in the back, Pandora, and hold on tight. I'll get in the front with Daddy and we'll try and get home alive.'

Pandora hoped Richard was joking.

'The police are always awfully good about my driving, you know,' said Rev. Townsend. Pandora was aware of the huge silver cross he had around his neck. Thirteen brightly sparkling paste diamantés were set into the cross. 'I think they see my cross and my dog collar and assume I am on my way to assist the dead or the dying. I've never been stopped yet.' The vicar put his foot down on the accelerator and tore down the ramp in the car park. 'Bloody thing's been rebuilt since I was last here,' he said as he reversed up yet another ramp.

Richard closed his eyes. He turned to Pandora who was white with fright. 'Just pretend you're at the circus and we're playing bumper cars. We'll get out of here in a few moments. Daddy hates car parks.'

Finally they emerged at the ticket exit. The vicar beamed at the ticket collector. 'Been rebuilding again, have you?' he said jollily.

'Don't think so, sir.' The man looked puzzled.

'Well, never mind. God bless you, my son.' And the vicar roared off down the tunnel and thence out into the very unbeautiful environs of Hounslow proper.

Richard caught a look of surprise on Pandora's face. 'Don't worry, my pet,' he said, smiling at her as the car whizzed down the dismal roads. 'Wait until you get to Devon. God's own country there. You'll love it.'

'Will it be green with little fields and houses with thatched roofs? That's how I've always imagined England.'

'It will be, darling. In fact, the vicarage has a cottage at the gate where the cook and the gardener live, and it has a splendid thatched roof. Doesn't it, Daddy?'

'It has indeed. Drat that fellow! Who does he think he is? I have right of way, young man!' the vicar bellowed out of the rolled down window. 'Absolutely no manners, the young have these days. None at all. Yes, thatched cottage. It's Norfolk reed, of course, but it's so hard to get anybody to do it these days, dear. Richard, you owe your mother an apology. You did not write back after she sent you such a long letter. Do say you're sorry. She gets so frightfully hurt.'

'Daddy, she knows she can telephone me whenever she wants to and I'll pay for the call. Telephones have been invented to put an end to all this boring business of letter-writing. Anyway, Mummy's letter was like a roll-call of cows all about to calf at the same time. It's a positively indecent read. If Aunt Louise has had her varicose veins stripped from the backs of her legs, I should think she might quite like to keep that piece of information to herself. The state of the cook's prostate gland might also be best left a secret. As it is, Mummy sits in that little study of hers, pretends she's Jane Austen, and makes detailed notes on everything.'

'She's started another idea,' Philip said. His voice sank. 'She's gone mad over health food, my dears. We all get lined up in the morning, and asked if we've *been*. If you have, you get let off the prunes, but if you haven't then it's prunes for breakfast. I hate prunes. I really have always hated prunes. All my life, I've hated them.'

'What do you do then, Dad?'

The vicar looked shiftily across his shoulder at Pandora, who was listening entranced. 'You look like a girl who can keep a secret. Promise you won't tell? Scout's honour, and hope to die, and all that? Well, Richard, sometimes I tell a lie.'

'Thank God, Mum's English and doesn't do a forced inspection.' Richard remembered Hortense.

'We get lots of beans to eat as well on this new health food diet.' The vicar sighed. 'Mummy's cut out lard, so I have to sneak down to the cook's cottage for my toast and beef dripping. There's nothing like a piece of bread fried in lard and beef dripping. Oh yes, about all the beans. I have banned beans for Sunday luncheon. I pointed out to your dear mother that the whole row of Townsends including the vicar simply cannot sound off like cannon shot. The last time the bishop was down, she was so thrilled with her newfound recipe for Boston baked beans, the poor fellow could hardly contain himself at evensong. I tried to carry the day by swiftly bringing the congregation to its feet to sing a hymn. The bishop had three hymns in the middle of his sermon. Which rather surprised him. I thought I was rather quick-thinking. On the way out, I explained that several rats had died under the transept. So the day was saved. Your mother was mortified and now we have beans on a Monday when there is no evensong.'

Pandora shook her head. It all sounded quite odd to her, but she needed to take some more pills to keep her body aware of the universe. So she asked if they could stop at a gas station.

'Petrol station in England, my pet.' Richard pointed ahead. 'One coming up,' he said.

While the vicar filled the car, Pandora went into the ladies' room. It was unbelievably dirty. She gingerly took some water from a broken tap in her hand and swallowed her pills. These were her reality pills, a legacy from Marcus, and Pandora hoped very much that with enough support and love from Richard she could kick the habit. She had so many pills by now: ones to put her to sleep, ones to wake her up, ones to help her endure each day. Even now, everything seemed unreal. She felt as if she were sliding in between different lives. Marcus, Marian, sometimes Norman, her mother, and now all this newness. Newness was such dangerous stuff. You never knew what might happen next. Pandora stood staring at her face in the mirror. She opened her slim, brown, snakeskin handbag and replenished her lipstick. She looked fine, except for her eyes. Her pupils were pinpoints, but then only another drug-user would know anything about that. And it didn't sound as if Richard's family did any of that sort of thing.

Mummy looked endearingly like a vicar's wife should. She put both her firm little hands on Pandora's shoulders and hugged her whole-heartedly, kissing Pandora warmly. Pandora was amazed at Molly Townsend's wonderful, soft, russet-apple skin. 'It's all the bloody rain we get down here, darling,' Molly explained.

Pandora looked at Richard. 'Mother swears like a trooper. There's no stopping her. So don't worry about it.'

'Come along, everybody. The whole family is waiting in the dining-room, and they're all awfully hungry.'

'You have cooked Richard and Pandora a proper lunch, haven't you, Mummy?' Philip sounded really anxious. 'You haven't brought them all the way across the ocean to feed them hay, or something like that?'

'Indeed I haven't, Philip. I've cooked Richard his favourite dish.'

Richard grinned. 'Jugged hare,' he said delightedly. 'You see, Pandora, you . . .' And then he thought better of it. 'You'll love it,' he said. 'Tastes like chicken, only better.'

Pandora took his hand.

The whole family resembled a small army of some twenty people, some of whom were children. And there was Aunt Louise minus her varicose veins. Cook looked remarkably cheerful for a man with prostate trouble. Trout, the gardener, grinned at Richard and said, 'Never too old to do a bit of ferreting, sir.'

Richard nodded. 'As soon as we've settled in.' For the moment, the major sweat was to see that the recipe for jugged hare remained a secret between his mother and the cook.

For what seemed like far too long to Pandora, people were shaking her hand, offering her sherry, and talking loudly in a strange sound. They all understood each other without any trouble at all. She listened, trying to follow some of it. Mostly, it seemed, you swallowed all the first consonants of the words and repeated little phrases like *don't you know* several times. Gareth, the brother with four children, didn't have any Rs in his vocabulary at all.

His wife Nan was a social worker. She took an instant dislike to Pandora. Nan's stomach still sagged between her knees from her last pregnancy. She was built like a small bulldozer, and that was how she behaved in life. 'I never take no for an answer', was her motto. She took one look at the sleek and lovely Pandora and decided this was definitely no.

All sound stopped as the cook walked into the dining-room like a drill sergeant. Under his arm he had an evil-looking hammer, its head decently wrapped in chamois-leather. 'Permission to sound for lunch, sir?' he said loudly.

'Permission granted.'

Chalker struck the big Indian gong two thunderous blows. The room shivered, the glass rattled, and even the children fell silent. Philip settled Pandora on his right-hand side and marvelled at his luck that Richard should be such a splendid fellow and bring home such a pretty little thing.

Across the table, Pandora was aware that Nan was watching her closely. Upon hearing that she was a social worker, Pandora realized that she had better be wary. The whole family seemed to talk at the tops of their voices, yelling up and down the table, while bowls of soup followed by the famous jugged hare were passed down the middle. Pandora looked at her plate. The meat looked moist and delicious, drowned in a red wine sauce.

In a rare moment of silence, Richard heard Nigel, Nan's most disgusting child, say loudly, '. . . and Cook told me that we're eating Peter and Flopsy today.'

Up the table was a loud wail. 'We aren't eating Peter and Flopsy today, are we, Grandma?'

'Of course we are, dear. They were just the right weight and in fine good health.'

Rosemary's little six-year-old eyes filled with tears. 'Oh, my poor Peter Rabbit! And Flopsy!' Tears rolled down her cheeks.

'Anyway,' Nigel said, pleased to have been the centre of attention, 'Cook told me they've been cooked in their own blood.'

Pandora blanched. Not only did she know the names of the poor animals she was about to eat, but they were positively swimming in their own blood. These people were barbarous. 'I forgot to tell you,' she smiled at Molly. 'I'm a vegetarian.'

228

'Are you really, darling?' Richard looked at Pandora with surprise. 'You ate a perfectly huge steak the other night.'

Pandora leaned forward. 'I am a vegetarian as of now, Richard.'

'Oh, I see. It's the blood. That's it. You silly little oaf, Nigel. Why couldn't you keep your mouth shut?'

Nan bristled. 'I think it's very clever of him to know how to cook jugged hare. After all, it's a very famous English dish.'

'If you don't mind, Mrs Townsend, I'm a little light-headed and jet-lagged. Could I just skip lunch and go and have a sleep?'

'Of course.' Molly rose from her chair. 'I'll take you up myself.'

Molly chattered all the way along corridors that seemed to meander endlessly, until finally she came to a room with an ebony door handle. 'I think you'll like this room. It is very old and has the best four-poster in the vicarage. Trout has brought in your suitcases. We don't have housemaids, I'm afraid, so you'll have to unpack yourself.' Molly pushed open the door and Pandora had to smile.

It was just the sort of room she had always wanted to own as a child. All blue and white. The curtains on the four-poster bed were tied with swags of white lace. There was a picture window with a deep, wide seat, lined with blue and white cushions. Across the green valleys Pandora could see the cows of her dreams.

'I'll leave you now, dear, and I'll come back for you at tea-time. I say,' she smiled, and her face, gnome-like, puckered up, 'Richard is really gone on you, you know. That's what we used to say in my day. He's really gone on you.'

'Well, to tell you the truth, Mrs . . .'

'Do call me Molly, dear.'

'I'm quite gone on him too.'

'Oh, that's good. He's my last and my favourite. Richard's always been the odd one out, but so funny and so clever. Such a nice boy, too. I must run now and let you have a sleep.' She waved her little fingers and closed the door.

How can the English be such barbarians and so civilized at the same time? Pandora thought. Anyway, she thought as she lay down on the bed, I'm going to sleep.

Chapter Forty-one

Tea was taken in the garden. There again, the whole family turned out and gorged themselves on English scones and clotted cream. Pandora kept wanting to pinch herself. In a fit of educating herself during her Marcus days, she read a lot of H. E. Bates. She also found a book by E. F. Benson which described in wicked detail the daily lives of English village folk. For Pandora, still swaying in and out of reality, watching all these large wicker armchairs set out on an emerald green lawn gave her a headache. Tea, actual English tea, was a horrible tasteless invention, and Cornish clotted cream closely resembled a bad yeast infection, so closely that Pandora refused to try it. 'But you must,' said the ever-helpful Nan. 'Cornish clotted cream is so famous.'

'So is thrush,' Pandora hissed back.

Nan reared back and went a dull red.

The men were over at the ramshackle tennis court. Pandora very much wished she could join them. The children were in the paddocks riding various retired horses that used to belong to their fathers, so there was nothing for it but to sit among this brood of women and try to think of something to say.

Mentally Pandora ticked off the names. Molly, she was good fun. Delilah, married to Michael the banker, had three children. Delilah was very plain. She sat knitting something small, no doubt for Frances who was quite pretty and very pregnant. Frances's husband James, Richard informed her, worked in the Foreign Office, and Frances was frightfully well-connected. At this moment Pandora wished Frances might be frightfully well-connected to a drug-dealer. If she was going to have to sit every afternoon with this group of women, she might die of boredom.

Molly, seeing Pandora's empty plate, said, 'You missed lunch, Pandora, and if you don't like scones and cream, why don't I get you some bran muffins? They're awfully good for you-know-what.'

All the pairs of eyes agreed that *you-know-what* was best served by eating bran muffins. Pandora weakly consented. Anything, she thought, to get through this bitch of an afternoon. Was she really being a bitch herself, because she was jealous that she had no children and never would? She sat back and listened to Delilah talking to Nan.

'I explained to the playgroup teacher that Agatha is four and is really ready to read. She knows all her numbers and all her letters. But the stupid woman said I was just another pushy mother, and what Agatha needed was more time to play in the sandbox.'

'That is drivel,' Molly interrupted. 'All children should be able to read quite easily by the age of four. I taught all mine myself. *Dick and Jane* with their dog Spot. All the boys were wonderful, except of course for Richard. Far too lazy. I started, you know, Pandora, by hitting him on the head with the book when he got it wrong. Bloody waste of time. He has a head as thick as a tree trunk. So in the end I bribed him. Worked like a charm.'

'Always has for Richard,' Nan snapped. 'I hope you've got an awful lot of money, because Richard likes to spend.'

'Nan!' Molly was outraged. 'You mustn't be so vulgar, dear. Richard is the most generous soul I've ever met.'

Delilah laughed. 'Come on, Molly. It's always with other people's money.'

Pandora found this last piece of information interesting. It would be a nice change to be married to a spender, after the miserly rule of Marcus who only put on her back what would make him look good. Even the jewellery had never been given with love. Mostly as bribes. Hush money. Well, he had left her a lot of money and a house to sell, so she had plenty of cash to spare.

'Richard has his job at the *Boston Telegraph*,' Molly reminded Nan.

'Yes, if he keeps it. He's always going on about writing a novel, though.'

Pandora smiled. 'Why not?' she said. 'It would be marvellous if he became a novelist.'

'And pigs might fly.' Nan smiled like a toad that had just swallowed a bejewelled butterfly. 'Richard has the attention span of a six-year-old.'

'I have *what*?'

Nan jumped.

'Nan said you'd never write a novel because you have the attention span of a six-year-old,' Molly reported.

Richard rumpled Nan's hair. 'She's a jealous old cow, aren't you, Nan? Dropping all those calves . . . Ugly little buggers, the lot of them.

Anyway, of course I'm going to write a novel one day. And Nan, I'll be sure to put you in it.'

Nan pushed his hand away. 'Do grow up, Richard.'

'Shan't,' Richard said gleefully. 'Shan't ever grow up. Pandora and I will go to the Serpentine. There's a statue of Peter Pan in Kensington Gardens. Have you read *Peter Pan*?'

Pandora shook her head. 'No, I haven't read anything very much.'

'Well, while we are here, I'll put my whole library at your disposal and you can read *Peter Pan* first. It's my absolute favourite book.'

The men sauntered back and more silver pitchers were produced to fill teapots. Conversation was now on general matters, of cows' hooves, too much rain for hay-making, and the latest betting on the local cricket match. 'Have you been to an English cricket match, Pandora?'

Pandora shook her head. She was glad she was wearing dark glasses.

'Come on, old thing,' Richard said. 'Let's go for a walk and let the whole family get on with their trivia.'

He kissed his mother on the top of her head and Pandora felt very pleased to see how fond they both were of each other. She felt a pang of envy. She stood up and followed Richard up the lawn and across to the tennis court.

'Well, I like her,' Molly said, glaring at Nan. 'And while she is my guest, Nan, you are to be polite to her.'

Nan's lower lip hung down, exposing purple, inflamed gums. 'There is something odd about her, Molly. I smell a rat, and I'm going to get to the bottom of this.'

'I think she's all right,' Frances said. 'She's just a bit common, like most Americans. They can't help it. Mummy says they're a young country.'

'I think she's beautiful,' Philip said, watching Pandora's slim figure hand in hand with Richard. 'I think he's found himself the right girl at last. Make him settle down. That sort of thing.'

'Don't forget, dinner's at eight,' Molly called out to the retreating couple.

Richard waved a hand. 'See why I live in Boston?' he said. 'That's family life. I can only stand it for a few weeks. It's all too claustrophobic for me.'

'I'm not used to so many children,' Pandora said, wishing she had worn more sensible shoes.

'I don't even like children,' Richard said.

'Oh.' Pandora stopped for a moment. 'Is that really true, Richard?'

He nodded. 'Honestly. Occasionally I find a brat I like, but mostly they are all of them awful until they are about eighteen. Then you can talk to them.'

'I can't have children, Richard.' Pandora's heart was beating with fright.

'Oh good.' Richard smiled. 'That's another reason for marrying you. All those other women I nearly married kept insisting that they must have brats. An awful idea!'

They were walking across the moorland. The bracken was thick and soft. Quite naturally they sat down together. Richard gathered Pandora into his arms. He kissed her very gently on the forehead and then on her lips. Pandora drew back. She could feel the beginning of the sexual heat in his embrace. 'I'm not ready yet, Richard. I'm afraid it will take time for me to feel anything. Those were such awful, degrading years.'

'I know, darling,' Richard said. 'And I can wait quite easily. After all, we have the rest of our lives together.'

Pandora lay in the bracken with her head on his breast, and she thought: This kind of happiness is too fragile. It's as if a glass-blower has me on the end of his rod and he is blowing joy into my soul, and any minute now he'll give too strong a puff and I'll shatter into sharp, tiny shards. All this will have just been a dream. She snuggled into Richard who was quite happily asleep.

The sun went down and the wind grew wilder. Pandora stroked Richard's face. 'Where am I?' he said, looking puzzled. Then he grinned. 'I'm in the arms of the woman I love. Come along. It's time to go home and change for dinner. After dinner I'm going to spare you the family card games tonight. I'll take you up to your virginal little bed and I'll read *Peter Pan* to you.'

'How they all can eat!' Pandora remarked to Richard as they sneaked off upstairs after saying good night to Molly.

'Mummy, do tell Nan that I can't wait to do dreadfully salacious things to Pandora in her bedroom. Won't you, darling?'

Molly giggled. 'It's so nice to have you back, Richard. The others have all got so stuffy over mortgages and education and all that sort of thing. Good night, Pandora, and sleep well.'

Richard lay on the big four-poster with the book in his hands. He looked at the familiar drawing of a naked Peter Pan sitting on a toadstool playing his panpipes. Pandora went into the bathroom, had a shower, and chose her prettiest pink silk negligée. She brushed out her hair and sprayed herself with Shalimar. As she pushed open the door of the bathroom, she saw Richard's face. Across his rugged features there appeared something resembling awe. 'I have never seen anything so beautiful in my life, Pandora.'

Pandora moved towards the bed. She tucked herself into the thick white sheets and she smiled. 'Nobody will believe you are just reading me a goodnight story.'

'Who cares?' said Richard.

Pandora listened to Richard reading. As Peter Pan flew away, she felt her heart might break, but she sat very still with her long hair covering her face. When Richard got to the moment when Peter flew back to his mother's house only to see her with another baby in the nursery, with Peter's entrance through the window blocked by iron bars, Pandora could bear it no longer. Wildly sobbing, she threw herself into Richard's arms.

He dropped the book in astonishment. 'Pandora, it's just a story.'

'No, it's not,' she sobbed. 'It's not a story at all. It's the story of people like me, unwanted people. We're all over the world, Richard. You can find us anywhere, the Army of the Unwanted.' She was hysterical by now.

Richard tried hugging her and rocking her gently. 'You're not unwanted, Pandora. You're wanted by me. For ever. We'll be married. I'll always love you. I promise you.'

Pandora could not be comforted.

On the island of Little Egg, Julia reported back to Janine. 'It's painful to watch her cry like that.'

'I know,' Janine said. 'But it will straighten out that part of her life. She has put it so far away that only in this kind of trance can she remember these things. And maybe she needs to grieve. Poor Pandora. But it's not long now, and she will be back with us.'

Chapter Forty-two

Staying awake at all was becoming a real problem for Pandora. Blotted out in sleep, she felt safe and comfortable. Her huge pill bottle she carried carefully everywhere. Once Richard, after reading her *The Little Prince*, asked if he might make love to her. He did so very gently. Pandora reassured him that she enjoyed their lovemaking, but the truth was she had felt nothing. No sensations at all, except to be glad to hold his head in her arms and to kiss his calm clear eyes and watch the joy on his face as he came with happy cries of relief. 'Shhh,' Pandora said and she put her hand over his mouth. 'You'll wake up Nan.'

Richard threw himself back on his pillow. 'She's probably already awake with her bum in the air and her ear on the floor. Who cares?' He leaned over to kiss her, but Pandora was asleep. He frowned. He was worried about Pandora's sleeping, but then she had been through an awful ordeal, poor thing. He looked at her lying there and he hugged himself with satisfaction. He was in love, really and truly in love with a wonderful woman. Next week they would fly back to Boston and begin their lives together. Marian had been sent instructions to pack all Pandora's possessions and have them sent to Richard's apartment. Marian wrote a short note to Pandora, explaining that she really didn't want to leave her home and her family, but she would always think of Pandora and pray for her.

Pandora was glad to see two of the families leave the vicarage. That just left Delilah and Nan. Molly on her own was good fun, and Pandora enjoyed her earthy country humour.

The day she and Richard were to fly was a particularly hot day. There was nothing unusual about the day except that Pandora awoke with a headache. It nagged at her persistently and she knew, however much she might try to avoid it, she would have to face Nan's piggy face at the tea-table. She took an extra Valium.

As she sat with the sun beating down on her head, she felt faint. Within a few seconds, she had tumbled to the ground.

Richard leapt up from his chair, picking her up and carrying her into the hall. He put her down gently on a Victorian chaise-longue. Molly rushed off to ring the family doctor, and Nan took her long-awaited opportunity to get to the bottom of the trouble. She opened Pandora's capacious handbag and there she seized upon a large bottle full of multi-coloured pills. Nan's eyes gleamed. She stomped into the hall, leaving the handbag lying on the lawn. 'You needn't ask a doctor, Molly my dear. Here,' she said, waving the bottle of pills in Molly's astonished face. 'Look at this.'

'They're pills, aren't they?' said Philip.

'Yes, indeed. They are pills. But let me tell you what kind of pills. Those are *drugs*,' Nan hissed.

'Shut up, Nan,' Richard said. 'Shut up, you stupid fat-mouth, you bitch.'

'That woman,' Nan's mouth was slathering with moisture, 'is a drug-addict.'

Pandora opened her eyes. 'Where am I?' she asked, looking up at a row of concerned faces.

'You fainted,' Richard said gently, holding her hand, 'and I carried you in. The doctor will be here in a minute.'

'My handbag, Richard . . .' Pandora felt panic-stricken.

'You won't find what you're looking for in your handbag, Pandora. This is what you're looking for, isn't it? You're a drug-addict. Come on, admit it. That's what you are.'

Pandora looked at Nan in dumb misery.

Richard grabbed the bottle from Nan and then hit her hard. Nan fell on the floor, her mouth open wide with surprise. 'Gareth, what on earth are you going to do about this?' Nan gasped.

'Nothing,' said her husband. 'I should have done it myself years ago. Sorry, Pandora. Nan's an interfering old bitch.'

Pandora's eyes filled with tears. Molly gave her a big hug. 'Don't worry, darling. Don't be embarrassed. I used to be sloshed regularly on whisky for years. I was young and the vicar's wife and had to go and visit smelly, bad-tempered old people. All that going to church to keep Philip happy . . . I started with a nip in the morning, then a nip at elevenses, then a nip at lunch, another at tea-time. Eventually it was nip-nip-nip, all day long. And I'd fall asleep and never hear the babies cry or anything. Marvellous time I had, absolutely marvellous. But the bishop got to hear about it. One day I was so pissed, I stuck the two youngest in the pram and went down the village to do some shopping. Unfortunately,

I forgot to put any clothes on. So the bishop had hundreds of telephone calls. He was forced to speak to Philip, and I had to give it up. Which reminds me, the sun is over the yardarm. So why don't you and I have a large gin and tonic? I giggle on gin. Always have.'

Pandora smiled.

'The doctor will be here in a minute,' Molly continued, 'and he can join us for a drink. He'll be awfully understanding about pills. Really, I wish he'd give Nan pills, sanctimonious little bitch.' Molly was happily bumbling along to the drawing-room and Richard had his arm around Pandora's waist.

That explains all the sleeping, he thought. Poor girl.

Dr Jimson listened later to Pandora as she sat and told him her life story. Quite why it tumbled out the way it did amazed her, but he was a calm, very gentle man with owl-grey eyes set over a big nose, and he sucked his pipe as he listened.

'It's no wonder you're addicted to those pills,' he said. 'In my opinion, there are two ways out. You can go into hospital and gently be weaned off them, or you can throw the lot down the lavatory, go through a few hellish weeks when you won't sleep and you'll think you're going to die, but you won't die. And the day will come when you will look back and wonder why it took you so long to take the leap.'

Pandora smiled.

Dr Jimson looked at her very seriously. 'I hear you're thinking of marrying young Richard.'

Pandora nodded happily.

'Take my advice, young lady. I brought the lad into the world, you know. Molly's last child. She spoiled him dreadfully. Don't marry him, dear. He's not marriage material.'

Pandora's face fell. 'I'm sure I can change all that.'

Dr Jimson shook his head. 'I've seen hundreds and hundreds of hopeful brides say those very words to me. Years later I've treated them for their depressions, for asthma, for cancers . . . You know cancerous relationships breed cancerous cells. I've always said that. Not all cancers, of course. No, enjoy Richard. Have fun with him, but take my word for it. He's not marriage material.'

Pandora stood up. 'Well,' she said, 'thank you. I'll certainly think about what you said. I've made two mistakes already, and I don't want to make a third.'

*

Dr Jimson stayed for dinner. He seemed very fond of Richard. Pandora was puzzled. Nan and her family had left the vicarage, much to everyone's relief.

Later on that night, Pandora said, 'Do you think I should go to a clinic to get off these things, Richard? Or should I throw them down the toilet?'

'After the last experience you had in a clinic, darling, I think you'd be much better off throwing them all down the loo. You do that now. I'll flush, then we will get into bed and I'll read you *Sir Gawain and the Green Knight*. It's such an exciting story.'

They both leaned over the lavatory bowl while Richard gave the handle a huge tug. There was a roar of water and coloured pills, and a roar in Pandora's head. What had she done?

Chapter Forty-three

'Look, Richard,' Pandora said after a night of dreadful sleeplessness. 'I think I can get used to doing without the pills, but Dr Jimson rather worried me.'

'Did he, darling?' Richard was running his hands over Pandora's back. 'You have such lovely skin,' he said. 'It's silky and soft like baby's skin. I could stroke you for hours.'

'Oh, do listen, Richard. I'm serious. Dr Jimson likes you, but he warned me not to marry you.'

'Did he really? I say. That's a bit much. Don't let that worry you, darling. He's an old grouch. Used to go and steal his chickens. He took ages to find out it was me.'

'Why on earth would you steal his chickens?'

'To eat them, of course. We used to have midnight parties when we were teenagers. All my brothers would raid old Cook's larder. I'd poach a salmon, and them strangle a few chickens and meet the girls in the woods and have a huge bonfire and drink lemon shandy.'

Pandora had to smile. 'Back home,' she said, 'it wasn't so innocent. We all drank tequila and had sex.'

'Tell me about it.' Richard pulled Pandora close. 'When I got to Boston, well, it was like Christmas every day. Everywhere there were girls with their nipples bursting out of their T-shirts, and their shorts were so tight you didn't even need to guess the colour of their pubic hair. There I was, an eligible English bachelor. It was like a non-stop orgy. Lovely, really, come to think of it. Quite lovely. After all those years of fiddling with bra straps and straining to get a finger in between the thighs, and all the ahhs and ohhs, and mostly nos. You see, English mums have a vice-like grip on their girls' vaginas. No sex until you are at least announced in the *Telegraph* and a picture of your bride appears as a virgin in *Horse and Hound*. After the engagement's bruited about, lists go up in Fortnum and Mason, and Peter Jones, and all the silver toast racks start arriving. So if a poor chap changes his mind after a few bonks, he's considered a dreadful scoundrel. America was such a wonderful change.'

'Richard, stop trying to distract me. No, Dr Jimson thinks you were very spoiled by your mother and that you will never really grow up.'

'Pandora . . .' Then he giggled, but not completely. 'You'd hate it if I became all posh and never smiled, wouldn't you?'

'I would,' she said. 'Oh, what I'd give for some tranquillizers.'

Richard hugged her. 'Let's get up, eat a huge breakfast, and then go for a long walk. Tomorrow we're off back to Boston. You'll be so busy sorting out the apartment you won't have time to miss your pills.'

Pandora groaned. 'I hope so,' she said slowly. 'I dearly hope so.'

Pandora did miss the pills. For nights she could not sleep. She clung to Richard during those long nights. 'The pain isn't a kind of pain I understand,' she said. 'It's more like I'm all exposed. All my nerve-endings are raw. I feel that if I drew my fingernails up my arms, they'd leave tracks.' She couldn't eat. She got thinner and thinner. She stared at herself in the mirror of horror. She needed the pills, her brain told her. They kept her away from the pain.

'The pain of what?' Richard asked after a particularly difficult night.

'The pain of just being alive. That's all.'

On Monica's first visit, Pandora knew she would be delighted with Richard. Their apartment was long and elegant. The windows looked over Boston Common. The furniture had been sent over from England. Mostly early, well-carved, Victorian furniture that Pandora loved to polish. To begin with she was very lonely, but then, in a sense, glad. She needed that time to herself to throw off the effect of the pills. If she found herself shaking and vomiting, at least she need not explain. She did get a letter from Vincent Singer telling her that the divorce was final and that the house was sold. Half a million from the sale of the house was hers. An additional quarter of a million from the sale of the contents was included in the cheque. Richard was delighted.

Monica, indeed, was just as delighted with Richard as she was with the news that her erstwhile useless daughter was now a rich woman. Monica stayed in the apartment for a gruelling two weeks, finding much to complain about, but finally departing with a sum of money to secure herself a house of her own and security in her old age. 'See that you don't louse this one up, honey,' were her cheerful words as she left.

'You get married as soon as you can. Men like Richard don't grow on trees, you know.'

Pandora nodded wearily. She was doing her best. Now the divorce was through, organized specially by Vincent Singer. Her ex-husband was somewhere safe in Mexico, so slowly the dreams and nightmares of Marcus were beginning to fade and a new life starting to emerge.

Richard insisted on buying Pandora a magnificent diamond engagement ring. Slowly she began to meet his friends. Peggy and Roy, both friends from the office, she liked immensely. Peggy often came round at the weekends and took Pandora off on shopping sprees. Richard's habit was to get up late at weekends and go off with his men friends to watch basketball in the winter or the Red Sox in the summer. Sundays were devoted to golfing. 'What do women do if they don't have kids?' Pandora asked after the first six months of weekend widowhood.

Peggy shrugged. 'I don't know,' she said. 'Roy and I have been "seeing" each other for the last six years. That means I see him in the office. He sees me at my apartment, or we go out to dinner. Sometimes I go to his apartment, but his habits are gross.'

Pandora nodded. 'Richard's a bit like that. I've got a permanent stoop from picking up his clothes. I guess we women go out shopping, take each other out to lunch, and just wait. At least women with kids have their kids for company.'

'Yeah,' Peggy said, 'but lots of those men screw on the side.'

'Thank God,' Pandora said, 'Richard would never do a thing like that. He's untidy. I never know where he is or when he's coming home, but I trust him absolutely.'

Pandora was saying the same thing five years later. Peggy and Roy got married in those five years, but were soon separated. Peggy was inconsolable. 'I don't know where I went wrong,' she said. 'Roy just said he felt our marriage was Claustrophobia City and he valued his independence.' By now Peggy had two little girls, so Pandora found herself visiting her very housebound friend. Loyally she invited Peggy regularly to dinner parties and to events she attended with Richard. They had married a year after Peggy and Roy, but to Pandora marriage made little notable difference to their relationship except that they moved to a much bigger house and they opened a joint bank account.

Pandora found her life quite full. She helped in the gift shop at a little art gallery in the mornings and she spent the afternoons getting ready to entertain Richard's increasingly wide circle of friends. On several occasions Vincent Singer sent large cheques from the sale of the shares, as stipulated in the divorce settlement. Now they could and did entertain in great style.

Hortense had returned to haunt Richard and to amuse Pandora who enjoyed her energetic, genuinely Bohemian attitude to life. 'You're spoiling that guy, Pandora,' Hortense would say as she watched Pandora buy Richard yet another silk shirt from Turnbull and Asser.

'But then, he spoils me too,' she said. 'He's always buying me things or making surprises for me.'

Hortense made a face. 'Are you sure you're happy?'

'What an awful question, Hortense! Who is happy? You tell me. What is happiness supposed to be? An endless amount of orgasms? I have those, though Richard's been very tired lately. I must get him a check-up. A new dress? A trip? I don't know, Hortense. Those are the sort of questions you struggle with when you are eighteen. But when you're moving from your twenties to your thirties, you just get on with life.'

Hortense lay on a pink silk sofa, her grubby skirt over her chubby knees and her sweat-stained armpits exposing bushes of hair. 'I think being happy is finding a kind of peace within yourself. You know when the priest says, "The peace of God that passeth all understanding"? That's where I want to be, on that threshold, my feet planted firmly. Sometimes I get it when I'm painting in the middle of the night, just me and the canvas and the soft stroke of the brush and the smell of paints. Lovely, it is.'

Pandora smiled. 'You're lucky,' she said. 'I have this dream that one day Richard and I will find our island in the Caribbean and there we will find our perfect peace together . . . I wonder where he is, Hortense. I've got ten people coming for cocktails, and eight to sit for dinner. I do hope he hasn't forgotten.'

Richard arrived half an hour late with a bunch of roses and a bottle of Shalimar. 'Don't be cross, darling. I'm not late. I set out to get a little pressie for you, and the Shalimar was hard to find.'

All the guests looked hot, except Pandora and Richard. They were a legendary couple in Boston. Everyone envied Richard. He had a wife who adored him, who went to watch the Red Sox with him, knew all their batting averages, and, in the freezing winter, loyally sat watching the Celtics play basketball. Richard, unlike most other men in his newspaper office, also awoke to a cooked breakfast and always knew, whether they were entertaining or not, that he would return home to a three-course gourmet dinner.

The group surrounding Pandora and Richard was now becoming more 'European'. That impressed Pandora's friends immensely. Richard remained the flame in the centre of the circle. The days and the weeks and the months and the years carouselled by in a series of trips, operas, dinner parties, visits to England to see Molly and Philip. For Richard's thirty-sixth birthday, Pandora bought him a red Cadillac. The car stood in the drive of their house as she drew Richard to the window and opened the curtains. His joy in her present was all that she hoped it would be. For the next few weeks, Richard was somewhere in Boston in his red car. Friends called up to make jokes about it. In particular, Gretchen Müller.

Gretchen and her husband Friedrich were newcomers to the group. Friedrich was head of a German banking corporation. He rather frightened Pandora. He had a wedge-shaped face with watery blue eyes. His eyelashes were sparse and very short. He was thin. His body was military and he barked rather than talked. She had no reason to dislike him. He was well-behaved in a stern, Prussian manner. It was Gretchen she so much admired. Gretchen, unlike Hortense who was one of life's happy failures, was a true survivor. 'My people died in the camps,' she said in her sibilant German accent. 'I feel guilty to be alive. To love, to eat, to have sex.' Those lines usually appeared at the end of some dinner party when Gretchen was well-tanked-up and about to persuade some man to go down the hall with her to find her host's nearest bedroom for a quick fuck. 'What is good food without a good fuck?' she would demand. Usually Friedrich yanked her away before the event took place. Sometimes he was not fast enough and an exhausted phone call from Gretchen the next morning gave Pandora a chance to hand out absolution.

She talked a lot to Richard about Gretchen. 'I really admire her, you know. She just gets on with life. She's so vibrant . . . Darling, what would you like for breakfast?'

Richard turned over. 'Oh, I don't know. You choose.'

'Let me think.' Pandora smiled. 'Bacon and fried tomatoes. There. Did I read your mind?'

Richard muffled his head into the pillow. 'You always can,' he said.

Pandora got up, put on her silk peignoir, and went towards the kitchen. She noticed, as she passed the roll-away writing desk, a large amount of bills sitting up at the top of the table. Idly she ran her hands through the pile. Richard hated administration of any sort but wouldn't allow a secretary to take care of their personal business, so Pandora always ended up paying the bills. As it was, he objected to the presence of the maid who came three times a week to clean the house. 'Why should I pick up your clothes, Richard, when you always drop them on the floor?' she had said many times. Pandora could hear a sharpness in her own voice that she disliked. 'All you have to do is to walk as far as the laundry basket.'

'Don't nag,' would be Richard's reply, and his eyes would widen and his tone become harsh.

She complained to Gretchen sometimes. 'Oh pooh,' was Gretchen's advice. 'Throw the clothes in the fireplace and burn them. That would teach him a lesson.'

'No, it wouldn't,' Pandora said. 'He'd just go out in his red car with his line of credit cards and buy more. I've heard of women addicted to shopping, but Richard is ridiculous.'

By this time, Gretchen, Friedrich, Pandora and Richard were really a foursome. Gretchen kept Richard laughing with her bawdy stories and unpredictable behaviour, while Friedrich and Pandora tended to talk about music and the art galleries. Pandora had found a great interest in German *Lieder* and Friedrich suggested she join a group that met regularly on Thursday nights. Richard seemed amenable. She usually came back flushed and happy with the haunting sounds of the birds in the German valleys singing in her ears.

For many of their ten years together, Pandora was really happy with Richard. They shared the same love of music: Mozart, jazz, opera. They travelled well together and life seemed like a beautiful multi-reflective golden ball that hung suspended over both their heads. Pandora wanted the magic years to go on for ever, like the picnics they took with them in an English wicker picnic hamper.

As Richard grew older, Pandora saw him change slowly. Many times he was rude and disdainful, but she passed it off as just a temporary mood. Something upset him at the office. She noticed that he very easily became jealous of the attention she received from other men. Slowly she pulled back into her shadow, letting Richard tell his interminably long stories. Sometimes she tried to break in to save Richard from embarrassment: she could see the bored glaze in people's eyes. But Richard seemed impervious, blind to their reactions. The endless flow of his self-important, self-obsessed dialogue washed over Pandora at all hours of the day and night. The only time he stopped talking was when he watched television.

Erosion was the only word Pandora could think of. Pandora knew she made Richard impatient and angry. She also knew that she found Richard stunted and childish. From a past that had once been a paradise of love and laughter, shared adventure, and at times great empathy and passion, the desert proceeded to erode outwards from the middle of the paradise.

It began between the sheets, where two bodies no longer fitted like shoebags, where backs were turned and pillows acted as fortresses between the two parties. Breakfast was no longer a shared event, and dinners alone were silent and angry affairs. Pandora was bitterly unhappy and retreated into her world of art and music. Richard was home less and less. Hortense, ever able to home in on trouble, said Richard was going into a mid-life crisis. He did talk more and more of giving up his job and going off to write his book. Pandora shrugged. 'If that's what he really wants to do, he should do it,' she said. Never for one moment did she think that it was Gretchen whom he wanted to go with him . . .

That guilty day of discovery was now clearly in front of her mind's eye again . . . The complacent look on Gretchen's face when she said, 'He will be joining *us* in a moment,' and, later that night, the scarlet evidence . . . There was a moment when a hand reached out and plucked the splinter of pain from Pandora's soul . . .

She began to stir in the sand. Janine and Julia were bending over her. 'She is coming back to us,' Janine said. She sat on the sand. 'Bring her back slowly with the drum.'

Pandora, still standing in the room in Boston, heard the call of the drum. It set up such a yearning in her that she was unable even to grieve for her loss of Richard. She listened while he explained his unmet needs. Pandora was no fun any longer. She was predictable. He, Richard, needed to go out and meet life with someone like Gretchen, who would show him how to live, really live. Their lives had become humdrum, boring. Pandora nodded. She knew all these things as a mother knows her child. He must go, and so should she. She, to follow the call to the ocean, and somewhere to meet the wish of her life – her dolphins. And he, with Gretchen, to find what he was looking for.

'Life,' Pandora said, aping Hortense's voice, 'is a series of journeys. Goodbye, Richard.' And she kissed him.

She ran downstairs and threw her suitcase into a waiting cab. The last she saw of Richard was his white face staring at her from the window of the apartment.

'Where to?' the cab-driver asked.

'Logan Airport, please.'

'OK, you got it.'

Another door shut, she thought, crossing her legs and looking at her expensive silk tights from Paris. She was wearing a black soft suede coat with matching black boots. Her handbag was from Cartier and her watch from a little watchmaker in London's Burlington Arcade. She appreciated the look of respect in the cab-driver's eye.

'You're one hell of a classy dame,' he said as she left the cab. 'D'you wanna night out on the town?'

'No, thank you,' Pandora said, grinning. 'I've got a hot date on an island with some dolphins.'

The cab-driver watched Pandora walk away. Some guy got lucky, he thought. Look at the way she swings her ass . . .

Pandora felt her eyes open. She gazed at the faces hanging over her. 'I'm back,' she said, and she stretched herself out. She felt long and lean, like an earthworm finding a sodden piece of earth. All her body was loose, all tensions gone. Like after making love with Ben. She could see Ben's face looking down at her. His face was full of concern. 'I'll carry you home,' he said. 'You'll be weak.'

Janine smiled at Pandora. 'I'll be over with bush tea to get your appetite started again, and then you can begin to tell us what you learned.'

'Not tonight,' Ben said very firmly. 'Tonight Pandora needs a good rest away from you and all your witches and spells.'

Even Ben admitted to himself that, during their lovemaking, Pandora felt free to take her pleasure from his body at her own will. Before he had often felt that her great need was to please him and that for her there had always been a slight holding back. Now she lay curled up beside him, not in her usual defensive attitude with her fists balled and pulled in front of her face, but with her hands rested relaxed on the clean sheet. Her breath was calm and steady. Whatever happened in that cave did her good, freed something inside her. And for that Ben was grateful. He might never find out what it was, because he would be excluded from the talking by the women, but he had to admit something had worked.

Chapter Forty-four

Over the next few days, Pandora felt herself very light-headed. Janine and Jane spent those days cleaning out the cave again. 'We need to clear it of all your old memories,' Janine said to a mystified Pandora. 'After all, you wash yourself and your body after a hard day's work, don't you? Well, this is the same idea. We will give the cave a good psychic cleaning out and then you can recount what you think you've learned.'

'Funny,' Pandora was sitting at the bar. 'I'm not frightened all the time.' She was watching Lizzie, hands on her hips, having a screaming match with Lionel Marshal, the manager. 'Your stinking white bitch of a mistress is taking jobs away from people on Little Egg! You carry down all these white-haired blue-eyes from your fucking American corporation and you pay us cleaners less than the minimum wage.'

Lionel's face was purple.

'You see, before the dreaming,' Pandora continued, 'I'd be scared to see a man with an angry face, Janine. Now I think Lizzie's absolutely right. Lionel would never get away with his behaviour in America. Also, I have made a decision that as soon as we have had this session, I'm going out to visit Dad and spend time with him.'

Janine stopped pouring a drink. 'I'd stay away from here, Pandora, until after the hurricane season. Octo and I waited for the singing turtle to go. He was lying on the crest of the wave and he took a huge breath and then we followed in the boat and watched as long as we could with the sonar. He went deep, really, really deep, and that usually means there'll be bad hurricanes this season. Several people on the islands heard the duppies howling when he left. They were those who died in the '32 hurricane whose bodies are still in the caves.'

Pandora pulled at her beer. 'I couldn't stay away that long, Janine. I'll be here. If a hurricane comes, I'll be here with all of you. I'd feel much worse if I were somewhere else worrying about you. Besides, I've learned not to be afraid any more. The only thing I haven't decided is whether I want to stay married to Richard.'

'Hush,' Janine said. 'We will talk about that in the cave.'

'OK. I'll go over to my post box and see if there's anything from Mom. She's too busy on the phone to Chuck to bother with me, which is a good thing. Then I'll find Eve, my diving buddy. She's back for a week, and I'll go diving.'

Way down, hanging in space off an underwater wall, Pandora felt the peace again. For the moment she remembered nothing of the dreaming, but even Eve noticed a change in her. 'You look radiant, honey,' she said as they kissed.

'I feel radiant. I don't quite know what it is. It feels like I have a small flower growing inside me. It's still very fragile, but it is there. Before there were only stones and old broken bits of bottles and pills glued together, but I feel as if I've been gardened. My inner self has been raked clean.'

She was thinking of her flower as she hung in the water and then shot off sideways after signing to Eve. Where was the turtle? she wondered. She moved back to the reef and hung over a multi-faceted fire coral. The usual blue-spotted parrot fish swam around her, demanding attention. Then a big grouper with a massive pout nosed at her hand. She held it open to show him she had no food for him. He swam away, disgusted. Angel fish swished by, far too beautiful to acknowledge the intrusion of an awkward human. Pandora grinned.

She rejoined Eve and signed for home. Slowly they swam back to the shore and then lifted their masks and sat in the warm shallows. Ben's barracuda friend came out from under the wreck to say hello. 'Gee, Eve, do you remember how frightened I was of that poor barra?'

'You were scared of your own shadow, honey,' Eve said.

'Well, I'm not now. I'm writing to my dad tonight and asking if I can go and see him next month. Imagine! I know where my dad is and I can visit him.' She sat gazing at the sea and the long arm of the reef that protected the island's south side from bad weather. 'They say this hurricane season's going to be bad.'

Eve nodded. 'I've heard that as well. We'll be boarding up in Florida. I've got all my fresh water and cans of food ready. My old man says I've got enough supplies for a year.'

Pandora could see Ben's dive-boat coming in through the reef. 'Ben's back,' she said. 'I'd better get home and cook.' She looked at Eve. 'Now

I go home to cook for Ben because I want to. I don't feel I *have* to, and that's a big difference.'

Eve chuckled. 'I just get takeaway.' She waved as Pandora waded out of the water, pulling off her diving gear.

Chapter Forty-five

It was a creamy, starlit night the night that Janine and her sisters took Pandora back up to the cave where she had redreamed her life. As they walked up the mountain, snatches and visions of scenes from the dreams came back to Pandora. Janine looked at her. 'Don't try to organize your mind, Pandora. Just leave all the information alone; when you feel ready, it will come out like a piece of silk pulled through a golden ring. Don't edit information, or you will change the reality of your past with the knowledge of the present. Let that happen gradually.'

'You know a lot about this sort of stuff, don't you, Janine?'

'Yes, I do. All our family do, but it doesn't make us any wiser in our own relationships. You seem puzzled, Pandora.'

Damn. Pandora blushed, hoping the shadows would hide her embarrassment. 'Well, I guess with all that knowledge, I wonder why you still act as a prostitute, I mean go with people for money.'

Janine paused for a moment. 'It's the only way I can make enough money for Octo and myself to eventually retire and run a bar. He smuggles drugs or whatever he can do to make money for us both.'

'That's not very moral, is it?' Pandora said, ashamed to hear the words coming out of her mouth.

'No, it's not at all moral, Miss America. But who are you to judge, after your long history?'

'I know,' Pandora said softly. 'That is something I'm beginning to realize.'

'We're nearly there,' Janine said.

Jane carried the drums.

'No white cockerels?' Pandora said. 'Thank God.'

'No, this is just a private way to talk on an island where even the stones have ears. Julia cooked a conch soup with dumplings, and we can just relax.'

Pandora felt an unfamiliar swing in her walk. Her limbs felt as if they were at one with the mountain. Before the dream, she would have struggled up the mountain, her body feeling so alien to the terrain that the two elements would fight all the way up, until she reached the destination dishevelled and panting. Tonight she walked with the mountain and it reminded her of those long rolling pads at the airport. 'I'm going to see my dad next weekend,' she said happily as they sighted the opening of the cave.

Julia, carrying the pan of soup, stepped into the cave, followed by Janine and then Jane. Pandora stopped for a moment and looked out and then down to the jagged coral below her. The sea stretched far away and the moon hung full and satisfied before her. Is all this really happening? she wondered. She heard the flutter and the furious clicking of an owl's beak. Beside her hand a white luminous flower gave out a powerful smell. The sweetness of the summer trailing the carrion rotting smell of the dead leaves of winter. Yep, she thought. It is all happening. She drew a deep breath and slipped into the cave.

For a moment she blinked while she got used to the darkness. Then Jane lit two lamps and the shadows flittered on the walls of the cave. The floor had been swept flat and clean, so her sleeping shape and pillow of wild herbs were gone. Jane sat quietly with her drums while Julia went to the back of the cave and brought out four bowls and spoons. 'Let's eat first and then talk.'

Janine felt about in the capacious pockets of her skirts. 'I have a bottle of grapetree wine with me. Miss Rosie gave it to me. She made it herself,' She passed the bottle to Pandora.

The wine was harsh but thirst-quenching. Pandora handed the bottle on to Julia. They ate mostly in silence. Pandora wondered where to begin.

After Julia removed the dishes, Pandora leaned her back against the wall of the cave and listened to Jane playing on the drums. Was there really the broken heart of a murdered woman known as the Mother of the Earth in those drums, she wondered, or was this dreaming and drugging and sleeping all a form of Haitian play-acting? Pandora found herself beginning to feel quite irritated and sceptical. What was she doing here with these women? Then slowly, as the sound of the two drums mixed together, she felt her anger subside and she felt her armour plate begin to open.

'All my life,' she began, 'I felt I was nobody. I was an abortion that went wrong. I really have no right to be here tonight, but I fought and I manifested myself against my mother's will. I learned in my dream that those people like me, who have to manifest themselves because they are unwanted, manufacture a way of life to keep themselves safe.

They have no other mandate for life. There is no pleasure in their being born, no rejoicing. They don't know what pleasure is. So they do not trust this thing called joy or pleasure, but feel safer in misery and sorrow. Misery and sorrow are with us always. Joy and laughter can quickly be removed. Also, because I was never held or kissed by my mother, and my father for a long time was forbidden even to pick me up, I knew little about affection, except for punching and slapping. That was love and attention. I could see all this happening in the dream, but mostly I saw how I never gave myself permission to give my life any direction. I just walked along the precipice of my mother's violence, my father's disappearance, and then into a life with Norman. I knew when I was in the dream I should never have married him. But inertia was always my way out, so I just followed the track that took me to Norman's bed. And had Marcus not been where he was, I would still be in Norman's bed, or dead from the beating.

'Oh, you have no idea how grateful I was! Norman wanted me and I had been grateful to him, even for the beatings. He felt enough for me to hurt me. He was always sorry, and often he cried when he saw what he had done. I licked the tears off his face many times, and I forgave him. Unlike my mother, who would never forgive me. I was glad Norman was born and wanted me enough to marry me. I was even more grateful when I discovered that Marcus wanted me as well. This highly trained Harvard psychiatrist wanted this woman from the train tracks. I was also, for once, doing something my mother approved of.

'I watched myself take the pills in the dream. I watched the other women in the group take the pills, too. For a moment I felt, as we sat in our "group circle", as if we were all mostly human but our souls were unmanifested, so we had no control over ourselves or our lives and we mostly deserved what happened to us. Marcus never said he was sorry. He just bought sorry presents and I was grateful. No one had ever given me fur coats and pearls; nor had I pictured in my wildest imagining that there would be anybody from the train tracks of my world who could ever afford to give me things to make me beautiful. If Marcus hadn't been caught, I would still be there, or dead from the pills.

'I watched myself meeting with Richard. Here was someone who made me laugh. Here was someone who taught me to make love gently. Took away all the pain and the violence.' She paused. 'And I did it again.'

'What did you do again?' Janine asked.

253

'I made him central to my life, as I made my father the centre post of my whole existence. So when he left, he took the central part of me with him and I was an empty gourd. The sounds I made were hollow. The voice I spoke with had no depth to it. I didn't even have seeds to bear children with. So when I married Richard, I was a rich woman. With Marcus, every painful sexual excess had a price attached to it, a credit card excursion to a shop. With Richard it was different. Richard liked to play. I was grateful to be taught how to play, so again I gave him everything I had. To begin with, he took things diffidently. And then he became more arrogant. The money enabled him to be the centre of attention, and I saw in the dream how quickly we *were* the in-couple in Boston. I also saw myself in the shadow of the crowd. Soon I un-manifested myself until I was an excellent hostess. I ran a beautiful house, and he had sex if he felt like it. I saw the desert in our bed and in our life and there was nothing I could do to stop it. Gretchen was no surprise. At least she had life. I had none. I was cold and worn out.'

'What did you learn from the dream, Pandora?'

Pandora took a deep breath and from somewhere deep down inside her a much stronger voice spoke. 'I learned that I do exist and I need not merge into a man to feel I am alive. I learned that I am a person in my own right. I am not just a couple, or a *we* or an *us*. What I do is mine and can't be taken away. What I must do now is go and find my father. I feel that once I liberate him from that great lie my mother told him, both of us will be healed.'

'And Richard?' Jane said softly.

'I don't know yet. I really don't know.'

Jane calmed the drums and for a moment the dying music held the women together in a spell of peace, a benediction for women everywhere.

'You know,' Janine said, 'it's very different between men and women. In the old days here, Pandora, all the young men went to sea, so for years, women ran this island. The men came back, but they were very peripheral to the life here. Women like Miss Rosie and her friends all had their own incomes, or bartered for what they wanted, so it wasn't as if having a man in your life changed who you were. Then we started to get Western tourists and then, worst of all, television from America. And all the young girls got into this idea that you lived your life through and for men.'

Jane laughed. 'But now we younger ones have changed all that. I want a career of my own. Maybe I'll still marry. Maybe not. Who knows? But my generation of girls will not live like you have, Pandora.'

Pandora sighed. 'I know,' she said. 'I was an idiot. But not any longer. It was so awful to lie there and see myself let all those things happen to me.'

Janine looked at Jane. 'You can brag now,' she said, 'but look how you behave any time you see another woman with a man you have your eye on.'

'Sure. That's called affirmative action. I learned that from Eve. Don't let them take what's yours.'

Pandora stretched out her legs. 'Eve seems to have most of her life sorted out, but I'm nearly there.'

Janine rose. 'Come on, Pandora. We'll go down the mountain together. The others want to stay the night here.'

As they walked down the mountain, they held hands in the silence. When they reached Ben's house, Pandora kissed Janine. 'Thank you for the dreaming, Janine. It helped me enormously.'

Janine's face was cold in the moonlight. 'All you have to do now is decide about Richard.'

'I know,' Pandora said. 'I'm disappointed that it didn't come clear in the dream.'

'You still have things to clear before the answer comes. Good night, Pandora.' And she hugged her tightly.

Chapter Forty-six

Getting off Little Egg was always a problem. Ben stood with Pandora in the little shack that served as an airport. The plane was late. 'Trust Big Egg,' Ben said gloomily. 'If they had their way, there would be no flights to Little Egg, no tourists, and they would get all the tourist money to themselves.'

Just then they heard the drone of the aeroplane engines. Pandora was both nervous and excited. She had decided to take a train across the various American states to get to Phoenix. 'I know so little about America,' she said, explaining her idea to Ben who thought she was quite insane.

'Why not a plane ticket – zoom – and you're there?'

Pandora laughed. 'No,' she said. 'I want to go by train and see towns and faces and places. Dad has sent me a detailed list of all the places he visited, so I'll go there, too. It will give us something to talk about after all those years apart.'

She hugged Ben before she left, knowing how much she would miss his calm, self-assured presence and his warm, sweet-smelling body. 'Goodbye, Ben,' she said as she walked to the aeroplane. She boarded the plane and then gazed down as the plane lifted itself off the tarmac and headed across the sea to Miami.

Miami Airport, after the months of peace and silence, was a nightmare for Pandora. She began to feel a state of panic take hold of her by the shoulders. Her eyes began to squish up and to fill with tears and her legs shook. Oh no, she told herself very firmly. That's the old, helpless, defenceless Pandora. This is just an airport and these are just people hurrying through.

She walked along slowly, following the human tide that swept her to the luggage carousel. Would her suitcase be there? It was, and Pandora pulled it off the carousel with a feeling of triumph. She just had managed passport control; only Customs was left. As she waited, she watched families move in clusters around the airport. The men mostly handled the passports and the airline tickets while the women struggled with the children and the hand luggage. Must there always be a server and a served? she wondered as she watched the families go by.

Maybe, she thought as the comfortable Amtrak train pulled out of Miami. I feel so different because for all these months without Richard I have not been a server. The only person I have pleased is myself. That thought sounded selfish. The nuns would never have allowed that thought to manifest itself in their convent. A boy's mother was the central core of a boy's life. From her he learned everything and his whole world existed around the fact that she loved him and served him. Relaxed in the air-conditioned train, Pandora could hear Reverend Mother's voice. 'Then, when he becomes a man and marries a wife, his wife takes over the central core of his existence and loves him and serves him as did his mother.'

But, Pandora argued with that thought, I had no choice in shaping Richard or Marcus or Norman. I just got crammed down three holes. And I was expected to cope with three damaged men. Anyway, I'll stop thinking about that part of my life.

Next to her a tall man, with his Stetson pulled down to his ears and his cowboy boots jammed uncomfortably under his seat, said, 'Excuse me, ma'am. Would you mind if we changed seats? You sit next to the window, and I'll sit on the aisle.'

'Sure,' Pandora said.

'Thank you, ma'am.' They changed seats. 'Tony's my name,' he said, holding out a large welcoming hand. 'I'm on my way to Dallas. Just been diving in the reefs of the Red Sea. Glad to be back on dry land for a couple of weeks.'

Pandora looked out of the window. Most of the passengers were kindly, busy, very ordinary people. Many were moving for jobs. Some were travelling to see more of America, and a few were itinerant hobos. But as the train ran down through towns she remembered from her father's letter, she felt a closeness arising between herself and the yet unseen man.

El Paso, and the hot New Mexican desert. The sand seemed to go on endlessly. Tucson: anonymous, quiet. But now really close.

Pandora felt as if she had a fever. This was the myth she had carried with her all these years, the cause of so much of her heartache. The shame, and the fear of an unknown sin now washed away by her mother's confession.

She craned her neck as the train pulled into the Phoenix station.

There were several tall men standing about the platform. One of them was her father.

And then she saw him. He did not see her, but the same green eyes she had inherited from him were looking anxiously at the train windows. She walked down the aisle slowly. Such joy must be savoured. She walked down the steps and on to the platform. He was still looking. His face was more gaunt than she remembered, but his hair was still strong and thick, though iron grey. She quietly walked up to him and slipped her hand into his. 'Dad?' she said.

He looked down at her, puzzled for a moment. 'My little girl,' he said. He sounded bewildered. 'It's my little Pandora.' He picked her up and hugged her.

She, in his arms, once again felt as a baby bird feels in its nest. 'Oh, Dad,' she said. 'I've waited so long for this.'

Both of them were crying. About them, people busied themselves. Bus stations, train stations and airports are places where crying goes unnoticed. Grown men sob. Children shriek. Women wail, as people are torn apart or reunited. After a moment, Frank said, 'Let me carry your luggage, honey. We can't stay here bawling like babies.'

Pandora sniffed and wiped her eyes.

They walked out to the car park. Frank opened the door of the pick-up truck for her. Pandora hopped in. She could see her suitcase sitting forlornly in the back of the pick-up. Louis Vuitton, she thought, does not enjoy travelling by pick-up truck. 'First,' Frank said, 'I want to tell you that I got married again.'

'Yeah? You didn't say anything in your letter.'

'I know I didn't. But I kind of wanted to explain myself. Ruth is my wife's name, and she really is a good wife to me, Pandora. She has two daughters. They are both married, but when they were home, I helped raise them.' His voice choked. 'It took away some of the pain of losing you.'

Pandora put her hand on her father's forearm. Just to feel his arm was a pleasure.

'Ruth is always home, Pandora. She cooks, she takes care of me, and she loves me. I could never get that from your mother, you know. Your mother had the damnedest ideas in her head. First of all, she thought she had to have her own money. Then she thought looking after me was unnecessary because I was a grown man and should be able to look after myself.' He shook his head. 'But the damnedest thing of all is that I still love your mother with her sassy tongue. Sometimes

I feel guilty when I'm sitting with Ruth by the fire. I always kept in touch with her, you know.'

'I know, Dad, and I just want to say this before we get to your house. When Mom was on the island, she got drunk one night and she confessed that all those nasty things she said about me and you . . . She said they weren't true.' Pandora found herself shaking. 'I asked her why she said all those dirty things, and she said it was because we made her jealous.' There was a silence in the cab and then a deep groan.

Frank lifted his head. 'Thank you, God,' he said. 'I knew all along she was making it up, but you were too little to understand.'

'Why was she so jealous of us?' Pandora had wanted to know the answer to this question for so long.

'I guess because she'd never been wanted or loved herself until I came along. We were like oil and water. I loved her, still do love her, but she didn't want a knitting-book marriage, not like all the other girls in the place. She wanted what she called equality. Ruth ain't like that. She takes care of the inside of the house and I take care of the business. I'll show you my little repair shop, just a few blocks from the house.'

'Are you happy, Dad?'

'Yeah, I'm happy. But I miss the fire in Monica.'

Pandora laughed. 'You should see her now. She came down to the island bitching and moaning, and now she's going into business with a guy called Chuck. She says she's planning to marry him on the beach when I get back, and then they'll start up the business.'

'Do you think they'll be happy together, Mom and Chuck?'

'Yeah, I think they will. They'll fight, but Mom never minded that. Chuck is a real hustler, and so is she. They'll be fine.'

'See?' Frank pointed to a white framed shop across the road. The sign read *F. Mason. Electrical Repairs.* 'That's my own store. All owned, nothing owed to the bank.' A few blocks away he pulled up in front of a pretty little white stucco condo.

Waiting at the door was a small, pleasingly plump woman. She took Pandora by the hand and led her into the sitting-room. 'Frank, take Pandora's things up to her bedroom, dear. I've heard so much about you, Pandora, and I've been longing to see you. Both girls and their families are coming round tonight for a barbecue. They are all so looking forward to meeting you as well.'

Inwardly Pandora groaned. More family life. Privately she had hoped to spend a quiet evening reminiscing with her father and downing a couple of beers. 'That sounds wonderful,' she said. 'I'd better go upstairs and shower.'

Mrs Mason nodded and walked back to her cream and pine kitchen. So this is Pandora, Ruth thought. The woman who confessed to sexual torture and a barbiturate habit. Frank cried for days after he saw the article. Mrs Mason patted her stomach. Well, at least Frank had a decent home now, a loving wife and family. She very much hoped Pandora would cause no ripples in their idyllic existence.

Chapter Forty-seven

Over the years with Richard, Pandora had become well-used to the idea of his mother's English way of life. In Molly's house, Philip reigned supreme and all Molly's thoughts were directed at keeping him a happy and contented man. The sons, when they were there, were also served, but all the men took scrupulous care to see that none of the women carried heavy parcels or opened doors for themselves. The radical ideas of the women's movement had not extended its roughened hands into the pleasant Devon countryside. Quietly Pandora noticed Molly and the female in-laws, including herself, shoulder the burden of a vast vicarage. Upon his arrival at his mother's house, she knew Richard would let out a huge sigh of relief and revert to behaving like a six-year-old with his brothers.

It had been many years since she had witnessed an American family together. Living alone with her mother and then childless in her marriages, most of her friends had been single or without children. She could hear the booming arrival of various flotsam and jetsam of her father's second family. She stood in the little bedroom that must have belonged to the girls, and she wondered about them and then about herself. Two brass daybeds nestled up against the bedroom walls. It was a long room, papered with pink roses and swags of blue ribbon. A big mirrored cupboard ran along one side of the room and then there were shelves. Shelves and shelves of dolls. Sitting primly on the bottom of both beds were yet more dolls.

Pandora opened a door of the cupboard in order to hang up her few meagre dresses. There, row upon row of flounces and rustles of silk dresses hung spotlessly in the cupboard. Nervously Pandora hung up her brown sun dress and a black cocktail dress; after apologizing to the dolls she put a pink gingham dress on a bedside chair. Sugar and spice, she thought, that's what little girls are made of. At least most girls. Maybe if I'd had a room like this, I'd be less of a mess.

While she took a shower in the pink, shaggy bathroom, she mused about her mother. No wonder she couldn't love me, she thought. She'd never been loved herself. Dad tried, God knows, but he was looking for something she couldn't do for him, which obviously Ruth can. It's taken me thirty-seven years to realize that my mother is a human being.

And with that she shut off the shower and stepped back on to the deep pink-pile bathroom carpet. The room felt claustrophobic after the freedom of the island, but she appreciated the luxury. I wish Ben were here, she thought. We could roll all over that carpet.

She could hear more arrivals, so she took herself back to the bedroom, wrapped in a thick pink robe. She put on her dress and slipped on a pair of sandals. The things felt so unfamiliar to her feet.

Most of the family were spread outside in the backyard. She recognized Ruth's two girls. They looked so alike, they might have been twins. 'I'm Debbie, and this is Doreen.' Debbie was the louder of the two. Children, all under the age of seven, were tearing about the place. The two men were standing by the barbecue talking to her father. Frank looked very relaxed. He was obviously in charge of the barbecue section of the meal. Ruth bustled in and out, twittering vague admonitions to the children who seemed to be allowed to bite, kick, shriek, and answer back. Both mothers assumed blank expressions of maternal love and devotion and seemed not to notice the noise or the damage to the garden.

'Pandora, honey,' Ruth's voice came fluting out of the kitchen, 'come and give me a hand. The girls are setting the table.'

Pandora entered the kitchen and knew she must make some comment. All she could think to say was, 'You have a simply beautiful kitchen, Ruth.'

'Indeed I do, Pandora. It's all done by Frank. That's what he does in the evening. He goes to his workshed at the end of the garden and he makes things for my house and my girls. Anything they want, they just ask. Those boys of theirs can't fix a thing. What a different generation! Here, I'll give you the Cheese Wiz, and you just put some on these crackers.' Ruth paused and gazed at Pandora. 'You know, you're not a bit how I expected you to be. Frank always described you as shy and skinny.'

Pandora smiled. What would Ruth say if she told her about dreaming in a cave on an island where a turtle sings warnings?

'Somehow, after all you've . . . ahem . . .' Ruth paused embarrassed.

'Don't be embarrassed. I'm over it all now, and I have changed.' To get Ruth off the subject of herself, she said, 'You've really done wonders for Dad, you know. He looks really happy.'

Ruth took her hands out of the sink and smiled. 'Well, he was so bedraggled when I first met him. He'd never had a decent home life. Your mother drank a lot.' Ruth put up her hand. 'I'm not one to criticize, but Frank needed a real home, a wife to come home to, and a good dinner.'

Pandora nodded. 'You're probably right,' she said. 'Most men want just that, Ruth. But what about those women who don't want to centre their lives around a man and his needs? What happens to them?'

'Well,' Ruth's voice sharpened, 'they eventually lead very lonely lives. Family is everything.'

'I think family *is* everything,' Pandora said slowly, 'but what it really means is that mothering is everything.'

Ruth beamed. 'Of course, dear. You're absolutely right. I've put everything I've got into Frank and the girls, and now, all these years later, I have my reward.'

Cheese Wiz on crackers, and visits twice a year, Pandora thought cynically.

'I trained both my girls from when they were tiny to be housewives. Can you cook?'

Pandora shook her head. 'Sure, but now I only do it if I want to. Otherwise, I don't bother. I used to cook all the time in my married days, but I made two vows when I got to the island. One was that I'd never admit to cooking, and the other was that I'd never admit to being able to type.'

'You're not one of those feminists, are you?' Ruth said, laughing.

'No, I'm not anything. I just want to be a person in my own right. A whole person, Ruth, not part of someone else. I've done that for far too long.' She saw that she had gone too far. And whatever she, Pandora, felt, she had no right to pick away at Ruth's life. 'Anyway,' Pandora said, 'you're doing a wonderful job, and I'm so pleased you married Dad.'

Pandora's Cheese Wiz snacks were a success. The meal was a colossal event. The men stood for as long as possible around the barbecue and then brought in huge T-bone steaks covered in barbecue sauce. Doreen produced a bowl of salad liberally sprinkled with Thousand Island dressing, and Debbie finished the meal with a meringue cream pie. The children stuffed their faces, talked with their mouths full, continued to roar and shriek, while the adults talked over the din. Ruth shot in and out of the kitchen like a yoyo, followed by Doreen and Debbie. Pandora sat at her place, feebly saying, 'Can I do anything to help?' but was waved down as the matriarchs went through their well-rehearsed routine.

After the meal, Frank made a half-hearted offer to wash up, and was loudly scolded. 'You work hard all week, dear. You go outside with the boys and have a nap.'

Pandora hung about the back of the kitchen with a dish-towel. The children were firmly glued to the television in the sitting-room, and she felt invisible. *The unwanted don't have a family life because they don't know how to make one, I suppose.* She listened to see if she could gain insight into how Debbie, Doreen, and their mother filled their lives. Doreen said, '. . . a bigger car, Mom. The boys are swimming regularly and I have to get them over to swim meets and then back in time for Little League.'

'Randy's a Little League coach this year,' Debbie said. 'I really must find a stain-remover for that new bureau I found in the flea market. Do you remember, Mom? The one I telephoned you about?'

'Yes, dear.' Meanwhile Ruth's hands were busy. Small but fleshy, she had firmly created this little corner of her world, and those seemingly sweet little hands would fight to the death anything that tried to come near or to contaminate her pretty, nice-smelling abode.

Both of her daughters wore matching bows above their ears, lace collars and flat shoes. They talked in magazine phrases. They were all so earnest on Pandora's behalf. 'We were so sorry you had such an awful time with that terrible man.'

Both girls registered shock when Pandora explained that she had just left a third husband.

'We thought you were just having a vacation on a Caribbean island,' Doreen said. 'You mean you left that Englishman, the one Dad said was so good to you, and you *live* on an island?'

Both girls clasped their hands and gazed at Pandora. 'Why did you ever want to leave a nice man like that?'

'That's a good question, Doreen. I'm still waiting for an answer.'

Randy appeared at the door yawning. 'The other two are still asleep out there, but I could do with a cup of coffee, Mom. Then I'll mow your lawn for you, if you like.'

Debbie grinned. 'That's more than you do for me, Randy.'

He shrugged. 'But you're my wife, honey.' They all laughed.

Chapter Forty-eight

'Pandora?'

Pandora was sitting in the doll-bedecked bedroom with her chin on her knees, contemplating her face in the dressing-table mirror. The mirror was round and surrounded by pink lights. The whole contraption was wrapped in swathes of frilly material. Pandora was not keen to inspect her face too closely. Those are my life's roadmaps, she told herself.

'Pandora?'

Damn. That was Ruth calling. She got out of bed and padded to the door. 'Yes, Ruth?' she called down.

'It's nearly ten o'clock. I've been keeping breakfast warm for you.'

Pandora felt guilty. She didn't even eat breakfast, but it felt too mean just to ask for a cup of coffee. 'I'll be right down,' she said.

Ruth tut-tutted around the kitchen, thinking: No wonder she couldn't keep a man.

Pandora, face rinsed and hair combed, arrived downstairs shoeless.

Ruth looked at Pandora's bare feet. 'You really should wear shoes, Pandora. You might step on something and hurt your foot. Besides, your feet will widen.'

'I know,' said Pandora cheerfully. 'But I have always hated wearing shoes, and your carpets are so wonderfully soft.'

Ruth beamed. 'I use Carpet-Soft. It makes such a difference. For years I used Carpet-Clean, but it never really brought out the best in my carpets. Besides, Carpet-Soft gives a double-coupon, and I'm collecting for a dinner service. I've only got four more coupons to go.' She led Pandora into the kitchen. Ruth took out a plate of waffles and bacon.

Pandora tried not to heave. 'I think I'll have a cup of coffee first, if you don't mind,' she said.

'Of course, dear.' Ruth was busy at the sink, washing a salad. 'Frank'll be home for lunch in a few hours. Then we can go shopping together.'

'That'll be great. It's been ages since I've seen a mall. We have two big supermarkets on the island, but everything's got to be shipped or flown in. Sometimes I go crazy for fresh lettuce, and I never thought I'd feel murderous over fresh tomatoes.' Pandora decided to tackle her breakfast and make the best of things. Most of the night before had been taken up with cleaning up after dinner. The men watched basketball and, finally sleepy, children were put into cars and the family gathering was over. Small sleeping children appealed to Pandora. 'It's the fact they wake up that bothers me,' she had remarked to Doreen.

Doreen had given her a very odd look. 'Are you one of those people who prefers animals to children?'

'I sure am,' Pandora had said, shutting the car door firmly.

Now, alone with Ruth, Pandora felt inhibited. She had so little to share with her. Their lives didn't remotely touch each other.

Ruth had no such problem. 'What happens about birth control on the island?'

'Birth control?'

'Yes. You know: the pill, IUDs, all that stuff? I guess the women go to the hospital? I'm past all that, thank goodness, but my doctor thinks I should try HRT. Hormone Replacement Therapy,' Ruth said, as if the momentous news could change Pandora's life for ever. 'I'm in the change now, and I find it very uncomfortable. Not that Frank and I ever do very much. Well, you know what I mean.'

Pandora nodded, embarrassed.

'As soon as my periods stopped, I never felt a single sexual twinge again. Frank's very good about it all.' She giggled. 'If I want something bad enough, I let him make love to me.' She giggled some more. 'I think all women do that. Men are always so grateful for sex. Don't you find that?'

Pandora thought of Marcus. 'Not all of them are,' she said. 'What time will Dad be home?'

'Oh, he'll be here exactly at half-past twelve. I'll put the casserole in at eleven-thirty and he'll walk into a beautifully clean house with the smell of chicken pot pie. It's his favourite.'

'At least on the island,' Pandora said, faithfully trailing after Ruth with a duster, 'you just take a broom and sweep the whole thing out.'

'Oh, I'd hate that,' Ruth said. 'I love housework. I love to see everything clean and shiny.' She carefully wiped down the spaces between the stair carpet and the railings. 'Now, Pandora, if you get my little dustette from under the stairs and do the stairs for me, we'll be ready for Frank for his lunch.'

On her knees, Pandora smiled. She hadn't vacuumed anything since the day she left Norman. It quite amused her to watch the fluff rise up into the small suction, thin-lipped Hooverette. She made patterns in the carpet. There's the white sand outside of Ben's house and there's the swing where we make love . . . An urgent lust overtook her and her body shook with the fever of it.

She finished the Hoovering and quite deliberately switched her thoughts away from Ben. 'Anything else to do?' she asked politely.

'Just set the table for three, dear. I'm just putting a finishing touch to the pie pécan. I always feel so European when I say it that way. Sort of French, you know?'

Just as Ruth predicted, Frank opened the front door at precisely twelve-thirty. He had a newspaper rolled up under his arm, and Ruth rushed into the hall to kiss him hello. Pandora stood watching. Frank pecked his second wife on the cheek and then walked over to Pandora and gave her a big hug. Pandora felt herself relax. All the sinister years were now behind them both.

Frank sniffed. 'Chicken pot pie?' he said, beaming.

'How did you guess?' Ruth said, clapping her hands together.

'It's Wednesday, isn't it?'

A ritual, that's what that sentence was, a marital ritual. Pandora had her rituals with Richard. 'Pressie, darling,' he'd say, dropping a package on to her knees. 'What did you buy for yourself this time, Richard?' 'Turnbull and Asser shirts. You know me too well, darling,' and Richard would bend down to kiss her. Keeping Richard in a wardrobe fit for a journalist-about-town was an expensive pastime for Pandora. His sartorial tastes out-paced his journalist's salary.

Frank pulled Pandora's chair out. 'You look sad, honeybun. Are you missing the island?'

'No, Dad. Just a sad memory. But it's gone. I'm going to the mall with Ruth this afternoon. I never thought I'd get excited about a mall in my life, but I'm quite looking forward to it.'

'Mrs Johnson brought in her mother's old clock, Ruth. You should have seen it. A big black marble thing. Beautifully made inside. I cleaned it out for her, balanced one of the flywheels, and she went off happily. Then Tania came in to say that old Giles Mortimer died yesterday, so you'll need to get my funeral suit out.'

'Oh dear. But it *really* is a blessing.' Ruth cleared the three lunch plates. 'Poor old man. His wife died only a year ago, Pandora, and none of us thought he'd last as long as he did. He was totally dependent on her, wasn't he, Frank?'

'Uh? Oh. Yes. Totally.' Frank was trying to look at sports scores in the newspaper on the empty chair next to him.

'Frank, you know you have to wait for your coffee before you read your newspaper.'

Frank turned his face away from the paper, and for a moment Pandora saw the look of an outside Tom-cat tamed from its wilderness. 'Sorry, honey,' Frank said.

Ruth carved a neat slice of her pie and put it on to his plate. Pandora watched her father's calloused fingers fumble with a dessert fork.

'That was lovely,' Pandora said, feeling overfull and uncomfortable. Lunch on Little Egg was a meat patty bought from Captain Billy's.

'Off you go now, Frank. I'll bring your coffee in a minute.'

'Thank you, dear.' Frank ambled off to the sitting-room to recline on the recliner and read his newspaper.

'You wash,' said Ruth, 'and I'll take him in his coffee. And then after a few minutes you'll hear him snore. I let him have half an hour, and then he'll go back to the store. Then we can go off for an afternoon in the mall.'

Wowie kazowie, Pandora thought.

As she walked up the stairs, she heard her father snoring. All that food . . . She sat down in front of the mirror and put on the lights. Ugh. There were handbags under her eyes and wrinkles on her forehead. I'll buy some face cream, she thought, and maybe a lipstick.

Chapter Forty-nine

For Ruth the trip to the mall was the highlight of her day. Pandora, at first excited by the idea, was amazed to find herself asphyxiated and then frightened by the throng of humans making their way in and out of the shops. She realized that she knew no one in that huge mall, and no one knew her. She found herself smiling and lifting a hand to a face. The face would turn suspicious and surly. 'Gee, I'm not used to being so anonymous,' she remarked.

Ruth was busy pushing her way to the supermarket. 'They have a special offer on toilet tissue,' Ruth said, her eyes gleaming. She grabbed a shopping trolley and swung into action.

When they reached the special offers, Ruth filled her trolley to the brim. 'Ruth,' Pandora said, 'you've got enough rolls for several years there.'

'Yes, but think of the saving!' On the front tray of the trolley, Ruth had a yellow box full of coupons. As they trundled down the aisles, they checked and double-checked for cheaper and cheaper deals. When they reached the fresh produce counter, Pandora felt a pang of lust for the fresh green lettuce and the big, shiny tomatoes. Then she saw a few naked, whiskery coconuts so far away from home. She yearned to tuck them under her arm and take them back to the sun and the sea. For a moment, Pandora felt that the huge over-stuffed market was somehow unnecessary and obscene.

'What happens to all the stuff nobody buys?' she asked the girl at the check-out.

The girl looked at Pandora. She chewed her gum reflectively. 'They grind it all up and it goes into the sewers,' she said with impatience.

'Couldn't they feed the homeless or give it to the Salvation Army?'

'Nah.' The girl was pushing Ruth's food over a laser scanner. 'Somebody might get food poisoning and sue.'

Pandora looked at the red light of the laser scanner. 'Is that safe?' she said.

The girl wiped the glass cover. 'I guess so,' she said. 'I find my hand gets dry and my nails grow funny, but it must be OK, or they wouldn't let us use it, would they?'

Pandora stared at the pretty, bland, unthinking face and realized that was once how she was: the 'they' in her life telling her what to do and how to do it. You aren't born helpless. Small children are active, inquisitive, experimental creatures. 'They' teach you to be helpless. 'They' know best . . .

'Pandora, you're daydreaming.' Ruth expertly swung the brown bags into her arms. A wodge of coupons lay in the girl's hands. 'We'll take the bags to the car and then we can go to the Dairy Queen. They have my favourite ice-cream there.' Ruth was like a child. Her face glowed in anticipation.

Pandora felt mean and spiteful. She desperately wanted to get away from the mall. The pungent smells of different perfumes made her feel sick. She felt lost and faceless. Even outside in the car park the air was lifeless and stale. Ruth put the bags carefully into the boot of the car. She used her time so methodically as if the day trembled and threatened to turn black if she misused a minute. Ruth shut the boot, walked around the car checking that all the doors were properly locked, and then put her keys back into her purse. 'Come along,' she said. 'You're in for a treat.'

Dairy Queen, Pandora remembered from her teenage years, was where all the tramps, the homeless, and she and her friends would hang out. Mostly Pandora was high on some pill or other. She discovered it wasn't any different today. They took their seats at a round table and Ruth said, 'Take your pick, Pandora. I always have a chocolate ice-cream with a cream topping and then nuts.'

'I'll just have a coffee,' Pandora said faintly.

Across the way a young woman savagely slapped her two-year-old toddler and Pandora glared at her. The woman lowered her eyes and the child howled. Pandora felt sorry for the woman. She was probably tired and strained and on welfare. She and the child looked none too clean. Ruth came back and sat down on her chair with a sigh of satisfaction. She looked about the restaurant. 'I used to come here all the time with my father,' she said. 'We used to sit together on a Sunday afternoon. That was my time to be with my father. We were a family of five children, so he gave each of us a special time when we could just talk to him.'

'You were lucky to have a father in your life.'

Ruth nodded. 'I was lucky. I had a wonderful childhood and a wonderful husband. I thank God for my children and my grandchildren every night.'

Pandora looked at Ruth who was contentedly spooning ice-cream into her mouth. 'Ruth,' she said, 'are you ever unhappy or bored?'

Ruth's eyes opened wide. 'Pandora, when do I have the time to be either? I'm busy all day and every day.'

'I know.' Pandora felt treacherous asking these questions. Why shouldn't some women be perfectly happy being housewives? 'Don't you ever want something just for yourself, Ruth?'

Ruth thought for a moment. 'No, not really. I watch the soaps all day, and so much happens in all those people's lives, that I feel it's all happening in mine. I love "General Hospital". That's my favourite. I sit down with a fresh cup of coffee to watch that.'

'I see. I wish I could find life that easy.'

'I always told the girls that the secret to a happy life was not to ask too many questions.' Ruth finished her ice-cream, licked the spoon decisively, and put it neatly on the side of her plate.

Pandora realized she had slobbered her coffee into the saucer. Damn, she thought. Can't I get anything right?

Later that night Pandora sat in the back shed, watching her father make a wall cabinet to house Ruth's newly acquired dinner service. She watched his sure hands measure out the wood. There was a veil of fat around him. He was no longer hard and lean. His cheeks, under the merciless light of a bulb hanging from the ceiling of the shed, cast shadows in the shed. 'Are you happy, Dad?' Pandora asked.

'I guess so.' Frank chalked off a section for cutting. He looked rather shyly at Pandora. 'I guess I'm as happy as a man can ever be.'

Pandora heard pain in his voice. 'What do you mean by that?' she said.

'Well, I miss certain things, you know. I miss riding the trains. I miss . . . Well, I guess I miss freedom. Your mother always bitched, but she gave me my freedom to come and go as I pleased. Sometimes I would get itchy feet and just have to go.'

Pandora grinned. 'And you brought me all those nice presents back.'

'Yeah.'

'Do you remember the goldfish?' she asked.

'Sure, I remember the goldfish. You fell in the stream trying to get them back.'

'That was mean of Mom.'

271

'Yeah, but life was mean to her. Now Ruth had great parents. There isn't a mean bone in her body.' He carefully glued the two wooden sections together.

Pandora heard Ruth's voice. 'Supper, Frank! Wash your hands before you come in.'

Frank sighed. 'I wish she wouldn't do that,' he said. He went to the sink in the corner of the shed.

'You're lucky. She just asks you to wash your hands,' Pandora observed. 'Richard's mother asks us if we've *been*, in front of everybody.'

Frank laughed. He put his arm around Pandora as they walked back to the house. 'What are you going to do about that husband of yours?'

'I don't know, Dad. But I'm beginning to think that I don't want a man to be the central pivot of my life, if that makes sense. I don't want the total responsibility of taking care of him. I feel it sucks up almost all of who I am.'

They were standing quietly in the starlit evening. It was a calm night and the Arizona air smelled sweet. 'I know what you mean, believe me. Men feel it, too. Maybe in the old days, when there were big families, men and women were just too tired to ask themselves questions. Now we all have time, lots and lots of time . . . Nothing to do with it.'

'Frank!'

'We're coming!' And Frank let his arm fall from Pandora's shoulder. 'It's a difficult question, that one,' he said.

Pandora followed him. He's bored, she thought. He's very, very bored.

After Ruth and Pandora finished the washing up, Pandora dutifully sat in the over-stuffed chairs in the den and watched the monstrous colour television for the rest of the evening. At eleven o'clock Ruth made malted milk drinks and they went off to bed. Pandora lay in her cot-like bed with a sense of despair growing like a huge cancer inside her. Not long now, she thought, and I can go back to the island. Only four more torpid, boring days. I'm bored, she thought. I'm so fucking bored I could die. And Dad's trapped for the rest of his life. And he knows it.

272

Chapter Fifty

Four days later Frank took Pandora to the train station. Ruth had already said her weepy goodbyes. Pandora felt Ruth was really rather glad to have her perfect, orderly house back again, to be able to live in her world of soap operas, and to have all conversations with Frank safe again. Ruth did not want to discuss AIDS or any other social issues. So now the terrorist to peace and quiet was departing, she was actually quite relieved.

Frank hugged his daughter tightly at the train station. 'Well, whatever happens, Pandora, you know where I am, and I'll be there for you whenever you need me.'

'I know.' Pandora felt sad at leaving Frank, but guilty because so much of her wanted to get back to the island. 'You should come and visit me on the island, Dad.'

Frank shook his head. 'No. Ruth couldn't take the humidity.'

Pandora wanted to say *Damn Ruth! Come yourself*, but she knew she couldn't say it, so she smiled and waved.

She brought three big books with her, and she purposefully read her way across Arizona and the other states back to Miami, Florida. The train raced along the tracks and ate up the miles that were to take her back to her happiness and her home.

Monica was already on the island when Pandora got back. She was at the airport looking girlishly excited. 'Chuck and I are getting married this Saturday on the beach,' she said breathlessly. 'We thought we'd wait for you to come back.'

'Are you sure you want to get married again, Mom?'

'Oh, yeah. I'm sure. Chuck and I give each other plenty of space. He does his thing and I do mine. Ben says he'll see you later. He's been called in for a diving trip.'

Pandora looked at her mother and found herself smiling. The island had had a good effect on Monica, she felt: she had lost weight and was brown from the sun. Maybe it would work between Monica and Chuck. The whole thing was such a lottery.

The sun was setting on the golden beach by the hotel. Janine had not allowed Chuck any alcohol before the ceremony. Chuck was pleading, but Janine was adamant. 'You're going to get married sober, so as you can't say you were too drunk to know what you were doing,' she said firmly.

Chuck was wearing white chino pants, a blue shirt, and a tie. Monica wore a grey lace dress that made her look years younger than she really was. Pandora had curled her hair, so it hung softly around her face. Pandora, standing behind them both in a simple lime green dress, listened as the ancient vows, so simple to say and so impossible to keep, were said out loud by her mother. 'To have and to hold, from this day forward, till death us do part.'

The Pastor's voice boomed out the amen and the gulls passing by agreed loudly. Pandora stood there, guiltily aware she had failed to keep those vows twice and was now about to do it for the third time. Monica and Chuck kissed each other very happily, and Janine and Octo signed the register as witnesses.

The reception was held by the swimming pool. Miss Rosie was beaming, and in among all the islanders who attended the event, even Miss Maisy was seen to be enjoying herself.

Later that night in Ben's arms, Pandora said, 'I do hope it's all right for them, Ben. I really do. My mother deserves some happiness in her life.'

Satiated with making love, Ben sleepily agreed.

Pandora lay on her back, listening to Ben snoring. What a curious business marriage was! Having had all this freedom from Richard, she realized that she didn't miss him. To be away from his constant demands for attention was a relief. She fell asleep dreaming of sitting on an Amtrak train with Ruth beside her, eating ice-cream and every so often looking up to say, 'Of course I'm happy. I'm too busy to be anything else.'

Ben was away on Big Egg when Richard's letter arrived. He was bored and dissatisfied and now he wanted to see if he could come to the island and they could both try again. Pandora was far from pleased. First of all, she realized she didn't want Richard to invade her space, and secondly, she was feeling more and more intensely the need to live alone. With Ben away she enjoyed the silence and the peace. One day

Ben would marry his island girl and the house would be full of children. But for now Pandora had found her equilibrium and she was at peace with herself and the world. How dare Richard think he could just swan in and take it all away?

She went down to the bar to find Janine and have a grouch. Octo was sitting at the bar, looking worried. 'There's a big system off the western coast of Africa, moving west,' he said. 'Let's hope it's not coming our way.'

'Is it a hurricane yet?' Janine asked.

'No, it's just forming. But I've had a feeling in my bones that this year we're heading for a bad one. Nobody listens though. Only those who lived through the hurricane of '32. The younger ones just think it's all a joke.'

Janine gave Pandora a beer. 'I'm just finishing up. Let's go for a walk,' Janine said, 'and you can tell me all about Phoenix, Arizona.'

Pandora made a face. 'Not much to tell, Janine. All plastic America. That's why Americans keep escaping down here.' Both women were walking shoeless along the beach. Tiny sand crabs scuttled sideways into their holes. 'Look at all those conch shells, Janine.'

Janine nodded. 'They say there's going to be a change in the weather. They come close to the shore. I think we should get the cave ready. Most of the bed linen is up there, and fresh water. I'll get Octo to put a pile of coconuts up there, and, Pandora, be sure to bring up thick sweaters with you. If it does come this way, don't mess about; make for the cave.'

All up and down the island, as the days passed, the islanders anxiously listened to the radio, or those who had televisions passed on the news to those who did not. By the fourth day the swirling mass had taken shape and was officially deemed a hurricane. Hurricane Betty was whirling her way towards the Caribbean. With any luck, she would take a slight turn and head for South America. All this talk of hurricanes unsettled Pandora, but there were so many experts that after a while she got rather bored with the subject. She did pack a small suitcase. She also helped Monica make a shopping list for the new store, and saw her off to Miami to 'shop till she dropped', as Monica joked.

Two days later the hurricane had gained speed, but was turning slightly away off its course towards the islands. Octo shook his head. 'I don't trust this one,' he said. 'I'm taking my boat and moving it in to the reef on Fire Island.'

275

Miss Rosie agreed with him. Many did not.

Ben telephoned to say he was staying on Big Egg because he had a sister there and he needed to nail up her windows. 'Go and get plywood and nail down all the windows. Before you leave, nail a board across the front door as well,' he instructed Pandora. 'If the hurricane comes straight at us, you will be given a time to leave the house, so please go. You will, won't you?'

Pandora promised she would.

For a whole day the hurricane sat. The centre got tighter and tighter. The second day it was still sitting sullenly on the television screens. That night, Janine said she and her sisters were going up anyway. Pandora preferred to wait. Half the island were in the caves that lined the mountains. Some of the tourists had flown off the island to get out of the way of the hurricane, and the others were drinking themselves into a stupor and betting nothing would come of it.

By six o'clock on Wednesday evening, Pandora had finished nailing up her windows. 'Tomorrow I'll go up,' she promised herself. She looked up at the sky and she felt puzzled. The sky was a weird colour. It looked like a mad painting, a flat yellow mud colour. No birds were singing, just a terrible silence. No crickets. No frogs. She looked at the sea. The sea was slippery. It lay inert. I'll take a sleeping pill, Pandora thought, and have a good night's sleep. I'll put my suitcase down by the front door and tomorrow morning I'll nail up the door and go and join them. She felt guilty about taking a sleeping pill, but the lack of wind and utter lack of sound had given her a curious headache.

She picked up the phone, but the line was dead. Damn. She wanted to say goodnight to Ben. Still, she was tired after all the effort of boarding up the house. So she boiled herself an egg and then, after a quick shower, she put on a clean nightdress and fell into bed.

She awoke hours later to the sound of dreadful screaming. She moved in the bed, wondering what on earth it could be. The house was shaking and swaying, and then she realized that the hurricane must have unleashed its forces that night and torn across the sea and was about to hit Little Egg and any other island that was in its way. Pandora got out of bed and reached for the light. No electricity.

She did have her diving torch. By now she was afraid. She pulled on her thickest sweater and a pair of jeans. She put on her sneakers and tried to open the door. The wind was pushing against her, but eventually she managed to get out. She realized it was all she could do to walk upright in the wind, and it would be crazy to try and carry her suitcase. Once outside she could see the palm trees genuflecting to the power of the wind. Behind her the sea, which had been so still and so calm, was coming towards the beach in big rolling waves. She turned and began to run towards the mountain.

For a while she was alone and then she joined other stragglers. An enormous tree was down at the foot of the path leading to the mountain, so everyone had to go on foot. A seething mass of people struggled up the steep sides of the mountain. Old people carried by their children, babies crying, and all the time the terrible sound of the wind screaming. Rain poured down. Great heavy drops of battering rain.

Soon the pathway was a mud slide and every step forward was a step back. Pandora had mud under her fingernails as she clawed her way up the track. Beside her a little girl was clinging on to her leg. 'Hold on tight!' Pandora screamed over the wind. 'Don't let go!' Just then the first of the tidal waves hit the island.

There were terrible sounds of screaming and crying as people were washed away by the force of the water. Pandora found a tree and wrapped her arms around it and held on tightly. She tried to wrap her legs around the child, but her legs gave way as the suction of the receding water pulled the child away. Pandora was too frightened to cry. She was about to let go herself. The pull of the wave had exhausted all her strength.

Then she was aware of a big pair of arms picking her up and throwing her like a piece of wood across his shoulders. Thank God, she prayed. It was Octo.

Pandora came to, lying in the cave, with Janine leaning over her. 'Where's Octo?' Pandora asked.

'He's gone to get his mother,' Janine said. 'You're all right now.'

Pandora felt safe enough to shake and to cry. 'Janine, so many were washed away.'

Julia sat silently, the drums in her lap. Pandora could hear the sounds from the drums, the terrible sound of a mother crying for her lost children. Jane was at the back of the cave cooking something hot. Janine went to the front of the cave with Pandora. They linked arms and leaned out into the wind. Below they could see Octo struggling to get up the path. In his arms he carried a curious creature. Her enormous head was lolling on his shoulder, and the rest of her minute body lay in his arms. The wind was louder and stronger. 'Come on, Octo!' Janine screamed.

Pandora held her back. 'You can't go out there, Janine. You'll be blown away.'

Step by step they watched Octo struggle, but then he slipped and for a frozen moment the women watched the man and his mother fall in slow motion into the roaring cascading sea, hungrily waiting for its victims.

Janine threw herself on the sand and howled. The other two girls rocked with grief. Pandora sat numb, too shocked to think, except to wonder if he had not come to rescue her, perhaps he could have saved himself and his mother.

The night passed for all four of them in sleeplessness. The wind screamed and roared and the sea answered back. To Pandora, it felt like a fight to the end between the will of good and the will of evil, the wind being Lucifer, bending everything to his will, and the sea being God. She sat upright, looking out into utter blackness. Then after hours, oblivious to time, she fell sideways on to the sand floor, asleep.

Chapter Fifty-one

When she awoke it was to the sound of silence. Julia was also awake and boiling a can of hot water. Mercifully Janine was still asleep. 'Oh God, Julia! What will Janine do without Octo?'

Julia shrugged. 'She will grieve for a long time, Pandora, but life goes on.'

'Do you think he could have saved his mother if he didn't have to go looking for me?'

'No, don't think that way. That's the Western way of thinking. His time had come. His worst worry was that he should die and leave his mother, even though Janine would look after her for him. He has moved on with her in his arms, just as it should be. We are the ones left to grieve.'

The four of them huddled on the floor, drinking their coffee. Then, standing up, Pandora looked out at the grey lowering sky. 'We must wait for a while to make sure the hurricane doesn't hit us again. In the '32 hurricane, people came out of the caves when they heard the silence. They didn't realize they were in the eye of the hurricane, and then they were all killed when the hurricane's back wall hit them.'

Jane talked to the drums. The sounds of the drums were peaceful, a gentle lament for the eternal knowledge of the mighty forces of the world, reminding man he was but a blink away from death at all times.

Pandora looked out of the cave. Below her she could see people moving slowly down the muddy boulder-filled track. 'I think it's really over,' she said. She could hear the sounds of birds singing. She saw two big frigate birds diving on to the beach.

Julia looked out. 'It's going to be an awful climb down, but I want to see what's left of our house, if anything.'

'Here.' Pandora put a blanket around Janine's silent shoulders. 'I'll help you down.' She pulled Jane out of the cave and carefully the three women helped Janine to negotiate the slippery mud and rocks as they slowly, step by muddy step, slipped and slid down the track. There was no avoiding the bodies caught in branches: faces known to them all.

Pandora felt the conflicting emotions of euphoria that she was alive and guilt that they had died and she had not. A small baby lay by the side of the track, its eyes wide open. Pandora gently closed the eyes and put the baby hands across its breast. '*Madre de Dios*,' said Julia and she crossed herself. 'There's Virgil, in under that boulder. He won't make any dirty movies any more.' Virgil's mouth was pulled back in a rictus of pain and fear.

On down they went until Pandora found the only way she could endure the awful sight was to resolve to block out the dead. There were no dying. The water had drowned everything it snatched. Octo had saved her life and lost his own. Pandora had never been so close to death before. She felt she had tasted it, a thin, metallic taste.

Finally they were at the foot of the mountain. Crews of men were hauling up the uprooted trees by hand. There was no electricity. The island ambulance darted back and forth to the hospital. Pandora could hear the hospital's auxiliary generator pumping – a hospital built by Little Egg, and no thanks to Big Egg. She wondered for the first time how Ben was. No telephones. She could see the telephone poles strewn along the road.

'You take Janine back to your place. I'm going to check on mine.' Pandora was anxious: she had not nailed down the front door. 'I'll catch up with you later.' Pandora walked slowly along the road. She passed people also slowly making their shocked and disbelieving ways back to their homes. She saw houses without roofs, gardens with upturned trees, trees embedded in houses. One house had only one wall left, and hanging by itself was a portrait of the Queen. People didn't stop to talk to each other. They shambled by like the lost tribe in a fog of sorrow and misery. Pandora was wet through her blanket, heavy around her shoulders.

When she turned the corner, to her delight the little house was quite untouched. The door was open. And then Pandora saw Miss Rosie with her broom, brushing the sand briskly out of the house. Pandora ran the last few yards and flung herself into Miss Rosie's arms. 'Octo is dead, Miss Rosie.'

Miss Rosie gently took the blanket from Pandora's shoulders. 'I know,' she said. 'I saw their souls like fireflies leave their bodies. They will be rejoicing tonight. The good Lord took many souls unto himself. Still,' she smiled, 'he left my weary old bones here.'

'Oh, Miss Rosie! I couldn't bear it if anything happened to you.'

'Nothing will happen to me, child, till my time has come. Come and take all these wet things off. I have some hot water on. You mustn't catch cold. More people die from the cold and the disease that the hurricane brings with it. All the wells will be contaminated, except one on the North Side. The British Navy will be here by the evening, and they will help clear up.'

Pandora took off her clothes and unpacked her suitcase. 'I don't think I'll be the same again, Miss Rosie.'

Miss Rosie's bright eyes smiled at her. 'A hurricane is a mighty event. I'll think more carefully about what I do or say.' Miss Rosie handed Pandora a cup of island soup. 'This will make you sleep. I'll stay here and when you wake up you'll feel much calmer.'

Pandora curled up in the bed and obediently drank her soup. She murmured her thanks before she fell asleep.

Ben came back on the first available aeroplane. The final figures were one hundred and twenty people dead, seventy severely injured. Most houses sustained damage, and many were totally washed away. For three days the skies were leaden with rain. Large pools of slimy green water lay everywhere. The Navy arrived with blankets and food and shelter. Finally the rain subsided and the sun began to come out.

Most of the time, Pandora sat on the beach, thinking about Octo and how she would miss him. Janine grieved with her.

The sun grew warmer and the island began to get back a semblance of order. The sound of sawing and hammering could be heard. All the dead that had been found were buried. Those that were injured grew better. Broken branches flowered. 'The world really does go on, you know, Janine.' Pandora looked at the flat calm water that had momentarily turned so treacherous. 'Shall we take Ben's boat out for a ride?'

Janine nodded.

Together they pulled the boat from under the house and down the beach into the sea. 'I'll leave the engine. Let's just row. I could do with the exercise.' Pandora sat with the oars and Janine lay on the back seat, staring at the now bright blue sky. Pandora rowed out into the middle of the lagoon. There was no air. Everything felt motionless. Looking ahead, Pandora could see what looked like a school of unusually large fish. 'Look, Janine,' she said, standing up. 'What's that up ahead?'

Janine stood up and put her hand over her eyes. 'It's the dolphins. They've arrived.'

Pandora felt a surge of emotion. The creatures were coming towards the little boat. Three big dolphins were leaping out of the sea, followed by others. Pandora sat, quietly holding her breath in case she frightened any of them away. Soon inquisitive snouts were pushing at the boat. She could see the dolphins pass under the boat and then playfully slap their tails on the surface, spraying both the women with water. One of the biggest dolphins leapt out of the water and jumped right across the bow of the boat. 'I'm going in to swim with them, Janine.'

Janine was smiling. 'You go,' she said. 'I'll wait for you.'

Pandora took off her bathing suit and dived cleanly into the water. She felt, as she sank down through the water, the bodies of the dolphins roll beside her. She came to the surface, laughing and stroking playful noses. The dolphins squealed at her. All the world was coloured by a pure light. All the blue was bluer. The heavens bowed down to the earth and the dolphins gave their joy and their blessing to both women. Pandora rolled over on her stomach and held on to the flipper of the biggest dolphin. She planed across the water, singing with happiness.

For a while the dolphins stayed with them, and then slowly they moved away. Pandora climbed out of the water into the boat. 'Your face is shining, Janine,' she said.

Janine nodded. 'I've been praying for the dolphins to come to return the joy to our lives, and I can now let the memory of Octo go in peace.'

When they got back to the house, Ben was standing ankle-deep in the water. He looked at Pandora. 'You've been swimming with dolphins,' he said.

'How do you know?' Pandora asked, puzzled.

'Anyone who swims with dolphins shines like a light. It's the joy they bring, and their knowledge of the universe.'

Pandora walked into the house. Ben's right, she thought. I do feel alight.

Overhead a small private plane was preparing to land at the airport. Ben came to the door of the house. A few minutes later the telephone rang. Pandora took the call. 'Are you all right, Pandora?'

'Yes, I'm all right, but where are you, Richard? You sound so close.'

'I'm here on the island. I got a lift with this man who was taking some medicines for the hospital. I've been awfully worried about you. We all are. Mummy is frantic.'

Pandora was silent for a moment.

'Where can I meet you, Pandora?'

'Go to the hotel. I'll see you there.' She made a face. 'Richard,' she said as she put the telephone down.

'What are you going to do?'

'I don't know, Ben. I'll go and see him, and then I'll come back.'

'I'll wait.'

'Thanks, Ben. You're a good friend.'

Ben smiled.

Pandora pulled a cotton wrap around her bathing suit. She took the moped and purposefully took the long way round to the south side of the island. She knew she was dreading the thought of even seeing Richard again. She felt her inner peace shatter. She wished she could get off the moped and throw herself into the sea and watch the fish busily getting on with their lives. She would even rather dive off the dock and find Ben's barracuda and stroke the ugly face she'd come to love. The early years of love and friendship with Richard were still warm memories, but the final years tamped those memories down firmly, like a bung in a cask of sherry. Those days will never come again, she reminded herself. Richard's having sex with Gretchen was not the main problem. That she could forgive and live with. It was the betrayal of herself, the fact that Richard could lie so plausibly. Richard was never to be trusted again. Even if he promised to be faithful, Pandora knew it would be no use. Adultery starts in the head, and she would always watch Richard with suspicion. Where there is no trust, love cannot flourish.

The moped had a will of its own, and inexorably it made its way to the hotel parking lot. Wearily Pandora parked, slung her island thatch-palm basket over her shoulder, and wished she had a fistful of tranquillizers. She walked through the hotel lobby and out to the bar. Janine waved and smiled. 'Your husband is over there,' she said, pointing at the volleyball court.

Pandora grimaced. She could both hear and see Richard leaping up and down with the tourists, eagerly knocking the ball over the net. He called encouragement to his teammates. 'That's the ticket! I say, good shot!'

She stood and watched him. He was wearing typical English white shorts, baggy round the knees. She had to smile, recalling the times she had tried to talk him into American-style close-cut shorts. 'But Pandora,' he always replied, earnestly wrinkling his brow. 'They taught us at school those sort of shorts lowered your sperm count. I don't want to think of my fertility as lowered. Poor little buggers, staggering around in the heat. No, I am English and I wear English shorts.'

He also was wearing a grey airtex shirt and English plimsolls.

She slowly dragged her feet through the sand towards him. 'Richard?' she called. He didn't hear her. He was too busy showing off. 'Richard!' she screamed with irritation. Finally she caught his attention.

'Pandora! Just hang on, darling. We'll just finish this game.'

Pandora sighed and squatted on the sand. How often had she heard that phrase? Too many times. Hours and hours of watching Richard play golf on English golf courses, or cricket in Devon, baseball in Boston. If she added up all those hours of yawning boredom, she could add years to her life. Because the truth is that life with Richard had become a non-life. Richard had life; she didn't. Richard, she thought, looking at him instantly at home on the island, will always have a life of his own. For him the world was not a scary place, whereas she was shit-scared most of the time. Richard had life in both hands. Now he was coming back to her. Even though he had almost bankrupted her with his spending, he had lied to her and been unfaithful, he felt perfectly able to fly back into her life and expect her to fall into his arms.

There was a loud roar as the game finished. The few tourists who had stayed through the hurricane disbanded, and Richard raced up the beach to Pandora's side. 'You look smashing, love,' he said, his eyes glowing. 'I've never seen you look so well, or so beautiful, darling.' He slid to his knees. 'Oh, Pandora, I missed you so.' He put his hands in her hands. His voice was pleading.

She looked into his handsome face and felt her resolve shake.

'When I heard about the hurricane, I realized how much I loved you. The thought of anything happening to you . . . Please, darling. Please take me back.'

'Richard, you can't just walk back into my life like that. Anyway, I'm living with Ben, and I'm very happy with him. He's kind and gentle.'

'Unlike me, I suppose?'

'Yes. Very unlike you.'

Richard's face darkened. 'What does this Ben fellow do?'

Pandora shrugged. 'He fishes and takes out dive-boats sometimes and does some work for the Department of Public Works.'

'Are you in love with him?' Richard's voice was sharp, and Pandora remembered the lance of his anger.

'No. I'm not in love with Ben the way you mean it. I love Ben as a friend and a lover. But I've never loved anybody the way I loved you in those early years.'

'Then why can't we get back together?'

Pandora looked at him very carefully and said slowly, 'Richard, whatever you do or say, you will never grow up. I can't live your teenage life. I was warned not to marry you, and I didn't listen. I was a fool.'

Richard stood up. 'I need a drink,' he said desperately.

Pandora followed him to the bar. They settled at a table nearby. Janine shot a look of quiet sympathy at both of them. She had lost Octo for ever, and now she watched Richard lose Pandora, and she felt sorry for him. Richard was too coarse a soul for Pandora. Janine dreaded the day that Pandora would leave the island, but she knew that Pandora would take the wisdom of the island with her. Richard would grieve but not for long. The world was full of pretty women waiting for Richard, but always in his heart he would know that he had lost the only woman who loved and truly understood him, and that ache would last his lifetime. Janine knew that ache and she pitied him.

'So,' Richard said glumly. 'There's no point in my staying on the island, is there?'

'Of course there is, Richard. You and I may not be lovers any more, and in time we can get a divorce, but for now we can be friends. I'll take you diving and show you around my island. You'll love it, I promise you.'

'What are you going to do with the rest of your life, Pandora? You've always been so helpless.'

'No longer, Richard. No longer. Here I learned to grow within myself. Here I found what I was looking for. You see, I never really had any sense of self before.'

'You're telling me!' Richard's tone was belligerent again.

'Don't get cross, Richard. Just listen. Thanks to Octo and Janine and all my friends on this island, I learned what inner peace was. You know that phrase "the peace of God that passeth all understanding"? Well, I've found it, Richard.'

Richard watched Pandora's face. She had changed. There was an inner radiant light around her.

'A little while ago,' she said, 'a pod of dolphins swam into the reef. I dived into the water, and for those minutes, I was a dolphin. They welcomed me. My body grew flippers and my skin changed. There was this tremendous connection between all of us. There was no separation at all. It felt like an electric current full of love, wisdom, and compassion.

That's what the dolphins offered to me, and now that's what I'm going to offer the rest of the world. When I'm ready, I'll go back to college and get a Master's in social work. Then I plan to spend the rest of my life helping other women who, like me, felt they were worthless and unwanted. Before I came here, I didn't have an inner world, just a bleak, joyless exterior. But now I have found my inner world, I want to share it.'

Richard looked puzzled. 'You're not talking about all this American pop-psychology, Pandora, are you?'

She laughed. 'Forget it, Richard.' She stood up. 'I tell you what. Why don't you come for dinner with Ben and me? I'll cook you lobster in coconut sauce. You'll love it. I promise.'

'I suppose so.' Richard sat in his chair, looking like a thwarted little boy. His lower lip hung down.

'I promise you. I'll be back to collect you at seven.' Pandora kissed the top of his head lightly and was gone.

Richard at that moment had never felt so alone in his life, the feeling like ice dripping down the back of his neck and into his soul. He jumped to his feet and walked up to the bar. 'Anyone for tennis?' he said, his British stiff upper lip a-quiver.

'You're on, mate,' said an Australian.

'Right-o. I'll just get my racquet and meet you on the court.' *Can't let an Aussie beat an Englishman*, Richard muttered to himself as he went off to collect his tennis racquet.

'How did it go?' Ben asked, hugging Pandora.

'Better than I thought. Tonight I'll pick him up for dinner, and you can meet him. He clarified something for me, just by asking about my plans. I realized, Ben, that in time what I want to do is to teach other women not to totally lose themselves in a man. Some women are happy that way, and they won't need my help. Millions aren't. Millions of women out there are living quiet, desperate lives, drowning. But nobody notices.'

Ben sighed. 'I'll miss you dreadfully, Pandora.'

'I'll miss you too, Ben, but we both know that you'd hate to live off the island. It would be like putting a frigate bird in a cage. And I need to go and get on with my life. I don't feel I have to have a man in my life any longer. For a time, I'm happy to be on my own, to make my own decisions. And it's all very exciting. Maybe in years to come, a man might come into my life who doesn't want to devour me. Then I'll think about it. But I'll always come back here, Ben, and visit you, because I feel Little Egg is my home. That's what's so wonderful about all this. I have finally come home.'